MURDER ON

FIFTH AVENUE

MURDER ON

FIFTH AVENUE

A BILL DONOVAN MYSTERY

MICHAEL JAHN

ST. MARTIN'S PRESS ✖ NEW YORK

Readers are invited to write to Michael Jahn at
medj@WORLDNET.ATT.NET

A THOMAS DUNNE BOOK.
An imprint of St. Martin's Press.

Library of Congress Cataloging-in-Publication Data

Jahn, Mike.
    Murder on Fifth Avenue : a Bill Donovan mystery / by Michael
Jahn.—1st ed.
        p.   cm.
    "A Thomas Dunne book."
    ISBN 0-312-18632-0
    I. Title.   II. Title: Murder on 5th Avenue.
PS3560.A35M877   1998
813'.54—DC21   98-4795
                                                                CIP

First Edition: July 1998

10   9   8   7   6   5   4   3   2   1

For my mother, Anne Jahn,
who taught me to love books

MURDER ON

FIFTH AVENUE

1. "MAKE ME ONE WITH EVERYTHING"

Friday, November 29, the day after Thanksgiving, was brilliantly sunny but very cold. The long line of tourists and other potential customers waiting to get into F.A.O. Schwarz at the start of the holiday shopping season watched their breaths freeze and waft slowly upward in the lifeless air. That very busy corner of Manhattan, diagonally across Fifth Avenue from the Plaza Hotel and Central Park, could be a wind tunnel at times. But on that day no air snaked around the tall office buildings and across the famous facades of such Fifth Avenue stores as Schwarz, Tiffany's, Cartier, and Bergdorf Goodman. Only the murmur of voices (many speaking foreign tongues) and the distant sounds of the season—recorded carols and the tinkling of sidewalk Santas' bells and those rung by assorted beggars—distracted the crowd from the task of getting into the world's most famous toy store. Even the clown posted outside to amuse patrons during the half-hour waits was silent, a mime.

Donovan had forgotten his gloves again—Marcy had threatened to sew them to his cuffs—and as a result his hands were stuffed deep into the pockets of his navy blue greatcoat. He hated to wait in line and as a general rule pulled rank to avoid it. But something about the impending birth of his son made him eager to join the ranks of the other holiday toy buyers, a gleefully anonymous celebrant of the rituals of parenthood. Marcy had been in a bed at Fifth Avenue Medical Center for the previous week, taking medicine to fight off premature delivery and preeclampsia—high blood pressure during pregnancy. Donovan was on partial leave for a month to keep his wife company while both awaited the magic moment. But there was no reason for Donovan not to wander out to buy his son's first rattle.

He fingered the cellular phone that at any moment could bring the call to rush back to the hospital and watched a sidewalk vendor animatedly explaining a gyro—a Greek sandwich that had become ubiquitous around Manhattan—to a grandmother from somewhere out in the heartland. The smoke of grilled roasting meat curled around the edge of the man's tall aluminum pushcart and hung suspended in the frigid air. The pushcart vendor seemed interesting, a pudgy man of perhaps forty years whose fat cheeks and scraggly beard hung below an immense white turban that completely covered the sides and top of his head. His cart also was colorful, decorated with red, blue, and yellow signs hawking pretzels, hot dogs, sausages, soft drinks, and assorted ice creams. There also was an "Allah Is Great" bumper sticker on which someone had scribbled a street address. Next to it: an aging snapshot of what Donovan recognized as one of the Great Buddhas of Bamiyan was accompanied by a bit of doggerel:

SAID BUDDHA TO THE HOT DOG VENDOR
"MAKE ME ONE WITH EVERYTHING"

By the time the line of customers crept up to the vendor's patch of sidewalk, the grandmother had been talked into buying a soft pretzel and rejoined her family outside the entrance to F.A.O. Schwarz. Donovan eyeballed the turban, having noticed the Eastern ecumenicism—Muslim and Buddhist sentiments back to back—and sensing that beneath the turban lingered someone interesting to talk to. Donovan got the man's eye and asked, "Sikh?"

"And ye shall find," was the reply.

Donovan groaned despite inner gratitude at having found a conversation. "One clown is enough," he said. The mime was nearby, his impression of Marcel Marceau's man in an invisible box largely veiled by frozen breath.

"You want something?" the vendor asked.

"I want to know where you're from," Donovan replied.

"Afghanistan," the man said, looking around nervously— as if making a joke, or dodging bullets, Donovan thought.

The captain decided to play along. "Then why this kind of turban?"

"It keeps my head warm."

"I thought maybe you were a Sikh," Donovan said, a bit disappointed that no punch line lurked at the end of the turban talk.

"Not a chance. I like their headgear, that's all. They make the warmest turbans you can buy. As for me, I'm a Muslim. I worship Allah. What do you worship?"

"My wife," Donovan said.

Tossing in a disapproving frown, the vendor replied, "You've got it backward. A man's wife should worship him."

"Trust me. There's less argument this way."

The man shrugged. "So are you going to eat or did you just come here to entertain me?" the vendor asked.

"I came to this edifice"—Donovan cocked his head in the direction of F.A.O. Schwarz—"to buy a toy for my unborn son."

"You're becoming a father? For the first time?"

"What are you, a lawyer?" Donovan asked.

"Your wife is giving you a son. No wonder you worship her. Here, have a pretzel on me." He tried to hand Donovan a twisted bit of bread the size of a baseball mitt flecked with rock salt. But Donovan waved it off.

"Too much salt. What do you get for a gyro?"

"For you, five bucks."

"Five bucks?!" Donovan exclaimed. "For half a pita bread stuffed with lettuce, onions, tomato, and two slices of goat meat?"

"It's lamb, and you get three slices," the man said. "Plus the yogurt sauce."

"Five bucks is still too much money. And that 'lamb' was last seen eating tin cans outside Kabul. I can get a real gyro anyplace else for three dollars."

"Such as where?" the man said, growing combative.

"There's an Israeli joint on Broadway and a Hundred-fifth Street that makes a great one," Donovan replied.

"You want to talk about too much salt, you try an Israeli gyro," the vendor said. "Now, the Egyptians don't do too bad. There's this place on Second Avenue."

"I know it. The Muslim cabdrivers go there. But to be honest with you, the only really good gyro is the Greek one you get in Astoria."

The man frowned. "Who has the time to go to Queens to eat when you could eat a perfectly good one here, on Fifth Avenue? Besides, the round-trip subway fare brings you up to five dollars. An Astoria gyro isn't cost-effective. How much is your time worth?"

4

"I'll have a pretzel," Donovan said. "But I want to pay for it."

"If you insist," the vendor replied, pushing the thing at Donovan again.

"How much?"

"For you . . . two bucks."

"Two bucks for a pretzel that a moment ago was free?!" Donovan exclaimed.

"That's what the price is."

"I can remember when these things went for fifty cents."

The man was unimpressed. "Maybe you can also remember when the Knicks won titles."

"No one's memory is that good," Donovan replied, fishing two bills from his pocket and forking them over. Then he watched the steam from the hot dough freezing in the air, while flicking the salt onto the sidewalk.

The line moved forward by another customer, and Donovan moved with his pretzel to the far end of the pushcart. He assumed that was the end of the conversation, but the vendor seemed to be enjoying the encounter as much as he was. For the man appeared at that end of the wagon, brandishing a can of Coke.

"One buck," he said. "Now, that price has been stable for at least two years. Go ahead; tell me you can get it for sixty cents over at the Korean store on Lexington Avenue."

"I'm not going to drink a cold soda on the coldest day of the year. You're from Afghanistan. Get me a cup of hot tea. Black Russian tea, if you've some left over from those convoys you guys used to raid."

"You're a dreamer," the man replied.

"I'm cold," Donovan said, biting off a bit of pretzel and chewing it while watching the clown duck inside F.A.O. Schwarz to warm up.

Donovan became aware of the fact that the vendor and he were about the only ones talking out loud. The rest of the crowd was silent or talking in hushed tones; whether due to the cold or in respect for the approaching holiday was impossible to tell. The background music—bells ringing here and there and carols beaming from various speakers—seemed that much louder. A wisp of a breeze came up and whisked off the smoke from the grill, just as a jaunty "God Rest Ye Merry Gentlemen" filled the winter air.

Donovan sighed gently and his heart warmed as he thought of Marcy and his unborn son. The trace of a tear appeared in his eye. It was so long in the making, not just the boy but also the very marriage itself, the improbable union of an Irish cop from the West Side and his wealthy, multiracial wife, framed in years of professed love and false starts, coming togethers and breaking aparts, that led up to a family. Within the month, maybe within days, a new child would be born. A new life would enter the world.

Suddenly the air was pierced by screams, screams followed by three shots coming in rapid succession and, Donovan could tell, from a large-bore weapon. There was also the breaking of glass, the ear-piercing wail of a burglar alarm, then more screams. The sounds came from down Fifth Avenue, perhaps a block away. But their immediate effect was to make Donovan's vendor friend jerk his hand inside the cinch holding up his pants.

Donovan saw the glint of black metal on the handle of an automatic. Tossing aside the pretzel, he grabbed the man's hand and immobilized it while shoving a gold captain's badge in his face.

"Are you a cop?" Donovan asked.

The man shook his head nervously. All the color was gone from his face.

"Well, I am, and I'm telling you to stay out of it. And if that's not licensed, get rid of it before I get back."

The vendor was speechless. Donovan sensed it was a rare occurrence. "Understand?" he asked.

The man bobbed his head up and down.

"Happy holidays," Donovan muttered, letting go of the man's hand. Donovan drew his Smith & Wesson and pushed his way through a crowd that parted quickly for him.

Traffic stopped dead in the middle of Fifth Avenue, the world's most famous boulevard, to watch the scene on the sidewalk. Tourists, many of them European or Asian and babbling in an array of languages, jostled shoulder to shoulder for better views of the carnage. The ten-foot-high plate-glass window of Sarkana, the legendary international jewelers', was shattered. Three monstrous bullet holes—they looked almost big enough to push broomsticks through—sat at the centers of three spiderwebs of cracked glass. The force of the explosions had splintered the "bulletproof" glass in patterns that over-lapped and gave the dark-tinted glass a misty appearance. It was as if a lace curtain had been drawn over it.

Several customers gawked through the glass. One man wearing a Russian fur hat tried to peer through one of the bullet holes. In the meantime, several women held each other and cried, their just-bought packages dropped at their feet. Among those shoulder to shoulder in the crowd surrounding this scene were two sidewalk Santas and three Santa's Angels. The latter were sent out each holiday season, by a coalition of Christian charities, to beg coins for the poor. Wearing trade-mark red capes and hats, both of which were trimmed with white fur, they rang bells and encouraged passersby to drop coins into gold buckets that swung from red tripods. One of these devices was overturned near the shattered window, the coins spilled from the bucket onto the concrete, there to mix with the slivers of broken glass. Sirens converged on the scene from all directions. Donovan could see two squad cars trying to bully their way down Fifth Avenue through the bumper-to-bumper traffic. A lone foot patrolman was elbowing through the pack of onlookers.

Donovan joined him, showing the gold badge. Startled by the appearance of this well-dressed senior NYPD detective, the patrolman shouted (to be heard over the burglar alarm), "Captain? I . . . Unh, did you get the call, too?"

"I was shopping and heard the shots," Donovan said, edging between two Italian tourists who stared, wide-eyed, at his revolver.

"The call was 'shots fired at Sarkana, one down.' "

"Who?"

"I got no idea. How many shots did you hear?"

"Three," Donovan replied.

"What the hell's going on?" the officer asked.

Before anyone could answer, the two men were inside the lustrous store, waved inside by a panicky store manager. Off to the right, a man's body lay flat on its back surrounded by a king's ransom in jewels. Donovan was reminded of a pharaoh who had been entombed with his finery. A diamond-encrusted bracelet was clutched in the victim's right fist, while his bloody chest was sprinkled with diamond cuff links. A pearl necklace, itself decorated with a tear-shaped arrangement of diamonds, rubies, and sapphires, lay at the feet of a young blond woman—clearly the dead man's companion. She had fainted and was being attended to by two saleswomen, one of whom was fanning her with a glossy store catalog.

"Who runs this place?" Donovan asked, holding up his badge so that anyone who was interested could see it.

"I . . . me, I do," the store manager stammered.

"What's your name?"

"James Hargrove. I'm the manager."

"Did you see what happened?"

"I . . . yes, I was standing right next to Mr. Melmer."

"Melmer?" Donovan asked, looking down at the body, which was being examined by the uniformed cop.

"Erik Melmer. He's the CEO of Melmer International in Düsseldorf. He came here to buy a gift for his fiancée."

"Her?" Donovan asked, nodding at the unconscious blond.

Hargrove nodded.

The uniformed cop stood back up and said, "They don't come no deader than this guy, Captain."

"Oh, my God," the manager responded, his voice still shaky.

"Are you OK?" Donovan asked. "Do you need to sit down?"

"I'm all right; I'm all right. It's just a shock, that's all." He brushed some fragments of glass off his freshly pressed Armani jacket.

"Was the girlfriend hit, too?" Donovan asked as the cop went over to check her, too.

"I don't think so. She fainted. I never saw anyone faint before," Hargrove replied.

"Have you ever seen anyone shot before?"

"No."

"I think she's OK, Captain!" the patrolman called out.

"Call an ambulance anyway," Donovan said, exchanging his revolver for his cell phone and handing the latter to the officer.

More officers succeeded in pushing their way through the crowds. Donovan had them cordon off both the body and the space outside surrounding the bullet-riddled window. As he worked, Donovan led the still-recovering store manager around Melmer's body to the edge of the display case the man had been standing by when an unidentified assassin with a seriously large handgun sent Melmer to meet his maker.

The display case had a top surface that was flat on the store side but sharply angled on the window side, the latter to allow those outside to peer in at the baubles. The effect also gave shoppers the sense of being celebrities, for anyone rich or merely brazen enough to have a gem taken from that display case was sure to attract a small crowd of gawkers.

"Did you see the one with the gun?" Donovan asked.

"No," Hargrove replied. "I mean I was aware of the window-shoppers, but didn't pay any attention to them."

"All of a sudden there was shooting?"

Hargrove looked out the window at the crowd, which now was pushed back by uniformed policemen and their ubiquitous yellow crime-scene tape. Viewed through the shattered glass, the scene had the surreal quality of something viewed through crinkled cellophane.

"There was a commotion," the manager remembered.

"Like what?"

"Like . . . I remember now that people moved suddenly. It was as if they were surprised by something."

"By someone pulling out a big gun, maybe?" Donovan suggested.

"That could be," the man replied, excited by the recollection.

"Tall or short, man or woman?"

This time Hargrove shook his head. "I couldn't tell you," he said. "There was a commotion, movement outside, and then the glass exploded and Mr. Melmer was thrown backward. He didn't utter a sound. He just clutched the bracelet and fell."

Hargrove allowed himself a look back at the body, then said, "It's going to be some trick to get the blood off the diamonds."

"It always is," Donovan replied.

Returning his attention to the window, the manager said, "You know, Captain, this window is supposed to be bulletproof. And not just run-of-the-mill bulletproof, but the highest-grade protection. We paid a great deal of money for it."

Donovan reached out and held the tip of his finger near one of the bullet holes, the idea being to gauge its size. "No glass made will protect you from the cannon that made that hole," he said.

"Really? But we paid—"

Donovan took out his Smith & Wesson again and popped a bullet out of the cylinder. He held it up near the hole. "This is a thirty-eight-caliber slug," he explained. "It's a little over a third of an inch in diameter. As you can see, it would fit easily in that hole." He replaced the bullet and gun. "The bullets that made those holes were much bigger, almost certainly special rounds fired from a military weapon."

Hargrove seemed nearly relieved. Donovan recognized what he called the "overwhelming force" syndrome. That is, why feel guilty about something that was way beyond your ability to prevent? Hargrove clearly could go to his superiors and say, "They fired a cannon through the window; what do you expect from me?" And he would probably keep his job.

"The ambulance is en route," the patrolman said, handing back the cell phone.

Donovan nodded but shoved the phone, and a business card, back into the man's hands. "Call the number you see there and tell Sergeant Moskowitz to get up here and bring a team."

"Sergeant Moskowitz," the officer replied, making a note on the back of the card.

"And don't let him give you any guff about it being cold, the Sabbath, or whatever."

"Sure thing, Captain," the officer said, amused at the notion he would order a sergeant around. He went off to find a corner in which to make the call.

Turning back to the store manager, Donovan said, "So you didn't see anyone outside the window."

The man thought for a moment, then replied, "Just the usuals—women tourists, a few men, a Santa's Angels volunteer."

"Ogling jewels? A Santa's Angels volunteer ogling jewels?"

"Dreams are free," Hargrove said.

"Nonetheless, the idea of a uniformed charity worker, nominally here to do the work of the Lord, ogling jewels intrigues me. Male or female?"

"Male . . . of course."

"Why would a male Santa's Angels volunteer be so interested in . . ." Donovan looked around, then pointed at the pearl-and-jewel necklace still draped over the dead man's torso. "In that? How much does that cost?"

"For you, one-point-seven million," Hargrove said.

"Jesus, and I thought the gyros were expensive in this neighborhood. Is there any chance you have baby rattles here? Do you have anything under a million? If not, can I postdate a check?"

Hargrove smiled faintly, then said, "Sure we have baby rattles. Nice silver ones. A hundred dollars. The engraving is free. How does that sound?"

"That sounds good," Donovan replied. "I'd rather shell out the hundred bucks than get back in that line outside F.A.O. Schwarz in this weather."

The woman who had passed out was stirring, responding to the fanning being given her by salespeople. At the same time, the sidewalk outside was filling up with cops. They had blocked off the two nearest of the five traffic lanes and filled up one of the others with official vehicles. Doing so assured that the everyday gridlock that afflicted Fifth Avenue from Fifty-seventh to Sixtieth Streets would extend up through the Metropolitan Museum of Art on Eighty-second. An ambulance arrived, and the attendants were duly escorted into the store. They put the woman, now jabbering incoherently in German, onto a gurney and wheeled her out. Upon their departure, a morgue wagon pulled up. Blue-jumpsuited attendants stormed into Sarkana and began bickering with the uniformed cops about having to wait until Forensics came and released the body. All in all, the stifling sense of death that permeated the fancy store had been replaced by the refreshing sound of New Yorkers arguing. Following a fatal but brief interlude, life had returned, full tilt, to the city that never sleeps.

Donovan said, "Places like this videotape everything, don't they?" He looked around for cameras and found two pointing down at the display case and its adjacent body.

Hargrove's eyes widened. "Of course! The cameras! You want to see the tape."

"Are there cameras outside?"

"There's one," the man said excitedly. "We put it there in case someone tried to throw a brick through the window to steal things from the display case. A brick wouldn't make a dent, of course. But a military weapon . . . ?"

"I'll take that tape," Donovan said.

"Can you wait?" Hargrove asked, edging eagerly away from the scene.

"Long enough to buy a rattle," the captain replied.

"**H**ere's the cigars. You owe me four hundred and eighty bucks." So said Detective Sergeant Brian Moskowitz in handing Donovan an elegant-looking wooden box labeled "Albarron y Gonzalo."

Donovan stood in the cold outside Sarkana and stared blankly at the package. Then he looked down at his assistant —while muscle-bound and tough as a bull, Moskowitz stood several inches shorter than his boss—and said, "What's wrong with this picture?"

"When I got the call to rush up here, no questions asked, I assumed you had become a dad and wanted me to bring the cigars," Mosko replied.

"I want you to handle the investigation," Donovan said. "I'm on leave."

"I can do that, too. So why isn't the baby here yet?"

"It's not even close. Marcy's only at thirty-four weeks. The usual pregnancy lasts forty."

"So what's she doing in the hospital?" Mosko asked.

"Preeclampsia," Donovan said. "Now do you know any more than you did ten minutes ago?"

"What's preeclampsia?"

"High blood pressure during pregnancy."

"How come she has that? Marcy is healthy as a horse."

"She's forty years old," Donovan said.

"She doesn't look it," Mosko replied.

"I guarantee you, right at this moment she feels every year. So tell me about the stiff."

Moskowitz plucked his notebook computer off the hood

of his car and looked at the screen. "Erik Melmer was head of Melmer International, which is one of the leading manufacturers of"—the sergeant squinted at the screen—"of contrast media in Europe."

"What's contrast media?" Donovan asked. "A photography thing?"

"No. A medical thing, it says here. Something to do with ultrasound."

"Ultrasound like we've been using to look at the baby," Donovan said.

"Apparently there's a big market for contrast media. That's what the book said, anyway. Melmer was forty-seven years old and divorced. Supported an ex-wife and two kids living in Cologne. His fiancée is—listen to this—Princess Anna of Karlsruhe. They got engaged last August."

"What the hell's Karlsruhe?"

"Beats me. I know it's in the Black Forest . . . not exactly Moskowitz country, if you know what I mean."

"Is she one of those Eurotrash princesses whose families haven't sat on any throne—except maybe a porcelain one—for two hundred years, yet they still claim to be royalty?"

"Could be. I think Karlsruhe is a former principality. But she lives in Düsseldorf."

"Does this Anna have a last name?"

"Hebbel. Anna Hebbel. She's twenty-seven. Melmer and her had been living together for the past year and were to get married next month."

Donovan shook his head. "Not even Eurotrash royalty deserves what happened to her."

"Yeah, I agree. She's in Fifth Avenue Medical Center under sedation. Maybe Marcy can look in on her."

"Marcy is flat on her back trying to remember what her feet look like. Anyway, she doesn't *Sprechen Sie Deutsch*. Does

Princess Anna have any relatives in this country?" Donovan asked.

"Not that I'm aware of."

"Put in a call to the German consulate. Maybe they can help."

"You got it."

"And while you're at it, send someone up to get the identification of the Afghan gyro dealer parked outside F.A.O. Schwarz."

"Let me guess. You got agita and want to sue."

"He's carrying a gun and seemed a bit jittery when the shooting started."

"Imagine that."

"Just do it," Donovan said. "I don't want him arrested. I just want to know what his story is. Now, what about the store's surveillance tapes?" Donovan asked.

"Right over here," Mosko said, and led the way to Howard Bonaci's crime-scene van. The specially outfitted Dodge van contained a miniature crime lab as well as photographic and videotape facilities. Donovan got the city to buy it as an inducement for his old crime-scene wiz to transfer from the West Side Major Crimes Unit. It stood by the curb just outside the inner ring of yellow crime-scene tape, the one that marked off that part of sidewalk where the shooter stood. It was empty now, save for a technician who was poring over the upended Santa's Angels collection tripod.

Moskowitz slid open the side door and urged his boss inside. Donovan unbuttoned his overcoat and complied, squeezing in behind a console that included two monitors and a videotape deck. He sat next to Bonaci. The crime-scene chief's skinny, nervously moving fingers wandered over the pushbutton controls.

"Howard, my son, so good of you to be here this day after Thanksgiving."

"No problem, Boss," Bonaci replied. "The only thing I would get by staying home is more leftovers."

"I love leftover turkey. I could eat it all year."

"Not my wife's you wouldn't. It's tough as rubber and dry as a bone. I got some in the fridge, though, if you want to see for yourself." He reached back and tapped his finger on the pint-size refrigerator that served as repository for fragile evidence as well as for lunch.

"No thanks. I'm still getting over the turkey sandwich I got from the Korean joint yesterday."

"You ate this sandwich in the hospital room?" Bonaci asked, cueing up a tape.

Donovan nodded. "Sitting at the end of Marcy's bed."

"This must have been some Thanksgiving."

"Are you kidding? It was great. I got to be with my wife and child. How much more can a man be thankful for?"

"You got a point," Bonaci said. "Check this out." He pressed a button.

"What are we looking at?" Donovan asked.

"The tape from inside the store. Watch."

Donovan did as he was told. He watched as a camera showed, with relative clarity, Melmer and Hebbel examining jewels as the midafternoon sun streamed in the tinted window. Hargrove stood near her elbow, watching closely. All seemed breezily engaged in a transaction that, to the average man or woman, would represent a lifetime of assets.

Then Hargrove's head seemed to flick in the direction of the window. In that instant, a spray of tiny glass fragments was followed by Melmer wincing. He seemed startled.

"That's bullet one," Donovan said.

Another spray of glass came a split second later. This time all three jerked reflexively, and the woman's mouth opened as if to scream.

"Bullet number two. I couldn't tell if he was hit or not."

Then Melmer jerked backward as the third bullet clearly made a thumb-sized hole in his chest, and lurched forward as the slug, now exiting, made a fist-sized hole in his back. The man fell backward onto the floor, his fingers in a death grip on the diamond-encrusted bracelet.

"That's three," Donovan said.

"The store manager looked out the window," Bonaci added.

"So he told me. He said he saw a movement."

"He should have seen more than that. Look at the outside tape."

"You got something useful from the outside camera?" Donovan asked.

"Better than useful. We got the perp. Watch."

He switched tapes and pressed a few more buttons. Donovan watched as the monitor showed what appeared to be a normal holiday-season crowd of window-shoppers. They carried green-and-red shopping bags and riotously colored boxes, which they held in arms already fattened by layers of winter clothes. Breath froze in the air, and frost particles clung to scarves. In the center of the crowd, conspicuous in a bright red cape with white fur trim, with collar and cap arranged in such a way as to hide the face, a Santa's Angels beggar stood at the center of the window holding a collection tripod.

"Watch the guy in the center," Bonaci said.

"The Santa's Angels man? Hargrove said there was one in the crowd."

"That's him. Watch him closely."

Bonaci slowed down the tape. All of a sudden the red cape fluttered and a hand flicked into the bucket normally used to collect coins for the poor. When it came out it held a large silvery object. That was when several window-shoppers reacted, lurching away from the beggar. The gun came up and was pointed at the window. Donovan and Bonaci watched as three slugs tore into the glass, which buckled like a tarpaulin buffeted by a gale-force wind but didn't break. Three holes, and the spiderwebbing Donovan had seen earlier appeared in a flash.

Then the crowd fell apart in panic and the Santa's Angels beggar tucked the gun under the cape and fled the chaos, running off in the direction of downtown. The collection tripod tumbled over.

Said Moskowitz, who had been watching over Donovan's shoulder, "We're interviewing as many of the people in that crowd as we can find. So far no one saw where the perp went."

"And there are a lot of Santa's Angels beggars out on the street this time of year," Donovan said.

"At least a couple every block," Mosko agreed.

Donovan leaned back and stretched. "You know, I have the feeling I've been to this movie," he said.

"What are you talking about?"

"Do you remember Andrea Jones?"

Thinking, Bonaci said, "Yes . . . no, I forget."

"She was using her great-great-granddaddy's navy Colt to leave powder burns on assorted lowlifes around town."

"Where was I when this happened?" Mosko asked.

"It was twelve or thirteen years ago, so more than likely you were working out in gym class at South Shore High," Donovan said to his twenty-something aide.

"Not a chance. I didn't start pumping iron until I got outta college and my hair began to thin. It's a compensatory mechanism for me." He patted the back of his head, where a distinct white glow was pushing through his curly black hair. "So what happened to this Jones woman?"

"Marcy shot her," Bonaci replied. "I remember now."

Moskowitz whistled between his teeth and said, "Boss, I got to say I admire your ability to get along with strong babes. But what's this got to do with Melmer being killed?"

"Andrea Jones once disguised herself as a bum in order to get a point-blank shot at a mob guy," Donovan said.

"Are you suggesting the Santa's Angels beggar who shot Melmer was anything more than a guy who went cuckoo and blew away an innocent man?"

Donovan rolled the thought around in his head, then said, "I would like to know more about Melmer."

"I'm working on that," Mosko replied. "Although, on the face of it, I don't see what there can be about a man who makes contrast media for medical equipment that could get him killed."

"There must be business rivals," Donovan said. "And there's an ex-wife."

Mosko mentioned, "Hey, if you want to kill a guy, you don't wait until he's standing behind bulletproof glass on Fifth Avenue."

"I don't know. . . . It's a nice smoke screen," Bonaci said.

"I also would like to know more about handguns that fire substantial rounds," Donovan said.

"Now you're in my area of expertise," Bonaci replied, brightening. "There are military handguns that can fire through bulletproof glass."

Mosko said, "But why would anyone need a *handgun* that can fire through glass? I mean if you want to blow a hole in a store window you can use an elephant gun or, for that matter, a damn rocket launcher."

"You can't carry an elephant gun in your Vidal Sassoons," Donovan said. "And a handgun that fires rounds through bulletproof glass is ideal for assassination through bulletproof limo windows."

"Oh," Mosko replied, chastened.

"The only one I could tell you about offhand is the Kammacher seven-point-six-five-millimeter, which fires a round said to be effective through some bulletproof glass at short ranges," Bonaci said.

"That slug is too small to make the holes I saw," Donovan replied.

"Now, that same outfit might have a larger-bore weapon. But the recoil problem would be tremendous."

"That sounds too big for a Santa's Angels coin collector to handle," Donovan said.

"Another problem is where the hell anyone would get a Kammacher," Bonaci added. "It's not only that they're made in what used to be East Germany for sale only in Europe. It's that the Secret Service went nuts the one time—I think it was five years ago—a U.S. company applied for permission to import them. And, interestingly enough, that outfit wanted to sell them to the Secret Service. I tell you, these are big weapons, not like your pocket thirty-eight. I don't see how anyone could smuggle one into America, let alone slip it into New York City."

By way of calling attention to the possibilities that existed for smuggling stuff into New York City, Donovan tapped the cover of his box of Cuban cigars, which sat on his lap.

"Cuban cigars!" Bonaci said excitedly. "Where'd you get them?"

"His Uncle Stanley," Donovan replied.

Moskowitz looked down and kicked a piece of litter across the pavement.

"Uncle Stanley wouldn't also be into illegal weapons imports, would he?" Donovan asked.

"Not that we talk about at the table," Mosko replied, somewhat irritably.

"It seems to me if a man can get a box of—very expensive—Cuban cigars, shipped via Toronto, for a New York City police captain, he can get a damn gun."

"Stop giving me a hard time," Mosko said.

"I wouldn't call a Kammacher automatic a 'damn gun,' " Bonaci added.

"Check and see if any of these substantial firearms are in the U.S.," Donovan said.

"You got it." The crime-scene chief seemed excited by getting an assignment that touched on an area of personal interest.

"If these guns are assassination weapons, that lends credence to the notion Melmer may have been a deliberate target," Mosko said.

"Yes, it does," Donovan replied.

"Maybe there is something about contrast media manufacturing we should know about."

At that moment, a jumpsuited crime-scene investigator came up and handed Moskowitz two plastic evidence bags. They were the size of sandwich bags and contained oddly lustrous, barely deformed pieces of metal.

"What's this?" Mosko asked.

Donovan said, "Only one of the shots hit the target. There were two others."

"This is them, Cap," the crime-scene man said. "We dug them out of a plaster column about ten yards behind the victim."

Mosko thanked the man, who then disappeared back into the crowd of police officers and crime-scene investigators.

Moskowitz, Donovan, and Bonaci took turns inspecting the slugs.

"Nine millimeters?" Donovan asked.

"I'm pretty sure of it," Bonaci replied, his brow more than usually furrowed. "And metal-jacketed, too. This is serious ammunition."

Donovan said, "I'm no firearms expert, but what's with that metal? That doesn't look like any metal jacketing I've seen before."

"You're right. I haven't seen it before, either. And for having gone through the world's best bulletproof glass and an inch or so of plaster these slugs are damned pristine."

"I'll have some tests run on them," Bonaci said. "I'll find out what that metal is. And if they match the one in Melmer—"

"They will."

"Then there's a very big weapon in the hands of a madman," Bonaci said.

"And on Fifth Avenue at the height of the holiday shopping season," Moskowitz added.

Donovan said, "Somebody call up this Kammacher outfit and see if they have a gun that fits this ammo. Then see if they know how it may have gotten into our country."

"Boss, it's Friday evening in Germany," Mosko replied.

"Somehow I doubt these German manufacturers of assassination weapons are at the synagogue worshiping," Donovan snapped. "Get them away from the dinner table or wherever they are and ask them what the hell's going on."

"You got it," Mosko said, and left the van.

"Metal-jacketed and some weird kind of metal," Bonaci

mused, in respect or awe, holding the evidence bags up and letting the light glint off the bullets.

Donovan got back onto the pavement, checked his watch, and scowled. "It's getting late," he said.

"You wouldn't be giving out those cigars today, would you?" Bonaci asked.

"Not yet. Tell me, Howard, do you think a silver rattle from Sarkana is too ostentatious for my baby boy?"

"Silver? Nah. My grandma got me a silver rattle, engraved with my initials and date of birth. My mom still has it."

"Did you ever use it?"

"It has dents," Bonaci replied with a shrug.

"I have to finish my shopping," Donovan said, and went back into the store.

"The line must have been long," Marcy said when Donovan walked into her room. To pose this question she peeked around her belly, which billowed up the white hospital gown as if someone had inflated a basketball beneath a linen table-cloth. To one side was an IV pole. Its several bags were attached to intravenous lines that fed into her arm. Behind it a large electronic monitor sat on a shelf. It beeped at the rate of about 160 beats per minute, the baby's pulse.

He kissed her lips. Then he kissed her belly, saying, "Hi, Danny. . . . It's Daddy." He touched his fingertips to her belly, awaiting a movement. None was forthcoming. "It would be my luck to get a baby who has nothing to say," Donovan remarked, then sat in a chair and handed Marcy the package from Sarkana.

"I never made it into F.A.O. Schwarz," he replied. "Someone was shot in Sarkana, so I bought the rattle there."

"I thought you're on leave."

"I'm on partial leave. Don't worry. I can keep an eye on things from your side."

She grumbled but said, "Who was shot?"

"A rich German tourist, and I only got involved because it happened a block away. Open the package."

She worked at undoing the wrapping, which included a silver ribbon and a black-on-black gift box. "This is very chichi wrapping to put on a baby gift," she said.

"I work with the tools at hand," he replied.

"Tell me what happened."

"A guy named Erik Melmer was buying jewels for his fiancée when someone pumped a slug into him right through the window of Sarkana."

"Right through the window? Cool."

"Using a high-powered handgun."

"Did you catch the shooter?"

"Nope. All we know is that he was dressed as a Santa's Angels beggar."

"Collecting coins for Christmas, he pulls out a high-powered pistol and shoots a tourist? Talk about holiday spirit. So this was a random act of violence?"

"Maybe yes, maybe no. Anyway, Melmer's fiancée is in this hospital building someplace."

"She's down the hall."

Donovan looked toward the door, then back at his wife. "Excuse me, but isn't this the perinatal intensive care unit?" he asked.

"It is. She's pregnant and they were afraid she might lose the baby."

"She didn't look pregnant fainted on the floor of Sarkana."

"I heard she was at twenty weeks. Not everyone shows as much as I do."

"Credit your exquisite bone structure," Donovan said, kissing her again.

"Thank you," she replied, finally getting the package open. She held up the silver rattle—which was shaped like a tiny barbell—and shook it. The rattle made little tinkling sounds. "I love it," she said.

He was at the door, peering down the hall. When he came back, he asked, "Would her room be where the two suits are standing guard by the door?"

"It would."

"They look like Secret Service agents."

"The nurse tells me they're private cops. What do you want from me? I'm stuck here in this bed. Stop working and sit down by your wife."

He did as he was told.

She said, "I started to get contractions right after you left. Dr. Campagna put me on tributylene and magnesium sulfate."

Donovan peered at the lower of the two electronic lines bumping their way across her monitor. It hovered around 20. "The monitor looks good now," he said.

"It was up to thirty-five a few hours ago."

He held her hand and leaned back in the chair. "Will any of this hurt the baby?"

"No," she replied assuredly.

"That's good," he said, and closed his eyes for a moment.

He lapsed into thoughts of playing catch with his son in Riverside Park, the way his dad had done with him so many years before. But Donovan was roused from this thought by the unusual amount of traffic in the hall. There were male voices speaking in German, plus the occasional sound of a nurse arguing. Donovan stood.

"Can't you relax?" Marcy asked.

"Can you relax with all this stuff going on? I'll be right back."

"You're going to be a father soon," she snapped. "No more working. And especially no getting shot at."

"That's not likely to happen in the hospital."

"This is New York."

He went down the hall, showing his badge to a tall and somber-looking man in a cheapish grey suit that fit him a bit too tightly. The fellow had given Donovan the eye before he was within five paces, which signaled extreme jitteriness.

"Captain Donovan, NYPD," he said.

"This is a private room," the man replied with a trace of a German accent.

"Is this Anna Hebbel's room?" Donovan asked.

The man nodded. He was joined, meantime, by another security guard, who came out of the room. This one was shorter and better-tailored but hardly friendlier-looking. Between the two of them Donovan caught a glimpse of the woman he had seen in Sarkana, but lying in a hospital gown, eyes open, motionless, being attended to by two doctors, a nurse, and several other civilians.

"Yes," the first guard said.

"I'm investigating her fiancé's death. I would like to extend my condolences."

"If you would wait a moment."

The two men withdrew and conferred and then got several others involved in the discussions. After a minute or two, one of the doctors joined Donovan in the hall. He was a short man, well dressed. A custom-made sky blue Oxford shirt shone beneath the usual white coat. A mother-of-pearl fountain pen decorated the breast pocket.

"I am Dr. Shreffler, Mr. Melmer's physician when he is in New York. May I help you?"

"Captain Donovan, New York Police. I just wanted to extend my condolences to the princess and see how she is."

"She is under sedation—"

"While pregnant?" Donovan asked pointedly.

The doctor sighed, then said, "You are quite right, Captain. No sedation is appropriate. I merely don't want her to get upset—more so than she is, of course—which being interviewed by a police detective would surely do. Is there anything I can ask her for you?"

"No, not right now anyway," Donovan replied, tossing in a shrug. "I just wanted to say how sorry I am. We try to be responsive to the victims of crimes." He handed the doctor a card, then added, "Give her this and ask her to call me in a few days. We'll need to ask her a few questions before she leaves New York. Maybe she saw something that will help us catch the killer."

"I'll do that," Shreffler replied.

"Where were they staying?"

"They have an apartment in Trump Plaza."

"I hope the baby is OK," Donovan said.

"I'm sure he'll be fine," Shreffler replied.

"Tell me, Doctor, can you think of anyone who would have a reason to kill Mr. Melmer?"

"No. He was a lovely man with no enemies that I know of. But I will ask Princess Anna. Now, if you will excuse me . . ."

Donovan thanked the man and went back to Marcy's room, the two security guards retaking their places by the door and watching him every step of the way.

"Well?" Marcy asked.

"Her baby will be fine," Donovan replied, sitting back down. "Her late fiancé has no known enemies."

"That's very nice, William. Now take off your jacket and

put away your attitude. You're on vacation to attend to your wife and your unborn child."

Donovan grumbled but complied. Both of them knew he had a hard time relaxing and was never entirely off duty— at least not anymore. At one point not quite a decade earlier, he gave up drinking, his longtime remedy for the conflicting feelings of guilt and obligation that kept him up nights. That problem began with the murder of his father—also a prominent policeman—a crime that remained unsolved.

The older Donovan might still have been alive were his son, a young patrolman in 1968, not off enjoying the company of his antiwar friends on the Columbia campus one crucial night. Of course, no one had assigned him to be with his father that night. The two Donovans weren't even attached to the same precinct. And, if the truth be known, they didn't get along that well at that point, having parted company on the subject of Vietnam. But in Donovan's heart a portion of responsibility for his father's death rested with him. One day he would solve the crime that had hung over his heart for nearly three decades. He often sat up nights pondering decades-old evidence and thinking.

But that only came after he stopped spending countless hours and many hundreds of dollars each month on scotch. At midlife, and with the support of Marcy and his friends, Donovan gave up his bar-brawling days and soon discovered a new ability to get things done. Among them: being promoted to captain, getting a citywide command, and reacquainting himself with books and learning. Gone were the friends of shabby backgrounds and questionable incomes as well as the passel of saloons that ran very nearly the entire length of Broadway.

Donovan began prowling bookshops and patronizing sidewalk book vendors. He became a computer maven. Monitors hummed in both his downtown and home offices; his briefcase notebook computer could download information from his other PCs through a cellular modem. A cell phone replaced the roll of quarters he used to carry around for use in pay phones or, occasionally in the wee hours of those scotch-filled nights, as impromptu brass knuckles. With his fingers wrapped around it, the ten-dollar stack of coins helped settle many arguments with the pastiche of shady characters—both in and out of uniform—with whom he spent his off-duty hours.

That was Donovan's past. Now, in his early fifties, he had attained something resembling peace. He had financial security and professional respectability—a citywide command as New York City's chief of special investigations, which let him pick the most interesting cases. And in his personal life Donovan had love and family at last; Marcy and he were married after nearly a decade and a half of breaking up and getting back together. And they were about to welcome the baby they had been talking about nearly that long: Daniel Magid Donovan, his son.

"I don't want you even thinking about working until after the baby's born," Marcy said, taking his hand and moving it to her belly.

As he felt the baby move beneath his fingers, Donovan shut his eyes, smiled peacefully, and felt, no doubt about it, very good indeed.

3. "START A FAMILY," THE MAYOR SAID

The weekend slid by. As had become the norm, Marcy's life consisted of watching TV, listening to the monitor beep, and taking occasional walks in the hall to let the creases unfold from her back. On those forays, she and Donovan walked arm in arm, taking turns pushing the IV pole from which dangled her medications. On each trip they passed Princess Anna's room, but after Donovan's first encounter with her doctor the door was always shut and guarded. Late on Sunday afternoon she disappeared along with her entourage. Donovan found her room open and snooped around it for a while, emptying out the personal trash basket kept bedside but finding little of interest: a menu from a Mexican restaurant on East Ninety-sixth Street, a collection of balled-up facial tissues, and several plastic toothpicks. Finally Donovan stole the water glass from her table and slipped it into a plastic bag. Donovan's days were otherwise filled with reading the papers, getting coffee from the cafeteria, and trudging to the Korean place on Lexington Avenue in search of palatable food.

It was on a sunny and warmer morning early in December that Moskowitz showed his face in Marcy's room, bearing his notebook computer and a box of Perugina chocolates.

"Hiya, Sergeant Barnes," he said, amused by the sight of a police sergeant pregnant and propped up in bed.

"Retired sergeant," she replied.

"Whatever." He balanced the box of chocolates on her belly and gave her a kiss on the cheek.

"Thank you for the chocolates. And my last name is Donovan, not Barnes."

"How come a radfem like you didn't keep your last name after you got married?" Mosko asked.

"For one thing, I'm not a radical feminist," she replied, a bit testily. "For another, it took fifteen years to get him to marry me. . . ." She patted the knee of Donovan, who had swiped a semireclining chair from the intensive care waiting room and was leaning back, doing the *Times* crossword puzzle. "Given that, you don't think I'm going to use his name?"

"Morning, Boss," Mosko said, helping himself to a

straight-backed chair and setting up his computer atop her food table.

"Hi, Brian." Donovan looked over the top of his newspaper and smiled at his assistant before returning his attention to the puzzle.

"Do you want to hear the daily report now?" Mosko asked.

"Daily report?" Marcy asked.

"Well . . . I thought that's how he was working his partial leave. He'd get a daily report but otherwise be free to do what he wants."

Donovan put down his paper and tossed his pencil onto the food table. It skittered over the top of the Perugina box and landed in her applesauce. Marcy gave him a dirty look.

"Can I have a chocolate?" he asked.

"No. They're for Dr. Campagna."

"I thought I was buying these for you," Mosko said.

"Are you nuts? Pregnant women can't have chocolate. There's caffeine in it."

He looked at the box, then at the array of intravenous tubes feeding into her long and slender arm. "Are you having fun with this?" he asked.

"I've never been happier," she replied. "Honey . . . give him the money for the Perugina."

"How much?" Donovan asked.

"Twenty."

He handed over a bill, then grumbled, "This pregnancy is costing me a fortune."

"Insurance covers most of it," Marcy said.

"But not cigars, rattles, and chocolates."

"Think how happy all this is making her . . . honey," Mosko said.

"Let's hear the report," Donovan snapped.

Moskowitz switched on his laptop, then flipped through assorted screens until he found the one he wanted. "First, the bullets. They were nine-millimeter, all right. And metal-jacketed. Your basic but, in this case, *very rare* assassination round." Mosko gaped at the screen, clearly reading something for the eighth or ninth time and trying to believe it before passing the info along to his boss.

Donovan read his thoughts and said, "Let's hear it."

Mosko cleared his throat and exclaimed, "Would you believe *depleted uranium!*"

Donovan pondered for a moment, then turned to his wife and said, "I really need a chocolate."

"No," she replied tersely.

Mosko said, "That's how the report came back from the lab. The metal jackets on those bullets were made of depleted uranium."

"Isn't that radioactive?" Marcy asked.

"About as much as a glow-in-the-dark watch dial," Mosko said.

"Depleted uranium is used in armor-piercing antitank ammunition," Donovan added. "I never heard of it being used in handgun bullets. For one thing, you would think that the physics of shooting through armor is different than the physics of shooting through glass."

"Wouldn't you consider bulletproof glass to be armored?" Marcy asked, using her sensible tone of voice.

"I suppose," Mosko said. "Anyway, the slugs in the wall matched the one in Melmer."

"I'm surprised that slug stayed in the man."

"Bonaci says an armor-piercing round would lose a lot of momentum coming through tissue."

"And what about the gun?"

"According to Bonaci's source, there's only one handgun

in the entire world that fires a steel-jacketed nine-millimeter round that's made of depleted uranium. And that's the Kammacher Stedman."

Donovan offered a quizzical look.

Reading from the screen, Mosko said, "It was developed in the mid-nineteen-eighties for the Stasi."

It was Marcy's turn to look perplexed.

"East German secret police," Donovan clarified. "After the fall of communism and the demolition of the Berlin Wall, the Stasi was disbanded. A lot of them are still being hunted down for cold war atrocities. But what about the gun?"

"Kammacher went private—it was a state-owned company under communism—and tried to sell the Stedman, among other weapons, to the combatants in the Middle East: the Syrians, Palestinians, Iranians, Afghans, and Lebanese among them."

"How did they do?"

"They only made a few—three of them, to be exact, prototypes really—and it turns out there wasn't much of a market. For one thing, the slugs cost a hundred bucks each."

"And close-in assassination ain't the terrorist's thing," Donovan said.

"You're right," Mosko agreed. "Those schmucks like to strap dynamite to their bodies and blow themselves up along with school buses. And Israel, knock wood . . ." He went to rap his knuckles on her food table but saw it was Formica. Then he looked around for *any* wood that was within reach but found none. So he shrugged, knocking his knuckles against an imaginary piece of wood floating in the air, and returned his attention to the monitor. ". . . did a great job of keeping the few that were sold outside their borders. So—"

"Kammacher was forced to sell them to a fairly limited black market," Donovan said.

"You got it. They got rid of all three of the prototypes. The Russian mob bought one. We know because a French businessman was shot through the window of his armored limo in Kiev and the perp was caught with the gun. And one weapon supposedly turned up in Kabul as well."

"Afghanistan," Donovan said. "Interesting."

"Why?" Mosko asked.

"How many bulletproof limos do you imagine there are in Kabul?"

"I would think the president, the prime minister, the chief mullah, or whatever they have over there, has one. At any rate, there's another Stedman out there, but no one knows where it is. There's a rumor floating around the Internet that the third prototype was bought fairly recently by an American collector, but no word as to if it got into the country or *what* happened to it. Anyway, Kammacher decided not to put the weapon into full production in 1993 after the State Department slammed the door to America shut."

"Is there any chance the third Stedman got into the country anyway?" Marcy asked.

"Apparently, it did," Donovan said.

"At the moment, I only have hearsay. I didn't have too hard a time getting someone from Kammacher on the phone over the weekend. But the State Department is going to be harder," Mosko commented.

"Why would it be harder to get the U.S. State Department on the phone than a German arms manufacturer?" Marcy asked.

"It's a bigger bureaucracy," Donovan said.

Mosko added, a bit cautiously, "Maybe you can give it a shot."

The reason for his caution was instantly apparent. "He's on leave," Marcy said. "It's one thing for him to take reports from you once a day." She paused, dramatically, then added, talking to her husband, "Once a day. Did that transmission come through?"

"What did you say?" Donovan replied, toying with her. "I didn't hear you."

A bit steamed, she replied, "Earth to Donovan. Did you get that?"

"I got it; I got it," he said. "Calm down or you'll give yourself a contraction."

"It doesn't work that way."

"With you everything is tied into emotions," he said, looking at her monitor to see if the indicators changed. They didn't this time.

"What's all this stuff?" Mosko asked, pointing at her electronics.

"It's a fetal monitor," she replied.

"You look like RoboMom."

"Thank you very much. I find you very attractive, too. Anyway, this man is my husband and about to become a father. I don't want him working. Giving you advice once a day is enough."

"The mayor did say to start a family," Donovan allowed.

What he meant by that remark was that his previous big case, a series of murders in a landmark Broadway theater, got so many headlines the mayor of the city of New York, up for reelection and in need of the ink, begged him to lay low.

"Start a family," the mayor had said. "Settle down," Hizzoner had added as he married the two of them, providing two reclining chairs and a bag of popcorn as an inducement to take things easy. A year later, newly reelected and in an expansive mood, the mayor had the police commissioner grant the city's most famous detective a month's partial leave so he could be by his wife's bedside as she prepared to give birth.

"I just thought that maybe he could use his contacts to get the State Department to open up," Mosko said.

One of Donovan's childhood friends was a West Side Democratic politician who currently served as political adviser to the president. A simple phone call to him could open many doors.

"I'll see what I can do," Donovan said cautiously.

Marcy gave him another dirty look.

"Without getting too involved in this Melmer murder," he added.

He and Marcy exchanged glances, and after a second both smiled. They touched hands.

"I love you," she said.

Moskowitz rolled his eyes. "OK, so you call Washington. Ask them if it's true what Kammacher says, that the State Department went apeshit after Kammacher wanted to sell Stedmans here and if they know what happened to the third one."

"When did this happen?"

"They said '93. That's all I know."

"I'll check it out," Donovan replied.

"On to the matter of witnesses. Nobody we were able to interview could give us a sketch of the guy in the Santa's Angels getup. He pulled the gun; they looked at the gun."

"It's always that way," Marcy said. "Witnesses always focus on the weapon."

"Up to the point he pulled the gun, he was a guy in a Santa's Angels cape and hat. A white guy, maybe in his twenties, and not too tall. That's it. Nobody got enough of a look at him to give us a sketch."

"Did anyone see where he went?" Donovan asked.

"Downtown. He disappeared into the crowd."

"Who would notice him?" Marcy said.

"What about the other beggars—the three in the crowd outside Sarkana after the shooting?" Donovan asked.

"We talked to them plenty. They saw people running away from the site, including one of their own. But they couldn't ID him. Those guys don't all know each other anyway. Most of them are day laborers hired every November."

"How many do they hire?"

Mosko said, "I called the Santa's Angels this morning. They had—are you ready for this?—a total of one hundred people collecting money in the twenty-five blocks of Fifth Avenue between Thirty-fourth and Fifty-ninth Streets."

"That's all?"

"I'm getting a list. The breakdown is seventy-five red-coated beggars with tripods and twenty-five Santas. Three beggars and one Santa per block."

"And the Republicans say the economy is bad. Can we get a list of these people?"

"I'm working on it."

"I don't suppose that Santa's Angels checks criminal records before hiring beggars and Santas," Donovan said.

"I got no idea."

"It is possible to have an ex-con Santa? A rehabilitated drug dealer, for example, out there ho-hoing and waving a bell in the name of God?"

Moskowitz cleared his throat nervously. Donovan was no fan of organized religion, and a lecture on the subject was far from out of the question. The more careful among his men found themselves avoiding topics likely to precipitate tirades.

"What about white-collar criminal Santas, guys who just spent time in the pen for insider trading?"

"I think they hit the college lecture circuit, Boss," Mosko said.

"What about Mafia informant Santas? Maybe the Santa's

Angels calls up the Federal Witness Protection Program each Christmas and say, 'Send me over a hundred.' "

"It's possible."

"What about hit-man Santas?" Donovan asked finally.

"Or Santa's Angels bill-collection guys," Marcy said.

"It's not a bad cover to use in stalking and killing someone. What did your inquiries about Melmer get you?"

Relieved to be off the subject of religion, at least for the time being, Moskowitz peered at his screen and said, "Zilch."

"Whaddya mean, 'zilch'?"

"I mean that no one at Melmer International would talk to me. But it was the weekend."

Peeved, Donovan muttered, "I got to make a few calls, honey."

"So call. We have a phone. You know, one thing strikes me here. If you're dressing up as a Santa's Angels Christmas beggar meaning to shoot someone in particular, you're going to have to know his exact schedule."

"Like, 'Melmer will be in Sarkana with his fiancée between three and four P.M. on Friday, November twenty-ninth'," Mosko said.

Donovan nodded. "And you'd have to plant yourself outside Sarkana's window without arousing the ire, or even the notice, of Santa's Angels quality control."

"Say again?" Mosko asked.

"I mean they must have supervisors who walk up and down Fifth Avenue making sure that such-and-such block, say the one where Sarkana is, doesn't have too many collection guys. I can hear this conversation: 'Sorry, Mac, but there are already three beggars and one Santa on this block. You're gonna have to haul your ass down to Forty-seventh, where one of our ex-cons just jumped parole and took off for Mexico, leaving a spot vacant.'"

Mosko seemed vaguely amused. "I'll check it out."

"Were there any prints on that tripod and bucket?"

"Only about a thousand. It will be hard to tell if any belong to the perp. Bonaci blew up that piece of videotape and says it looks like the guy was wearing gloves."

Donovan picked up the Perugina box and turned it over, looking to see if there was a seal on it. If there wasn't, he could get inside later on, when Marcy went to the bathroom. But there was a seal, and she grabbed the box back and put it on the end table on the opposite side of her bed.

"This killer is no madman," he said.

"And why not?"

"Your basic lunatic doesn't go to such trouble to shoot someone. Your average loony buys a cheap gun or uses whatever he has on hand and shoots the first guy who comes along who pisses him off. Some poor slob who reminds him of his father, his mother, his high-school guidance counselor, or whoever he thinks fucked up his life."

"He doesn't shoot through a store window," Mosko said.

"After donning a disguise and carefully securing one of the only handguns capable of shooting through bulletproof glass," Donovan added. "I have a lot of experience with exotic weapons, and in each case the man or woman using one is making a statement. This killer is telling us something."

"Melmer was a deliberate target," Mosko said.

"That very well could be. Of course, another possible statement is 'no one is safe, not even behind bulletproof glass.' But that seems a little esoteric and even a bit off the point, considering we don't know much about Melmer yet."

"Let's try harder to find more about him."

"Check for prints on this," Donovan said, handing Moskowitz the purloined water glass.

"Where'd you get that?"

"His fiancée's room. She was down the hall."

"In the perinatal ICU?"

"The lady is with child," Donovan said. "Twenty weeks. You might also find out where Melmer and his lady were twenty weeks ago."

"Eighteen weeks," Marcy corrected.

"Right; pregnancy is measured from the first day of the last menstrual period," Donovan said.

"Not from the day you eggulate," Marcy added.

Moskowitz elevated a bushy black eyebrow. "Say again?"

"Not from the day you eggulate," she said.

"Ovulate," Donovan translated.

"Pop an egg," Marcy said.

"I learn so many new words working for you," Mosko commented, making a note. "Do you expect her prints will turn up in the Interpol computer?"

"You never know."

"How do you know she used this glass?"

"Lipstick," Donovan said, pointing out the red smudge below the rim. "She was the only woman in the room today, not counting nurses, who aren't allowed to wear lipstick."

"They let you wear makeup in ICUs?" Mosko asked.

"They do on the day you're being discharged," Marcy said.

"Actually, you can get away with quite a lot around here," Donovan added, retrieving his newspaper and using it to cover an embarrassed but pleased-with-himself grin.

"Such as sneaking into rooms and disappearing with evidence," Marcy said quickly.

"Speaking of disappearing, that's what happened to your gyro dealer," Mosko interjected.

"Gyro dealer?" Marcy asked.

"I asked him to check out an Afghan in a Sikh turban selling gyros outside F.A.O. Schwarz," Donovan said in a voice that indicated he found nothing unusual about that combination.

"I see," she replied. "You weren't planning on eating one of those gyros, were you?"

"Perish the thought."

"You know that lamb is very fatty, and at your age—"

"I'm pretty sure it was goat," Donovan said.

"Goat? You were going to eat goat?"

Mosko said, "In any event, the man was gone by the time we got there."

"Which was?"

"Four o'clock."

"Let me get this straight. Four o'clock on the day after Thanksgiving, the busiest shopping day of the year, and this man up and bolts from his primo spot outside F.A.O. Schwarz? Other vendors could kill for that location. Perhaps literally."

"You said he had a gun. What kind?"

"Black automatic. That's all I know."

"What? Did he *show* it to you?"

"He went for it when he heard the shots," Donovan said. "I was talking to him as a way of passing the time while waiting in line to get into Schwarz—"

"Goat meat," Marcy muttered, shaking her head.

"I grabbed his hand, identified myself, then told him to lose the gun by the time I got back if it wasn't licensed."

"I guess it wasn't," Mosko said.

"So the upshot is the man had an illegal gun and was scared enough of something to feel he had to use it," Donovan commented.

"Scared of what?"

"Of something. Of hearing gunshots. Maybe he flashed back to his days as a member of the mujahideen fighting the Russians outside Kabul. Who knows? Anyway, I told him to get rid of the gun, not take a powder entirely. He could have stuffed it in a garbage can. He could have made that mime outside the store eat it."

"Only you could get the mujahideen and a mime in the same thought," Marcy said.

"Is this guy connected with Melmer, do you think?" Mosko asked.

Donovan shrugged. "He's an Afghan with a gun who took off after hearing the shots. I'm pretty sure he lives in Queens, by the way."

"Why do you say that?" Mosko asked.

"He had an address scribbled on a bumper sticker. The address was written by a left-handed man, and he was left-handed. It was Fifteen sixty-two thirty-two seventy-eight Queens Boulevard. Check that out. He also knows the gyro place on Second Avenue where all the Muslim cabbies go."

"Oh, that sure is on *my* route home," Moskowitz replied.

"If it helps, he has a sense of humor," Donovan added. "The man was another New York City rip-off artist, but an entertaining one. He wears a Sikh turban because it keeps his head warm."

"I doubt he's connected with Melmer," Mosko said.

"Me, too."

"But I'll have someone look into him."

Donovan got his pencil out of Marcy's applesauce and wiped it off using one of the napkins that came with her breakfast. He scrutinized the crossword puzzle while Moskowitz shut off the computer and put it in the leather shoulder bag he used to carry all his stuff.

"You know, you ought to bring your laptop here from home in case you want to do things," he said.

"The man is on leave," Marcy replied. "Talking to you once a day is enough of a burden."

"You're cute," Mosko said. Then he leaned forward and touched her belly. "So is this the kid?"

"That's my baby," she said.

"Our baby," Donovan added, without looking away from his paper.

"Danny Boy," Mosko said.

"Daniel," she replied. "He is not named after an Irish song. It's a Hebrew name: Daniel Magid."

"*Magid* means 'storyteller' in Hebrew," Moskowitz said.

She knew.

"You realize, of course, that the initials DMD will make people think he's an oral surgeon," Mosko said.

"You're a hideous man to even think that."

"With my luck he'll become a reporter for the *Post*," Donovan said. The captain's battles with tabloid and television reporters were legendary.

"Daniel is going to be a novelist," Marcy remarked.

"I'll be supporting him forever," Donovan moaned.

"In any case, he's our angel," Marcy said. And with that she leaned down and kissed her belly. "I love you, Daniel," she added.

"I gotta get out of here," Moskowitz said.

It was Thursday, December 5. Marcy had been in the hospital for a full week, and in that time Donovan more or less had moved into the private room with her. He put back the semi-recliner he had stolen from the intensive care lounge, accepted the gratitude of the nurses for so doing, then went out in the dead of night and stole a full recliner from one of the suites where the residents slept. He packed one of his old L.L. Bean canvas carrying bags with shaving and other stuff as well as changes of clothes. And he brought in a portable CD player and FM radio along with several handfuls of jazz and classical CDs. And reading material, including several back issues of the *Times Book Review* and *New York Review of Books*. (Donovan's shortcut to learning a wide variety of subjects was to read reviews of books about them; he told Marcy his technique was "the *Classics Comics* approach to knowledge.")

The sun was just setting when Moskowitz wrapped up his daily briefing by reaching into his leather shoulder bag and pulling out a brass menorah and a small wrapped package.

"Happy Hanukkah," he said, setting up the menorah on the food table that hovered over Marcy's belly and planting the package atop her outstretched hand.

"Happy Hanukkah," she replied. "What's in the package?"

"It's for Danny Boy," he replied. "For his first Hanukkah."

"His name is *Daniel*," she said firmly. "What's in the box?"

"Open it," he replied. Waving a pack of matches, he said, "Do you want me to light them?"

"No. That's William's job."

"He's not a Jew," Moskowitz said. "He's an ex-Catholic atheist."

"I'm surrounded is what I am," Donovan replied, looking up from an essay on Benjamin Franklin and the American dream. "I'm outnumbered two to one."

"Three to one," Marcy said, patting her belly.

Donovan grumbled and watched as his wife tore open the package and pulled out a large plastic rattle that glowed in primary colors.

"Mickey Mouse," she said. "How quaint."

"I figure the kid will want a rattle he can *use*. Not one to put on the mantel and show to guests."

"Thank you, Brian," Marcy said, beckoning him to bend over so she could plant a kiss on his cheek.

Donovan put away his reading, stood, and stretched. "Today is the first day of Hanukkah, right?"

"You know that," Marcy replied.

"It's also the annual ceremony for the lighting of the Rockefeller Center Christmas tree."

"So?"

"Kind of a coincidence, wouldn't you say?"

Moskowitz offered a quizzical look. "What coincidence?"

"Scheduling the Christmas tree lighting for the first night of Hanukkah," Donovan said. "Both the Christians and the Jews are lighting up on the same night, trees on the one hand and candles on the other. It sounds suspicious to me. We better investigate."

"I got to be honest, Boss; I don't know what the hell you're talking about. In my book, this don't rank very high on the galactic scale of paranoia."

Marcy smiled and said, "What he means is he's bored and wants to get out of this room. Take him to the Christmas tree lighting and buy him a cupcake or whatever his people sell to mark the occasion."

Donovan plucked his suede jacket off the back of the door and slipped it on. "Can I get you anything?" he asked her.

"I don't think there's any such thing as Christmas cupcakes," Moskowitz said.

"What you can do for me," Marcy said, "what you can do for your son, is convert."

"From what to what? From atheism to Judaism? It doesn't work that way. First you're a Jew; then you become an atheist. That's how it works. I can cite you hundreds of examples, and that's just among the guys I grew up with on the West Side. Besides, your father is still a Christian after how many years of being married to your mother? Forty-three? So I'll still be an atheist and glad for it when I'm ninety-five."

Marcy said to Moskowitz, "He thinks organized religion is responsible for all the woes of the world since year one."

"I don't want to get him started," Mosko replied, hoisting his bag onto his shoulder and heading out the door. "I can't take another go-round with the religion lecture."

"It was you who brought the menorah," Donovan said.

"Next time it will be a Christmas cupcake," Mosko replied.

A short time later, they walked casually down Fifth Avenue, looking with partial interest at the Santa's Angels and the tourists dropping coins into their buckets.

The Norway spruce stood seventy feet tall, an Everest of a tree, broad at the base and tapering symmetrically to a thin tip crowned by a gigantic white star. Twenty-six thousand lights and ornaments hung silently in the dark, awaiting the moment the mayor would flip the switch to make them glow as bright as the office windows, lit far into the night for the Christmas season, that towered above and enveloped them.

The tree was set in a mammoth pot placed up against the railing that surrounded the Rockefeller Center skating rink. Branches that until the week before had graced a suburban estate sheltered Paul Manship's eighteen-foot-high, eight-ton, gold-leaf-coated statue of Prometheus bringing fire to Earth. On the tree's other side they also sheltered a space, for the dignitaries, that was cordoned off between the spruce and 30 Rockefeller Plaza. Four red velvet ropes enclosed a patch of sidewalk the size of a backyard deck. The mayor stood in it, accompanied by the Roman Catholic cardinal (his childhood pal), and assorted other luminaries, most of them considerably less luminous than the megawattage about to be unleashed in the branches of the sturdy, old, but inexorably dying, tree.

Dozens of blue-clad police officers milled about, separating the big shots from the dozen or so TV crews lined up to immortalize the tree-lighting ceremony. Outside the inner ring of dignitaries, cops, and journalists was the crowd, estimated at ten thousand, that had shown up, Christmas presents and videocameras in hand, to watch the mayor flip the switch that officially started the holiday shopping season.

Donovan and Moskowitz eased their way through the crowd. The smell of Christmas was in the air, as were the sights and sounds. Donovan thought of his childhood and turkey dinners with chestnut stuffing and mashed potatoes smothered with gravy and butter, served alongside a tree surrounded by wrapped packages. He thought of his wife and son and felt good, very good, humming along with "God Rest Ye Merry Gentlemen" and slipping through the crowd in as uncoplike a manner as possible. Moskowitz trailed behind, glancing warily at the gigantic tree and listening with ill-concealed amusement to his boss, the nonbeliever with the tough-guy past, humming a Christmas carol.

"So what's with Christmas trees anyway?" Mosko asked, wondering if it wasn't time to break the spell.

"It's a nice tradition if you're not allergic to them and don't have cats," Donovan replied.

"I mean what's a tree got to do with Jesus or the Holy Land? I been to Israel a couple of times and I didn't see a single pine tree."

"This is a Norway spruce," Donovan replied.

"I seen even fewer of them," Mosko insisted.

"You want to know what the tree thing is about?"

"Yeah. I figured you would know. Does it have something to do with the tree the Romans cut down to crucify him on?"

"I don't think so," Donovan said dully. "To the best of my knowledge, the Christmas tree is a pagan tradition from northern Europe. They used to bring a tree indoors every year before the snows closed in. It was a ritual to ward off evil and ensure that the trees outside would survive the winter."

"That still doesn't tell me what a Christmas tree has to do with Jesus," Mosko said.

"*Nothing.* What's a gefilte fish got to do with Abraham and Sarah?"

Mosko replied, "The day there's a seventy-foot gefilte fish standing on Fifth Avenue I'll tell you."

"I got a better idea," Donovan said. "Let's ask the cardinal to resolve this." With that, he led his friend off the Fifth Avenue sidewalk and onto Channel Gardens, the slender mews, decorated at that time of year with man-size white wire angels and lined by expensive shops, that led into the heart of Rockefeller Center. At the center's core, the Christmas tree towered over the scores of national flags that surrounded the skating rink with a riot of patriotic colors.

The two detectives eased their way through the masses of onlookers and the knots of uniformed police officers that lingered among them. Donovan and Moskowitz skirted the rink, looking over the railing at the several dozen skaters who displayed their varying skills before a very large crowd in a wholly spectacular setting. Over by the VIP area, the Boys Choir of Harlem was wrapping up "God Rest Ye Merry Gentlemen."

Casting his eyes about, looking over the crowd in search of important faces to wave to, the mayor spotted his favorite detective and waved Donovan over. Then Hizzoner tapped the cardinal on his festive red sleeve to alert him. Both exchanged knowing glances and faint smiles.

Donovan and his family went back many years with both men. While still a parish priest back in the dim recesses of twentieth-century history, the cardinal had heard confession for Donovan's father. Both mayor and cardinal knew Marcy's father when he was district attorney, of course. And Donovan himself hadn't exactly been invisible. He certainly wasn't invisible to another dignitary at the ceremony, Deputy Chief Inspector Paul Pilcrow, Donovan's longtime nemesis.

Pilcrow was Donovan's boss. The captain reported to Pilcrow, but reluctantly so, reflecting a dislike so mutual it came back as if on a tether. In reality, Donovan reported to the commissioner and the mayor, with Pilcrow standing between and finding fault wherever he could. The deputy chief was a man who worshiped at the altar of order. It grated on him that his most brilliant detective was among the world's least orderly persons. But Donovan was too important to fire, at least short of being caught with a smoking gun in his hand. Pilcrow was always looking for one and had proved himself not beneath suggesting that Donovan had fallen off the wagon (his continued sobriety being a condition of the captain's badge). Pilcrow also hated Marcy but, while pigheaded, was not so stupid as to take on a pregnant former‑policewoman who happened to be the daughter of a media bigwig and a state supreme court justice.

Famous for sucking up to the mayor whenever possible, Pilcrow stood with the dignitaries, his chest puffed out, trying to make small talk, something he was far from good at. Such behavior was part of Pilcrow's long-running campaign to be appointed the city's second black police commissioner.

He saw the captain and Moskowitz approaching and his face tightened. Jumping between Donovan and the mayor, Pilcrow asked, "What are you doing here, Captain? I thought you were on leave for a month."

"Everyone's been pushing religion on me lately," Donovan replied. "I thought this evening's ritual would be a good place to start."

Pilcrow made a noise that sounded a little like a novice driver grinding gears on an old Honda.

"How is your wife?" Pilcrow asked, at last.

"She's doing well, thanks."

"Any day now?"

"Any week now. How's your back healing?"

Pilcrow scrunched his shoulders to indicate discomfort. He had been wounded the year before while butting into one of Donovan's cases. The pain between Pilcrow's shoulder blades was a frequent reminder of the perils of standing too close to Donovan when he was working. This night when all anyone expected was the annual tree lighting, however, Donovan didn't seem to Pilcrow to be working. Even though Moskowitz and he slipped through the red velvet barricade and joined the dignitaries, the captain was looking not at them but up at the monumental tree, which stood massive and dark amid the glittering holiday lights of Rockefeller Center and Fifth Avenue.

He stared at the base of it, then looked it up and down, then finally ducked his head under the lower branches. When he pulled his head back out, Donovan said to Moskowitz, "This is a good tree for climbing."

"You're a city boy. When did you ever climb a tree?"

"In the park. And at my aunt's house on the Island when my dad sent me out there summers, figuring that the fresh air and clean living would turn me into a Boy Scout or something. I'll tell you; I got to be pretty good at climbing trees."

"My back hurts on cold nights like this one," Pilcrow said, edging the sergeant out of the conversation.

"Generic ibuprofen and hot baths," Donovan replied, patting Pilcrow on the arm reassuringly before walking around him to respond to a beckoning gesture from the mayor.

Donovan hadn't seen the mayor personally in a year, not since the city's top official had married Donovan and Marcy in an impromptu ceremony held in Times Square at the crest of New Year's Eve. Their paths crossed infrequently during the normal course of events, but often in memorable circumstances. In the course of the last one, Hizzoner played justice of the peace at a ceremony that made the front page of the *Times*.

"Maybe the boss wants to check on my progress, how I'm doing as a husband," Donovan mumbled to himself as he left Moskowitz in Pilcrow's clutches and stepped over to where the mayor and the cardinal awaited their turns to speak. Lowering his voice so as not to seem disrespectful to the dignitary currently at the microphone, a fiftyish woman in an expensive fur who was thanking the Connecticut family that had donated the tree, the mayor shook Donovan's hand and said, "You're about to become a father, Bill. Congratulations."

"Thank you, Your Honor," Donovan said, beaming.

"Do you know if you're getting a boy or a girl?"

"I'm going to have a son."

"That's great."

"My blessing on mother and child," the cardinal said, raising his right hand in a saintly manner.

"Thank you."

"You remember Captain Donovan, don't you?" the mayor asked.

"Who could forget? Tell me, Captain, did you enter into a spiritual *paxis in terram* to match the secular one?"

"If you mean did I get religion? Nope. Sorry, still an atheist. Nothing personal, Your Eminence."

"Your father must be turning over in his grave," the cardinal said.

"Why? Because I quit the Church, married a girl who's half Jewish, or stopped drinking?" Donovan replied.

"Take your pick," the mayor said.

The cardinal smiled. "You will see the Lord differently when your son is born," he said.

"There are no atheists in the delivery room, is that it?" Donovan said. He elevated his eyes as if seeking God but saw only a big Christmas tree that sat in darkness waiting for the mayor to flip the switch.

"What brings you here?" the mayor continued. "There's no threat to His Eminence or me, is there?"

"I hope not, sir. Marcy's in Fifth Avenue Medical Center waiting for the baby to come, and I thought I'd take a walk."

"Give her my love," the mayor said, then turned away and to the podium. It was time for him to take over the annual tree-lighting chores. Soon Donovan heard the familiar baritone, so clipped of phrase yet elegant of adjective, intoning that year's version of the annual rite.

It said: "My fellow New Yorkers, we are gathered here this beautiful evening amidst the best tourist season this city has seen in twenty years. More millions of visitors are gracing these streets than ever before. We see them every joyous day, strolling up and down Fifth Avenue, prettily wrapped packages tucked under embracing arms. . . ."

Donovan muttered, not quite to himself, "I hear the relentless hand of commerce ringing the cash register."

"Everything in this life is a reflection of God's love," the cardinal replied.

"You sound like Marcy's rabbi," Donovan replied in a loud stage whisper.

"We have the same tailor," the cardinal replied, touching pudgy, round fingertips to his skullcap.

The mayor's voice boomed on: "We see them every glistening evening, enjoying the dazzling lights of midtown. Last year we saw the beginning of the rebirth of Times Square, whose magical lights spell 'Happy New Year' to the world. This year we celebrate the different magic of Fifth Avenue, the world's most fabulous marketplace. . . ."

The continued talk of money was making Donovan more and more uneasy. So when Mosko sidled over, tilting his head to whisper in his boss's ear, Donovan welcomed the interruption.

"Hey, Boss, I got the tree thing figured out. . . ."

Whatever the punch line was, it was obliterated by a flash of chaos. For the glass-and-concrete canyon that was Rockefeller Center was filled with the deafening roar of large-caliber gunshots. One shot, then another.

Now, when a gun goes off on a New York City street the sound seems to come from everywhere and only the very experienced or the phenomenally lucky can guess in which direction the terror lies. The mayor froze in midsentence, his eyes wild and white and scared with the thought of death. His two-man security detail lurched forward to protect him. But Donovan got there first, coiling his legs and springing to tackle the mayor and hurl him to the pavement, covering his body with his own while wrenching his Smith & Wesson from its holster. At the same time, Moskowitz tossed the cardinal to the pavement and squatted, looking around for the would-be assassin. Mosko's Penzler automatic pointed up at the still-dark tree.

"Where'd that come from?" Donovan yelled.

"Don't know!" Mosko yelled back.

"Is anyone hit?" a security man blurted, kneeling beside Donovan and his boss.

"I don't think so," Donovan replied.

"I'm OK; I'm OK," the mayor stammered.

"Me, too," the cardinal added, feeling along his red-robed body in a search for holes.

There came screaming then, from a block away or so. And a general panic began in the crowd and spread away from the site.

"Those shots sounded like the ones I heard last week," Donovan said, scrambling to his feet and offering a hand to help the mayor up.

"Another shooting?" Hizzoner asked. "What the hell's going on here, Bill?"

"I'll find out," Donovan replied, and ran off. Moskowitz was right behind him.

"I'm in charge here," Pilcrow said then, charging into the scene and sounding like Alexander Haig after the Reagan shooting. As happened in that case, no one listened.

Those in the crowd who didn't run from the shots were gaping at the spot from which they had come. It was at the corner and a bit uptown. A handful of uniformed officers were hustling toward the spot, elbowing past tourists and shoppers whose holiday spirit had been jostled by yet another bloodletting.

As Moskowitz, younger and, despite all Donovan's working out, faster, went on ahead, the captain grabbed one of the cops. To this sergeant he said, "The suspect could be dressed like a Santa's Angel. Stop all you see and check IDs. But be careful."

"Gotcha, Captain."

There were several Santa's Angels around, just standing and gaping like everyone else, for the most part, the sound of tinkling bells having vanished for a time. Four more Santa's Angels stuck to their posts on the less-crowded east side of the avenue. The sergeant got two more uniformed cops to help him and went off to see whose those red-robed beggars were and what they were up to. Leaving Moskowitz to play front man at the site of what the captain was sure was another killing, Donovan spent ten minutes prowling the edge of the swelling crowd of onlookers, just looking. At one point he watched quietly as the sergeant grilled a Santa's Angel who made the mistake of turning surly and refusing to identify himself. Then Donovan wandered over to Madison Avenue, looking for the route *he* would take were he an assassin escaping his handiwork.

When Donovan got to the edge of the crime scene he found a shoulder-to-shoulder crowd that was jammed against the storefronts and spilled out into the street, bringing the incredibly jammed holiday traffic to yet another standstill. The focal point of the crowd was the festively decorated window of E & J Tuttle, a fabulously expensive store Donovan remembered from his childhood. That was when his mother and aunt took him on their annual window-shopping trip along Fifth Avenue in the weeks between Thanksgiving and Christmas. They never bought anything—much too expensive—although Donovan vaguely recalled a chameleon that he took home in a cardboard box and fed crickets caught in Riverside Park.

As a child Donovan had loved those yearly excursions to wallow in the riches of Fifth Avenue during the Christmas season. Now he gulped hard at the sight of Tuttle's old and famous Christmas display shot up like a target. The gigantic display window—or what was left of it—highlighted an assortment of larger-than-life nutcrackers watching while a gigantic robot Santa rode a fire-engine red sleigh through a starry winter sky behind a team of mechanized reindeer. But now the window was smashed. The robot Santa Donovan had planned on taking his son to see had slivers of glass showered atop its red cap and speckled throughout its white beard. And children were being led away from the scene by horrified parents who were at a loss to explain how precisely assassination helped make it a season to be jolly.

Donovan tucked his Smith & Wesson back in its holster and moved quickly through the crowd. As he did so he met a breathless Moskowitz on the way out.

"Who's dead?" Donovan asked.

"Another Christmas shopper," Mosko said. "Inside the store."

"The same shooter?"

"A Santa's Angels beggar," Mosko reported.

4. A HELL OF A PONTIAC, OR TWO VOLKSWAGEN BEETLES

"I didn't know it was possible to pay thirty-five hundred dollars for lingerie," Donovan said, looking in the bullet-riddled window—bulletproof, of course—that separated passersby from the extravagant collection of ladies' finery displayed in another display window. In particular, he gaped at a silk night-gown, blood red and edged with gold, that seemed flimsy enough to get the mannequin upon which it was draped arrested for public indecency.

"Me neither," Mosko agreed.

"I can remember when you could get a hell of a Pontiac for that amount. Or two Volkswagen Beetles."

Behind the robot Santa, a handful of exquisitely coifed and dressed salespersons gaped out the window, through the spiderweb of cracks joining and spreading out from the two holes, at the scene outside: a roped-off sidewalk surrounded by police cars, other official vehicles, and hordes of gawkers. Unaccustomed as they were to gore, the fashionable store's personnel looked as one might at a public beheading of the sort the Saudi Arabians favor. The prominent displays of blood and guts—two in as many weeks—were far beyond the pale of their expectations.

"Who's the stiff?" Donovan asked, shifting his gaze downward. A man's body lay bloodied and broken behind the mannequins and a small display case filled with expensive perfumes.

Mosko consulted some notes that were written on the back of an envelope pending transfer to his computer. "The ID in the pocket reads: 'Terry Seybold.' He's thirty-seven and lived in Southport, Connecticut."

"What did he do for a living?"

"A card in his pocket says he's manager of a stock brokerage office in Westport."

"So he lived and worked in Connecticut. What was he doing here?"

"Shopping," Mosko said, reaching out with the tip of his shoe and touching a white-on-white box from E & J Tuttle.

Donovan crouched down and carefully lifted the top. Inside was a gown identical to the $3,500 one he had been gawking at in the window. It was packed in soft paper that crinkled like pine needles being crushed underfoot on a weekend walk in the woods.

"The man wasn't hurting for money," Donovan said. "Was he married?"

"His ID says no."

"Then who was he buying this *shmatta* for? A girlfriend?"

"Lucky lady," Mosko said.

"Me, I'd rather have the two VWs. But each to his or her own."

Donovan inspected Seybold's clothes, looking at the lining and stitching of his coat and jacket and the leather on his shoes. Then the captain stood and brushed some dirt off his jeans. "He's wearing about five grand himself," he said.

"And that don't count the silk undies. The guy was shot in the chest, which pretty much ruins the togs."

"Pretty much. Can we tell yet what kind of slug killed the man?"

"Are you asking, 'Was it a nine-millimeter fired from a Kammacher Stedman?' It could be. We have several witnesses."

Moskowitz indicated the crowd of onlookers, which if anything was larger than the one that had gathered to witness the aftermath of the Melmer slaying. Added to it were several local TV stations' remote vans, hunching up through the traffic, their saucer-shaped antennae perched atop telescoping antennae that rose from squat vehicles, heavy with electronic equipment, that seemed always to hum like microwave ovens.

"Including the press, I see."

"Yeah. They just got here. They want to talk to you."

"And me in my civvies," Donovan said, straightening the old and honorable suede jacket he wore over a black turtleneck sweater and jeans.

"You're on leave, remember. You were bored, so we went for a walk. Anyway, the witnesses described a white male about thirty years old. Average height."

"Hair color?"

"Nobody noticed. They heard two shots—well, one woman says she heard three shots, but we're downplaying that."

"Why?"

"There's only two holes in the corpse. There must have

been an echo. Fifth Avenue is fairly narrow, and the buildings are tall."

Donovan led his assistant back out of the store and glanced up. So did a handful of people in the crowd outside. One way to get attention on a New York City street was to stand looking up. Several people would always imitate you. Donovan always felt that was due to the Big Apple resident's persistent fear of having a suicide fall on him.

"There were a lot of echoes in Dealey Plaza, too," Donovan said.

"Where?"

"In Dallas, where JFK was shot. That's why a lot of conspiracy theorists think there were two shooters."

"I thought that was because of the Oliver Stone movie."

"You're putting the chicken before the horse, my friend," Donovan said.

Moskowitz smiled.

"How many bullets did you find?"

"Two. Both in the body."

"So our killer's aim is getting better as he moves downtown," Donovan noted. "What else did the witnesses see?"

Mosko consulted his notes again, then said, "Less than the last time. There were shots. A Santa's Angels guy suddenly was running off."

"I see he didn't leave behind a tripod this time."

"I guess not."

"Maybe Friday's was his only one. Where do you get those things, by the way? Do the Santa's Angels wholesale them or can one of its beggars design his own?"

"I'll ask. The guy wore a regulation cape and a hat, plus jeans."

"Jeans are new. I don't remember them at Sarkana. Was there a videotape of this one?" He scanned the facade of

E & J Tuttle, which was polished black marble and stainless steel. "I don't see any security cameras."

"There aren't any," Mosko confirmed. "I guess this outfit doesn't worry as much about smash-and-grab artists." That peculiarly urban brand of robber typically smashed in the front of a store—in extreme cases by driving a stolen car into it—and grabbed as much loot as he could before the cops arrived.

"They go after jewels or TVs or something else anyway, not lingerie," Donovan said. "Where did today's perp go?"

"Downtown," Mosko replied, "in the general direction of Rockefeller Center."

Donovan looked down that way, again leaning over the display case. Several persons in the crowd outside imitated him.

"Maybe he wanted to catch the tree-lighting ceremony," Donovan said.

"Or catch the Christmas show at Radio City Music Hall."

"In any event, he melted into the crowd of shoppers, Santas, and other Santa's Angels coin collectors. I mean *I* didn't see him, and I looked around for where someone might run. Did anyone see the gun?"

"No. Shots. Man on ground. Man running. That's the gist of it."

Donovan was staring off into the crowd, focusing on a familiar face. Then he smiled and waved.

Mosko looked to see who it was, then gave his boss a quizzical look. "A member of your fan club?"

"Are you telling me you don't recognize Paul Duke?" Donovan said.

"The TV guy?"

The anchorman for WTV's *The Morning Show* was one of those impossibly handsome men who only turned up in Hollywood or on television. A regular item on *People* magazine's annual "50 Most Beautiful People" list, Duke was tall and dark, with perfectly coifed black hair and Mediterranean features that were vague enough to allow speculation about Spanish, Italian, Greek, Jewish, or Arab ancestors. His reputation as a serious journalist—serious as television reporters go, anyway— was formed during the war in Afghanistan, when Duke stood atop a mountain ridge not far from Ghazoor and challenged Russian choppers to strafe him. This fearlessness, as much as his looks, got him the coveted morning news job on WTV. Duke's studio, visible from the sidewalk at Rockefeller Center, was a tourist attraction. Each day hundreds, if not thousands, of camera-toting visitors pressed their faces against the bulletproof glass to watch the handsome, debonair, and fearless Duke read the morning's headlines to a nationwide audience counted in the millions.

Duke's path had crossed Donovan's on several occasions. The captain was an occasional guest on the show, usually to comment (or not comment, as circumstances warranted) about some horrible crime he was investigating. Every so often Donovan was put on camera to talk about a faraway homicide. The last such instance came a few years back, when the captain was a regular commentator during the O. J. Simpson trials. It was Donovan's opinion that the LAPD shouldn't have hopped that fence to get into the suspect's estate without a search warrant. "Starting a fire in a garbage can and pulling the alarm always worked for me," he told Duke one time, precipitating a torrent of protest from defense lawyers. In consequence of his many and often colorful appearances on the show, Donovan was a favorite of Duke, who now beckoned him from behind the police barricades.

"I'm going to go talk to him," Donovan said.

"Why?" Mosko asked. "He just wants to ask you about the killings! What can you say?"

"The usual platitudes: 'We will fight them on the beaches, will fight them in the alleyways; we will never give up.' "

"I thought you hated reporters."

"Generally speaking, I do," Donovan said. "But Paul's different."

"He's better dressed," Mosko allowed, after taking another, longer look at the still-gesturing man. "And that haircut must cost a fortune."

"I wonder what he's doing here," Donovan mused.

"He's a reporter."

"No, he's an anchorman. He gets a mil a year to sit there in front of the cameras and pose while reading a story a reporter handed him. He never goes out in the street anymore."

"What about the Afghan war?" Mosko asked.

"That was gutsy to stand up to Russian helicopters, challenging one to fire on him," Donovan said. "But the chances of it happening were really pretty small. Duke traveled with a camera crew, after all, and let's give Russian pilots credit for being able to tell the difference between an American network TV crew and a mujahideen guerrilla band. Besides, I don't think that Duke is ballsy all the time. In fact, I'm pretty sure he stays indoors for a reason." He drew Mosko's attention back to Duke, who was waving more frantically by way of ignoring two midwestern-looking women who were waving autograph books in his face.

"So what's he doing here?"

"I don't know. Maybe he was coming down Fifth in his limo when this happened and decided to play reporter. Maybe he knows Seybold. They both have houses in Connecticut, if that means anything."

"This is why you want to talk to him—you, a guy who hates reporters? Because it's odd for him to be here and you want to know why?"

"Curiosity is the basis of all learning," Donovan said grandly.

"It also killed the cat," Moskowitz replied.

"Get some uniforms to keep those local TV crews away from me," Donovan said.

Mosko nodded, then added, "I'm going to see what more I can find about this guy Seybold."

The evidence technicians had begun to arrive and were setting up their equipment and staking out their turf. Uniformed officers pushed the crowd back and erected barricades. In addition to the crowd of shoppers and tourists, several very well dressed business types had appeared from the executive offices of other shops and were having a worried convocation in the middle of Fifth Avenue, now gridlocked to a halt once again. Bonaci's crime-scene van was making its way down a side street, fighting the nearly impenetrable traffic.

Donovan left his assistant in charge, went to the police barricade, and slipped out of the protected circle and into the mass of milling bodies excluded from it. He was aware that, well off to one side, uniformed cops were keeping the TV crews sent to cover the murder from descending on him. They didn't seem happy about it.

Upon seeing Donovan coming, Duke shooed away the admirers and stepped out into the street, finding an open spot between a stalled number 5 bus and a cream-colored stretch limo that, like all the other vehicles, was going nowhere fast.

"Bill Donovan!" Duke exclaimed, pumping the captain's hand.

"Hello, Paul. What in the world has prompted you to leave the studio and walk among the proles?"

"The proles? Oh, the people. Well, I thought I'd pay a visit to my fans." He nodded at the growing group of admirers that gawked at him from the sidewalk.

"Which is why you turned up at a murder scene, risking life and limb from the ladies," Donovan said.

"I heard about it from our news staff," he replied. "You were listed as investigating officer. I thought I'd pay you a visit."

"I'm flattered, but I'm on leave." Donovan indicated his casual attire, which he had augmented by slipping his gold badge onto the outside of his breast pocket.

"On leave? But you're here."

"I was a few blocks up, keeping Marcy company. You met her in the studio a year or two ago."

"Of course. Who could forget the lovely Marcy?" he said.

"You heard we got married?" Donovan asked.

Duke laughed. "Heard? Yes, I would say so."

"We're expecting in the next couple of weeks."

"So you're having a baby? That's great. Congratulations." He shook Donovan's hand another time. Duke seemed genuinely happy for them.

"She's up at Fifth Avenue Medical Center . . . in the ICU, for a complicated set of reasons."

"Is everything OK?"

"Oh, sure. Just precautions. Her doctor is Mr. Careful."

"You can't be too cautious these days. And Fifth Avenue is a great hospital. A number of my colleagues at the network have been there. Do you know what you're having? Boy or girl?"

"Boy," Donovan said, beaming. "I'm going to have a son."

"Picked out a name yet?" Duke asked.

"Daniel Magid."

"Ma—?"

"Magid."

"That sounds like a family name. After Marcy's mom?"

"No," Donovan said emphatically. "Jews consider it bad luck to name a kid after a living person. *Magid* means 'storyteller' in Hebrew. Marcy wants him to be a writer, like her mom."

"Refresh my memory. Marcy's mom is . . ."

"Deborah Magid . . . her maiden name . . . the editor of *Perfect*."

"The women's magazine. That makes her a powerful woman, doesn't it?"

Donovan shrugged. "She's my mother-in-law, which makes her powerful even if she were a cleaning lady."

"I see your point. And your father-in-law, everybody knows Justice Barnes. Bill, your son is coming into the world bearing a powerful pedigree."

"Yeah, I guess he'll live down my side of the family. So is this your limo?"

The cream-colored limousine they were standing next to began to inch forward as the gridlock eased—at least on the downtown side of the crime scene. The bus also began to move and, showing no consideration for either celebrity or the power of the police, threatened to crush the two men against the big car. They stepped to the back of the latter, with Donovan trying to see through the dark-tinted windows.

"It's mine."

"What kind of mileage do you get on this thing? About the same as on a tank?"

"To be honest with you, I have no idea. But that sounds about right."

"I would think that a limo only attracts crowds," Donovan said. "How many autographs do you have to sign when you step out of it?"

"None. The trick is to keep moving. By the time these tourists have both recognized you and conferred among themselves to make sure it's really you, you're gone."

"And New Yorkers, of course, would sooner give up their rent-controlled apartments than ask a celeb for an autograph," Donovan said.

Duke nodded.

"We like to think there are so many stars living around us that hitting on one for his signature would be like asking the janitor for a stock tip," Donovan added.

Duke looked at the body, then quickly away and up at the store window, then back at Donovan. "Who's the victim?" he asked.

"Is this official? Are you playing reporter?"

"No. Just curious."

"The dead man is a Connecticut stockbroker named Terry Seybold. Know him?"

"I don't think so."

"He looks a bit like you," Donovan said.

"Poor man," Duke replied, with a smile.

"We should all be so unfortunate."

"Tell me, Bill," Duke said, moving closer and slipping into a conspiratorial tone. "Did I hear correctly? Is there a killer out there using a handgun that can shoot through bulletproof glass?"

"It's too early to tell," Donovan replied.

"What's your gut feeling?"

"My gut feeling is that it was done by the same guy. But we don't have tonight's slug yet—presumably it's in the victim—so you'll have to wait."

"Is there a gun that can shoot through bulletproof glass? A handgun, I mean?"

"Sure. How's your firearms knowledge? I ask because guns ain't my specialty, really. . . . People are. I only tell you what was told to me."

"I know a few things."

"The Kammacher Stedman will do it. It fires a depleted-uranium nine-millimeter round. That was the weapon used at that killing up at Sarkana. There are only three such firearms in the world, and only one of them is unaccounted for."

"Why would anyone want a handgun that powerful?"

"Assassination through bulletproof limousine windows," Donovan said, nodding in the direction of the limo, which had pulled to the curb near the next corner. "The gun was developed in Europe for that purpose."

"I see," Duke replied, rubbing his chin and falling silent.

Donovan let him have his thoughtful pause, then jumped on it. "Why are you worried about being shot?" the captain asked.

Duke's reply came in a startled, defensive voice: "I'm not worried."

"You just left your posh limo, braving autograph hounds, to find out about the presence hereabouts of a gun that can fire through bulletproof glass. And you tell me you're not worried."

"I'm curious. In covering the Afghan war I picked up an interest in weapons. Exotic pistols in particular. Who could blame me? I was surrounded by them. There were a lot of handguns floating around—all types. I even got one automatic off a dead Russian. But I never heard of a round that could fire accurately through bulletproof glass." Duke glanced at the window of Tuttle. "I understand the killer put three bullets in the victim at Sarkana."

Television reporters, Donovan thought. *They never get things straight.* He said, noncommittally, "He hit the target."

Duke seemed uncomfortable and looked longingly toward the safety of his limousine. At that moment, Donovan found it hard to imagine him standing in Afghanistan, raising his fist at Russian helicopters. *Maybe the man is only fearless about threats he can see,* Donovan wondered. *There's something about the notion of a gun that can shoot through bulletproof glass that chills the soul. You spend six figures on a secure limousine, maybe even hire an armed bodyguard as a chauffeur, and an anonymous crazy can still get you when you pull to the curb to drop off your laundry.*

"It's a crazy world," Duke said at last.

"Paul, who wants to shoot you through your limousine window?"

"Nobody," the man insisted. "Guns are just an interest of mine. You know how it is—I have to maintain my tough-guy image." With that, he gave Donovan a comradely punch on the shoulder, the sort of gesture the captain remembered from his high school days.

"Well, while you're tending your machismo, let me know if there's anything I can do for you," Donovan said.

"Oh, sure, absolutely. I appreciate that. I have your number in my Rolodex. Are you still on Riverside Drive?"

"Yep. Rent-controlled apartment and all. I'm currently preparing to dismantle my home gym and turn it into a nursery."

"You haven't done that yet?"

"More Jewish superstition. Marcy won't buy anything for the baby before he's born."

"Not even a crib?"

"It was all I could do to talk her into letting me buy a rattle," Donovan said ruefully.

"You're going to be one busy fellow the day after your son is born," Duke commented.

"Tell me about it. On my side of the family, we'd have built the Taj Mahal by now. So, are you still living in Southport?"

"Me? Sure. And I have an apartment in town."

"He lived in Southport," Donovan said, indicating the body, now surrounded by a swarm of evidence technicians lorded over by Howard Bonaci. "Are you sure you don't know him?"

"Terry . . . what did you say his name was?"

"Seybold," Donovan said, then spelled it.

"Sorry." Duke shook his head.

"Want to see what he looks like?"

Duke hesitated but, perhaps sensing his machismo was being tested, rose to the occasion. He followed Donovan to the corpse and looked down on it as a technician uncovered the face. Duke tensed up, then looked quickly up at the store window, as before.

"You didn't see bodies in the Afghan war?" Donovan asked.

"It's different when they're American."

"Funny, but I haven't found that," Donovan said. "I thought you took an automatic off a dead Russian."

"All right, you got me. I bought it from the mujahideen fighter who took it off the dead Russian. I hope you don't blow my cover on that. I told that story to *People.*"

"Your secret is safe with me."

"Since I'm being completely honest with you, the mujahideen didn't like me all that much. They expected me, a rich American, to give them millions of dollars for their struggle. When I finally said, 'Hey, I'm a TV reporter just here on business—let's not get carried away overestimating my commitment to the cause,' they were pretty pissed off."

"You had to come down from the mountains posthaste," Donovan speculated, and Duke nodded.

"My visa was expiring anyway," Duke added. After a moment's awkwardness, he changed the subject, and in a predictable direction. Looking at a snappy, rose pink negligee with a $2,500 price tag, he said, "What I like about being single is not having to buy stuff like that."

"Do you know Seybold or not?" Donovan asked.

Duke shook his head. Then he walked away from the body and back in the direction of his limousine. Something in his body language tipped off the chauffeur, who jumped out of the driver's-side door and rushed around the gigantic vehicle to open a back door for his boss. The driver looked beefy and suitably bodyguardish, an ex-marine sort of guy.

Donovan followed Duke to the car, then stuck out his hand. They shook.

"Sorry if that upset you," Donovan said.

"I'm not afraid of bodies," Duke replied, taking a deep breath. "I must be coming down with something."

Donovan decided to allow the man his smoke screen. "Take two generic ibuprofen and take a hot bath," Donovan said. "The single ladies of New York need you healthy."

Duke smiled. The discussion was ending on comfortable turf. Although Duke's reputation as a lady-killer was as legendary as his looks and tough-guy image, he never tired of talking about it. "It's a shame you went and got married, Bill. We could do the town. I know some dynamite babes."

"I'm married to a dynamite babe," Donovan said.

"Of course you are," Duke replied, getting into the car. "My best to Marcy."

5. "IT'S NOT LIKE THIS HAPPENED AT SOME CHEESY SHOPPING MALL"

"**T**he guy was shopping for his fiancée," Moskowitz said, angling his computer to get the glare from the streetlights off the screen. He had it set up on the hood of a patrol car that was parked near the body.

"Who's she?" Donovan asked.

"One Amy Willets, a graduate student at the Yale School of Drama."

"Wait a second. How old was Seybold?"

"Thirty-seven."

"And the girl?"

"Twenty-five," Mosko replied.

"You mean this guy is thirty-seven and he's going to marry a woman who's—" Donovan caught himself in mid-sentence, sighed, and shrugged. He had just remembered that he was twelve years older than his wife.

Moskowitz smiled. "You were about to say something, Boss?"

"Never mind," Donovan snapped. "Has she been told?"

"Yeah, by the Connecticut cops."

"Try to find out if Seybold had enemies. When was the wedding supposed to happen?"

"In June. They just announced their engagement last month. It was in the papers."

Donovan looked down at the body, then scuffed his left foot idly on the concrete. "Did any of the witnesses notice Seybold before he became a statistic?"

"What do you mean?"

"I mean was he talking to anyone? Did they have words? Or did the killer just march up to the window and shoot through it and Seybold had the bad luck to be standing there?"

"He was talking to the store manager," Mosko said.

"Who's that?"

"Martin Kimble."

"I want to talk to him," Donovan said.

"So do I," Mosko added. "But he ran off to consult with the home office. He disappeared before I could get my hands on him."

"Disappeared as in left the premises?" Donovan asked.

"Ran off. Took a powder. Hit the road."

"Send somebody to find him. In fact, send an army to find him. Tell this Kimble—home office or no home office—that material witnesses who disappear before talking to the cops piss me off."

"I'll put it just like that," Mosko said, calling a detective over and giving him an instruction.

Donovan added, "I don't get this. On Friday, November twenty-ninth, and again this evening, a young guy who's engaged to be married is shot to death on Fifth Avenue while shopping for his bride-to-be. On Fifth Avenue, the world's most famous shopping boulevard. It's not like this happened at some cheesy shopping mall." Looking sharply at his assistant, Donovan added, "Or in Brooklyn, where you might expect violence."

"C'mon; you can get some real good buys on Ralph Avenue and nobody's been killed that I know about."

"They just lost all their hubcaps. Tell me, could there be a connection between Melmer and Seybold?"

"Other than that they were both good-looking young guys who were planning on getting married?"

"Other than that. Did you find out where Melmer was eighteen weeks ago?"

Mosko consulted his computer, then said, "Umh . . . here, in the city."

"Doing what?"

"Staying in his apartment at Trump Plaza. He was here on business."

"What kind of business?" Donovan asked.

"I dunno," Mosko replied. "The man was in the medical stuff business. I guess he was selling medical stuff."

"Try to be more specific. Call his secretary and ask her."

"Why is this important?"

"It's important if he was meeting Seybold, for example. Our latest victim was a stockbroker. Now, if Melmer was in town on business related to the stock market, we might have a match. Is his firm publicly traded?"

"You mean like on the Big Board?"

"Like that." Donovan nodded.

"I got no idea. But I'll find out. You know, this is the sort of stuff you're good at."

"I'm on leave."

"Yeah, but you seem to be hanging around this case, don't you?"

"I was in the neighborhood, you guys were bugging me about Judaism, so I thought I'd wander over and connect with the tree."

The sergeant said, "Since you're spending so much time sitting next to her while she takes naps or watches TV, maybe you could plug in your laptop and do your Internet thing."

"I can't use the cellular modem in the hospital," Donovan said. "One night I logged on to CNN Online and it set off the fetal monitor. Bell went off at the nurses' station and they came running. They thought she was having contractions."

"So plug it into the wall," Moskowitz replied.

"My laptop is home in my study."

"I'll send a cop to pick it up."

"Marcy will flip."

"She's forty and the size of a house," Mosko said. "Her flipping days are over."

"You don't live with the woman," Donovan replied. "OK, have someone get my computer for me. No, never mind; I have to go home tonight to work on dismantling my gym."

"It seems like only yesterday we got you that," Mosko said ruefully.

"I'm only moving it down the hall to the maid's room off the kitchen."

" 'The maid's room.' I love you guys with your big old apartments. Has there ever been a maid in there?"

"Not that I'm aware of, and I've lived my whole life in that apartment. Apart from a few years in the sixties when I was . . . well, never mind. I'll do my 'Internet thing' for you. But I'm still not officially working. For one thing, these two deaths may not be related—"

"Sorry, Boss, but I think they are," Bonaci said.

"Do we have the same shooter, definitely?"

"I can't give you a definite yes until I get the bullet outta there." He looked down at the body, which was being zipped into a bag. "But I'd bet on it."

"Do those look like nine-millimeter holes to you?" Donovan asked.

"They're big ones, all right. And the descriptions of the shooter match the descriptions of the Sarkana killer."

Donovan said, "The first Santa's Angels killer was first seen ogling jewels in the window he was soon to fire through. Today's Santa's Angels Army killer was seen doing what? Admiring the lingerie?"

"None of the witnesses noticed him until the gun went off," Bonaci replied.

"And then he ran downtown," Donovan said, leaning against the hood of the car and looking in that direction.

"Toward Rockefeller Center," Mosko added. "Where your friend Duke works."

"If I killed someone, I would run away from the crowd, not into the center of it," Bonaci added.

"When a tree wants to hide, it goes into the forest," Donovan said, thinking once again of the gigantic Norway spruce. It had been lit by then, the mayor and cardinal having recovered sufficiently to complete the ceremony. "Did you have any luck reaching the Santa's Angels people?"

"I have a guy making calls to find out where they come from," Mosko reported.

"We need a roster of volunteers and paid workers—the names of everyone they have on Fifth Avenue this season. Also the names of supervisors, if any. How do those cloaks, hats, and tripods get distributed? Where and when do they turn in the day's receipts? Is there a mustering point?"

"You mean like a union hiring hall?" Mosko asked.

"Yeah, like that. Do Santa's Angels guys show up at the hiring hall every morning at seven to see if there's work for them? And, more to the point, is it a place where we can check IDs and videotape their faces?" Donovan said.

"Friday's tape wasn't good enough to compare faces, if that's what you have in mind," Bonaci said.

"No, but you might get a match with the eyewitnesses. You guys find out where the mustering point is and any other details you can. Like how many of tonight's Angels were also on duty November twenty-ninth. And get ahold of the names of those supposed to be working this block."

Donovan looked across the street, in the direction of a ringing bell. There were Santa's Angels volunteers—two red-cloaked beggars and a Santa—working the sidewalk. "I asked a uniformed sergeant to talk to those guys," Donovan said. "Track him down and see what he got."

"You got it," Mosko replied.

"And while you're at it, find out if anybody knew Seybold's schedule ahead of time."

"I got that already," Mosko replied, consulting his computer. "He had on his calendar that he was driving into the city. His secretary knew about his plans."

"Did anyone else?"

"No. She said he told her he was going to buy a surprise for his fiancée's birthday."

"When is that?"

"Sunday," Mosko replied.

"Seybold had a cell phone in his pocket," Bonaci said, producing the plastic bag that held the device.

Donovan took it and looked it over. The digital phone was one of the small, expensive ones. "Get the record of calls made on this for the past week," Donovan said.

"For the past week? Wouldn't for today be enough?"

Donovan gave his assistant a withering glance.

Mosko said, "No, of course it wouldn't be enough. I can tell you, though, that he didn't call in before he died. The secretary said he left the office late and drove straight here."

"Do you think the killer knew his schedule and was waiting for him?" Mosko asked.

Donovan tossed up his hands.

"Do you think the killer was lying in wait for Melmer?"

"I think I need more information before thinking anything," Donovan said at last. "I'm hungry. You don't happen to have a sandwich in that fridge of yours, do you?"

Bonaci shook his head. "I got a container of strawberry yogurt and a knish."

"What kind of knish?"

"Cheese. But it's left over from Saturday."

"Forget it," Donovan said, pushing away from the hood of the patrol car and looking around for the telltale smoke of a sidewalk vendor. On a nearby corner, a black man in a chef's hat was serving up fajitas and burritos.

Donovan said, "Maybe I'll get a . . . Hey, what about my gyro vendor?"

Moskowitz switched screens on his computer, then said, "Gyro vendor . . . gyro vendor, let's see. Oh, the Afghan you met the day of the first killing. The guy with the automatic who split. I checked out Fifteen sixty-two thirty-two seventy-eight Queens Boulevard. It turns out to be one of those Muslim meat shops."

"Muslim meat shops?" Bonaci asked.

"Where they sell the stuff prepared according to the Islamic kosher laws, or whatever they are," Donovan said. "They call it *halal* meat."

"That could be his supplier," Moskowitz said. "Now, we just can't walk in there and ask if they know this guy. At least, I can't go in and ask. I'm trying to find a Muslim police officer who can do it for me. In the meantime, I have someone checking with the city bureau that licenses sidewalk vendors to see who was assigned that spot in front of F.A.O. Schwarz."

"That's a primo location," Donovan said. "These guys fight over less important corners. The name and address of the guy I talked to must be on record somewhere."

"I'll find him, Cap."

Bonaci asked, "Why are you so interested in this street vendor? I mean, he can't have been the Sarkana shooter—he was arguing with you at the time."

"We were having a discussion," Donovan said.

"Most likely he ran because that gun was unlicensed. Maybe he also has green card problems."

"You know I don't like guys who run away from me," Donovan said. "They switch on my gene for pursuit. My pal from Afghanistan did that when he took off after I spotted his gun. And Kimble bolted after witnessing a murder."

"We'll find both of 'em," Mosko said.

"Do it fast," Donovan replied.

Not too long later, Donovan walked into his wife's hospital room to find her on her back with the head of the bed elevated halfway. Her robe was pulled up, exposing her huge, perfectly round belly to the early-afternoon light. She was getting ready to inject herself in the upper thigh. Her doctor stood on the far side of her bed, near the window, eating a Perugina chocolate and scanning the last several hours' worth of printout from the fetal monitor.

"Skin-popping heparin again, huh?" Donovan asked, sliding into his chair and unfolding the brown paper bag that held his dinner.

"It's subcutaneous injection," she said sharply. "Not skin-popping."

"I know what I see," he replied, watching as she pinched a fold of skin and slipped the short, slender needle under it. A few seconds later, the anticoagulant was spreading through her system; in the time since she had begun the successful pregnancy Marcy had learned that it was clotting in the womb, not bad luck, that had caused the earlier miscarriages. Those were the tragedies that had put so much stress on her relationship with Donovan.

Then she pressed an alcohol pad on the site and handed the detritus of the operation—the needle and its wrapping—to him. "I hate it when you hand me your garbage," he said, but nonetheless walked across the room and deposited the needle in the red sharps container on the wall. On the way back, he snagged a chocolate from the Perugina box and popped it into his mouth before she could notice.

"Good afternoon, Captain," said Dr. Campagna, folding the six-foot strip of printout into a manageable size and slipping it into a folder.

"Doctor," he replied, chewing and swallowing.

"She's doing very well. The baby is doing very well. You should be proud of both."

"I am. How is her coagulation status?"

"It should be all right. I'll check the newest figures in a moment. I would say, though, that if you don't let her get stabbed or shot she won't bleed to death."

"I won't let that happen," Donovan replied.

"He's said that before," Marcy commented, giving him a look. In fact, she had been shot, and in the stomach, a decade and a half earlier during an undercover operation that he ran. Only the fact that he, too, was wounded saved the relationship.

"What about bleeding during delivery?" Donovan asked.

"I'll stop the heparin well before. Also the tributylene and mag sulfate. And the baby aspirin."

"What about the insulin?" Marcy asked. To an already full palette of pregnancy complications had been added gestational diabetes, which, like the rest of the problems, would probably go away after she gave birth. But four injections a day—two insulin and two heparin—had left her tummy and thighs black and blue.

"That you'll take right up until you deliver," Campagna said. "Of course, the baby will have to go into an incubator for a few days as a result."

"Why?" Donovan asked.

"To stabilize his blood sugar. Don't worry. It's just temporary."

"Will I be able to nurse him?" Marcy asked, looking sad.

"Sure. But you'll have to do it in the nursery, not in your bed."

"At least it's something," she said, leaning back and pushing her gown into place.

"How long will it be before her bruises go away?" Donovan asked.

"Several weeks. The combination of anticoagulants and all those injections make the bruising worse."

"I'm afraid if anyone sees her I'll get hauled off for beating my wife," Donovan said.

"As if you would," she said, taking his hand.

"As if I *could*," he added, thinking of her black belt in kung fu.

Marcy asked, "Can you tell me yet if I'm going to have a vaginal delivery?"

The doctor looked down at her and smiled enigmatically. "All I can say is I like to deliver babies on Saturdays," he replied.

"What's that mean?"

"You're going to have a C-section," Donovan said.

"Do you have any Saturday in particular in mind?" Marcy asked.

Campagna thought for a moment, then said, "Two weeks more, at least."

"Two weeks!"

"Maybe three."

"Three weeks will be Christmas," she protested.

"I live alone and have no family, so Merry Christmas," the doctor replied. "Or Happy Hanukkah. Whichever you celebrate."

"In our family we celebrate both," Donovan said.

"Which are you?" the doctor asked the captain. "The Christian or the Jew?"

"I'm the atheist," Donovan said.

"Captain, I assure you that will change after your son is born."

Donovan harrumphed, and the doctor smiled at him. Donovan liked Campagna. He was a character, a short and driven man who delivered three hundred babies a year at an average, the captain had discovered, of $7,000 per. Even Donovan's barely remembered high school math yielded an income of $2.1 million. Some of that was spent, it turned out, on a passion for soccer that took the doctor around the globe to see World Cup events. Campagna himself was hardly an athletic figure. He was pushing seventy and smoked filtered cigarettes, a pack of which always was jammed into his shirt pocket. And smoke figured into one of the great stories about this man, who was the chief of maternal and fetal medicine at Fifth Avenue Medical Center.

One time, huffing and puffing as he pushed a sonogram cart down the hall at three in the morning, Campagna tripped on the newly washed floor and hit his head on the back of the cart. He was rushed unconscious into a treatment room, where the attending physician looked at the doctor's age and pack of cigarettes and assumed he had fallen as the result of a heart problem. When Campagna woke up he had a pounding headache and a case of nicotine withdrawal that was made considerably worse by the sight of the myriad wires sprouting from sensors on his chest. He stripped them off and, clutching his smokes and holding his gown about him, scurried down the hall. Frantic hospital personnel found him on a fire escape, puffing away and stamping his bare feet to ward off the bitter cold of a February morning. The yarn became a centerpiece of the Campagna legend, along with his threat to quit medicine and open a pizza parlor the day a managed-care cost cutter tried to tell him how to treat a patient. As a result of his fame as a leading authority on high-risk pregnancies such as Marcy's, couples came from around the world to have their babies under his care.

Campagna walked across the room to a small grey metal desk that sat next to a pint-size refrigerator like the one in Bonaci's van. That was where Donovan stored the yogurt, fruit, and seven-grain bread he bought for Marcy to pick at during the night. Campagna left the folder on the desk and went to slip the box of chocolates into the fridge. He stopped in midmotion and waved for Donovan to come get a piece.

The captain did just that, braving a look from his wife. "How many of those have you had?" she asked.

"Just one."

It was her turn to harrumph.

Donovan picked up a hazelnut chocolate that was wrapped in gold foil and unwrapped it while the doctor switched on the computer monitor that sat atop the desk. He tapped in a password and, after consulting the folder, Marcy's Social Security number. A row of numbers presently appeared on the screen.

Donovan bent over to look at them. "Lab results?" he asked.

Campagna nodded. "And the rest of your wife's medical history, going back ten years."

"Is anything wrong?" Donovan asked.

"No. I just wanted to recheck her clotting status."

"How is it?" Marcy asked from across the room.

"Good."

The doctor switched off the monitor.

"I think I might like being a doctor," Donovan said.

"We have our uses, I guess. Do you have any other questions? I have to go."

Donovan said, "Is Gicana going to re-sign with Italy?"

His eyes widening, Campagna said, "Roberto Gicana is a soccer genius. If he doesn't, it will be the end of the world. I cannot even consider the possibility of an Italian team without him."

Campagna shook Donovan's hand, then went and took both of Marcy's hands and squeezed them. "Have a restful night," he said.

"How can I rest when the baby is hiccuping every half hour?" she asked.

"How does he feel?" Campagna asked, grinning.

"He makes me giggle. But sometimes I wish he would stop."

"You cannot tell the baby what to do," Campagna said.

When the doctor was gone, Donovan sat back next to his wife.

She said, "So tell me about it."

"Tell you about what?"

"About the second murder. About how you threw the mayor to the ground and covered his body with your own. It was on the news and the nurses were talking about it."

Donovan took her hand and said, "I heard shots. I reacted. There was no serious chance of my getting hurt—if the killer was shooting at the mayor he could have killed him by then—except maybe that Pilcrow might have tripped over me trying to get attention."

"Was *he* there?" she asked.

"Unfortunately. Anyway, the party turned out to be around the corner. A guy was shot inside E & J Tuttle."

"Fancy," she said.

"And, until this evening, a pretty safe place to shop."

"Who was killed? The TV didn't say."

"A stockbroker from Connecticut," Donovan said.

"Through the window like the one a week ago?"

"Yep. I'm not sure if the perp was celebrating the first night of Hanukkah or the lighting of the Christmas tree."

"Same perp?" she asked.

"Probably."

"You're not going to be able to stay out of this investigation, are you?" Marcy said.

"I'm going to try," he replied, leaning back in his chair and closing his eyes.

They held hands silently for a long time, then switched on CNN and watched the coverage of the disrupted Christmas tree lighting. Nurses came and went, taking readings off the fetal monitor and checking Marcy's IVs. The baby moved off and on and hiccuped some, and when those things happened she pressed her husband's hand against her belly. For a while, when the nurses were gone, Donovan rested his cheek against her bare flesh, which was hot and ripe.

Later on he took a cab home, where he spent an hour taking his Universal gym apart and lugging the pieces down the hall to what once was the maid's room. The new layout of the Donovan apartment was shaping up: master bedroom, baby's room, study, living room, dining room, maid's room (soon to be the exercise room), kitchen, and two and a half baths. All this in a white turn-of-the-century Federalist-style building, the lower floors of which were laced with ivy.

At midevening Donovan showered and put a load of laundry into the wash. He dressed and packed his laptop into his briefcase along with a file full of printouts that Moskowitz had sent to the apartment. These were the day's reports, part of the price Donovan had to pay for spending most of the month in his wife's hospital room. When he got back to Fifth Avenue Medical Center, Marcy was asleep, lying flat on her back with one arm curved around her head, her face aglow even while dreaming, her café au lait skin glistening in the light from the fetal monitor.

Donovan unpacked his briefcase quietly and was about to crank up the laptop when he thought, *The hell with the case; I'm off.* Unless told otherwise, he would let Mosko handle it. Better to spend the time staring at Marcy. He eased himself into the recliner and turned so he could see her face. Donovan lowered his head onto a pillow and, before too long, fell asleep dreaming, like her, of babies.

6. MELMER'S BLACK FOREST COOKIE

It was ten the following morning, the first Friday in December, and Marcy had moved far enough to her right to let Donovan squeeze onto the bed alongside her. Her head was nestled against his shoulder, and she had one leg hooked over one of his to keep him from falling off. The head of the bed was cranked halfway up and they were watching a travelogue about Tanzania when the door flew open.

Deputy Chief Inspector Pilcrow straightened his jacket and strode into the room, clearing his throat into his hand as a way of announcing his arrival.

Moskowitz came through the door behind him, flashing Donovan a palms-up "What could I do?" look.

"Don't get up," Pilcrow said as Donovan lurched toward unwrapping himself from his wife.

Donovan sank back down against the pillow. "Deputy Chief," he said, resigning himself to his fate.

"Good morning, Bill. Hello, Marcy."

"Hi," she said flatly.

"Boy, you're really coming along. How long will it be now?"

"Two or three weeks," she replied.

"And it's a boy, I hear. That's great. Congratulations to you both."

He extended his hand for both to shake but pulled it back when he saw the array of IV lines sprouting from Marcy's free arm. Instead, he grasped Donovan's left hand and gave it a mushy squeeze.

"What's up, Paul?" Donovan asked, although he knew quite well what it was. Pilcrow only made personal appearances to deliver bad news.

"I'm afraid I'm going to have to cancel your leave."

Marcy squeezed her eyes shut and looked away.

"This is about the two murders on Fifth Avenue?" Donovan asked.

"It is."

"What about these two killings is important enough to get you up here in person?"

"You know that they're related?" Pilcrow said.

"It seemed that way as of last night," Donovan replied.

"Well, they definitely are. We've gotten a message. Sergeant Moskowitz can give you all the details, but basically, at seven-twenty-seven this morning the Midtown Merchants Association—"

"The sort of chamber of commerce for all these swanky stores along Fifth Avenue."

"Correct. It received an anonymous note that took credit for the two killings and threatened a continuing campaign of murder that would be sure to destroy the Christmas shopping season."

"How much does he want?" Donovan asked.

"Ten . . . million . . . dollars," Pilcrow said, spacing the words out to lend weight to them.

"Is that a lot these days?"

"It's enough to get your leave canceled. The mayor wants this madman caught ASAP."

"I saw the mayor last night and he didn't say anything," Donovan said.

"You mean looking up at you from the sidewalk where you threw him?" Pilcrow replied.

At that point, Marcy looked back in Pilcrow's direction, her eyes blazing. She was about to speak when Donovan beat her to it. "My wife is expecting our first and maybe only child. She needs me by her side. I worked hard for this leave of absence . . . this *partial* leave, during which I still get daily briefings on active cases."

"I understand that," Pilcrow said.

"And ten million dollars doesn't seem like that much for an association made up of stores that pay a hundred grand a month each in rent. Why don't they just pay it?"

"They will if need be."

"Frankly, Paul, I don't see why I should do anything that would hurt my wife and child just to save the bottom lines of—"

"The Midtown Merchants Association."

"—a bunch of multimillionaires who don't need the extra dough," Donovan argued, pulling his arm out from around his wife and sitting up on the side of the bed. "And what about you? You're an African-American with three generations in Harlem. How much do you really care if E & J Tuttle makes a few million less this fiscal year? That store isn't even owned by an American, let alone a New Yorker. It's owned by a billionaire Japanese businessman."

"How do you know that? I haven't seen that in the papers."

Donovan shrugged. "I plugged in my laptop in the middle of the night and poked around the Internet. Something is bothering me about these murders."

"You got that off the Internet?"

"Yeah. It's not the be-all and end-all, but it's a good research tool."

"I thought you didn't care about the Midtown Merchants Association," Pilcrow said.

"I don't. It's the puzzle that intrigues me."

"Well, the mayor and the commissioner, your old pals *and protectors*"—he spit out the last two words—"care about the Midtown Merchants Association. And that means I care. Now you care as well. I'm sorry this is eating into your personal time, Captain, but I'm making it official. Your leave is canceled."

With that, Pilcrow turned and stalked out of the room. Furious, Donovan scrambled off the bed to go after him, but found himself caught in Brian Moskowitz's brawny arms.

"It ain't worth it, Boss," Mosko said, holding Donovan back.

"Yes, it is. Getting fired. Sued. Thrown in jail. It's worth every bit I would have to pay."

"You're becoming a daddy. You can't go around punching out superior officers."

Donovan relaxed, and Mosko let him go. "Maybe not, but it sure would feel good to throw one more right cross before I get too old and lose the ability forever," Donovan said.

"So you're going back to work?" Marcy asked.

"You heard the man," Mosko replied.

"I am and I'm not," Donovan said. "He can put me back on the job, but he can't tell me how to do the job."

"What do you mean?" Marcy asked.

"I can conduct this investigation from right here," he said, patting her bedside.

"How can you do that?"

"I'll be here when I'm not on the job," Donovan said. "When I'm on the job, I'll most likely be just a few blocks away. This is Fifth Avenue Medical Center, I mean."

"You can do that?"

He nodded. "Call me on the cell phone if you need me and I'll run right back. I'll only go back to the apartment when I absolutely have to."

"Such as to take showers," she said.

"Campagna will let me use the residents' quarters for that, I suspect," Donovan replied.

"I love you," Marcy said, reaching out for him.

He leaned over and kissed her on the lips. "I love you, too."

Mosko tapped his foot on the floor.

"But don't get fired over me," Marcy added.

"It's not just you."

"Over Daniel and me."

"He can't just fire me. He would have done it long ago if it were that easy."

"I hope you're right," Marcy said.

Donovan sat down in his recliner and gestured for Moskowitz to pull up a chair.

"The man wants me to work," Donovan said. "Let's work. What have you got?" he asked.

Mosko said, "You have a meeting in half an hour with the Midtown Merchants Association."

"Is this necessary?" Donovan said.

"What do you think?"

"Of course it isn't. They'll just tell me the same thing Pilcrow told me: 'Please, Captain Donovan, save our bottom lines. Stop this grinch before he ruins Christmas.' "

Marcy smiled.

"They do have the ransom note," Mosko said.

"They didn't make you a copy?"

"They want to make a presentation of it, I guess."

"Oh, God, this is going to be worse than I thought. They'll glad-hand me and offer all the help in the world. But they'll make it clear they contribute millions to the city's economy and, if my luck runs true to form, to the mayor's soft-money fund as well."

"There could be a little pressure." Mosko smiled.

"I should have just decked Pilcrow and taken my chances," Donovan said.

"I don't know how it was in the neighborhood you grew up in," Mosko replied, "but in Canarsie it ain't a good idea to beat up deputy chief inspectors."

"As attractive a proposition as that may be," Marcy said.

"Easy for you to say, having done it," Donovan noted.

It was about two years earlier that Marcy had kung-fued Pilcrow onto his ass in order to prevent his interfering with Donovan while the captain was hot on the trail of a killer. She had claimed—successfully, she thought—that it was an accident. But since that event Pilcrow's dislike of her—stemming from her half-Jewish parentage—had turned to out-and-out hatred.

"Where's this meeting taking place?" Donovan asked.

"At the Wolf studios in Rockefeller Center," Mosko replied.

"Why there?"

"Your friend Duke? He's in on this, too."

"How so?"

"It seems he's on the board of the Midtown Merchants

Association and has volunteered to help them catch the grinch."

Donovan grumbled, "Standing foursquare in the middle of Fifth Avenue, no doubt, shaking a fist at the heavens and defying the killer to come and duke it out with him. Same as he did in the Afghan war."

"Exactly who are we maligning now?" Marcy asked.

"Paul Duke," Donovan said.

"Oh, he's *cute.*"

"He's cute on television. They make him up to look like a million bucks. In person he's just another guy."

"William," she said with a smile, "I believe you're jealous."

"I am not," Donovan insisted.

"And I did meet him. Remember that last time you appeared as an authority on police procedure? During the second O.J. trial? I was in the studio with you."

"Oh, that time. I remember now."

"Paul came into the greenroom. I'm sure he was flirting with me."

"Well, you're a mother-to-be and in no position to be flirted with by TV stars," Donovan snapped. "Besides, he's my friend."

"Your friend whose cottoning up to you last night seems suspicious given today's turn of events," Mosko said.

"It was suspicious then."

"You didn't tell me you saw Paul Duke last night."

"I figured why trouble you?"

"Thank you very much."

"He showed up, limousine and all, asking questions about the murder weapon." Donovan turned to his assistant and asked, "Was Seybold killed by the same gun as Melmer, by the way?"

Mosko nodded. "The results came in late last night. It was a Kammacher Stedman. The slugs matched."

"Yesterday Duke seemed nervous about the possibility of being shot through the window of his limousine, although he denied it. Today he wants to be the spokesman for the murder investigation. What do you think gives?"

"I don't hobnob with celebrities," Mosko said. "You figure him out."

"Something's wrong," Donovan replied. "The man is afraid of something and is dealing with it by snuggling close to the cop on the beat."

Marcy shrugged. "That shows a basic intelligence at work."

"And of course the ransom note will be featured prominently on his newscast, if it hasn't been already."

"It hasn't," Mosko said. "I asked."

Donovan stood and straightened his pants. "When did you say we have to be there?"

"It would be twenty-five minutes now," Mosko replied, checking his watch.

"What's the weather like?" Donovan walked to the window to see. He opened the blinds to reveal another brilliantly sunny day, crisp and very Decembery, falling over Central Park. The smoke from dozens of furnaces made cottony lines in the sky over Central Park West, on the other side of the park.

"Cold but not too bad. We can walk. Look; there's more news for you to chew on en route."

"Such as?"

"We got prints off that water glass you stole from Princess Anna's room and ran them through the NCIC and Interpol computers." Moskowitz read from a window on his notebook computer. "The lady's clean in the States."

"But in Europe——"

Mosko smiled while saying, "Princess Anna reveals herself to be Anna Fritsch, shoplifter and check kiter extraordinaire."

Donovan brightened, his face taking on a glow not unlike that on a fox who has just spotted a hare. "So, Melmer's Black Forest cookie has a past," he said.

"And there's more. Does her real name, Fritsch, ring a bell?"

Donovan thought for a moment, looking at Marcy, who shrugged, and then staring out the window. "No . . . yes, it does, but it's a long-ago and faraway bell."

"Think 1968," Mosko said.

"My favorite year," Donovan grumbled. "Fritsch. Yes . . . the Fritsch-Haegler gang. Those bombings of American-owned businesses in Stuttgart and Frankfurt."

"Stuttgart and Düsseldorf," Mosko corrected.

"Anna wasn't even born yet in 1968."

"No, but her mother was," Mosko said triumphantly.

Donovan brightened even more. "Kirsten Fritsch," he said. "The American-raised woman who led an adjunct of the Bader-Meinhoff gang. They did antiwar bombings and other stuff in Germany during the Vietnam era. She must be my age, if not older. I thought she was in jail for having blown up a GI."

"She was," Mosko verified. "The was in the West German lockup at Karlsruhe. That's where she gave birth to a baby girl. The year was 1971."

"Princess Anna."

"Yep. Mom got out of the slammer in 1979 and promptly dropped out of sight. No sign of her. No record of who the father was. Nothing in the record about the daughter until she scored her first shoplifting bust. That was in Berlin——West Berlin, then——in 1984."

"When she was thirteen. Whatta girl."

"Like mom, like daughter," Mosko replied.

"Bearing children under adverse circumstances also seems to be a familial trait," Donovan said. "Where's Mom now?"

"I got no idea."

"And where's Moll Flanders?"

"Who?" Mosko asked.

"What, they don't carry *Masterpiece Theatre* in Brooklyn?" Donovan asked.

"We got laws against the classics. Except maybe classics like professional wrestling and *Married with Children.*"

"Never mind. Presenting culture to you is like trying to teach a monkey to play the oboe."

"Hire a lawyer and sue me," Mosko said.

Donovan asked, "Where's Princess Anna?"

Moskowitz shrugged. "You saw her last."

"Let's go hunting," Donovan said.

The Wolf TV studios were designed specifically to be a tourist attraction, with on-air personnel sitting in front of gigantic windows against which the noses of tourists were perpetually pressed. Overlooking the skating rink itself, the centerpiece of Rockefeller Center, the spanking new WTV studios were so surrounded by glass and gawkers as to resemble a fishbowl, a high-tech one awash in blinking lights and flashing monitors. Donovan always felt a little vulnerable in it, as if being on national TV didn't make you feel naked enough by itself.

With Moskowitz by his side, he followed the production assistant who met them at the security door. They walked through *The Morning Show* set—a collection of pastel brown-and-blue chairs and sofas set off by maple desks and coffee tables, augmented by several high-tech pedestals bearing monitors—which was empty following the day's broadcast. They wound their way through the production facilities and editing suites to an elevator—also glass and overlooking the skating rink—that rose through the skin of the building to the third-floor executive offices. Eventually they were shown into a large conference room dominated by a crescent-shaped maple table at which sat Paul Duke and a woman.

She was fiftyish and very expensively dressed in a grey Bardosi suit and silk blouse, the same woman Donovan had seen helping officiate at the tree-lighting ceremony the night before. A contrasting silk scarf rode wrinkle patrol around the neck, which supported a once-killer face grown a bit gaunt and predatory with age. But she had auburn hair that, for the most part, hid the grey roots, and large brown eyes that roamed over Donovan; admiringly, he thought, despite his inappropriate jeans and suede jacket. Duke introduced her as Claudia Hummitz, executive director of the Midtown Merchants Association.

"I'm sorry to take you away from your wife," she said, adding, "figuratively speaking, of course."

He nodded. "Sorry I'm not dressed."

"Oh, don't worry about that. We just want to get this terrible business cleared up."

"Me, too."

"Captain, I can't stress too much what this tragedy is doing to business on Fifth Avenue. Did you notice how much thinner the crowds are today than they were a week ago?"

He hadn't. "I don't know how to measure that," he said.

"We do. We have a laser people-counter mounted on the corner of Fifty-third Street. Foot traffic is down twenty-five percent from last Friday."

"That was the day after Thanksgiving, the busiest shopping day of the year," Donovan said.

"Even allowing for a certain falloff, today's crowds are less. Everyone is afraid of being murdered."

"Not so long ago a madman of my acquaintance thought he could wreck a Broadway show by killing people in the theater. Attendance skyrocketed."

"That was Times Square," Hummitz sniffed, "not Fifth Avenue."

"Well, maybe blood doesn't sell on Fifth Avenue during the holiday season," Donovan said. "People are in the mood for chocolate and stuffed bears—"

"And Christmas cupcakes," Mosko added.

"So, you called the mayor and the mayor called me."

"He is an honorary member of our board and a great supporter of midtown merchants."

"I know. When we got married he bought us two recliners and a bag of popcorn. Maybe the popcorn came from a corner deli, but I'm sure the recliners were straight out of Bloomingdale's. Not Fifth Avenue, but close enough."

She seemed surprised, but pleased, to hear that Donovan also knew the city's top official. From his point of view, it was helpful to register a protest, however slight, at having his head gone over.

"Can you help us?" she pleaded.

"Let's see the note."

She pushed a maroon folder across the table. He opened it and found himself looking at a single plain sheet. In unremarkable type, it read:

GIVE TEN MILLION DOLLARS IN ONE-KARAT
GEM-GRADE DIAMONDS AND SAVE YOUR
HOLIDAY SEASON. WE WILL CONTACT ABOUT
DELIVERY. BETRAY US OR CALL AUTHORITIES
AND KILLINGS CONTINUE. NO ONE IS SAFE.

"Who's seen this?" Donovan asked.

"My secretary and me. I put it right in a folder afterward."

"And it came in when?"

"Actually, the call came in at seven-twenty-seven," she said.

"Call. What call?"

"You didn't mention a call," Mosko said.

"I didn't?" Hummitz replied. "I'm sorry. I got a telephone call at seven-twenty-seven this morning. The man said that he left an important message beneath the Rockefeller Center Christmas tree."

"Beneath the tree," Donovan said dully.

She nodded. "And that if I wanted to stop the killings on Fifth Avenue I should go get it."

"What was this like, a present? Wrapped in red-and-green paper and tied with a ribbon?"

She shook her head. "It was folded over and taped to the back side of a fence post. Have you seen the tree?"

Donovan nodded. "You might say that," he said.

"It's surrounded by a waist-high white picket fence," Duke explained, gesturing out the window.

Donovan went to look outside. A large crowd of tourists had already surrounded the tree, obscuring all but an occasional glimpse of the fence.

"He was right outside my window, Bill," Duke added, using the tone of voice anchormen employ for somber news. "I can look over my shoulder and see the tree."

"So what did he look like?" Donovan asked lightly.

"I didn't see him," Duke snapped. "I'm trying to work in there. Besides, the tree isn't that close. Only a few hundred yards." He left the impression that was quite near enough, thank you.

"Where's the tape?" Mosko asked.

"My secretary threw it out, I guess."

"We'll need to go get it," Donovan said. "There may be fingerprints on it. We'll also need your fingerprints and your secretary's."

"That will be fine," Hummitz replied. "We'll cooperate fully."

"You were at work at seven this morning?" Mosko asked.

"Every day."

"What hours do you guys work?"

"During the holidays it's seven in the morning to nine at night. But that's only for a month."

"What, will sales stop if you go home?" Mosko asked.

"No, but I like to give that impression," she said with a smile. "My members appreciate it."

Donovan sat back down at the conference table and asked, "What did the voice sound like?"

"It was changed. You know, like they do sometimes on *60 Minutes*."

"Electronically altered. You go into one of those spy stores and you can buy gadgets that will do it."

"Yes, like that. I remember this interview with a man in the Federal Witness Protection Program. His voice had that electronic sound."

"I don't suppose you taped the phone call," Donovan said.

She shrugged. "Sorry."

"So you got this call. What did you do?"

"I ran down to get the message, of course."

"I'm trying to picture this. You're sitting at your desk at the start of your fourteen-hour day. You're having your first cup of coffee. You get a call about the murders."

"Yes, just like that."

"Who answered the phone?" Donovan asked.

"Why, my secretary, of course."

"What did the caller say?"

"He told her, 'Put me through to Claudia Hummitz. I have information about the killings.' "

"So he asked for you specifically."

She nodded. Then, seeing the quizzical look on Donovan's face, she asked, "Is there a problem with that?"

Mosko replied, "I'm a mad killer. I'm striking out at Fifth Avenue stores. I call the switchboard at Tiffany's."

Donovan nodded. "Logically, you would call the most famous store on Fifth Avenue. Or the Associated Press, which is who terrorists usually call to take credit for stuff. But he called you."

"I'm not getting your point," Hummitz said.

"He knows who you are," Duke interjected.

"Oh," she replied, apparently taken aback. She had been squeezing a piece of facial tissue into a tiny ball with the palm of her right hand. It was an ad hoc worry bead, and Donovan noticed three or four like it around the Filofax and soft leather bag that sat on the table in front of her.

"And he knows what the Midtown Merchants Association is," Donovan said.

Casting about for an explanation that would let her sleep nights, Hummitz said, "I was in *The Wall Street Journal* a few weeks ago. A story about the upcoming holiday season."

"I have a vision of this terrorist reading *The Wall Street Journal* while polishing his weapon," Donovan commented.

"Maybe he's a Republican," Mosko added.

"This is New York. Anything's possible. Did you say anything to him?"

"What, this morning? Why, I said, 'Who is this?' "

"And he replied?" Donovan asked.

"He said, 'This is the Mountain Brigade.' "

Donovan gave Duke a hard look. "Recognize that name?" the captain asked.

"No," Duke replied after a moment's consideration.

Donovan thought that maybe the man was trying to look like he had the faintest idea of the answer. "When you were standing there in on that mountain ridge, daring the Russians to fire at you, you never tripped over the name of one of the major guerrilla organizations fighting the Russians?"

Donovan swore that Duke went pale. *That won't look good on tomorrow's newscast,* Donovan thought.

"You mean . . . this madman is after *Paul?*" Hummitz exclaimed.

Donovan shook his head. "Not necessarily. After all, if he was after Paul, he knows where to find him."

Duke cleared his throat uncomfortably. Donovan sensed the man was thinking of that big "bulletproof" window that his back was nearly pressed up against two hours a day, five days a week. That glass was all that protected him from an assassin in the crowd outside.

"Bill's right," Duke said suddenly, his chest puffing up. "The involvement of a terrorist group—"

"Alleged involvement," Donovan corrected.

"—with supposed ties to Afghanistan has nothing to do with me. Except that maybe the captain will let me assist him in his investigation."

Hummitz smiled and gave the anchorman an admiring look, the way a woman will sometimes do when a man in her life is acting gallant. It was the look Nancy Reagan always used staring at her husband when he was president.

Moskowitz gave Donovan a distressed look. This was the look he used whenever an unavoidable complication entered a case.

"I may be able to lend my expertise to the matter," Duke said.

"The New York Police Department always appreciates the assistance of the public," Donovan replied flatly.

"What does this Mountain Brigade do, other than hate America?" Mosko asked.

"I don't know the specifics, but I can find out on the Internet. All I can tell you now is they operate in Afghanistan, Pakistan, and Malaysia, and supposedly are bankrolled by Iraq."

Moskowitz scowled out the window in the direction of the Christmas tree. "So they come here to wreck the holiday shopping season? Does that makes sense?"

"They're striking out at the heart of capitalism," Hummitz said.

"I suppose," Mosko replied.

"We'll check them out," Donovan said. "In the meantime, tell me if you saw anyone while you were retrieving that note. For one thing, how did you know which post to look behind?"

"He said, 'Near the Wolf TV studio where the people gather.'"

Duke went a shade paler.

"This killer knows where the Midtown Merchants Association is, and he knows where the TV station is," Donovan said. "He's an observant man."

"Everyone knows about those crowds outside my window," Duke said.

"I agree," Hummitz replied. "There was a large crowd even at eight in the morning, waving placards at that idiotic weatherman. . . ."

Duke chortled. George Halloran was rumored to be a nasty drunk and not at all like his down-home, rib-tickling, homespun-humorist image. Seeing Duke's reaction to her calling Halloran idiotic made Donovan think there might be something to the rumors.

"Other than the weatherman, who did you see?"

"You mean in the crowd outside Paul's studio?"

Duke cringed.

"No, I mean around the tree."

"Just a security guard. And three Japanese tourists taking one another's pictures."

"Check out the guard," Donovan said to Mosko.

"You got it."

"See if he saw anyone loitering around the fence." To Hummitz, Donovan said, "What about in the crowd outside the studio? Did anyone stand out there? Were there any Santa's Angels people?"

"I just remember people with placards. 'Green Bay, Wisconsin,' or, 'Bozeman, Montana.' All those places, you know."

Donovan shook his head. "Anything west of the Hudson River is a mystery to me," he said. "I've heard stories about a place called California but can't verify that it exists."

"I've seen movies about it," Mosko added.

"No one stood out," Hummitz said.

"I could pull the tapes," Duke added helpfully.

"What tapes would those be?" Donovan asked.

"Why, the master shots made with camera two, of course. Those are the head-on shots they use when I read the news. They show everyone . . . all those hundreds of people, pressing their faces against the bulletproof glass behind me."

"Relax, Paul," Donovan said, reaching across the table and patting Duke on the hand. "We'll get the SOB before he can get you."

"That's not what I mean," Duke replied quickly.

"Sure it is," Donovan said.

Duke pulled himself up—he had been slouching in his chair—and asked, "Can we talk about this privately?" Then he gave a sideways glance to Hummitz, who flashed a little smile back at him. Donovan felt that, despite the admiring look she gave him earlier, she was enjoying the embarrassment suffered by the man. He clearly was taking some body blows to his macho reputation.

Donovan decided to change the subject. "Pull the tapes and make dubs for me," he said. "All those shot this morning a half hour before and after nine o'clock."

"Do you really think the killer is on them?" Hummitz asked.

Donovan shrugged. "I'll say this about Fifth Avenue: There are a lot of videocameras around. Eventually our man will turn up on one."

"Let's hope it's on mine," Duke said.

"I'll need to get into your phone records," Donovan added. "Chances are that call you got was made locally and not on record anyplace, but maybe he called long-distance."

"Like from a mosque in Teaneck," Mosko said.

"Now, now."

"Or from a gyro-supply shop on Queens Boulevard."

"What's this about gyro supplies?" Duke asked. "Do you mean gyrocopters?"

"Gyro sandwiches," Donovan said. "They're an obsession

104

of his." He nodded at his assistant, who replied by frowning.

"I'll gladly give you permission to access our phone records," Hummitz said. She checked her watch, then added, "If there's nothing else—"

"Sure, you can go," Donovan said. "And thanks for your help."

"Any time, Captain." She stood, straightened her suit, picked up her briefcase, and walked to the door. There she turned for a moment and asked, "Do you think I have anything to worry about from this man?"

"Who, him?" Donovan asked, nodding at Duke.

"No. I *know* about him." She shot the man another loaded glance. "I mean from the killer."

"No. He's after shoppers and tourists."

Duke also was on his feet but had gone to the window. There he looked out at the growing crowd, assessing, Donovan thought, the likelihood that one of those people was his would-be assassin.

Donovan added, "But just to be safe, I wouldn't spend too much time window-shopping. And I would be very careful about going into dark alleys with Santa's Angels guys."

"I don't go into dark alleys," she said.

"Anymore," Duke added, turning and smiling.

Her face turned hard, but she smiled and said, "Have a nice day, Paul; you, too, Captain," and walked out.

"Take it easy," Donovan replied.

The heavy conference-room door slid closed with a whoosh and a barely audible click. Mosko looked at the door, then at Duke, and asked, "Friend of yours?"

"We go back a long time," Duke said, still looking out the window.

"And into some dark alleys?" Donovan asked.

"Is this germane?"

"Probably not. But I'm curious."

Duke turned around, stuck his hands in his pants pockets, and said, "Can we talk alone, Bill? Nothing personal, Sergeant."

"No problem," Mosko replied. "I got things to do anyway." He got up from the table and hefted his shoulder bag.

Donovan said, "See if you can track down the little princess."

"I'll do that and a few other things," Mosko said, following Hummitz out the door by about a minute.

"Who's 'the little princess'?" Duke asked.

"A movie I'm renting."

Duke's brow furrowed, in either disbelief or astonishment.

"Hey, I'm becoming a dad," Donovan said. "I have to bone up on these things. How much do you know about diapers?"

"Not a damn thing."

"No kids? Not one little heir left behind on the road to fame and fortune?"

Duke returned to the conference table and knocked on it. "Just a string of broken hearts," he said. He sat back down and resumed slouching.

"Including Claudia Hummitz's?" Donovan asked.

"Why do you say that?"

"The two of you exchanged a few barbs."

"You can't break what you don't have," Duke said, adding a faint smile.

"It must have been a hell of an evening," Donovan replied.

"Three of them, actually, on consecutive Saturdays."

"Before or after you became the spokesman for the Midtown Merchants Association?"

"After. We were working late on a proposal last September and went out for a drink. One thing led to another."

"It's amazing how often it does," Donovan said.

"All was fine until I had too much to drink that third night and blabbed on about this woman I had had a fling with over the summer. Claudia freaked out on me. Strange. She's our age. But I guess not everyone who came up in the sixties is a sixties person, if you know what I mean."

Donovan knew what he meant.

"You should hang out with me some night," Duke continued. "No, you're married. Forgive me."

"Who do you want to talk about privately?" Donovan asked.

"You mean you're not really interested in what went on between Claudia and me?"

"Does it have anything to do with these murders?"

"Oh, God, I don't think so. There wasn't even a husband involved for me to outrage."

"I understand you've done quite a bit of that," Donovan said.

"You're been reading *People* again."

"I got my hair cut the other day and there it was, at the barbershop. Your pretty face right on the cover alongside Brad Pitt . . . whoever that is. How does it feel to be one of the fifty most beautiful people in America?"

"Tiring," Duke said with a sigh. "It gives you too much of a reputation to live up to."

"Not to mention tells all those outraged husbands where to find you," Donovan said.

"Yes!" Duke exclaimed. "And that's what I want to talk about."

Donovan's eyes widened. He said, "So there's some truth to the notion the killer I'm chasing is really out to get you?"

"That's what I'm worried about," Duke replied, looking down at his hands, which were clasped atop the table.

"Why didn't you tell me this yesterday?"

"I wasn't sure then."

"Now you are."

"I'm not the expert on homicide—you are. But it sure looks that way."

"What changed your mind?" Donovan asked.

Duke said, "The call Claudia got this morning. The one from the Mountain Brigade."

"At last count, Mountain Brigade was not an outraged husband."

"I'll get to that. Just hear me out."

Donovan folded his arms and stared at the man, imparting as much sympathy as was possible given what was being said.

Which was: "When I reported on the war in Afghanistan, I said a lot of things that infuriated the Russians."

"So did Dan Rather," Donovan replied.

"Dan Rather didn't wave his fist at their troops and defy them to shoot," Duke said.

"That was pretty gutsy of you," Donovan replied.

"I was drunk," Duke admitted. "It was like a frat-boy prank. I can't imagine why I did it."

Donovan said, "If Boris Yeltsin or whoever wanted to kill you, why wouldn't he just do it? In my opinion, governments that send assassins to kill their enemies don't involve themselves in a whole lot of rigmarole about store windows and Santa's Angels volunteers. The guy Stalin sent to kill Trotsky went straight for the target."

"But the CIA tried to poison Fidel Castro's mouthwash or something like that," Duke argued.

"Meaning?"

"Meaning that the Russians are trying to break me . . . to humiliate me, before killing me. The way I humiliated them."

Donovan shook his head. "Maybe I'm getting dense," he

replied, "but I don't see how shooting shoppers through store windows is meant to humiliate you."

"They want me to sit there on national television looking over my shoulder waiting to be shot and having a nervous breakdown," Duke said, slamming his fists on the table before getting up and returning to the window.

"*Quos vult perdere Jupiter dementat*," Donovan replied, in extraordinarily bad Latin.

"Huh?"

" 'Who God wants to destroy he first makes crazy.' "

"You're a Latin scholar?"

Donovan shook his head. "I read it in the paper this morning. In a book review about the Dreyfus affair. When stuck in a hospital room for weeks on end you do a lot of reading."

Duke fell silent. Donovan stared at him for a moment. When no further words were coming, the captain said, "You were going to tell me about the outraged husbands."

Duke smiled bitterly. "You know my reputation."

"According to *People*—"

"They're polite," Duke interrupted. "You should read what the *Enquirer* says."

"I would sooner have my flesh ripped by demons," Donovan said, using his favorite phrase for dealing with intolerable situations. "According to *People,* your affairs with married women have caused enough scandal to keep you in the news without getting you fired."

Again Duke smiled bitterly.

"But your highly publicized liaison with . . . what's her name?"

"Sandra Block."

Donovan continued, "The young wife of the Hollywood studio head—"

"Martin Block," Duke reported.

"Got you a warning from your bosses at WTV—keep your private affairs private or lose your million-a-year job."

"It's a million-five," Duke said, expelling a huge gush of air.

"Congratulations," Donovan replied.

"A lot of good that money will do me if I'm dead. Do you see the problem now?"

"I see several problems," Donovan admitted. "One of them is keeping your pants on, a lesson I would have thought you had learned by now in this age of AIDS. And another is paranoia."

"What do you mean, paranoia?" Duke asked.

"I think you're overreacting," Donovan said.

"Look at those people out there, standing around the Christmas tree," Duke replied. "And here . . . look down. . . . Come and look down."

Donovan walked around the table, went to the window, and looked down. He could see part of the crowd outside the studio windows, which at that time of day offered only taped segments and other modest attractions. The star was off camera, upstairs in the conference room discussing his nervous breakdown.

"Nice crowd," Donovan said, hoping to sound agreeable.

"Any one of them could be my assassin."

Donovan patted his friend on the back. "You know, Paul, I've been shot at a couple of times in my life. Often enough so that my wife routinely tells me to avoid it, if possible, in the future."

"Smart woman," Duke said, still refusing to make eye contact.

"And each time it happened it came like *that*." Donovan clapped his hands. "There were no rococo warnings, no cryptic threatening phone calls . . . just 'Jeez, there goes the bullet; thank God it missed.' And then I would shoot back, and all of the time so far my aim has been better than his."

"You don't sit with your back to a window for two hours every morning while a madman is out to get you carrying a gun that can shoot through bulletproof glass," Duke said, at last turning around.

Donovan again looked out the window and straight down, this time pressing his forehead against the glass to get a better glimpse of any potential assassins.

"I don't know, Paul. I see a lot of grandmas in that crowd."

"Two people were just shot to death by Santa's Angels volunteers," Duke said, his voice rising slightly.

"You have a point," Donovan acknowledged.

"Through bulletproof glass," Duke said. His voice had entered the plaintive register.

"Two points."

Donovan took the man and led him back to the table. The two of them sat on the edge of it, looking out at the gigantic tree.

"I can't take it anymore, Bill. My nerves are shot. I can barely concentrate on the TelePrompTer. All I can think about is a bullet crashing through that window and going into my back."

"Can't you draw the curtain or something?"

"Don't you think I thought of that? No, my producer won't let me. 'The people want to see you,' she says. 'And ratings go down when the folks at home can't see the crowds in Rockefeller Center in the background,' she says."

"Fire him," Donovan replied.

"Her. Are you nuts? Fire a producer? She could fire me. They'll never close the curtain or the set. I heard that Matt

Lauer over at NBC got sick of having tourists gawk at him every morning while he worked and tried to get the set closed. But no-o-o. Do you watch *The Today Show*?"

"I can't stand commercials, so I listen to *Morning Edition* on National Public Radio," Donovan replied.

"Jesus . . . an intellectual cop. What's the world come to?"

"This is New York, my friend," Donovan said. "Even the schmucks have Ph.D.s. So who's trying to kill you—Boris Yeltsin or Martin Block?"

"Yeltsin may be, given this morning's phone call."

"How can I say this politely, Paul? You're delusional."

Duke ignored the remark. "As for jealous husbands, it's not Block I'm worried about so much as Valery Koslov." Duke jammed his hands back into his pockets.

Donovan's eyes rolled. Valery Mikelovich Koslov was a multimillionaire Russian émigré with links to a faction of the Russian mafia suspected of extorting millions of dollars out of legitimate Russian businessmen and sports figures who made it big in the United States. Koslov's nefarious business made the headlines when a Russian-born professional hockey player had his arms broken for failing to pay a reported $10,000 a month in protection money. Following indictment for extortion and manslaughter—an unrelated charge—Koslov dropped out of sight.

"The Brooklyn DA wants him to surrender, but word is he doesn't trust anyone in a uniform," Donovan said. "It seems that in the old Soviet Union the cops would occasionally create shortcuts for what passed for courts in those days. So maybe Koslov is hiding out in the wilds of Brooklyn someplace or maybe he's beat it back to Mother Russia."

"I'm trying to tell you, Koslov is gunning for me," Duke insisted. "That's what the bloodshed on Fifth Avenue has been about."

"Please, tell me you didn't sleep with Valery Koslov's wife," Donovan said.

Duke looked away. "I'm not as strong as I seem," he replied, sighing loudly, apparently too embarrassed to face the captain.

"Strong ain't the problem—horny is," Donovan said.

"Gina Koslov is a beautiful woman, Bill, hard to resist."

"How old is she?"

"Twenty-four."

"And him?"

"Fifty-something."

"So you not only slept with a Russian mobster's wife; you slept with a Russian mobster's *young and beautiful* wife."

Duke tossed his hands up.

"You're a dead man," Donovan commented.

Duke turned paler yet. After a second he said, "Wow . . . just what I wanted to hear."

"Paul, I have to be honest with you: I don't know how much of this to take seriously. Frankly, I doubt any foreign assassins are on your trail. Judging by recent terrorist acts in this country"—a group of Arabs had recently been convicted in Federal District Court downtown for conspiring to dynamite bridges and tunnels leading into Manhattan—"their MO is blowing stuff up—and that doesn't include shooting holes in the windows of fancy Fifth Avenue stores."

"Egyptian fundamentalists are killing tourists as a way of stopping tourism," Duke said. "Why can't it happen here?"

"Because Fifth Avenue ain't the Valley of the Kings and Tiffany's ain't the Great Sphinx," Donovan replied. "Here the terrorists put a car bomb in the basement of the World Trade Center. Maybe flame an airliner. I advise you to forget that drunken night in the mountains of Afghanistan. Nothing you did over there is coming back to haunt you."

"I wish I had your confidence."

"On the other hand, Valery Koslov has shown himself unimpressed with star power and willing to avenge himself."

"That hockey player," Duke said.

"The same."

"What should I do? I'm afraid if I keep sitting with my back to that studio window someone is going to put a bullet in me. But if I come out in the open and ask for police protection, I'm going to get fired. They made it perfectly clear after the Sandra Block episode—'One more fuckup and you're gone.' "

"I know somebody I can ask about Koslov," the captain said, taking out a ballpoint pen and making a note on the back of a parking-garage receipt fished out of the depths of his back pocket. "If anyone can help me find him, this guy can."

"You're a pal," Duke replied.

Donovan scratched his chin and said, "Not to take the issue of firing too lightly, but aren't you rich? And at your level, don't they have to throw money at you to get rid of you? So they kick your horny little ass down the stairs. Don't they also have to toss another million or so along with you?"

Duke shook his head. "I'm tapped out. There's no golden parachute in my contract. I have huge expenses. And I know for a fact that I'm considered unhireable due to my legal problems."

"You're a good-looking guy who's popular with the women," Donovan argued. "Fox would hire you in a flash."

"Not true. I've already sniffed around there. I tell you, Bill, this job is my last chance. Lose this and I'm hosting an all-night cable show for peanuts—if I live long enough to tape the first installment, and you're telling me I probably won't."

"I'm telling you that while it's true you've made enemies, building up to an assassination by taking target practice on

Fifth Avenue store windows is a pretty weird way of doing business."

"Which is another reason I'm appealing to you," Duke said. "You specialize in unusual crimes and exotic weapons."

"My main requirement of life is that it be interesting," Donovan replied.

"I'm begging you—tell me what to do."

"Hire a bodyguard. Can you afford it?"

"My chauffeur is also my bodyguard. He didn't want me to get out of the car to talk to you."

"Take his advice. No more wandering into crowds outside Fifth Avenue stores, even if you do happen to see me in them. No sitting next to the window in your car. Go straight from your limo to the studio to your home. If you need to eat, send out for Chinese. And no fooling around with strange women."

"They're the most fun," Duke protested, smiling. He was lightening up a bit, perhaps seeing a light at the end of the tunnel.

"Who'd you hear that from, Dick Morris? No one is safe now that supermarket tabloids are waiting to throw money at any hooker who manages to snag a celebrity. For God's sake, lay low and take cold showers until I catch whoever is behind these crimes."

"Koslov . . . I'm sure of it."

"We'll see," Donovan said. "In the meantime, I'm going to have a man in that crowd outside your studio window beginning at eight A.M. tomorrow."

Duke brightened a lot. "Can you do that? That's great."

"When you're on the air, he'll be outside the window. In fact, I'm going to have a lot of men outside a lot of store windows starting tomorrow."

"Wow. What a great story."

"Too bad you can't report it without getting yourself

fired," Donovan said. "If you want me to help you, play ball. I'll give you an exclusive when I catch the bum. Now, can we go get those tapes?"

To Donovan, walking through a TV station after the day's business was done must be like walking through Mission Control right after a rocket launch. A lot of very expensive equipment blinked at no one. Few eyes remained to gape at the rows and rows of monitors, which in some places were stacked to the ceiling. Few feet remained to trip over the cables, some secured with duct tape, others strewn like yesterday's noodles across the grey industrial carpeting. Here and there a worker toiled in a corner. Following Duke through a maze of control rooms and postproduction facilities, Donovan noticed an old man adjusting color bars on a monitor and a raven-haired beauty fiddling with a drawing of Woody Woodpecker displayed on a video graphics machine. Neil Diamond sang "America" from a small candy-colored boom box.

"How'd you miss her?" Donovan stage-whispered to the star after they passed.

"What makes you think I did?"

"She didn't look up when you walked by."

"You don't miss much yourself, do you? She's saving herself for her husband," Duke muttered, his tone indicating he might be speaking of someone in the nineteenth century.

"Lucky man," Donovan said.

Duke led Donovan up a flight of metal steps, around a corner, and into Master Control, which looked down on *The Morning Show* set through a window that sprawled from one wall to another. A sickle-shaped hickory control panel sat below it, its back edge curling around six high-backed executive swivel chairs. Two of the latter were occupied: a woman of thirty or so years, with close-cropped red hair and an impish smile, sat next to the weatherman Duke had been maligning earlier. She had her hands outstretched to encompass three or four buttons and a small joystick.

"What is this, the bridge of the *Enterprise*?" Donovan asked, looking at the rows and rows of buttons, dials, and small monitors.

"This is Master Control," Duke said. "It's where they run my life from. There are six hundred and two buttons on this console. I sat here one morning and counted them."

"Do you know what they all do?"

"They all give me agita," Duke said. "Every single one. Hi, Rose. Hello, George."

The woman looked over and gave the two of them a smile. But George, being George Halloran, had a more complex reaction. Upon seeing Duke he scowled and the muscles in his thick neck tightened, causing a roll of pink skin to puff out. But when Donovan's face hove into view, Halloran popped into his public persona.

"Hi there," he said, jumping up and extending a plump hand. "George Halloran, and you are . . . I know you, don't I?"

"Bill Donovan, New York Police."

"Of course. It's been a year, hasn't it?"

"About that."

"What are you here for, the O.J. civil appeals verdict?"

Donovan shook his head. "I don't get scale for this appearance," he said. "I'm here to pick up a tape."

"This morning's master shot from camera two," Duke said to the woman. "I asked Rose to run a dub for me."

She reached under the console, where a soft brown leather carryall bag was propped against a stanchion. She plucked from it a black cassette and handed it to the captain.

"Here you go, Captain," she said.

"Thank you." He turned the tape over in his hand. It was without a label.

"Rose Waucqez," she announced, sticking out her hand. They shook.

"Good to meet you," Donovan said.

"I'm an assistant director of *The Morning Show.*"

"She rules my life and does an admirable job," Duke said.

"You need occasional guidance," Donovan commented, in a friendly sort of way.

"This is true," Duke replied.

"If you're not here to tape a segment on the O.J. appeal, what are you up to?" Halloran asked.

"I'm investigating the murders on Fifth Avenue," Donovan said.

"And our camera two can help you?"

"I'm interested in seeing faces in crowds outside Fifth Avenue windows," Donovan said. "I'm curious to see who was there during this morning's show."

"Speaking as someone who did two stand-ups—I went outside and shot my weather sequences while standing in the crowd—there were a lot of regular folks from around the country. Grandmas and grandpas and Little Suzies from the Heartland." Halloran was on a roll and moved closer to Donovan. That was close enough for the captain to get a whiff of alcohol stench, the smell that oozes from the pores of a confirmed boozer. Reflexively Donovan stepped back, clumsily backing into a chair and making a noise that called attention to what he was doing.

The jolly weatherman facade stiffened, then crumbled like yesterday's graham cracker. "Of course," Halloran said, fumbling for words, "it was cold out there and Little Suzie's Boston terrier peed on my foot."

"Be grateful she doesn't like Saint Bernards," Donovan said agreeably.

"Yeah," Halloran muttered, returning to his seat and lowering his three-hundred-pound, six-foot-three frame into it.

"Can I keep this or do you need it back?" Donovan asked the assistant director.

"Keep it. We have tons of tapes. But do we have a news item on how your investigation is going?"

Duke shook his head. "In return for an eventual exclusive I promised him to keep it off the air for the time being."

Waucqez frowned slightly, then shrugged. "I don't suppose there's much of a story in your wanting to see who was in the crowd outside our window," she said.

"Not much of one, no," Donovan agreed.

"What kind of a gun was used in those killings?" Halloran asked. "Do you know?"

"Most likely a Kammacher Stedman nine-millimeter."

"Oh. The assassination handgun. That's a nice piece of work, that weapon." The weatherman brightened considerably upon hearing a line of conversation that interested him.

"You've heard of it?" Donovan asked, also interested.

"Last year I was with a bunch of guys who could talk about little else."

"Where was this?"

"In Montana. What town was that, honey?" He nudged Waucqez with an elbow.

"Moose Horn. A little burg about an hour from Bozeman," she replied. "Don't call me honey."

"The two of you went together?" Donovan asked.

She pretended to scratch her forehead so she could roll her eyes without Halloran seeing.

"I was doing a setup at the Moose Horn Billiards Tournament, and Rosie came along to manage the crew."

"Don't call me Rosie," she said.

"Oh, c'mon, darling; have a heart. You're dealing with a sensitive old man who just is lookin' for a friend." Halloran was back in his cornpone public persona and living it up. Duke was nonplussed by this turn of events, but Waucqez seemed irritated.

"Turn it off, George," she snarled.

He shrugged and leaned back in his chair. The springs groaned under his weight as he began to swivel from side to side.

"Was it easier to do the weather from Moose Horn, Montana, than it was from Fifth Avenue?" Donovan asked.

"Easier. No Little Suzie in Montana."

"But lotsa moose."

"I never saw so much as a hoofprint. At that time, the state was full of reporters doing Unabomber stories. The moose were hiding in the hills. Anyway, I took . . . Ms. Waucqez . . . along to protect me. She's a crack shot, you see."

"Crack shot?" Donovan asked.

"It was beginner's luck," Waucqez said.

"Where did you shoot?" Donovan asked, taking a quick look at Duke to see if he was reacting. He wasn't.

"The town was also hosting a firearms exposition," Waucqez said. "George wanted to drop in on it, because George is a redneck who likes to drink shooters and beer and talk guns with the rest of the extra-chromosomal former marines."

Halloran seemed pleased with that description. He fairly glowed.

"My dad used to hunt deer with a handgun," Waucqez said. "He showed me how. Of course, I would never kill anything."

"What did you shoot?" Donovan asked.

"Oh, just a run-of-the-mill Wilson Combat Automatic," she replied, with a shrug.

"Just whose gun was this?"

"One of the rednecks at the exposition. Ask *him*." She tossed her red hair in the direction of Halloran.

"Well?" Donovan asked.

"One of the boys. A dealer, I think. I don't know the man. But what do you care about Wilson automatics? You're looking for the legendary lost Kammacher Stedman."

"The one that's unaccounted for. Do you know who owns it? And is it in this country?"

"One hears rumors about a rich Montana survivalist. A guy who's somewhere to the right of Hitler. Would never set foot in New York City—thinks it's ground zero of the international conspiracy of Jewish bankers who want to take over America and destroy traditional values. You know what I mean?"

"Sure I do," Donovan replied, rocking back and forth. "My wife took me to one of their board meetings last year. Go on."

"In any event, I don't know his name. I suspect I don't want to know his name. But for you, I'll ask around."

"I'd appreciate that," Donovan said. He handed Halloran his card.

"I'll give you a call if I hear anything."

Waucqez asked, "Is that all, Captain? 'Cause if it is, I have this segment I'm blocking out for George." She swiveled back to the control panel.

"What on?" Donovan asked.

"The Utah Snow Festival," Halloran said. "I'm flying there tomorrow. I'm thinking of doing my weathercast from the ski lift."

"Have a ball," Donovan said, shaking the man's hand.

"I will. Nice meeting you, Captain. See you tomorrow, Paul."

"Yeah," Duke replied.

"Stay cool," Waucqez said over her shoulder.

"I'll try," Donovan responded.

She added, "Paul . . . if you're on your way out, stop in and see June first. She wants to talk to you."

Duke said, "OK," but Donovan saw him grimace.

As they were walking out, the captain said, "That would be June Lake?"

"Regrettably," Duke replied, leading the way back down the stairs and through the studio.

"*People* says you two are—"

"No," Duke said sharply. "My coanchor and I are *not* involved."

Donovan, surprised by the strength of Duke's reply, said, "That was what we in the cop trade call an emphatic response."

Duke tossed up his hands and replied, "This is an old story. She's always been after me. I want to say to her, 'What is it about *no* that you don't understand?' "

"But being polite—and politically correct—you don't," Donovan said.

With Duke walking faster than usual, they reached that point where a corridor led straight to the exit. Through the glass panes on the door Donovan could see a handful of fans gathered outside. Beyond them, Duke's white limo idled by the curb. Moskowitz lurked just inside the door, talking on the phone.

"What about you and Rose?" Donovan asked Duke.

"Never! You must be nuts."

"Why? She's as cute as a button. I would think you'd flip for her."

"The woman is a director," Duke said. "Never sleep with one of those."

"Why not?"

"She has the power of life and death over me. See this wrinkle?"

He pressed a fingertip against a small crow's-foot on the side of his right eye.

"I see it," Donovan replied.

"If I get her mad at me, tomorrow morning I'm talking to ten million people and this wrinkle looks like the Grand fucking Canyon. You got it?"

Donovan got it.

"Directors can do that to you. It's better to stay away. But you're right; she *is* adorable. And *very* smart. I wish her well in love and life. Let's talk tomorrow, Bill. I have to go and see if June wants what I think she does."

"From what I can see of your life, there's only one thing that could be," Donovan said.

"That's the *last* thing that will happen," Duke replied. "Though it's not for lack of trying on her part. I'm not interested."

"On the other hand," Donovan said, "this *is* a TV studio. Maybe she just wants you to go out on a shoot with her."

Duke offered a mocking laugh. "On location? June Lake, the Heartland princess, set foot outside the carpeted studio? Actually go out on location with a camera crew and risk breaking a nail? My friend, June Lake has *never* gone on a shoot. She does everything in the studio, where expert camera work can make sure that the famous perkiness looks the same on Tuesday as it did on Monday."

"I'm sorry I asked," Donovan said.

When Duke has gone back into the studio, Moskowitz came over, storing his phone in his pocket as he walked.

"News?" Donovan asked.

"Guess who we found?" his assistant replied.

8. A VIKING WARRIOR WHO RECITES POETRY, THAT'S WHO

The window truck was getting to be a familiar sight on Fifth. Au Bon Pane, the company that supplied most of the glass panels to avenue merchants, had again parked its flatbed at the curb in front of a famous store. Atop the truck, six tinted glass panels were held not quite vertically, in such a way as to resemble a very narrow (but extraordinarily deep) church spire.

"Donuts and biscuits," Donovan said, looking at it solemnly.

"Say again?" Mosko replied.

"My dad's little Catholic joke. His way of saying, 'Dominus vobiscum.' "

"What's that?"

"I think it means 'the Lord be with you.' But since I haven't set foot in a Catholic church since 1962, you'll have to ask your old Irish mom. Doesn't that collection of glass look like a church spire?"

"Yeah. Our Lady of the Flat Trajectory. Can we go inside the store? We've got your chump."

E & J Tuttle was half-repaired. Four workmen were laying putty around the new bulletproof panel while two more installed a security camera. The blood had been cleaned up, and the myriad splinters of glass had been vacuumed from the floor. To change the mood, new and more cheerfully colored nighties decorated that part of the display window not taken up by Santa. Calming pastels had replaced smoldering reds and pinks. The price tags remained much the same, however.

"I wonder if sales dipped while they cleaned up the blood," Mosko said.

"Somehow I doubt it," Donovan replied. "I don't know what Hummitz and company are worried about. Death sells. Even on Fifth Avenue."

It was then that he spotted the chump he had come to meet. Martin Kimble was thirty-fiveish and thin, wearing an Armani suit and an expensive haircut. He smelled of cologne and perspiration, however, and his pale skin had gone pallid with fear. No doubt that was caused partly by having been on the lam for twenty-four hours and partly by the stoic-looking detective who watched, arms folded, as the young man sat in an upholstered chair and fidgeted.

"Is that Kimble?" Donovan asked from a score of paces away.

"That's him. We found him at his mom's house in Litchfield. That's in Connecticut."

"I know. I have a friend there."

"You? A West Side Democrat has a society friend in Litchfield?"

"This one drives a van for a living. He's a moving man; specializes in moving harps."

"Harps," Mosko replied.

"Delicate musical instruments. It takes a special skill to schlepp a harp. So, Kimble was at his mom's house? Is that where he lives?"

"Nope. He lives on Seventy-fifth and Second."

"He lives in the city but went home to spend the night

with Mom in order to recover from a homicide in his store. This is fascinating. Introduce us."

After the introductions Donovan said, "Store manager, eh?"

"Harvard MBA," the man replied, summoning up a credential in an effort to compose himself.

"It must be a big deal, being manager of a top Fifth Avenue store."

"I would say so, yes."

Donovan said, "You know, Mr. Kimble, I figure I go into five stores a week."

"Five stores."

"So I would say that, in my life, I have been into—let's see—thirteen thousand, seven hundred and eighty stores. Not counting a few unpleasant afternoons at the Garden State Mall and a positively disastrous two hours with a young nephew at Chuck E. Cheese."

Kimble was smart enough to sense that a punch line, perhaps a nasty one, was coming. He tensed up.

"In all that time, I think I've talked to three store managers. And you know what? In each case there was a body laying there and I was investigating a homicide."

"I'm not sure what you're getting at," Kimble said cautiously.

"I'm getting at the fact that a big shot Fifth Avenue store manager with a Harvard MBA doesn't talk to just any customer. Maybe he talks to a big shot customer when he's alive and the homicide cop who's mopping up after the guy is shot dead."

Kimble shifted his weight nervously from foot to foot.

"What the hell were Seybold and you talking about?" Donovan asked. "And don't tell me you were offering to gift-wrap that nightie he bought." ˌ

Kimble sighed. It was a big sigh of relief. He said, "This is because I went to call the home office."

Donovan imitated the man's sigh but did it better. "I'm a cop, Mr. Kimble, but I'm a New York cop. That means I'm open to any number of possibilities that, out in the sticks, would put you under immediate suspicion if not earn you a fast trip to the hoosegow. Do you know what I mean?"

Kimble shook his head.

"For example, I can understand—and forgive—a man who might want to talk to his therapist after witnessing a murder. Who might want to tell his boss that there's a big mess on the floor. Who might also want to consult an attorney before talking to a cop. Who might even want to have a few drinks."

Donovan gave Moskowitz a little smile.

That man said, "What the captain means is he ain't never heard of a grown man running home to talk to his mommy before answering a few simple questions from the police."

"Such as what you and Seybold were talking about," Donovan said.

Kimble sucked in his breath, then replied, "Actually, we were talking about that . . . nightie . . . as you call it. But you're quite correct that Terry wasn't just any customer."

"Now it's 'Terry,' " Donovan said.

Kimble nodded. "We knew each other quite well. It was Terry who brokered the sale of E & J Tuttle to Osamu Hirai."

Donovan smiled. "That being the Japanese billionaire I've heard about."

"Yes. I had to call his office to let them know what happened. Mr. Hirai doesn't like to hear bad news through the press."

"And how did he react?"

"Well, I didn't talk to him personally, of course. But the chief of his retail division handled the news well."

"And how did Mommy react?" Mosko asked.

Kimble looked around uncomfortably. The guest chair in which the detective kept him was placed next to a rack of baby dolls. Those nighties looked like they might have come from the Frederick's of Hollywood catalog were it not for the $700 price tags. In looking around to see if any employees could overhear the conversation, Kimble found himself staring into a C cup. It did nothing for what remained of his Harvard dignity.

"This is more complicated than you imagine," he said at last.

"Like I said, I'm a cop, but I'm also a New Yorker," Donovan replied. "Nothing is easy."

"Let's hear it," Mosko added.

Kimble sighed again. "Terry and I grew up together along with members of the Tuttle family."

"*This* Tuttle family?" Donovan asked. "As in, those who owned the chain of stores?"

"The same. It was a family enterprise, family and friends."

"The Tuttles owned it. The Kimbles and Seybolds worked for it."

"Correct."

"But the market took a bad turn and the family had to sell."

"The market wasn't that bad," Kimble said. "It was the Tuttle family that took a bad turn."

"Please explain."

"For generations, E & J Tuttle was handed down from father to son. Occasionally from father to daughter. But always to a family member."

"But no longer?" Donovan prompted.

"No longer. There was the problem of Tom."

"Tom?"

"Tom Tuttle. Uh, Thomas Hastings Tuttle."

"Who's that?"

"He was in line to inherit the presidency of the chain."

"Let me guess," Donovan said. "He moved to Vegas, supported himself by playing piano in a lounge, and married a stripper."

Kimble shook his head. "He would be better off were that true. Tom graduated from West Point and went into the Gulf War as a lieutenant. He was gassed—or whatever happened over there, poison or nerve gas or something else."

"I think it was a neurotoxin of some sort," Donovan said.

"Anyway, poor Tom had a breakdown, I guess you would call it. He dropped out. You know how, in the sixties, people would 'drop out' of the system?"

"I heard the expression," Donovan replied.

"The upshot is that he had some problems and the family no longer could count on him to run the company. So with no heir to assume the mantle of leadership it decided to take up Mr. Hirai's offer and sell out. It insisted, however, that they keep current management. Including me. And, as you know, Terry brokered the sale."

"And what of Tom?"

"We've lost touch with him. I know he wanted to be a novelist. The last I heard from him was a year ago. He was looking for a place in Alphabet City and planned to write a book."

"Does he have the money to support this habit?" Mosko asked.

"Not that I'm aware of. He went through his trust fund pretty quickly paying medical bills."

"And the family doesn't give him anything?" Donovan asked.

"They would if he would speak to them. But he cut off

all contact after the sale went through to Hirai. Tom was pretty upset about that sale."

"Upset enough to make him kill his old friend Terry?" Donovan asked.

Kimble looked down into his hands. He was squeezing them until the knuckles went whiter than usual. But he kept silent.

"I think the man just answered you," Mosko said.

Kimble looked up and stated, "We're worried about him."

"Who's 'we'?" Donovan asked.

"My family and his. The Kimbles and the Tuttles. Yesterday when Terry was murdered, I called the home office—the new one, in Tokyo, not the old one, in Providence. But then I went home to talk to the families."

"You suspected that Tom might be the killer," Donovan said.

Kimble nodded.

"Did you see him outside that window?"

"No. I was talking to Terry about that negligee he bought. In our business you quickly learn to ignore the people looking in the window. They're like wallpaper . . . always there."

"So you didn't see anyone?" Mosko asked.

Kimble sighed and said, "I did see the Viking. He was out there when the shots were fired."

"Viking?" Mosko asked, shaking his head. "What Viking?"

"He's talking about the guy who replaced Moondog," Donovan said.

"Moondog? Moondog?" Mosko turned from Donovan to Kimble and asked, "You got another chair? 'Cause sometimes in this business you gotta sit down."

"In my business, too," Kimble replied. But he didn't offer to get up or send for another chair.

Kimble said, "There's a man who, since March, has stood ten, twelve hours a day at the corner dressed as a Viking warrior reading poetry and panhandling. He's over six feet tall— without the Viking horns. Over seven feet with the horns and all. Rather hard to miss."

"And of course you know him," Mosko said to his boss.

"Nope. I just read the item in the *Times* mentioning him," Donovan replied.

"Is this guy homicidal?"

"He's a Viking. What do you expect he does, play checkers? Brian, I have no idea if the man is homicidal. He recites poetry . . . not his own. He's memorized what I suppose you would consider classics. . . . Poetry ain't my field."

"Glad to hear something isn't."

"And he collects coins from tourists who think it's cute to give quarters to poetry-reciting Vikings on Fifth Avenue. Nobody knows who he is, and to make sure of that he wears a kind of leather mask. And he never speaks."

"So who was Moondog?" Mosko asked.

"A blind composer of music who stood on the corner of Fifty-second and Sixth dressed as a Viking," Donovan said. "He died a few years ago, and when this new guy replaced him there was a hue and cry in certain quarters. True New Yorkers demand authenticity. So, Mr. Kimble, did Moondog Two look in the window?"

"I just caught a glimpse of him, but I think he was looking in the window."

"Maybe he was looking for an Xmas gift for the little lady," Mosko said.

Donovan said it was possible. "So he might have seen the shooter," the captain added.

"He might have been the shooter," Mosko said.

"Not at his height. Besides, it's hard to hide wearing Viking horns. Anyway, Mr. Kimble, let's get back to your old friend Tom."

"Oh, yes," Kimble replied, a bit disappointed that the diversion had ended.

"Do you know if he came out of the army with a special interest in weapons?"

Kimble shrugged. "Weapons I can't say. Death interested him, though."

"In what way?"

"He fancies himself a serious novelist. Wants to write literature. Do you know what I'm saying?"

Donovan knew.

"He has this fancy theory about death being the door to another reality. I can't connect with the logic."

"If anyone can, it will be the captain," Moskowitz said.

Donovan smiled. "Do you have a phone number for this guy Tuttle? Any idea how we can get in touch with him?"

Kimble fished a bit of paper from the pocket of his custom shirt. Torn off the end of a fancy envelope such as high-society invitations come in, it bore a number in the 212 area code.

Donovan took the paper and looked at it. "This in Alphabet City, isn't it?" Donovan said.

"I think so," Kimble replied.

Mosko looked over his boss's shoulder and said, "How do you know that the six-seven-three exchange is on the Lower East Side? It's a numerical exchange and not a letter code like Murray Hill eight or something."

"I guess you never ordered take-out from Sammy's Famous Roumanian Restaurant," Donovan said.

"Do they have a take-out menu?"

"They do for me."

Kimble stood, straightened his suit jacket, looked down at the workman who was trying to scrub the chalk outline off the floor, and said, "Terry was a good man. He was good people. And his fiancée is a wonderful girl. I feel so sorry for her. If it turned out that Tom is responsible . . ."

Donovan asked, "Does the name Erik Melmer mean anything to you?"

"No. I don't think so."

"He was the man killed last week in Sarkana."

"Was that the name? I'm sorry; I didn't pay that much attention. I thought it was a once-in-a-lifetime tragedy." Kimble laughed bitterly.

"He was CEO of Melmer International in Düsseldorf. Is there any chance that Terry knew him?"

"I doubt it," Kimble replied. "Terry didn't hobnob with CEOs as a rule. He was the manager of a suburban stock-brokerage office, not a Wall Street investment-banking firm. He only got involved in the Tuttle sale because of his family ties."

"Thanks for your cooperation, Mr. Kimble," Donovan said. "We'll be in touch."

When they were out on the sidewalk again, Donovan looked up and down Fifth Avenue. He couldn't be sure, but it seemed that the number of shoppers was indeed down, as Hummitz had said. In the thick of the normal holiday season, the Fifth Avenue sidewalks between Rockefeller Center and the Plaza were shoulder to shoulder. It could easily take three minutes to walk a block. (Normal walking time, as Donovan reckoned it on an average city street, was a shade under a minute a block.) But today not only could you take a step without bumping into a package-laden tourist, but you could also hear the bells of the Salvation Army volunteers that much louder. Fewer fur coats were out there to absorb sounds.

Moondog II also was gone. He was nowhere near his familiar corner. The words of Tennyson and Keats and the clinking of coins in his old brass pot were not heard that morning.

Donovan bought a bag of chestnuts from a street vendor and cracked one open, tossed the shell into the gutter, and nibbled at the meat while looking to see which of those holiday shoppers might be a killer. Moskowitz leaned against a NO PARKING sign, answering a long cell phone call from headquarters.

When the sergeant was done he waved the phone at the facade of E & J Tuttle.

"What's the story?" Donovan asked.

"Our underwear heir has a rap sheet, as you suggested."

"How long?"

"Ever been in a traffic jam on the Long Island Expressway?" Mosko asked.

"That bad, huh? OK, let's hear it."

"Thomas Hastings Tuttle, age thirty-two. Born Newport, Rhode Island. Graduated West Point. Commissioned in U.S. Army. Served in Gulf War as leader of a sniper group."

Moskowitz interrupted the narration with a pause that was more pregnant than Marcy could ever be.

"Go on," Donovan said.

"Got medical discharge. Treated at Veterans Administration facilities in Portland, Cleveland, and Hartford. Alleged to be suffering from Gulf War Syndrome. Arrested for assault, aggravated assault, and attempted murder."

"What happened with that last one?"

"It was plea-bargained down to simple assault after he paid the victim's medical bills. Tuttle also was picked up for vandalism, malicious mischief, vagrancy, and destruction of property. He became a one-man wrecking crew notorious for busting up neighborhood bars."

"How did I miss running into this guy?" Donovan asked.

"My guess is that he started drinking after you stopped," Mosko said.

"That would do it."

"Also, you were a West Sider. Tuttle was a menace mainly on the Lower East Side. One of his arrests was for trying to bust up the Shining Path Poets Cafe. They wouldn't let him read the stuff he wrote."

"I thought they encouraged violent revolutionary acts at that joint," Donovan said.

"They probably like their little *banditos* to take their chaos elsewhere," Mosko replied. "Anyway, that's it for Señor Tuttle."

"What's his current status with the law?"

"He has a parole officer—more fallout from the attempted murder—but failed to report last week."

"What day?" Donovan asked.

"Friday . . . the day the killings started."

"We need to talk to Tuttle. Do we have a current address?"

"Yeah, one that matches the phone number Kimble gave you. But the parole officer went there yesterday and the guy had cleared out."

"Cleared out?"

"Yeah, scooped up his futon, his CDs, his typewriter—"

"Typewriter?" Donovan asked.

"So the man is a troglodyte. The point is he took off, leaving no forwarding address."

"Find the parole officer," Donovan said. "Have him meet us this afternoon at the last-known address. Where is it, by the way?"

"On Avenue C, down the block from the Shining Path Poets Cafe," Mosko said.

"We'll go there."

Donovan handed Moskowitz another chestnut and cracked open one more for himself. The captain looked up and down the block again, hoping to spot Moondog II. But the Viking was as missing as Tuttle.

"That was a long call you took a moment ago," Donovan said. "Was there anything else?"

"Yeah. I finally got more from Melmer's secretary as to what he was doing in New York eighteen weeks ago."

"Which was?"

"Ever hear of the Diagnostic Equipment Manufacturers Association?" Mosko asked.

Donovan hadn't.

"They had their summer convention here last July, August. Melmer's company had a booth."

"In other words, he was here to sell contrast media," Donovan said.

Mosko nodded. "Medical diagnostic equipment is his main market. But last week Melmer and his fiancée were in New York strictly on personal business—buying holiday gifts and getting ready for their marriage. And Melmer's company isn't publicly traded. He didn't know Seybold. I had the office ask."

"Short of the possibility that they met at the sequined-bra counter at Bloomingdale's, I guess the Melmer-Seybold connection never existed," Donovan said.

"I guess not."

"Did Anna Fritsch ever call us like I left a message for her to do?"

Mosko shook his head.

"Call her apartment and make an appointment for me to talk to her," Donovan ordered.

"Why? Seybold and Melmer weren't connected. There's nothing she can tell you."

"Maybe I want to know what Eurotrash royalty is like," Donovan said. "I'm telling you, there's something wrong with her, and I want to know what it is."

"You just want some inside dope on her mom," Mosko replied. "This has something to do with those three years in the sixties that you won't talk about."

Donovan frowned and made a dismissing sort of motion with one hand.

"You're beating a dead horse, Boss," Mosko said.

"It's my bat," Donovan replied. "In the meantime, while you set up an appointment with her for me, let's go check out Tuttle's East Village pad."

"Do you want to do Alphabet City and Trump Plaza in the same day?" Mosko asked.

Donovan nodded. "One before and one after lunch," he said.

"Where would you like to eat?" Mosko asked.

9. ONE CHE BURGER TO GO, WITH FRIES

The bathtub was an old clawfoot model, one leg of which was duct-taped to the tub to keep it from falling off. Rust stains ran down the sides of the tub, mixing with soap scum to form a reddish grey abstract painting that mirrored a similar artwork on the ancient linoleum floor. The bathtub was a freestanding one, sitting not quite in the middle of the kitchen just to the left of the apartment door and across from a four-burner gas stove that dated to World War II.

Two tin pots sat atop it, a small one to heat water for coffee and a larger one whose most frequent use was betrayed by its contents: petrified glop that a few weeks earlier had been macaroni and cheese. A small refrigerator was as ancient as the stove; its condenser was on top like an exposed engine of a Ford trimotor airplane. Donovan opened the door cautiously, and for good reason. The inside was filled with rotting vegetables and moldy bread. A jar of hot Russian mustard had been left open. The stench assaulted both Donovan's stomach and his eyes. He slammed the door shut.

"Having been gassed in the Gulf War, you would think that Tuttle would be more careful about the atmospherics," Donovan said.

"The guy didn't have a much better pantry," Mosko replied, examining the cabinet whose doors, stuck permanently open by too many years of repeated painting, swung above the stove. "A copy of the Sunday *Los Angeles Times* from last July, a moldy box of vanilla wafers, and, hey, look: two cans of vegetarian baked beans. Tuttle at least *thought* of eating healthy."

"How much sodium?" Donovan asked from across the room, where he was going through the mail.

"Five hundred and sixty milligrams a serving," Mosko replied, after examining the label.

"He ought to think again."

"There's also half a bottle of Richard's Wild Irish Rose wine, the stuff alkies drink."

"Check it," Donovan said.

"What for?"

"I never knew a drunk to leave liquor behind when making a getaway. Silverware, yes. Booze, never."

Moskowitz uncapped the bottle and sniffed the contents. "Oil of some kind," he said.

"Any idea what type?"

"I have to ask Bonaci to be sure, but I think it's the stuff you use to polish the stock of a fancy gun."

"What kind of handgrip does the Kammacher Stedman have?" Donovan asked.

"Walnut. I'll bring this with us."

Donovan sat down at the folding card table that served to eat on, toyed with some cigarette burns in the vinyl top, and said, "There's nothing in the mail except a sale flyer from Stern's, an overdue notice from the public library, and a notice from the Shining Path Poets Cafe."

He handed his assistant the overdue notice. "Tuttle absconded with a copy of the annotated *Finnegans Wake*," Donovan said. "No wonder the poor man's deranged."

"I'll check and see if heisting Joyce is an indictable offense," Moskowitz said.

Tuttle's parole officer, one Harold Armis, lingered by the door, looking embarrassed and awaiting the moment he would be called on the carpet. He was a sixtyish man with pallid skin and a small amount of black hair that was combed laterally across his otherwise bare scalp, creating the impression of a football gridiron. His silver wire-frame glasses were perched at the end of a skinny nose.

"So, Harold, where's our boy gone?" Donovan asked at last.

In relief, the man expelled a lungful of air. "I wish I could tell you, Captain," he said. "Frankly, I was feeling proud of myself for checking up on him after he missed only one weekly meeting with his parole officer."

"You're a conscientious man."

"Most POs have such heavy caseloads—you know, ever since the mayor ordered the arrest of everyone who panhandles too loudly or pees on trees in the park—that they don't check on someone until after he misses two or three meetings."

"Which brings me to my next question," Donovan said. "Why did you check up on Tuttle? I mean the guy sounds more or less like a registered fuckup with literary pretensions. I've run across a few in my life. One of them actually published books. Was it the attempted murder?"

"Tuttle was just like you said—most of the time," Armis replied. "He drank too much, maybe dropped a couple of pills—he liked painkillers, I'm pretty sure, though he denied using them—and once in a while got into a fight in a bar. So far this is nothing you would call Perry Mason over. But Tuttle was wound as tight as a drum. He was capable of snapping—the way he did when he tried to kill Mr. Harachi."

Donovan spun around to face Armis. "Since he tried to kill who?"

"Whom," Mosko said, sticking his head out of the trash-strewn living room.

"I'm talking about Tomio Harachi, the victim in Tuttle's attempted-manslaughter plea bargain."

" 'Harachi' as in Japanese?" Donovan asked.

"You said it. A tourist in the city for a week. He dropped in at the Shining Path Poets Cafe after seeing an article about it in *New York* magazine. This was a night Tuttle was in there drunk, and not only drunk but in the process of being tossed out by the manager. You would expect under such circumstances that Tuttle would turn on the manager. No, he attacked Harachi, and out of nowhere, too. I mean the man was just sitting there eating his flan."

"There was no provocation?" Donovan asked.

"None whatsoever. Apparently, Tuttle hates the Japanese."

"When did this happen?"

"In February," Armis replied.

"That would be a month after the sale of E & J Tuttle to Hirai went through," Mosko said, appearing from out of the living room and announcing his arrival partly by kicking a Wendy's bag in front of him. Mosko flicked a bit of paper onto the table in front of Donovan. "That's a receipt from a theatrical costume shop in Times Square," he added. "Maybe Tuttle was trying to disguise himself as a normal person."

"He told me he was mad at his family and that it had something to do with the Japanese," Armis said.

"Did he give you the details?" Donovan asked.

"No. He gets mad when you press him too hard. And since, technically speaking, I'm his PO and not his psychiatrist, my only interest is in how well he's living up to the conditions of his parole."

"Which is not too good," Mosko said.

"That's right," Armis agreed.

Donovan stood, kicked the Wendy's bag back into the living room, and said, "Here's what I want you to do, Mr. Armis. Get a warrant for Tuttle's arrest on grounds that he broke parole."

"You got it," Armis replied, making a note on a piece of lined paper.

"Hopefully that will keep the press from finding out we want to talk to him about the murders on Fifth Avenue," Donovan said.

"Do you really think that Tom gunned down those two people I read about?"

"I would say he's a suspect. He has motive: He needs money and he has a grudge against the Japanese, who bought his family firm. I can't say if he had opportunity. Certainly his whereabouts are unaccounted for at the times of both killings. And God knows the man has the firearms knowledge to have pulled this off. Tuttle is a suspect, sure enough—"

"A damn good one," Mosko added.

"Yeah, but one thing I've learned is that the guy who seems more obvious to have pulled the trigger is seldom the one who really did it," Donovan said. "Tuttle is far from being the only suspect. I don't want his name to get into the papers and let the others think they're off the hook. Can you help me with that?"

"I'll do my best," Armis replied. He folded the piece of paper into his jacket pocket and edged toward the door. "If you have no further need for me, I'll get on that warrant."

"You don't happen to know who owns Sarkana, do you?" Donovan asked.

"You mean the jewelry store where the first murder took place?" Armis asked.

"The same."

"I have no idea. I take care of all my jewelry needs on Canal Street."

"Never mind," Donovan said, and waved as the man slipped out the door and pushed past the several Hispanic tenants who loitered out in the grimy hall, eavesdropping on the police investigation that suddenly had cropped up in their midst.

"I can't find anything else of use here, Boss," Mosko said. "The guy lived like a pig. What connection this has to literature is beyond me. But then, I mainly read the *Post.*"

"Three years with me and the man hasn't learned," Donovan moaned. "Come on; let's go read some poetry."

The Shining Path Poets Cafe sat in the middle of a block off Avenue C, nestled between a small locksmith shop and an even smaller bodega, the window of which held a box of Tide, a box of Pampers, a six-pack of Corona beer, and a display of hex-removing candles. The latter were tall votive candles in transparent red or blue jars that were painted with images of Christ and the Virgin Mary as well as with symbols of Santeria, the Cuban Christian-African spiritual mix. Donovan liked folklore as well as colorful candles. He occasionally had bought one of the spice-scented hex-removing candles from an equally old bodega on Amsterdam Avenue and 107th Street and lit it in the kitchen to see if it would scare the cockroaches. Then Marcy had married him and hired an exterminator.

Still, Donovan ducked into the shop and came out with a red-and-yellow candle that smelled of lilacs even through the brown paper bag in which it lurked.

Moskowitz eyeballed the bag. "A fifth of Ripple to have with lunch?" he asked.

Donovan showed him the candle. "To burn in Marcy's hospital room to make sure the baby is OK," he said.

"Do you really think this stuff works?"

"You can't be too careful," Donovan replied.

He led the way into the cafe, which smelled of cigarettes, red wine, pastry, and cinnamon-scented coffee. Donovan breathed deeply, expelled a goodly volume of air, and said, "Takes me back to some sixties book parties."

"When were you ever at book parties?" Mosko asked.

"I have lots of literary friends. Such as—"

"That meshugah music critic who used to lurk around Times Square before it got respectable," Mosko said.

"I was thinking more of some old beat friends of mine. Early sixties, son. Before you were so much as a gleam in your mammy's eye."

"Among them Kirsten Fritsch?"

"I never met the lady . . . that I know of," Donovan said.

"I don't understand your interest in her," Mosko replied.

"My instincts are good and you know it. Trust me."

The cafe was empty save for a thin man of sixty-some years who was poring over a copy of *Wired* while sipping scented tea. Otherwise, the small round tables sat with their shakers of Mrs. Dash salt substitute, their Jamaican hot sauce, and their fishnet-covered candles undisturbed by patrons. It was morning. Donovan walked along a plain wall made of cheap tongue-and-groove pine boards that had been whitewashed and used as a bulletin board for management and customers to tack up whatever fancied them. Among the items: a contemporary reproduction of a sixties Che Guevara poster, a Puerto Rican flag and accompanying broadside advocating independence for the island, a movie poster for *The Pancho Villa Story,* pages from a World War I army ordnance manual, pages and pages of handwritten and typed poetry, and a still photograph of John Wayne from his movie *Rooster Cogburn.*

Mosko stared at the latter. "Am I missing something?" he asked.

Donovan tossed up his hands. "Perhaps it's symbolic of anarchy, which is the essence of revolution."

"And what does any of this have to do with poetry?"

At that point a woman came up dressed in tight, faded, worn-at-the-knees jeans with a black leotard and a canvas vest of the sort photographers sometimes wear. Those are the vests that sport many small pockets in which to keep handy items like film, coins, batteries, and, depending on the mileu of the photographer, bullets or cocaine. Perched precariously atop her curly black hair was a red beret.

She stuck out her hand. "You must be Rachel Baez," Donovan said, grasping it.

"Good to meet you, Captain. Sergeant Moskowitz."

"Hello . . . Rachel Baez," Moskowitz said, looking at her red beret with a faint smile on his lips.

"Your office said you'd be over. What can I do for you?"

"We want to talk about Tom Tuttle," Donovan said.

She rolled her eyes. "Oh, that loser. I had a feeling the cops would come for him for one fine day."

"Here we are," Donovan replied jauntily.

"Who did he kill? How *many* did he kill?"

"One, two, or none. Where can we find him?"

"Look under rocks," she replied.

"Ain't too many on Avenue C. Mainly garbage cans."

"Look under them. Did you try his apartment?"

"He split," Mosko said.

She shrugged. "The guy was always moving around. Probably to avoid bill collectors. Hey, is it true he used to be rich?"

"Yep. He still could be again, if he only let his family help him."

"He was running from them. Said they stifled him."

"Regardless, Tuttle was pretty mad when they sold the family business—the one he expected to inherit—to the Japanese."

"Tell me about it," Baez said. "That idiot nearly took the head off a Japanese customer one night. Got sent to Riker's Island for it, too. Funny."

"Why funny?" Donovan asked.

" 'Cause we run an outreach program there. You know, poetry seminars for the prisoners."

"Revolutionary poetry," Mosko said.

"That's right," she replied.

"What the hell's revolutionary about poetry?"

Donovan held up his hand. "The explanation would be longer than you and I have time to hear," he said.

"You're right," she agreed.

"But it has something to do with raising your fist and trying to sound like Charles Manson," Donovan concluded.

"You're a tough man, Captain Donovan," Baez said. "If not entirely original."

"You're an interesting person, Rachel Baez," Mosko added.

"You should stay for a reading. There's one tonight. A guerrilla performance artist from Guatemala."

"What does he do?" Mosko asked.

"She."

"The sergeant doesn't want to know," Donovan said. "Look; I wonder if Tuttle left anything here. A guy who spends so much time in a club—plus moved in down the block to be near it—might leave behind a trace of his pitiful existence."

"That was very poetic of you, Captain," Baez replied. "He did, in fact, leave something behind. Something weird. Just yesterday morning, in fact. I wasn't here or I never would have let him in the door. Let me go get it for you."

The two policemen tapped their feet and looked at a menu while she slipped into a dark area, at the rear of the club, that served as an artists' mustering room. When Baez returned she carried an old canvas backpack with the stencil U.S. ARMY on it. A bit of horn peeked out from under the canvas flap. "You know what was so weird about this guy?" she asked.

"Beyond trying to destroy East Side bars and kill Japanese tourists?" Donovan asked.

"Yeah. He wanted like all the world depended on it to read his poetry here. And guess what it was?"

"Tennyson and Keats," Donovan said.

Her mouth fell open. "How could you possibly know that?" she asked.

"Is that a Viking helmet in that bag?" Donovan asked.

"Why, yes. Yes, it is. I told you the guy was weird. What he wanted this for I can't imagine." She pulled it out into the light. The Viking helmet looked like an old artillery shell onto which someone had glued cow's horns.

"Moondog?" Mosko asked. "Tuttle is Moondog?"

"Who's that?" Baez asked. "Not the blind composer who died a few years back."

Donovan shook his head. "The man who, since last March, has been imitating him, standing a few paces from the facade of E & J Tuttle."

"The famous store? You mean that Tom Tuttle is related to those people?"

Donovan nodded. "He was due to inherit it, but he flipped out after being gassed in the Gulf War and decided that his true calling was reading versions of Tennyson and Keats in the East Village."

"Sounds revolutionary once you put it that way," Mosko said.

"But you guys wouldn't have him, his family sold the chain of stores to the Japanese, and Tuttle punched out a Japanese tourist right here where we stand."

"Actually, it was over there, beneath the Che poster," Baez said. She pointed at the likeness of the old revolutionary.

"And after that he moved his Viking act up in front of his onetime inheritance and stood there, spouting poetry and collecting coins," Donovan said.

147

"But really staking out the joint waiting for one of the new Japanese owners to show himself," Mosko added.

"I wonder why Kimble didn't recognize the SOB, costume or no," Donovan said.

"Yeah! They were old friends."

"But it was Kimble who put us on to Moondog, and why would he do that if they were old friends?" Donovan scratched his chin and added, "What time yesterday did Tuttle drop this off?"

"Around eleven," Baez said. "He told the waitress he wouldn't need it anymore."

"We'll need her name."

"Sure, but she doesn't know anything."

"There is nobody on the planet who knows nothing," Donovan said grandly. "The least of us has a tiny piece of the puzzle."

"You're way beyond me," Baez said.

"Life can be very confusing," Donovan told her. "Forget what the revolutionary tracts say about policemen. Some of us are stumbling around looking for the truth like everyone else."

Donovan looked especially sincere when he said that. As a result, Baez looked at him warmly and said, "You have a way with words, Captain. You should come down here more often."

"Let me see the menu again and I'll consider it," he replied. She waved for someone to bring one over.

The captain scanned both sides of the single sheet, which was printed on coarse recycled paper. Then he said, "I'll take a Che Burger to go, with fries and a Coke. And my partner will have . . . ?"

"A Shining Path Burrito. I don't suppose you have Dr. Brown's Cel-Ray Soda?"

"Not a chance. But if you want to go over to Gem Spa, the egg cream place—"

"I know what Gem Spa is," Mosko said, clearly offended at his knowledge of Lower East Side eating spots being underestimated.

"You can get one there," she finished.

"I'll take a Coke, too."

Baez wrote up the order and handed it to a waitress, who appeared wearing camouflage pants and a black rhinestone-studded bustier. She scurried off while Donovan watched her with considerable amusement.

"Where are you guys going to eat this stuff?" Baez asked. "In the subway?"

Donovan shook his head. "At Trump Plaza, where else?"

Donovan and Moskowitz sat hip to hip on the Louis XIV settee, balancing their lunches on their laps. Mosko also had his computer on one knee, which made for an especially tricky balancing act. Between the odors from the burger, fries, and burrito, and the scent of lilacs from the hex-removing candle that sat in its bag at Donovan's feet, the two policemen were a blight on the afternoon of George Bliley, the valet. Impeccably dressed in a deep blue Savile Row suit and speaking in a carefully schooled voice that only an equally schooled ear could tell was more Manchester than West End London, he hovered nearby holding an Edwardian wicker wastebasket. His gaze shifted back and forth from the food to the Persian carpet, nervously awaiting the catastrophe of a dropped french fry.

"Your office said you would be calling, Captain," Bliley intoned, "and I'm most regretful that I was forced to keep you waiting."

"No problem," Donovan said. "We had to eat someplace. So this is Trump Plaza."

"This is Mr. Melmer's—forgive me, the late Mr. Melmer's—suite in Trump Plaza. They're all individual."

"No gold bathroom faucets in this one, eh?" Donovan said, munching a fry.

Looking pained, Bliley replied, "Indeed there are. Mr. Melmer changed many aspects of the decor, but not that one. He found it . . . entertaining."

"So would I."

"And, I must say, they never tarnish."

"That's the whole appeal of gold, Mr. Bliley. The only tarnish it collects is on your bank account. So tell me, who owns this place now that Melmer is dead?"

"His fiancée, I believe. Mr. Melmer took quite good care of her, even though the wedding had yet to occur. Would you like some napkins from the kitchen?"

Donovan had been fishing around for something to wipe a ketchup smear onto. At last he found a handful of paper napkins folded into a back pocket.

"No thanks. Who have you been taking instructions from lately?"

"Why, from his fiancée, of course."

"The princess," Mosko said.

"That is quite correct. I have been taking my instructions from Anna Hebbel, the princess of Karlsruhe," Bliley said.

"Do you like her?" Donovan asked.

"I don't have to like her or dislike her. She is the lady of the house." Bliley sniffed and waggled the wastebasket as Mosko crumpled up his burrito wrapper and looked about for a place to throw it.

"Oh, come on, Bliley," Donovan said. "This is New York in the nineteen-nineties, not London in the nineteen-twenties. You're not Jeeves the Butler and she's no goddamn princess."

"I beg your pardon," Bliley said, his shock apparently genuine.

"Ever hear the name Anna Fritsch?"

Bliley hadn't, so Donovan filled him in on the recently widowed woman's genealogy. As the details unfolded, so did the valet. All the starch went out of Bliley's carefully practiced stiff spine until he was as limp as the wrapper from Mosko's Shining Path Burrito.

"Are you telling me that my mistress is a cheap hustler with a criminal record?" Bliley said, stepping backward and sitting rather abruptly on a Regency love seat. He put the wastebasket at his feet and seemed to forget it.

"No," Donovan said. "I'm telling you that she's a cheap hustler with a criminal record whose mom was—*is, since, failing evidence to the contrary, she's still alive*—a convicted murderess."

Bliley lowered his head and shook it. "I paid five thousand pounds for the training that got me this bloody job and they told me I'd meet royalty."

"You still got gold faucets in the throne room," Mosko remarked.

Donovan balled up his hamburger wrapper and tossed it across the room, hitting the wastebasket perfectly.

"Three points," Mosko said.

"There couldn't be some mistake?" Bliley asked, looking up.

"Show him," Donovan said.

Mosko carried his computer to the man and showed him the screen. It displayed Fritsch's complete criminal record, which included a mug shot that was unmistakably hers. When he was done looking at it, Bliley said, "Princess Anna. Cheeky."

"So where is she?" Donovan asked. "I sent a message I wanted to talk to her."

"She bolted," Bliley said. "Took off this morning. Said she was going to spend some time with her mother in Germany and got a limo to take her to the airport. She said she's not coming back to this place that reminds her of the tragic death of her dear fiancé."

"With her mother?" Donovan echoed. "Where are they meeting, at a halfway house? At the annual barbecue of Adult Children of Felons?"

"I overheard her on the phone making reservations for a flight to Bonn."

"She was on the phone?" Donovan asked. "Pregnant and bereaved, she still had the wits about her to make her own plane reservations? How come she didn't ask you to do it?"

"I was packing all her things," Bliley replied. "I assumed she was being considerate."

"What time was the flight?" Mosko asked.

"The one o'clock Concorde out of JFK."

"It's left already," Donovan said, after checking his watch.

He stood and brushed some crumbs off his lap and onto the Persian carpet. He was about to apologize when Bliley looked up and muttered, "Oh, fuck it. I guess I'm out of a job anyway."

"Wait and see if she comes back. Once cheap hustlers become real ones they still need servants, no?" Donovan said.

"I suppose that's possible."

"Did Princess Anna leave anything behind?"

Bliley shook his head. "Not a bloody thing. I cleaned the entire house this morning. You're welcome to look."

Donovan nodded, and Mosko went off to do it.

"Except, of course, her rock."

"Her rock?" Donovan said patiently.

Bliley went to the mantel and took from it a round rock, brownish with white speckles, about ten inches in diameter but quite flat. It looked like something that had been poured into a mold.

Bliley handed the thing to Donovan, who hefted it. "It's light. Is it volcanic?"

"Yes, a souvenir of Princess Anna's disastrous vacation."

"Tell me about that."

"Mr. Melmer was here on business, as often happened. She was bored and decided to go off for a week by herself in the Caribbean."

"And booked a hotel room in Carricola," Donovan said.

"How could you know that?" Bliley asked.

"It's the only Caribbean island to have a volcanic explosion this summer," Donovan said, as if it were the most reasonable thing in the world for him to have known. But since it wasn't, he added, "I read a lot."

"I'm impressed."

"When was she there? When to when?"

"Oh my, this must be important, although I can't imagine why. I can tell you exactly. She was scheduled for July twenty-first through twenty-eighth."

"But the explosion cut off the island for nearly three weeks," Donovan said. "Several hundred tourists—all of them in this one hotel that became isolated near the eruption zone—were finally rescued by the Coast Guard."

"Yes indeed. She was one of them. Mr. Melmer was very upset about not seeing her for three weeks. But she assured him in frequent phone calls—I mean when the phones were working, that is—that there was plenty of food and good company."

"Especially the latter," Donovan said.

"She finally got out on that Coast Guard boat," Bliley concluded. "August fifteenth it was. She flew right back up to New York. And it was just a week or two after that they announced their engagement. They must have missed each other terribly."

"Terribly," Donovan said.

"And this rock is her only souvenir of her adventure."

"Not quite," Donovan stated.

"What do you mean?"

"She'll always have her memories."

"Yes. I see that you're a sentimental man." Bliley sighed and added, "Even if she is a cheap hustler, she deserves to have a man to be father to her unborn child. Would you like to take the rock? I mean she said she's not coming back."

Donovan thanked the man, arranging the rock next to his candle on the floor. It was then that Mosko came in from another room, bearing a broad grin as well as a thin leather folder.

"You know the good thing about these antiques from a cop's point of view?" he asked.

Bliley shook his head.

"The boards on the bottoms of the dresser drawers separate over time. Stuff falls through the cracks."

"What did you find?" Donovan asked.

"Princess Anna's passport!" he announced triumphantly.

Bliley looked astonished. Donovan was delighted. "No passport, no Concorde."

"She couldn't have gotten on the plane."

"She's still in New York," Donovan said.

"But she said she was going to spend time with her mum," Bliley objected.

"Surprise!" Donovan said. "Mum's in New York, too."

"**If** you want to be a doctor, Captain, come learn about ultrasound," said Marcy's doctor. Donovan peered over his shoulder at the tiny black-and-white screen and the keyboard below it.

"I like gadgets," Donovan replied. "And I like to see my son."

It was miraculous, the little picture. As Campagna ran the transducer over Marcy's undraped belly, the screen lit up with a tiny photo of a tiny life. Seen looking down from over his head, Daniel seemed a perfect little boy ready to pop out of his mother's womb and begin causing trouble, in the grand tradition of his father. Already he opened and closed the fingers of his right hand, which floated in amniotic fluid that appeared as clear as water. Far below, his umbilical cord twisted off to its attachment point on the wall of Marcy's womb.

"He has your nose," Marcy said, happily squeezing her husband's hand. "Isn't it perfectly adorable?"

Campagna looked at her, then back at the screen, and replied, "Your nose is lovely, Mrs. Donovan. The baby's nose looks more like yours."

Donovan smiled.

Seeing her husband's reaction, she said, "I had it done."

"Pardon me?" the doctor asked.

"I went to the wizard on Park and Seventy-third."

"A plastic surgeon?"

"He got it broke," she said, indicating Donovan.

"I think you're telling me more than I need to know."

"I don't mean that he broke it. I'd kill him if he ever laid a hand on me in anger. I mean that a long time ago, when I was an undercover policewoman, he sent me out on an assignment that resulted in my nose being broken."

"Really," Campagna said.

"The city paid for the nose job," Donovan added. "But, in fact, she had a beautiful nose before. And it wouldn't have been broken if she hadn't decided to duke it out with a man carrying a two-by-four."

"What was I supposed to do?"

"Shoot him," Donovan said.

"I wish things were as simple for me as they are for you," she replied, sighing.

Donovan reached out with a forefinger and touched the bottom of the screen. "What's 'DOC' mean?" he asked.

"Date of conception," Campagna replied.

"That's when Marcy got pregnant?"

"You mean you don't remember the night?"

"I remember every minute," he said quickly. "But it was an afternoon."

Mollified, Marcy smiled and once again squeezed his hand.

Campagna twice pressed the button that made Polaroid snapshots of the baby, then pushed the ultrasound cart a few feet away from the bed. He wiped the lubricant off Marcy's belly with paper towels and pulled the gown back down. When the photos appeared from a slot on the side of the machine, he handed one to each parent.

"You're a miracle worker, Dr. Campagna," Marcy said.

"No. You work the miracles. I merely stand by in case I can be of assistance."

Donovan patted the ultrasound machine and said, "Interesting gadget. I think I'll get one."

"What on earth for?" Campagna asked.

"Until my medical degree comes through, I can use it to

check hard-boiled eggs to see if they're done," Donovan replied.

"I suppose it would work for that."

"Does this thing store data and for how long?"

"This is the newest model. It knows everything about the baby—all pertinent data. It keeps records for all the patients on the floor for a week. Then the technician downloads the data into the mainframe, where it becomes a part of the patient's confidential medical record." With that, he switched off the machine.

After a few pleasantries and another trip to the box of Perugina chocolates, the doctor excused himself. When he was gone, Donovan closed the door and went back to the ultrasound machine.

"What are you up to?" she asked.

"I want to see if Anna Fritsch had an ultrasound while she was in that room down the hall," Donovan said. He switched the machine back on.

"Honey, those medical records are confidential," she argued, but with a wry smile.

"And so they are."

The screen came up blank save for a menu asking the operator for his password.

"And the machine is password-protected."

"And so it is," Donovan replied, typing in "Gicana" and hitting the ENTER key.

The screen came to life. "How did you get Dr. Campagna's password?" she asked.

"I looked over his shoulder. Roberto Gicana is the name of a prominent Italian soccer player. I saw Campagna using it the other day. It works to get into the medical records computer, too."

"This is highly illegal," she said, but seemed impressed all the same.

"And unethical. I'm trying to catch a killer."

He fiddled around with the menus for a time, trying this and that, occasionally muttering to himself. Such as: "She's German and doesn't have a Social Security number, which is how most medical records are stored, so let's try the name and see if we get lucky."

Donovan tried "Fritsch" and got nothing. But "Hebbel, Anna," earned him a couple of beeps and a bright sonogram of a tiny infant.

"Got her," Donovan said proudly.

"Does it give the sex? Boy or girl?" Marcy asked, craning her neck in that direction.

"Girl. Twenty weeks. Cute little thing, too." But, in fact, the image showed little more than one blur that resembled a head and another that looked like a leg. "Maybe Danny would like to meet her."

"Any babe that tries to lay a hand on my boy is in big trouble," Marcy said, petting her belly reassuringly.

"I thought you were going to be a progressive mom," Donovan commented.

She shook her head. "I want Daniel to be a virgin when he marries."

"The second half of my life is going to be a challenge, isn't it?" Donovan moaned.

"What was the first half of your life, a walk through Disneyland? You're a New Yorker: you like aggravation. When was the baby conceived?"

Donovan peered at the data displayed alongside the image. "Date of conception was August fourth," he said.

"And where were the parents then?" Marcy asked.

Donovan said, "The baby was conceived on the Caribbean

island of Carricola while Melmer was manning his booth at a trade show at the Javits Convention Center."

"Anna . . . what are we using for a last name?"

"Let's settle on Fritsch."

"Anna Fritsch gets pregnant by God-knows-who and flies to New York, where Melmer and her promptly announce their engagement. Do you think he knew?"

"My guess is 'yes,' " Donovan said.

"I agree. People are pretty sophisticated these days."

"*Technology* is pretty sophisticated these days," Donovan added. "Once upon a time a girl could talk a guy into believing that somebody else's kid was his, but no more."

"Melmer was a good man," Marcy said. "I think we can assume he loved her despite her carrying someone else's baby. But whose?"

Donovan shrugged. "I have to get my hands on the manifest of that Coast Guard boat."

"That assumes she wasn't made pregnant by a houseboy at the resort hotel," Marcy said.

"True," Donovan admitted.

"How important to the case is this information?"

"Melmer was killed by an unknown man," Donovan said. "The fiancée he left behind carries someone else's child. Maybe the real father is the murderer."

"Why would someone do that? To leave her with no option but to go back to him? And then what of Seybold? Why kill him? And who's behind the extortion demand? It makes no sense."

"Not at the moment, anyway. I need to know more. Including who was booked into that hotel on Carricola."

"How can you get that?" Marcy asked.

"There are ways," Donovan said, pressing the button that turned the sonogram on the screen into a Polaroid photo.

"What's the photo for?" Marcy asked, taking it from his hand and scanning it.

"To give to the father when I find him," Donovan said.

"William . . . what if this is a run-of-the-mill lovers' triangle that has nothing to do with the murders on Fifth Avenue?"

"That's too much of a coincidence to even think about. It's related; I just can't tell you how."

He shut off the ultrasound machine, then picked up the piece of volcanic rock and sat on the edge of the bed, tossing the rock into the air and catching it.

"You're just mad because she ran away," Marcy said. "You see suspects fleeing and you get this incredible testosterone surge. I can feel it from here." She laid her hand on his arm and continued, "You're hot."

"You, too," Donovan said.

"I mean that your blood is up. Isn't that how the Irish put it?"

"Since I stopped drinking and married a Jewish girl I've pretty much forgotten what the Irish do about anything," Donovan responded. "And on the subject of fleeing, they're all on the lam: Kimble tried running; Tuttle, Fritsch, and my Afghan friend actually did it."

"That last one would be the gyro guy," Marcy said.

"Yeah. Moskowitz can't find him. He even sent a Muslim police officer to talk to the owners of that halal shop on Queens Boulevard."

"Nothing came of it?"

"Nada," Donovan replied. He turned to his laptop, which purred away atop Marcy's food service table. He flipped through a few screens before finding the information he wanted. Then he continued, "And the city agency that licenses street vendors says only that the spot in front of F.A.O.

Schwarz goes to one Saihaj Bahador, a Sikh immigrant who has worked there every day for the past two years."

"Every day? The guy doesn't take off?"

"He works seven days a week, from eight in the morning until seven at night," Donovan said. "I guess he's one of those immigrants the Republicans say come here to get on welfare and poison the fabric of America. According to the agency, Bahador has an impeccable record and supports a large family."

"So where was he last Friday when Seybold was shot?"

"A good question. I think I'll ask him. He's back at work today." Donovan got up and stretched. "Time for a snack," he said.

"You're going out again? You just ate."

"I'm hungry."

"No more junk food. Please. You've slipped recently."

"At the worst I'll get a pretzel."

"Get one with no salt," she replied. "You're going to be a daddy soon, and I need you to live forever?"

"Well, that doesn't put me under too much pressure," he said, bending over and kissing her.

"You know how you always said your guiding principle as a cop was that good people should live forever?"

"I said that?"

"Often. And you said it offended you when crime prevented that from happening."

"Melmer sounds like he was someone who should have lived forever," Donovan said. "And Seybold wasn't a bad guy, either. I'm gonna get whoever killed them."

He walked across the room and plugged a tape into the VCR he had hooked up to the standard-issue hospital television. Then he tossed her the remote.

"Watch this for me," he said.

"If this is another of your Learning Channel documentaries, I'm not interested in Clovis points, Paleo-Indian burial mounds, or the attack formation Nelson used at Trafalgar," Marcy said, clicking the VCR on.

"You lucked out. This is two hours of your basic heart-throb, Paul Duke, reading from the TelePrompTer. It's the master tape from his show the day the extortion demand was left beneath the Rockefeller Center tree."

"Cool," Marcy said. "What am I supposed to be looking for? The guy leaving the note?"

"I don't know if the tree is in the shot," Donovan replied. "I'm hoping that maybe the killer wandered over and stared in Paul's window."

"I don't know what he looks like," Marcy protested.

"Look for Santa's Angels volunteers, seven-foot-tall Vikings, or mujahideen freedom fighters," Donovan said.

"Those people out there every day are grandmas from Iowa," she said.

"So look for an angry one," Donovan replied, slipping out the door.

As he headed down the hall, he heard her call out, "I'm retired! And pregnant!"

The line outside F.A.O. Schwarz was shorter than expected and didn't reach all the way to the sidewalk where the gyro vendor had set up his cart. As a result, this man catered to his regulars—office workers on late lunch breaks and cabbies who pulled to the curb, blocking the usually fierce midtown traffic just long enough to snag hot dogs.

Both cart and vendor were different. The cart was newer and without decoration. The one Donovan had seen on November 29 was plastered with stickers and other adornment, including the jokey Buddha snapshot. This cart was immaculate and frequently polished. A blue Windex bottle sat atop it, alongside a roll of paper towels. The only advertisement was a neatly printed wooden sign listing prices. (Gyros were $4.50, Donovan was gratified to see, and pretzels were $1.50, both cheaper than on the day after Thanksgiving.)

November's phony Sikh had been forty and fat, with a scraggly beard. This man was fifty and thin, with a magnificent beard that was carefully groomed and parted in the middle. He wore a black turban.

Getting his attention, Donovan smiled broadly and said, "Make me one with everything."

The man offered a polite smile. "I beg your pardon?" he asked. "May I get you a hot dog?"

Donovan shrugged. "I was fishing for a joke, but I'll take a pretzel."

"I do not understand," the man replied.

"One with no salt."

Donovan gave the man money and showed him his badge. At that, the vendor finally cracked a smile. A formal one. As he handed over the pretzel, he said, "You are a policeman. Is there something I can do for you?"

"I would like to know about the man working this spot on the day after Thanksgiving," Donovan said.

"There was no man working here that day," the vendor replied, raising his voice slightly to be heard over a chorus of "Deck the Halls" that suddenly blared over the store's outside loudspeakers.

"How would you know, Mr. Bahador? . . . You weren't here."

"This is my spot. No one else can work it."

"I assure you that someone was right here. I bought a pretzel from him. For two dollars."

Bahador seemed interested in the high price Donovan

had paid but said nothing about it. Instead, he said, "On that day I went with my wife to see the doctor. We are expecting another baby."

"Who are you using?"

"What do you mean?"

"What doctor?"

"Levy, at Columbia Presbyterian."

"Congratulations on your baby," Donovan said.

"Thank you very much. Who was this other man?"

"An Afghan pretending to be a Sikh. Do you know him?"

"As I told you, Detective, no one should have been here. If someone was, it was an interloper. If you have his name I will report him to the authorities."

"I was hoping you could give me his name," Donovan said.

Bahador shook his head. "It is possible that a vendor from one of the other corners took advantage of my absence."

"Where do you keep this thing anyway?" Donovan asked, pointing to the cart.

"I rent space in the Lexington Trader Garage, as do most of my colleagues."

"And where is that?"

"On the north side of Sixty-fourth Street between York and First Avenues," Bahador replied.

"How many of your colleagues use that facility?" Donovan asked.

"At least one hundred. Why don't you go over there and look? Will you recognize the man?"

"Yes. And his cart as well. Where do you buy your meat?"

"My halal meat, you mean?"

"Yes."

"In Paterson."

"New Jersey? Why there?"

"I live in Fort Lee."

"So you commute to the city to run a pushcart?"

"That is correct," the man said proudly.

"Times have changed," Donovan replied.

"I drive in, park my car in the garage, then push the cart from the garage to here. I support my family."

Donovan nodded.

"Have I done something wrong?" Bahador asked.

"Not if you don't know the man I spoke to," Donovan said.

"Did he do something wrong, may I ask?"

"Well, if you don't know him then it doesn't matter, does it?" Donovan said.

Customers waiting for service were beginning to get agitated, so Donovan excused himself and walked off briskly. But he didn't go far. He slipped around the corner and stood where he could remain unseen while keeping an eye on the vendor. That man served the customers on line, then took advantage of the first free moment to pull out a cell phone and make a call.

Donovan did likewise, telling the detective on his staff who answered the phone, "There's a suspect, Saihaj Bahador of Fort Lee, New Jersey, making a cell phone call from the corner of Fifth Avenue and Sixty-first Street. Get his cell number and find out who he's calling."

That done, the captain watched while Bahador spoke with increasing agitation to whoever was on the other end of his line. When the vendor hung up his phone, Donovan called his wife to say he would be out a bit longer than expected. Then he walked to the corner of Madison Avenue and caught a cab across town to Sixty-fourth and First, where the entrance to the Lexington Trader Garage was as dingy and urine-soaked as the entrance to any side-street parking tenement. A four-foot white sign, stained by rust, dangled over the entrance. It read: "Early birds, $7, 8 A.M. to 6 P.M." That much of a bargain could only come with serious problems. Among them: a stench that was overwhelming even in the frosty winter air, a dark and narrow driveway that plummeted steeply into a shadowy abyss lit only by a solitary bare bulb, and a screeching alarm that jarred Donovan's teeth when he set it off by breaking an invisible beam placed a few paces down the path.

A 1970s-vintage transistor radio blared Arab music. Its long-torn-off telescoping antenna had been replaced by a rusty coat hanger that someone had tried to twist straight. But only Donovan was there to hear the music, or so it seemed. There was no attendant; whoever was in charge of that garage had gone wherever Donovan's suspects had gone. The captain pulled out his Smith & Wesson and flipped his badge onto his jacket pocket. He thought of his unborn child and of Marcy and how he had promised her to avoid situations involving guns.

The attendant's booth had a fly-specked window made of glass in which chicken wire had been embedded to discourage breakage. A mouse hole big enough for money to pass through was at the bottom, along with a sign made of shirt cardboard listing the monthly prices. Among them: "Car, $250; Cart/car, $350; payable in cash on 1st." Another bare bulb hung limply at the end of ancient cloth-covered wire. It cast its yellow glare on a strip of flypaper that curled from the grimy ceiling, bearing hundreds of tiny corpses.

The door to the booth was ajar. Donovan nudged it open, then swung inside with his revolver in front of him. The booth was empty, although a half-eaten falafel sandwich was still warm atop the counter. The spice lightly scented the booth. The radio blared on from its place, on a shelf, next to an old black rotary phone. Donovan switched off the music.

The echoes faded from the gloomy dark. In their place

was the distant rumble of traffic and the occasional blare of horns as well as a persistent hiss from an overworked radiator. Donovan lifted the telephone receiver and dialed a number. When a detective answered, the captain said, "Yeah, Donovan again. Is five-five-five, four-seven-five-eight the number that guy called before? Too soon to tell? OK, well, get a patrol car over to the parking garage at Nine-seven-four East Sixty-fourth Street. I may have a bad situation here."

"You got it, Cap," was the reply.

"And tell Sergeant Moskowitz to get his buns over here, too."

Donovan was about to hang up the phone when he heard a sound, a rusty wheel, such as on a street vendor's pushcart, turning. He shot a glance out of the booth but couldn't see much at all, the window was so dirty. Mainly he could see some light coming down the steep driveway from the street and the glow of the other bulb, which hung halfway down a row of parked cars interspersed with sidewalk vending carts.

The detective on the other end of the line reacted to the silence. "You got a problem?" he asked.

"Hang on," Donovan said. Realizing it was too easy for someone outside to see him, he reached up and pulled the string to shut off the light in the booth.

In the instant he did so, there was the shriek of splintering glass followed a split second later by the roar of a nine-millimeter. He threw himself down onto the floor of the booth as the window—chicken wire or no chicken wire—exploded inward in a thousand fragments. The roar of the gunshot echoed throughout the dingy garage, and when his ears cleared he could hear a voice saying, "Captain! Captain!" over the phone.

Donovan scooped up the receiver and mumbled, "I'm under fire." Then he dropped the phone again and squirmed around until he could see out the door, his cheek pressed against the concrete floor, which was cold as ice and filthy from decades of spilled coffee, ground-in cigarette butts, and gum.

"I *had* to give up drinking," Donovan muttered, and worked his Smith & Wesson out in front of him, the stubby muzzle pointing down the row of cars and carts.

The hissing of the radiator seemed louder than before. Donovan kept quiet for ten, maybe twenty seconds. Then he pushed the door open a few more inches and yelled, "Police! Throw out your weapon and come out with your hands up!"

There was a muzzle flash down in the darkness and another roar. There was no more glass in the booth to break, and the echoes didn't sound as loud to him, lying as he was with one ear against the concrete. Donovan fired three quick shots in the direction of the muzzle flash. Before the echoes came he heard one impact on metal and another on glass; a windshield, he thought. After the echoes of the gunshots came the sound of heavy shoes running away.

Donovan scrambled to his feet and gave chase, running down the aisle of cars and aluminum carts, keeping close to them in case he had to dive for cover again. The sounds of the shoes stopped, and he ducked behind an old Chrysler. This time he heard only the sound of a metal door that had been thrown open. Its hinges screamed and then it crashed into what sounded like a basement corridor.

Donovan saw the rectangle of light where a door now stood open. Beyond it wasn't a corridor, but an alley. He got out from behind the Chrysler and jogged cautiously toward the door, his revolver out in front. The sounds of the street—engines, horns, and, in the closing distance, sirens—grew louder. But the sound of a man running away was gone.

When Donovan got to the door he flattened himself against the wall, then dropped to a squat and pivoted around the corner. He found himself staring into a basement-level alley flanked by brick buildings and marked on the far end by a black cast-iron fence and a wide-open gate. Garbage cans from both buildings lined the walls, on one of which an artistic janitor had meticulously painted a life-size rendition of a red 1959 Cadillac.

Donovan found himself alone in the alley. He walked briskly to the far end and went through the gate. A set of cast-iron stairs led up to street level. He climbed them and walked through a stone gate, the one the janitors used to take the garbage to the curb for twice-weekly pickup. The sidewalks on Sixty-fifth Street were empty save for a solitary woman pushing a baby in a stroller. But traffic had ground to a halt on First Avenue, and the reflections of flashing red lights were everywhere.

11. A HANDFUL OF HOT DOGS, WRINKLED LIKE LAST YEAR'S PICKLES

The garage was full of cops and their equipment. Several tall light stands flooded the underground chasm with white light that was blinding at times. Long shadows snaked across the dirty walls and over the rusted steam pipes that sweated orange water onto the hoods and roofs of cars. Radios crackled and cell phones beeped. Moskowitz had set up his notebook computer atop a newish aluminum hot dog stand. Its cellular modem was busy downloading files and e-mail from the office.

Donovan poked around the selfsame hot dog cart with

whose owner he had exchanged idle banter just a few days earlier. It didn't seem to have been used in a few days. The propane grills and steam trays were cold as ice trays, and a handful of Sabrett hot dogs languished, wrinkled like last year's pickles, in a vat of frigid water. The fat bubbles that had congealed atop that water picked up the cops' lights and shone like dirty pearls floating in an ice bath.

Halfway down the side of the cart, a .38-caliber bullet hole punctured the aluminum skin. It came from Donovan's gun, as did a similar hole in the driver's-side window of a 1992 Chevrolet.

Donovan glowered at the Great Buddha of Bamiyan.

" 'Make me one with everything,' my ass," Donovan said. "The sonofabitch who owns this cart tried to make me one with the floor of the attendant's booth."

"So much for your trying to achieve enlightenment through Eastern religions," Mosko said over his shoulder, his main focus remaining on the computer. "Forget their alleged quest for nirvana. Experience the religion that brought the world weekends, Moses, Sigmund Freud, Barbra Streisand, the captain and first officer of *Star Trek*, half of Goldie Hawn, and, if you insist on counting the guy, Jesus."

"I heard of him."

"He's not normally on those lists we keep of prominent Jews, but it's wrong to forget the guy entirely. I mean he had an impact. In time he got to be as big as, well, as John Lennon."

Donovan poked around the assorted drawers and cubbyholes found on the sidewalk cart. "What *are* you doing on Christmas?" he asked.

"We usually have a Jewish Christmas—two movies and a Chinese restaurant. There's nothing else to do in town."

"Last year Marcy took me to Ratner's," Donovan said.

"The year before that it was Sammy's Roumanian. Before that, *Schindler's List.*"

"What a warm and cuddly Christmas," Bonaci said, breezing past en route to supervise an evidence-gathering crew working out in the alley.

Donovan found nothing of interest in the cart and stepped back from it and folded his arms. "The bum tried to kill me," he muttered.

"Who, Steven Spielberg?"

"No, the Afghan in the Sikh turban. I guess his head got too hot and fried his brains."

"How do you feel?" Mosko asked.

"Incredibly pissed off."

"I think you're entitled."

"Marcy doesn't know about this, does she?"

"Nah. I called and told her you'd be a little longer yet, that's all. Now, if she just doesn't listen to the radio—"

"Damn! She turns on National Public Radio every day at five to get *All Things Considered.* They could carry the news. I'm in big trouble."

Laughing, Mosko said, "My friend, if you're more worried about what your wife thinks than about being shot at by a lunatic Afghanistani hot dog vendor, you're Jewish already. Make your wife and unborn child happy and convert. I'll call a rabbi for the bris."

"Leave me alone about religion," Donovan replied, squirming and crossing his legs. "I'm an ex-Catholic practicing atheist."

"How do you practice atheism?" Mosko asked.

"You don't believe in anything. For example, I don't believe you have a salary review coming up in three weeks."

"Oops," Mosko said, deciding in that instant to give full attention to his boss and the matter at hand.

"Did we get prints off this thing?" Donovan asked, kicking a tire.

"Only a million. But there's one that occurs more than the others. Assuming it belongs to the owner, we should be getting results soon. I faxed the prints to the database administrator, who will patch them into the FBI data bank and e-mail me the results if we get a match."

"When will this happen?"

"Any time now."

"Is this cart registered to anyone?" Donovan asked.

Mosko nodded. "It belongs to the owner of this garage, one Walid Maroofi."

"That name sounds Afghan."

"It is. Maroofi is a naturalized citizen and, get this, runs a service that gets jobs and places to live for newly arrived central and southern Asians, especially his countrymen."

"Including, possibly, jobs as parking-garage attendants," Donovan said.

"The thought occurred to me," Mosko replied.

"Haul his ass down here," Donovan snarled.

"I have men on the way to his apartment now," the sergeant said proudly.

"Where does he live?"

"Across the river. In Queens. Not far from that halal shop, in fact."

"Considering that I'm against everything that Archie Bunker stands for, it amuses me that his home borough is rapidly becoming Little Asia. You drive down Northern Boulevard and it's like taking the milk train east from Istanbul. Every stopover is another Asian ethnic enclave."

"True," Mosko replied.

"Does this Maroofi have anything to do with the Mountain Brigade?"

"The guys who sent the extortion note?"

"Allegedly," Donovan replied.

"I'll find out. I have a request in to Immigration."

Donovan fished a pencil and a Post-it notepad from his pocket and scribbled something, leaning on top of the cart. Then he pulled the top note off the pad and handed it to his aide.

"Who's Jerry McGinty?" Mosko asked.

"FBI, antiterrorist section," Donovan said.

"Where do you know him from? An old case I don't know about?"

Donovan shook his head. "A bar on Third Avenue. That you also don't know about. It's not what you think, though. I helped his cousin, just off the boat from Ireland, get a job there three or four years ago."

"Whatever works," Mosko said with a shrug, and got on the phone.

Donovan stuck his hands in his pants pockets and wandered back out to the alley door and from there made his way back to the street. It was getting near the end of the day, and the uptown commuter traffic on York and First Avenues was bumper-to-bumper. The side street was blocked by official vehicles, which had the predictable effect on the avenues. Horns blew nonstop, and with the arrival of each new green light came the roar of engines and the screeching of tires as drivers drag-raced the handful of yards allowed them.

Donovan walked to York and bought a cup of decaffeinated coffee from the Te Amo—a chain tobacco, candy, newspaper, and snack shop. He carried it across the avenue to a bench in front of Rockefeller University, where he sat and watched the Manhattan skyline. He called Marcy on the cell phone and managed to tell her what had happened without revealing that he had been shot at. She was sufficiently preoccupied with the results of the day's tests to avoid hard questions about what he had been doing, and for that he was grateful. He also was glad to hear music playing in the background. As long as she skipped the news, his secret was safe.

When it got too cold to stay, he walked back to the garage. Most of the technicians had cleared out, leaving Moskowitz and Bonaci supervising a handful of detectives. Two of them stood guard over a thin and extremely nervous-looking man—Maroofi, beyond a shadow of a doubt—who chain-smoked and alternated between gaping at the ceiling and the floor.

Donovan tossed his coffee cup into a trash can and let himself be drawn aside by Mosko, who pointed at a smiling face on a passport-type photo displayed on the computer monitor.

"Mojadidi," he said. "Yama Mojadidi."

Donovan bent over and squinted at the somewhat fuzzy photo. Then he smiled faintly. It was the pudgy fortyish man with the scraggly beard with whom Donovan had had that brief conversation just before being interrupted by the murder of Erik Melmer.

"This is the hot dog vendor I talked to," Donovan said.

"The one with the nine-millimeter?"

"That's him. His name is . . . what did you say?"

"Mojadidi," Mosko replied.

"Who is he?"

"He's a forty-three-year-old guy who came here on a visitor's visa a couple of months ago. He overstayed his welcome and disappeared into the underground. His last known address is in Long Island City."

"Another Queens boy," Donovan said.

"Yeah. In the shadow of that big Citibank building. I got

guys headed over there now, but I wouldn't count on him still being there."

"What do we have on him before he came to the U.S.?" Donovan asked.

"Not too much. He listed his occupation as air traffic controller. That was in Kabul."

"How much air traffic does Kabul get, other than incoming missiles?" Donovan asked.

"I guess enough to need guys watching radar screens," Mosko replied. "Anyway, Mojadidi came here by way of Karachi—"

"Coincidentally, perhaps, the same route a couple of the World Trade Center bombers took."

"And stayed out of sight until running into you the other day," Mosko said.

"Did you get Jerry McGinty on the phone?" Donovan asked.

Mosko nodded. "He never heard of either Mojadidi or Maroofi. He has heard of the Mountain Brigade, of course, but has no idea if this Afghan guerrilla group operates in the States. He's a little mystified by that possibility. As far as he knows, they don't have a worldwide agenda; they're just a local bunch of freedom fighters."

"What the hell is Mojadidi doing in this country?" Donovan asked.

"Ask Maroofi," Mosko said, nodding at the thin, chainsmoking man.

"That him?"

Moskowitz nodded.

"How'd he take to being brought here?" Donovan asked.

"He's scared. One minute he's running a seedy parking garage; the next minute he's surrounded by detectives. You know how these immigrants tend to be scared of authority."

"Which is why they came here, generally speaking," Donovan said. "Bring him over."

Moskowitz went to the man, introduced himself, told him who Donovan was, then returned with his muscular arm around the man's shoulders. Maroofi was fumbling for another cigarette when Donovan replaced Mosko's arm with his own and steered the by-then trembling Afghan toward the attendant's booth.

"Did my associate tell you who I am?" Donovan asked.

"He said you are an important man," Maroofi replied, flicking his thumb nervously at a Bic lighter—a souvenir one carrying a picture of the Statue of Liberty—and nearly dropping it before managing to light his smoke.

"He lied," Donovan said.

Caught off guard, Maroofi looked around at the muscular Moskowitz. "He lied? I don't understand."

"I'm not an important person," Donovan said. "I'm a nobody. But I'm a nobody whose wife loves him. You are an important person, because you have it in your power to find the man who tried to make my wife a widow. Don't you agree that it would be sad should my wife become a widow?"

"Yes. Yes." Maroofi bobbed his head up and down, his long and skinny nose slicing the cloud of smoke that Donovan could tell was a permanent fixture in front of the man's face.

Donovan led the man to the attendant's booth. The shattered window still lay in myriad pieces on the floor. The bits of glass crunched beneath their feet, the noise amplified by the concrete walls of the garage, which were painted dark grey years before but had turned to black following much neglect.

"I came down here looking for a hot dog vendor with a sense of humor, and look what happened to me," Donovan continued. "A man shot at me. I presume it was the same man I came to see."

From the corner of his eye Donovan could see Moskowitz staring intently at an e-mail coming in on his notebook computer.

"Fortunately, he missed. I shot back and, unfortunately, I also missed. Had this exchange of gunfire taken place out in the open—say on Fifth Avenue during the holiday shopping season—the two of us could have gunned down half a dozen bystanders."

Maroofi continued bobbing his head up and down, puffing furiously. Now and again Donovan waved some smoke away from his face.

At that point, Mosko waved to get his attention. Donovan said, "What?"

"You wanted to know who Saihaj Bahador made that cell call to?" Mosko called back.

"Who?"

"Him," was the reply.

Donovan's assistant pointed at Maroofi, who, hearing the conversation, coughed sputteringly and threw his half-smoked cigarette down onto the floor. He said, "I am a workingman. I am an honest workingman. I came to this country—"

"Not to get involved with these characters, certainly," Donovan interrupted.

"I helped get them jobs and this is how they repaid me," Maroofi said. He fumbled for another cigarette.

"Who shot at me today?" Donovan asked.

"That must have been Mojadidi," the garage owner stammered, lost again in the struggle to light up.

"Tell me what happened."

"He is my attendant here. I also allow him to take a cart

out and use a spot when it becomes temporarily vacant. As happened the day after Thanksgiving. Your assistant told me of your interest in that date."

"So this guy Mojadidi was out, using Bahador's prime real estate in front of F.A.O. Schwarz making a few extra bucks selling hot dogs, when I happened along and spotted his gun."

"I don't know anything about a gun. I don't associate with men who carry guns. He only told me he fled that day after a policeman questioned him. He has overstayed his visitor's visa, and Immigration is looking for him. So it made sense to me that he ran."

"I can understand the fleeing part, but why was he carrying a gun?" Donovan asked. "Fifth Avenue is hardly the O.K. Corral, if you know what I mean."

Maroofi didn't.

"You're not generally in danger of being gunned down there," Donovan explained.

"He must have been worried about being robbed, but as you say, that doesn't happen on Fifth Avenue," Maroofi replied.

"Having a gun—I assume it was an illegal one, since Mojadidi now is an illegal alien—is bad enough," Donovan said. "But using it to fire at a policeman is worse. To me that means that we're dealing with something more than a guy who's afraid of being sent back to Afghanistan. Is Mojadidi a member of the Mountain Brigade?"

"You mean the political party in my country?"

"If that's what they call themselves."

"I have no idea. I don't think he is political, especially. He is a Muslim, but not a fundamentalist. He doesn't have strong opinions about religion or politics. I don't know why he shot at you, but I am very sorry that he did."

"What do you know about him?" Donovan asked.

"He's interested in flying. I don't know much about him.

He answered my Yellow Pages ad. I have a listing for my placement service."

"Does he have family?"

"Mojadidi told me once that his wife was killed in the fighting."

"Which fighting? Against the Russians or the current civil war?"

"Against the Russians. His daughter also died tragically, I know. Mojadidi was very bitter about that. But he wouldn't talk about it much."

Donovan thought for a moment, then said, "You said he's a Muslim. But he had a snapshot of the Great Buddha of Bamiyan pasted on that cart. Unless you put it there, of course."

"Oh no, that belongs to Mojadidi. I am sure of it. He took that photograph himself years ago. He is from the Hindu Kush Mountains, which is where Bamiyan is located. I don't think he keeps the photograph out of religious devotion, however. He is, you know, Muslim."

"Just a souvenir of the old hometown, huh?" Donovan said, turning and leading the way back to the hot dog cart. Maroofi followed him, and together they leaned over and squinted at the yellowing snapshot.

Donovan had read about the Great Buddhas of Bamiyan. Massive sculptures—one is eighteen stories high—carved into the sandstone of the Hindu Kush Mountains seventeen hundred years ago, the Buddhas look down into the Bamiyan Valley upon the invasion route taken by Genghis Khan on his conquest of Asia. The gigantic statues also witnessed the battles by the mujahideen against the Russians and continue to watch the civil war, an antiaircraft battery sitting atop one of them.

A tiny imprint at the bottom of the photo showed that it

was taken in March 1993. Standing proudly at the feet of the Buddha and nearly invisible to the casual onlooker was a pretty girl, twenty-something, with straight black hair and huge, coal black eyes. She was barefoot and wore a light grey robe.

"Who's the girl?" Donovan asked.

Maroofi shrugged. "A tourist, I guess. The Great Buddhas were big tourist attractions for centuries. Not since the fighting, though."

"Mojadidi took her picture. She must be important."

Squinting even harder at the photo, Maroofi said, "Perhaps he was photographing the guns and the girl just happened to be there."

Donovan watched as the Afghan pressed a pointy fingertip against the antiaircraft emplacement, which was just barely visible, resembling a few wild strands of hair, over Buddha's head.

"Perhaps," Donovan said.

"I wish I could be more helpful," Maroofi responded, lighting his third cigarette in ten minutes.

"You could stop blowing smoke at me," Donovan replied.

The man flung his cigarette onto the ground and stamped it ferociously.

"So Mojadidi worked for you. Every day?"

"Yes."

"How did you pay him? By check?"

"I paid in cash," Maroofi said.

"And, of course, you couldn't file withholding on him 'cause he's an illegal. So I guess I'll have to get the IRS involved in this," Donovan said.

The man looked even more uncomfortable than before.

"I mean, so far I only have you down as harboring an illegal alien and complicity in the attempted murder of a police officer."

"Me? What did I do?"

"You own the phone line that Mojadidi was tipped off on. Bahador called to warn Mojadidi that I was on to him, and the sonofabitch took a shot at me."

"What they did is no fault of mine," Maroofi protested.

"Not true. You gave safe haven to a known illegal alien who carried an illegal gun, and he used it to try to kill me. Frankly, I think we may have to hold you in custody and shut down your garage for a few days while we sort all this out."

The thin man looked panicked and reached for another cigarette. But Donovan waggled a finger at him, and he jammed his hands together nervously and squeezed them. "You cannot do this to me," he said.

"Watch me," Donovan replied.

"You cannot shut down the garage. My customers need a place to store their carts."

"No problem. We'll padlock the joint after the carts are stored for the night."

"But my customers won't be able to get them out the next morning," Maroofi protested.

"Is that so?" Donovan replied.

"They will be furious."

"And, from what I've seen, armed. If I were you, I would hop on the first flight back to Kabul. It may be safer for you there."

The Afghan walked away from Donovan, downcast, thinking. Mosko watched him carefully, lest he bolt. But the man merely paced back and forth for a moment. Then he returned to Donovan and said, "Maybe I can help you find the man who shot at you."

"I had a feeling you could," Donovan replied.

"Mojadidi has an apartment in Long Island City," Maroofi said.

Donovan called his assistant over, then asked the Afghan, "Where in Long Island City?"

"On Twenty-first Street."

"Been there," Mosko said, shaking his head. "Tried it."

"Which one did you go to?" Maroofi asked. "The old apartment near Jackson Avenue?"

Mosko nodded.

"He gave that one up a few months ago. He moved down a few blocks to Hunters Point Avenue. I will write down the address for you."

He did so, using one of his business cards and the stub of a pencil.

"This address is right alongside the Long Island Rail Road yards," Mosko said.

"The rent is reasonable," Maroofi replied.

The building stood three stories high, its fake-stone facade barely rising above a mountain of used automobile tires that occupied a lot adjacent to the Long Island Rail Road's Sunnyside Yards. The building's ground floor bore a hand-lettered sign reading: "Flats fixed." But the shop was boarded up; the boards were plastered with eviction notices. One or two such papers also adorned the door that led to the apartments on the second and third floors, that part of the building where the linoleumlike exterior peeled off in slabs that reminded Donovan of skin peeling off a sunburned forehead. The day had grown late and the sun was setting behind the Manhattan skyline. Its accompaniment was the buzz of rush-hour traffic leaving the city and the occasional rumble of a subway train rattling along the elevated line. The mountain of used tires smelled even in the depths of winter.

Donovan got out of his Buick and stood with his hands in

his pockets, watching as Moskowitz directed the platoon of detectives that surrounded the building, flak jackets on, weapons drawn. Gesturing with a walkie-talkie, Moskowitz looked like a baseball manager moving his outfielders around. When all were in place and there was no way out of the building except for rats and roaches, Mosko walked over to his boss.

"You want a part of this?" he asked, drawing his Penzler automatic.

Donovan shook his head. "I got shot at once today. That's my quota. In fact, that's it for me for all time. From now on, *I* manage. *You* get shot at."

"Hey, I really like you; you know that," Mosko said.

"Go get him," Donovan replied, and watched while the sergeant tried.

Two men broke down the door, which was locked. Three more, toting shotguns, followed them up the stairs. Not all that eager to get shot at, either, Moskowitz brought up the rear. At the same time, cops trained guns on the ground-floor windows and the solitary fire escape. The passing of another subway train bound for the far reaches of Queens drowned out sounds from within the building. After a minute, Mosko's round face appeared in a third-floor window, peeking out from between the shreds of a yellowed window shade.

Donovan looked up at his assistant, who gave him the hands-up signal of futility.

"He ain't here!" Mosko yelled as soon as the subway was gone.

Donovan pushed away from the Buick, walked across the street, and went into the building and up the stairs. They were wooden and old, worn down by the decades until each step had twin scoops where the feet landed. The walls had been painted once but now were marked by graffiti and streaked by rust stains from plumbing that leaked when it worked at all. Far atop the stairwell, a small square skylight was coated with pigeon droppings.

"No gold faucets in this place," Donovan said, stepping into a one-bedroom apartment that was dirty and claustrophobic, the latter coming from low ceilings and linoleum that had turned brownish yellow with age.

A queen-size mattress sat atop a metal frame. Atop a recently draped white sheet was a paper shopping bag from the Sloan's supermarket down Jackson Avenue. In it: an economy-size bag of Snickers, two tins of hummus, a Spanish onion, a half-pint of extra-virgin olive oil, and a pint of plain yogurt. Donovan touched the latter with the backs of his fingers, carefully avoiding leaving prints.

"It's still cold," he said.

"We missed him again," Moskowitz observed. He was using the tip of a pencil to open a copy of the December issue of *Aviation Week & Space Technology*. Other detectives pored over the squalid quarters, peeking behind the nonworking radiator, sniffing the fumes coming from a Sears kerosene heater, looking in almost-empty closets, and checking a bottle of generic aspirin found in the medicine cabinet.

Donovan went to a window, raised the shade, and looked out over the mountain of tires. A commuter train had just filled up at the Hunters Point Avenue station. Three hours later, the old diesel engine would deposit a few hardy resort denizens at Montauk Point. At the moment, though, it rumbled and rattled across the spider's web of intersecting rail lines that was the Sunnyside Yards.

Donovan opened the window and shut it again after

catching a whiff of the used tires. "A rickety train. A mountain of used tires. Add a Kalishnikov assault rifle or two and we could be in Kabul," Donovan said.

"Maybe that's why Mojadidi rented the place," Mosko commented. "It reminded him of home."

"Did we find anything of interest?"

"No. Apparently the guy wasn't here very long."

"Apparently he's either the luckiest SOB in the world or else the best-informed," Donovan said.

"Well, we'll keep looking," Mosko replied, his voice halfway plaintive.

Donovan frowned at the useless comment. "I'm going back to my wife," he said.

"You want to bring her some Snickers?"

"No. Do you need me to drop you back in the city?"

Mosko shook his head. "I'll catch a ride with one of the guys," he replied.

12. "WHO *HASN'T* PAUL DUKE SLEPT WITH?"

Donovan shook his head in amazement when he stepped inside Marcy's room. Sitting by her side were the two anchors of *The Morning Show*, Paul Duke and June Lake. With them was a full network camera crew. It had set up three light tripods as well as an umbrella reflector that softened the light shining on Marcy's face, which was glowing with all its pregnant radiance. She had her bed cranked up and was snuggled between pillows. Most strikingly, she wore a stunning white-on-white nightgown on the sleeve of which was stitched the logo of E & J Tuttle. Wearing jeans and an Irish sweater, Duke sat back a bit and watched while June Lake, dressed to the nines in a beige suit and silk blouse, wrapped up an interview with the mom-to-be.

Dr. Campagna stood behind her, resting a paternal hand on her shoulder. He looked as pleased as the cat that caught the canary.

A woman carrying a clipboard spotted Donovan and gestured to him to be quiet. He crossed his arms and listened to Camapagna deliver a litany of advice on the subject of high-risk pregnancy until the camera and lights flicked off.

"We're taping a medical segment," the woman with the clipboard then snapped at Donovan. "Who are you?"

"The sperm donor," Donovan replied. At which she looked quizzical, then annoyed, then turned away.

"Hi, honey!" Marcy called out, able to see her husband now that the blinding lights were off. "I'm going to be on television."

Donovan walked to her side and kissed her. "That's great," he said.

"Where were you all day while I was being interviewed for national television?" Marcy asked.

"Out getting shot at," Donovan replied.

She laughed, then winked at Lake. "This is my husband William. He likes to kid around."

The woman got up from her chair, pressed her skirt back into place, and took Donovan's hand as Paul Duke introduced them. She was about five-seven, Marcy's height, with lots of wavy black hair, black-pearl eyes, and a four-alarm smile that inevitably was accompanied by a cocking of the head, Miss America-style, to one side. Marcy generally hated the beauty-contest look, Donovan thought. His multiracial wife had long ago perfected the aura of the ethnic goddess and generally despised the Barbie look. But that dislike apparently had been put on hold long enough to get on television.

"I'm always glad to meet Paul's friends," Lake said. "He has such good taste."

Donovan gave Duke a glance. The man shrugged.

"So what's the occasion?" Donovan asked.

"I'm doing a report on high-risk pregnancy. Since Dr. Campagna is the world's authority—"

"You're very kind, June," Campagna said. He had moved off the impromptu set and was fiddling with the medical records computer.

"—and your wife is so beautiful—"

Marcy glowed brightly enough to blind someone.

"—I thought I'd make them the centerpiece of my report," Lake concluded.

"How'd you hear about them?" Donovan asked.

"Oh, from Paul, of course. But I know Dr. Campagna from a shoot I did years ago. I'm sorry you got here too late to be a part of it. If we have to reshoot to add more material I'll be sure to get you in."

She gave him the look you give children you expect to be disappointed. But Donovan said, "I have no need to be on television. Thanks anyway."

"Bill was an expert commentator during the O.J. trials," Duke explained.

"Of course. Captain Donovan. That's where I've seen you. You were in the studio with Paul." Lake looked at him again, more appreciatively this time, as if he were a fellow celebrity. "I loved it when you said you would have gotten onto the O.J. estate by starting a fire in his garbage pail. You were kidding, weren't you?"

Donovan gave her the palms-up sign of ambiguity. Then he added, "In retrospect, I would have torched the whole place."

Lake sighed and said, "Ah, yes, dreams die hard, don't they?"

The camera crew was busy packing its gear into a handful of aluminum trunks and loading the latter onto a dolly. The woman with the clipboard was on the phone getting her voice-mail messages. Campagna was done with the computer and was eating a Perugina chocolate and gazing idly at the yards-long strip of printout from Marcy's fetal monitor. The inches-wide paper curled onto the floor and piled up in bouquets.

Donovan felt the fabric of his wife's new gown. "Where'd you get the rags?" he asked.

"From Paul," she said proudly.

Duke looked away.

"Well, I have to tell *Paul* that you can't keep it."

"I can't?" she said, her voice a mew and her mouth a pout.

"And you know why."

Of course she did. That meant Paul was a suspect. In something, if not in shooting shoppers on Fifth Avenue. But in replying Marcy said, "You're a captain now and can't accept gifts."

"As if I ever did," Donovan replied.

"I seem to recall a few beers," she said dryly.

"Ancient history. This is a thirty-five-hundred-dollar nightie and it will have to go back."

At that point, Duke chimed in, "It's not like I paid for it, Bill."

Lake added, "E & J Tuttle was delighted to 'lend' us this gown for use in the piece. Think of what it would cost them in advertising dollars if they paid to have one of their gowns—

with their logo on the sleeve—displayed on *The Morning Show*."

"Big bucks," Duke agreed.

"Nonetheless, you'll have to take it back," Donovan said.

"Whatever you want," Duke replied.

"Can I at least wear it until the baby comes?"

"Give it back before your water breaks," Campagna replied, looking up from the printouts.

Marcy grimaced and said, "I'll put it back in the box when I get up for my shower later."

Donovan smiled and squeezed her hand. "You're very understanding," he said.

"What's this about getting shot at?" she asked.

"I was kidding around, just like you said. Did you get a chance to look at the video?"

Marcy nodded. "Paul and June watched it with me."

"That must have been hard," Donovan said, speaking to them. "I don't think I could sit through watching two hours of me doing my job."

"It wasn't bad," Lake replied. "Paul and I know where the crowd shots come, and we helped your wife fast-forward to those spots."

"Did anyone stand out?"

"Yes," Marcy said proudly.

"Who?"

"Your Viking friend," she replied.

"He was there?" Donovan asked. "Let me see."

The *Morning Show* camera crew had moved out of the room, so there was a clear view of the room's TV screen. Donovan flicked on the VCR and handed Marcy the remote. She, in turn, handed it to Duke, who pressed a button. The tape had been wound to the spot where "Moondog II," aka Tom Tuttle, was seen in freeze-frame gaping in the window of the Rockefeller Center TV studio. At least, Donovan thought he could be Tuttle. For the head was covered with the horned helmet Donovan had picked up at the Shining Path Poets Cafe and the face was hidden behind a leather mask. But sprigs of mustache stuck out from the slit left for the mouth, and a certain angry fanaticism burned in the steel-grey eyes. The imposing figure, which looked very nearly seven feet tall, was draped from shoulder to calf in a forest green cloak big enough to hide an infantry regiment.

Tuttle was right at the front of the crowd, staring deep into the studio, his eyes ablaze.

Nervously fingering the remote, Duke said, "He's only there a minute. Then he takes off. Look! Look!"

He pressed a button and they all watched while Tuttle suddenly jerked his head, then all his body, away from the window and lurched through the crowd. Grandmas from Iowa jumped to either side to escape being trampled by the gigantic raging figure.

"So much for the power of poetry to soothe," Donovan said.

Duke shut off the tape, and the monitor on the wall reverted to showing CNN.

"Is that the killer you're after?" Lake and Duke asked, almost simultaneously.

"He's a suspect," Donovan replied.

"I never heard of this Viking," Duke said.

"Sure you did," Lake interjected, momentarily and lightly resting her fingertips on Duke's forearm. "Don't you remember we watched that piece about him on *CBS Sunday Morning*?"

Duke tossed his hands up, then brought them together and rubbed them nervously. She patted him reassuringly on the back, then pulled back her hand.

"I know his identity and I want to talk to him," Donovan said. "We're looking for him now. At what time of morning was this piece of tape shot that we just watched?"

Duke checked some notes he had made and answered, "We shot that segment between eight-fifty and nine."

"That day's killing occurred at nine-fifteen, so our Viking pal could have done it," Donovan said.

Campagna was done with the printouts and dropped them back onto the floor. The paper strip continued to flow from the machine, a thin glacier coated with chicken scratches. He packed up the folder containing Marcy's medical record, walked to the door, and stuck it in the plastic holder on the outside.

He said, "I'll stop by later tonight if I get a chance, Mrs. Donovan."

"Do you have another delivery?" Marcy asked.

"The quads are coming tonight," he replied.

"The ones whose parents flew in from Saudi Arabia?" she asked.

"Yes. My third set of quads this year. I should get an award."

"You're wonderful, Dr. Campagna," Marcy gushed.

The physician smiled, then reached through the little crowd by Marcy's bed and shook hands with Duke and Lake. To her he said, "Good to see you again, June."

She smiled back and waved as he walked out of the room and into the hall, brushing past the woman with the clipboard, who took advantage of eye contact with Lake to tap a fingertip against her watch.

"The crew has to go," Lake said.

"I'll see you tomorrow at the studio," Duke replied. He held back as she angled toward the door.

But she took him by the arm and pulled him with her,

saying, "For God's sake, let's leave this happy couple alone."

"I'll never be alone now that I'm having a baby," Marcy stated.

"Marcy, you can ship the nightgown back to me when you get a chance," Duke said. "Or just ask your husband to drop it off at the store."

Donovan nodded. Then he asked, "How'd you get here? Walk?"

"God, no," Lake said. "I won't let him set a foot outside the studio without his bodyguard."

Duke blushed. "She's mothering me," he replied sheepishly.

"We came in Paul's limo," Lake continued. "The poor man has been made a nervous wreck by all these terrible killings. For some reason, he's taking them personally."

"The killer was standing three feet away from me," Duke said tersely, indicating the TV monitor.

"The glass is bulletproof," she said.

"He has a special gun," Duke replied.

Lake smiled and made a dismissive gesture. "You *will* catch the killer, won't you, Captain? Before Paul has a nervous breakdown?"

"I always have in the past," Donovan replied.

"I'm sure you're as good as your reputation," Lake responded. And after a few pleasantries, she managed to pull Duke, who was shrugging and giving in to the inevitable, from the room. They joined the camera crew, a rattling caravan pushing aluminum boxes on heavy dollies, and followed it down the hall.

Donovan closed the door, then gave Marcy a long hug and a handful of kisses. After that he stole one of Campagna's chocolates and sat on the edge of the bed.

"What did you make of that?" he asked.

"I have to call my mother and tell her I'm going to be on TV," Marcy said, reaching for the phone.

Donovan caught her hand and held it. "I mean why do you think June told us they spent a Saturday night together?"

"When did she say that?" Marcy asked.

"When she pointed out that they watched *CBS Sunday Morning* together. That show comes on at nine A.M. Don't tell me they were in a conference room at work."

Marcy thought for a second, then replied, "I guess she likes him. I guess they slept together."

"Who *hasn't* Paul Duke slept with? Beyond Benazir Bhutto and Mother Teresa, of course."

"Didn't you tell me he was ducking June?"

"Yeah. When I went to the studio to pick up the tape you watched today. He acted like she was carrying the plague."

"Maybe they made up," Marcy said.

"Clearly."

"She *is* mothering him."

"He seriously needs direction of some sort," Donovan said. "Interesting that she knows what a nervous wreck he is. And he swore me to secrecy on that point. Said it would be the end of his career should anyone at the network find out. Oh, well, a man tells everything to the woman he sleeps with, I guess."

"I hope so," Marcy replied.

"In which case we can only be glad that Duke isn't carrying the codes that fire the nuclear missiles. Oh, well."

They rested and watched CNN for a while; then around ten Marcy drifted off and Donovan pulled his computer into his lap and logged on to the Internet. Ten minutes later he had followed a logical series of searches and links to produce, in sinewy tones of walnut and steel, a remarkably plain-looking nine-millimeter automatic, the barrel of which was etched with the words "Kammacher Stedman." The photograph came from the on-line catalog of Weber and Augsberg Classic Arms, the Zurich arms merchant that was among the few European weapons manufacturers that hadn't quite got around to apologizing for selling arms to the Nazis during World War II, despite the hoopla that arose half a century after that conflict's last bullets were fired.

The catalog showed three views—from the side, from the front, and from the top—as well as half a page of glowing reports about the weapon's armor-piercing ability. Donovan found the look of the thing to be unremarkable, a bit like the Glock nine-millimeter that some New York police officers had begun carrying. He was no authority on guns but realized that whatever the Afghan gyro vendor had been carrying, it wasn't a Stedman. That man's weapon was relatively slender, more like a Wilson.

What did catch Donovan's eye was a fact hidden in the glowing description. Only three Stedmans were ever produced, that was true. Moreover, only 100 *rounds* were ever manufactured. Most of those, 75 in all, were accounted for with the first two guns. Of the 25 bullets sold with the third, "lost" Stedman, 17 were fired in the course of its history as a collector's item. According to Weber and Augsberg's Web site, eight depleted-uranium slugs remained. But, Donovan noted, that site was last updated before the two murders on Fifth Avenue. In them, the killer used first three, then two bullets.

"There are three still out there," Donovan muttered, switching screens on his computer to begin searching for information on what the survivalists in Montana were up to.

A steep and narrow stairway—wooden and old, and creaking like a pair of angry crows, led to the second-floor office labeled SSA. The gold-leaf lettering struggled in vain to lend respectability to a weary old suite of rooms that would not have been out of place as the headquarters of a cheap import-export business. There was no need to push the door open. It opened and closed more or less constantly, syncopated like a grandfather clock, as Santa's Angels, some reeking of alcohol, others of tobacco, came and went, little slips of paper clutched between fingers more often than not twisted by age and arthritis.

Donovan and Moskowitz paused as an especially corpulent gent, his red cloak stretched over a genuinely plump belly, squeezed himself out the door and ventured down the narrow stairs, earning the glares of those who had to wait while he clogged their vital artery.

"What does 'SSA' stand for?" Donovan asked, pondering the gold leaf on the door.

"Seasonal Staffing Associates," Mosko replied.

"Do they handle just the Christmas season or is there more?"

"There's *lots* more. Bunnies at Easter. Remember the white fuzzy Easter bunnies that were begging coins outside St. Pat's and other local churches last spring?"

Donovan shook his head. "Marcy was eggulating at the time. I was busy getting her pregnant. The only rabbits I saw were the half dozen that died in the course of the impregnation."

"Oh, *that's* when she was eggulating. Say, they don't really kill rabbits anymore, do they? I mean it's just a saying, right? 'The rabbit died.' "

"To the best of my knowledge, they only kill a couple of chemicals," Donovan said.

Moskowitz led the way into the office, stepping in the door before the flow of Santa's Angels could resume and block the passage again. The room was large and square and smelled of 1947, something about cigar smoke and hissing radiators and a tiny AM radio playing the Andrews Sisters. A sixtyish man whose waistline bore the cumulative strain of too many egg, cheese, and bacon sandwiches was wedged between a rust-stained wall and an ancient oak desk chicken-scratched with penknife and dug-in ballpoint pen marks that indicated prior service in the local public school. Initials, hearts, and the customary obscenities were partly hidden by a huge vinyl desk calendar. On it, amid coffee stains and phone numbers, was a grid that showed Fifth Avenue from Thirty-fourth to Sixty-second Streets.

Donovan looked down on the grid and waited while the proprietor of the desk—one Walter Huncke, according to a plastic sign that sat next to a battered brass ashtray filled with cigar butts and spent matches—finished a phone call.

"You guys got experience?" the man asked without looking up.

"How much experience do you need to ring a bell and beg coins?" Donovan replied. "What is it, corporate downsizing has finally reach the nth degree—now a man needs a résumé to become a panhandler?"

"Who are you?" Huncke said, a flash of irritation in his eyes, finally lifted from the desk and telephone.

"Bill Donovan, New York Police. This is Sergeant Moskowitz."

"Oh, yeah," Huncke said, looking at Moskowitz. "You

called. What can I do for you ossifers?" He smiled at his little joke.

"One of your red-cloaked little beggars may have blown away a shopper on Fifth Avenue," Donovan said.

Huncke's smile faded, ground out into the ashtray with his cigars. He looked at the three hopefuls seated on wood-slat folding chairs across the room. What before had seemed like a trio of life's losers grasping for a few weeks' income now had the look of hit men. Huncke waved a fat forefinger at them. "Would you guys mind waiting out in the hall till I call you?" he said. "Close the door and don't let nobody in and you all got jobs through New Year's."

The trio complied happily, flush with new authority—control of a door being one of city life's power basics—and the promise of dough.

When they were gone, Huncke said, "This would have been that thing on Thanksgiving?"

"The day after," Donovan said.

"One of *my* guys did it? You got any idea which one?"

"If we did, he'd have been drawn and quartered by now."

Mosko said, "We need a list of Santa's Angels, along with everything you got on them."

"You want all of them?" Huncke asked.

"Every last wino," Mosko replied.

"Hey, some of 'em ain't that bad. The Santas, for example. All of 'em are clean as far as records go. I even do things I don't have to do to make sure they stay clean."

"Like what?" Moskowitz asked.

"Each Santa got to shave every day," Huncke replied proudly.

"Seems like a waste considering the beards they got to put on," Donovan said.

"Just like I told you. I go that extra mile to make sure this

197

is a merry and authentic Christmas season for all the children who see my Santas," Huncke responded.

"What else do you do?" Mosko asked.

"Each Santa gotta bathe at least twice a week. No one wants to give money to a Santa with BO, you know what I'm saying? That's even though it's so cold and windy out you can't smell nothing, not even dog shit."

"I'm sure that the tourist board appreciates your efforts," Donovan said agreeably. "Now, let's have a list of employees. And I'm interested in Santa's Angels, not Santas."

Huncke nodded and pulled open the wooden file drawer built into the side of his desk that lay to the right of his fat legs. There, carefully rested atop a jar of Maxwell House instant coffee and a large box of Sweet'n Low, was a crisp new manila folder. Donovan sensed that the man put the folder atop his personal food stash to make sure he could find it. Huncke transferred the file to the top of his desk and opened it gingerly. He said, "When the sergeant here called, I asked the girl to xerox the job application forms." He indicated a small metal desk, vacant save for a comb, a mirror, several tubes of Revlon lipstick, and an old AT-style computer. The desk was crammed into a corner of the room but near the window.

Huncke added, "I put Doris's desk closer to the window than mine because I smoke. This way she can stick her head out and get some air."

"That's thoughtful of you," Donovan said.

"Like I said, I take care of my people. Anyway, Doris is out getting her nails done."

"If I knew thirty years ago that it would be possible to make a living selling ultraspecialty items—nail jobs, cookies, socks—I would have gone into another line of work," Donovan said.

"Selling what?" Mosko asked.

"I haven't thought it out. Indulgences, maybe. So, Mr. Huncke, are there any serial killers in this batch?"

Donovan used his thumb to flip through the one hundred or so pages in the folder.

"Nah. A couple of guys who been through the school of hard knocks, maybe. But they're harmless."

"How about you letting us be the judge of that," Mosko said.

"Name them," Donovan ordered, tapping the pile of papers.

"The top three," Huncke said. Proud of his effort on behalf of justice, he took a fresh stogie from a weary old humidor and tamped it down on his desk calendar.

Donovan scrutinized the top application. " 'Jack Swain,' " he read out loud. "Fifty-seven. Lives in Bensonhurst. So who did he kill that you singled him out?"

"He didn't kill nobody. He did three years at Danbury for running a sports book."

Donovan shrugged. "No big deal. My old *paison* Gaetano did three at Danbury for running a numbers joint. Now he drives a limo during the day and in the evenings eats pepperoni and watches professional wrestling with his mom. They live together, in Bensonhurst, now that you mention it. He's harmless."

"Maybe your Danbury con knows his Danbury con," Mosko speculated.

"It could be. Danbury grads think of themselves as belonging to 'the club.' "

"Howard Klempert is harmless too, I think," Huncke said. He clipped off the end of the cigar and began fumbling around in his top desk drawer for a match. "He lives in Long Island City."

" 'Hunters Point Avenue,' " Donovan read off the second application.

"Above a butcher shop. I think he shares with another guy. I feel sorry for the slob—he's warmhearted and hard-working—and so I give him two tokens a day so he can get to work and back."

"What did *he* do?" Donovan asked.

"He did time for armed robbery a while back," Huncke said.

Moskowitz's eyes widened.

"What did he hit and when?" Donovan asked.

"A 7-Eleven in Union City. In the sixties."

"I think I better check this guy out," Mosko said.

"Do you know any more about it?"

"He told me he carried a gun at the time but didn't shoot nobody. He also said he did five years."

"Where?"

"Someplace in Jersey, I guess. Anyway, the guy is in his fifties now and, like you would expect for a guy that age, is in no shape to do anything physical."

Mosko smiled, earning himself a scowl from his boss.

"Did he say what kind of gun he used?" Mosko asked.

"He called it a 'popgun,' " Huncke said. "I don't necessarily believe everything these guys say. You know, they're applying for bottom-of-the-barrel jobs. Still, I have to check 'em out. I think Klempert is probably harmless. But you said you want to be the judge."

Donovan nodded. "What about Walter Tillis?"

"Now, *there's* an angry man. I mean one who's got a bee in his bonnet about *something*—I couldn't tell you what."

"His application says he's sixty-five and a Korean War vet," Donovan said. "That's way too old to be stalking people on Fifth Avenue."

"You would think so, but he bragged about being a two-time pistol champion. And I thought that might interest you."

"Really," Mosko said.

"Champion of what?" Donovan asked.

"His army unit," Huncke replied. "He's pretty proud of that."

"That's nice. He's got something good in his life to think back on. So what did he do that was so bad? Why are you fingering him?"

"He didn't *do* anything," Huncke said. "It's his attitude. The man is ready to boil over."

"And you have no idea what he's pissed off about?" Mosko asked.

"I don't have so much as a clue. Didn't you ever see these time bombs in bars? Tell me, Captain, did you ever spend an afternoon in a Blarney Stone?"

"Never," Donovan replied, rolling his eyes.

"Three Our Fathers and three Hail Marys," Moskowitz said, sotto voce.

"Well, if you had you'd know the type of guy Tillis is," Huncke went on. "Sits there hour after hour, staring into space and looking *mad*. Every so often swears at something on TV or growls at a guy who sits too close."

"I get that way in the subway," Moskowitz replied.

"If we arrested every guy who was pissed off we'd have to turn the Bronx into a jail," Donovan remarked.

"Isn't it one now?" Mosko said.

Unable to find a match, Huncke looked forlorn and tossed up his hands. "Can you guys help me out here?" he pleaded.

"We don't smoke," Donovan replied.

"Cops who don't drink or smoke. What's the world coming to?"

"Its senses, maybe," Donovan said.

With difficulty, Huncke pushed away from the desk, stood, and lumbered over to his secretary's work space. From her top drawer he plucked a matchbook. Then he went back to his desk and lit up as he lowered himself, grunting, back into his complaining chair.

Huncke carefully blew the smoke away from the detectives. He flipped the matches onto his calendar. Donovan noticed that the pack had red lettering on a yellow background and was subtle as a "Stop—Biohazard" warning. It read: "Sunnyside Tavern."

Donovan pointed at the calendar and asked, "Is this how you keep track of how the troops are deployed?"

"You got it," Huncke replied, leaning back in his chair, the tobacco giving him the glow of the newly addicted. "I got each man's post marked . . . see?" He jabbed the cigar at the corner of Fifty-fourth and Fifth. "Each X marks a Santa's Angel; each Z marks the big guy himself."

"How do you know everybody is in the right spot?" Donovan asked. "Do you have a supervisor who goes up and down the avenue checking?"

"You're looking at him," Huncke said, pointing at his chest with the cigar and spilling ashes onto his lap. He gazed down at them, deciding if it was worth the effort to clean up. Apparently he decided it wasn't. He shrugged and looked up at the captain.

"You do it?" Donovan asked.

"I'm the man," Huncke said. "Every morning at nine. Every afternoon at three. Again at seven in the evening."

"That's a long day for you," Mosko commented.

"It's a big responsibility, taking care of Santa's Angels," Huncke said proudly. "There's a lot of guys goin' out on the job every day. There's a lot of money coming in."

"How much?" Donovan asked.

"Come on now, Captain. That's a trade secret. Is it important?"

"I guess not. But how do you know it's all going to God's good work? Given the backgrounds of some of the guys you hire, don't you worry that a lot of money is being diverted to the corner liquor store?"

"Yeah," Mosko agreed.

"Two things," Huncke said. "One is actuarial data. That's what I call it, anyway."

"Actuarial data?" Donovan asked.

"Let me explain it this way. I know how much bread should be collected by a guy standing in a specific spot. After years of watching trends, you know?"

"*Trends* in panhandling? Christ, everything is data-specific these days. OK, I'll bite. Where are the best and worst spots to glom cash on Fifth Avenue?"

"I can tell you without even having to look it up," Huncke said. "The best is in front of Tiffany's and Cartier. The worst is in front of F.A.O. Schwarz."

"Explain," Donovan said.

"It's simple. In front of Tiffany's and Cartier you got shoppers who have no prayer in this man's earth to buy anything they see in the window. But they can make themselves feel better by dropping a quarter in a bucket."

"That makes sense. And what about F.A.O. Schwarz? I can tell you one thing—that not many people can afford the gyros the guy out front sells."

"That I can't help you with," Huncke said. "The issue here is toys, not food. People who are thinking toys are thinking affordable, and they're already thinking happy thoughts, so there's no subconscious impetus for them to give to charity."

"None of this would ever have occurred to me," Donovan commented.

"That's why the world needs experts," Huncke said in a self-satisfied sort of way.

"You said there were *two* things that made you sure you weren't being robbed," Donovan said.

"I check up on them," Huncke replied.

"How? Except for the three times a day you check locations, you sit here, right, ministering to the parade of guys coming through the door?"

"Right. Sorry. I meant to say Doris does it. She goes undercover for me, if you will."

"Undercover," Mosko said.

" 'Cause the guys know what she looks like. So she puts on a wig and changes her clothes—"

"Changes her nail color," Donovan said.

"Yeah, that," Huncke agreed. "And then walks up and down Fifth Avenue looking to see if she can catch someone stealing from the Lord."

"We'll need to talk to Doris," Donovan said.

"She's at the nail parlor, like I told you."

"Which one?" Mosko asked.

"Kim's Beautiful Nails, two blocks uptown on the right. The Korean nail place, not the Spanish one around the corner."

"Koreans have nail shops now?" Mosko asked. "Is there anything they aren't into in this city?"

"I haven't seen them riding to the hounds yet," Donovan replied. He closed the folder and handed it to Moskowitz. "Go talk to her."

"Will do," Mosko replied.

"Just two other things, Mr. Huncke," Donovan said. "Where do you keep the Santa's Angels outfits? Where do you keep the tripods?"

"That's easy. I got the tripods from a wholesaler of surveying tripods. I painted them and hung buckets. The outfits

I got from a theatrical costume shop in the Garment District. I keep both in there." He hooked a fat thumb in the direction of a back room.

"What I want you to do is count them both and let Sergeant Moskowitz know if the numbers of outfits and tripods matches up with the number of Angels."

"Whatever I can do," Huncke replied.

Moskowitz tucked the folder in his bag. Then the two of them exchanged a few more words of small talk with the proprietor of SSA before slipping out the door and walking down the narrow and creaking stairway past the line of men waiting all along it.

At the corner, Donovan bought a bag of chestnuts and cracked one open while watching traffic chug dutifully deeper into midtown. Mosko watched the cars full of Christmas shoppers from New Jersey, Pennsylvania, and Connecticut, the people all eager to walk the famous mile in front of the famous shops and absorb what holiday spirit was left following the depravations of a mad killer. Then he said, "This time tomorrow Fifth Avenue will be lousy with cops. Every corner. Every window. Every goddamned Santa's helper will have a cop watching him. We'll get the sonofabitch this time, Boss."

14. STALER THAN A CHRISTMAS CUPCAKE IN MARCH

But they didn't, in fact, get the sonofabitch. In fact, two weeks later the investigation was staler than a Christmas cupcake in March. On December 21, the NYPD was no closer to finding the Fifth Avenue killer than it was to halting illegal parking or curing the common cold.

None of the Santa's Angels leads checked out, not even Tillis, the one said to be a ticking bomb. He turned out to have been harassing passersby, who complained to the police, at precisely the times of the killings. And while Huncke's inventory of equipment came out that nothing was missing, a cop checking a Dumpster at a construction site on Fifty-third and Park came up with a sort of imitation that may or may not have been the prop used by the killer. No useful fingerprints graced its exterior; there was nothing traceable about it at all.

As for the other suspects, whatever hole Tom Tuttle had crawled into to hide, he had pulled the walls in on himself and disappeared utterly. No one could find him, not the police, not the parole authorities. So, too, with Anna Fritsch. An even more extensive search failed to turn her up. She didn't show up at the other end of that Concorde flight; there was no second passport. Neither did the woman, now twenty-two weeks pregnant, reveal her presence to the FBI, Immigration, the German consulate, Interpol, or anyone else. Donovan's men, try though they might, could turn up no clues to her whereabouts by badgering her doctor, who professed ignorance and had the lawyers to back it up, or by polling other local obstetricians.

The Mountain Brigade, after its dramatic extortion attempt and demand for ten million dollars' worth of diamonds in exchange for a cease to terror, appeared to have gone back into the mountains—whichever mountains they hailed from. And as for Yama Mojadidi, the New York City Afghan community appeared to have absorbed him down to the last fiber of his fake turban. When an entire ethnic community, especially a newly arrived and still struggling one, wants to hide one of its own, that man might as well be vacationing on Pluto. Once he disappeared from his hovel on the rim of the

Long Island Rail Road's Sunnyside Yards, Mojadidi was gone absolutely.

Despite the apparent disappearance of those who had made so many headlines threatening it, the holiday season on Fifth Avenue remained in dire straits. Though the perpetrator or perpetrators had apparently disappeared, the tabloids remained full of gory details about the two murders and the weekly newsmagazines all carried cover stories about what one of them called "the grinch that shot Christmas." And, of course, the late-night talk show hosts were ablaze with bullet-proof window jokes.

And so it came to pass that Donovan spent the first part of the seven A.M. hour of December 21 by sitting in bed with his wife watching *The Morning Show* as June Lake introduced the taped segment about high-risk pregnancy. There Marcy was, in all her dusky beauty, wearing the Tuttle gown, speaking glowingly of her unborn child and the doctor who was to deliver him just a few days away. Then came the phone calls from family to discuss how beautiful she looked and how wonderful the pregnancy was and how proud Donovan must be to become a father at his age.

Half an hour later, Donovan held his laptop, appropriately enough, in his lap while doing the latest in a long series of computer searches, requests for information, and correspondences with his many friends in the worldwide law enforcement community. This work session came after he shaved and showered and got a cup of coffee from the staff cafeteria in the subbasement and eavesdropped on a diagnostic consultation that was being conducted in one of those interminable rides on the medical-staff elevator.

Marcy had just got out of the shower—which she had taken, given her size and late-term lack of equilibrium, while sitting down on an aluminum chair that the nurses had placed in the shower stall. She was sitting on the edge of the bed naked, a towel around her hair, rubbing moisturizing cream onto her belly. Suddenly a ripple of hard flesh, a bump that moved, appeared in her skin and shifted an inch or so to the left. That happened to be the side on which Donovan was sitting.

"Ooh," she said, and pressed her palm against it.

" 'Ooh' what?" he asked, barely looking up from his laptop.

"That's the back of Daniel's head. He's moving toward you, honey."

"How can you tell that's not his bottom?" Donovan asked, reaching over and feeling the bump, moving her hand aside for an instant.

"Because his tush is up here," she said, patting that part of her belly that curved in to form a shelf atop which rested her breasts.

"I don't know how you can tell."

"Because he's supposed to be in that position, given how far along I am, and because I can feel every little bit of him, and because I saw the sonogram."

Donovan looked at the mammoth belly that soon would produce his son. "Isn't he supposed to be lower at this point?" he asked, pointing to the spot he had in mind.

"Yes. He hasn't dropped."

"Dropped?"

"His head should be down against my cervix, and it isn't."

"You're not due for four days yet," Donovan said, looking at his watch.

"It doesn't matter. Something is preventing him from dropping."

She put away the moisturizing cream and began to pull on her panties and bra.

"Is there a problem?" Donovan asked.

"If he doesn't drop, it will mean I definitely will have a C-section," she said, a bit ruefully.

"That's all it means? You were expecting that anyway."

"I know, but it would be nice to feel him being born."

"Can I still be in the room if you have a C-section?" Donovan asked.

"Of course. They just put a sheet up so you can't see the operation. They don't want you to see blood."

"It's happened before, on rare occasions," Donovan said.

"Not the same thing. When it's your wife, it's different."

"What do I do, then, sit there?" he asked, his eyes flicking back and forth from her to the monitor—more to the monitor as a particular screen got his attention.

"You hold my hand," she said.

"Easy enough," he replied, then added, staring full-time at the monitor now, "Whoa!"

" 'Whoa' what?" Marcy asked, leaning forward to see.

"It seems that I'm not the only dad-to-be among our recent acquaintances," Donovan said.

"Who's the lucky guy and why is this information being displayed on the Internet? Is it Brian?"

"Mosko has enough kids," Donovan said, shaking his head. "Guess who was among the guests trapped on the island of Carricola last summer with Princess Anna."

A smile crept across Marcy's lips. "It would have to be Paul Duke."

"Bingo."

"Otherwise it wouldn't rate a mention on the 'Net."

"No wonder he's so interested in this case," Donovan said. "It's not just that somebody—maybe—is trying to kill him."

"It isn't him who's the target of the killer," Marcy said. "It's her."

"Or her and him."

"You're not thinking of June Lake," Marcy said. "America's sweetheart? The only woman who's thought of as being perfect?"

Donovan coughed into his hand. "Stranger things have happened," he said.

"Can she even shoot?"

"Like you said, she's perfect," Donovan said.

"It wasn't me who said it. It was a thousand magazine covers. Look at any newsstand. Where was she when the killings took place?"

"I'll have to find out."

"The notion of June Lake being a killer seems very weird to me," Marcy said. "It's so Hollywood, the idea that a woman would *really* kill to get a man."

"Even if that man is America's premier hunk, now that Mel Gibson hasn't taken his shirt off in a movie in ten years?"

"I guess." Marcy swung her legs back into bed. "I also guess this kills the theory that the killer is trying to extort ten million dollars from Fifth Avenue stores."

"I never liked that theory much," Donovan said.

Marcy looked at the door and asked, "Where's the nurse with my breakfast?"

The phone rang. Marcy answered it saying, "Daniel's house." Then she frowned and listened and said to her husband, "It's your office."

Donovan took the instrument and said, "What?" into it. He listened for a while, then said, "Okay," and hung up.

"Tell me they're sending up bagels," Marcy said.

"Sorry. There's been another note from the Mountain Brigade."

"Oh. Maybe there *is* something to it."

"They want their diamonds delivered today."

"You are *not* making the delivery yourself," Marcy said firmly. "It's way too dangerous and you could be a daddy at any moment."

"Don't worry," he replied. "I have no intention of getting involved. The whole line of investigation is a fool's errand, and I'm not the fool who wants to waste time on it. However, I've been wrong before."

"Not when you married me," she said.

"And I do want to talk to Claudia Hummitz again, and she's the one who got the extortion call."

"What do you need her for? She's only the one who picked up the telephone when it rang."

"No one is only what they seem in this case," Donovan said.

When Donovan got to the office of the Midtown Merchants Association, Claudia Hummitz was sitting at the black leather banquette that sat across the room from her desk, wrapping around a glass coffee table, staring at her Filofax and an array of glossy catalogs from the Fifth Avenue stores that paid her salary. Her expression was blank, and she balled up a piece of tissue paper in the palm of her right hand. Three or four like it were clustered meticulously, tiny Kleenex cannonballs, next to the appointment book.

Her desk had been taken over by cookie-cutter young men, all thirty or so, wearing crisp Macy's suits and talking in clipped tones into cell phones. One of these, jacket off and folded carefully, was at work installing a fancy electronic device of one kind or another on the office telephone.

When Donovan got inside the office he was stopped by one of the men. This one, perhaps forty but dressed like the others and comporting himself just as crisply, as if he were on an eternal job interview, flashed a leather-bound ID in Donovan's face and said, "FBI."

"My condolences," Donovan responded, producing his badge. "Bill Donovan, chief of special investigations, New York Police." Having detected a hint of a Carolina accent in the man's speech, Donovan tossed in, "How are you boys doing here?"

"Very well, thank you, Captain. I've heard a lot about you. This is your case."

"You're welcome to a piece of it," Donovan said agreeably.

The man smiled and introduced himself as Dan Clark, special agent in charge. That name was, Donovan thought, one of those names that come up more often in Tom Clancy novels than in the ranks of real-life law enforcement officers. But this fellow seemed to be real enough, if a bit starched, and Donovan was delighted to work with him.

"What's going on?" Donovan asked.

"We were called in by the Midtown Merchants Association and have been in touch with your Deputy Chief Pilcrow," Clark said.

"My favorite people."

"The merchants group was of the opinion that the resources of the NYPD were being stretched a little thin trying to pin down the Mountain Brigade."

No, Donovan thought, *Pilcrow just wants to embarrass me; so be it.* "Our experience with mountains is limited," he said. "And, in my opinion, certain investigations have to follow a certain course and time line no matter what the professionals do or the amateurs think."

If Clark caught that insult to Pilcrow, he showed no sign of it.

Donovan continued, "Go ahead; jump in. Who *is* or *are* the Mountain Brigade?"

"We have been following two lines of investigation. One is that they're an Afghanistani guerrilla group that is part of the coalition fighting the Taliban."

"The Islamic fundamentalists who seem to be winning the civil war over there," Donovan said.

"Oh, you follow affairs in that part of the world?" Clark asked.

"I read the papers. And I have a certain fondness for Islam these days."

"Oh, why?" Clark asked, raising an eyebrow.

"It's the only major religion—other than Buddhism, of course—that hasn't tried to convert me recently. Go on."

"We have been getting reports that the Mountain Brigade has a wing in the U.S., here in New York City, soliciting money from members of the Afghan community so their brothers can continue the armed struggle back in the mountains of their homeland."

"I took note of those reports this morning," Donovan said.

"Where did you get that information?" Clark asked, his otherwise-neutral expression turning slightly in the direction of suspicion.

"They have a Web page," Donovan replied.

"Of course," Clark said. Donovan was certain this was the first the man had heard of it.

"Everybody has a Web page these days," Donovan said. "Even fund-raising American arms of foreign guerrilla groups. I'm thinking of getting one myself. Do you have any names for me? Such as of specific Afghans in New York?"

Clark shook his head.

"Ever trip over the name of Yama Mojadidi?"

"Who's he?" Clark asked, requesting the spelling and calling a crisp-suited aide over to write it down.

"A Queens lad originally from Afghanistan who took a shot at me a few weeks back. I'm still pissed off about it."

"No doubt. Got an address on him?"

"If I did—"

"Right, Captain. Now, the idea that the Mountain Brigade is trying to extort ten million dollars from Fifth Avenue merchants is attractive to us."

Of course it is, Donovan thought. The Feds always suspected the foreign-born first. Especially if the suspects were Muslims who could also be suspected of trying to throw a monkey wrench into the Christmas season at the same time.

"Striking at both God and country," Donovan said.

"I see you agree."

Donovan shrugged.

"On the other hand, the men behind this extortion attempt could be the Montana survivalist group under the leadership of Harlan Deaver. We've had our eyes on them for some time."

"Normally those guys just run check scams to raise money. And file phony liens against their enemies to foul up their credit ratings."

"You *do* keep up with things outside your turf. That's good."

"Nothing is outside my turf," Donovan said. "Because eventually everyone comes to New York."

"The story on these guys is that they will do anything to get money and screw the system. The notion of getting big bucks out of Fifth Avenue stores—"

"Particularly ones owned by Japanese billionaires," Donovan interjected.

Clark grinned for the first time during the conversation. "I see we *are* on the same wavelength," he said.

"If the Mountain Brigade is, in fact, behind these killings—"

"And the extortion attempt."

"A motive beyond getting the money to finance their secessionist campaign would be to strike at the foreign investors who are buying up American real estate."

Clark bobbed his head up and down.

"Do you have a problem with the idea that the group would never set foot in New York?" Donovan asked.

"No. They adjust when they have to. They say they hate the court system and don't recognize its authority, but they can spend hundreds of hours in courts filing false liens."

"True," Donovan admitted, looking over at Hummitz, who seemed to be growing bored with the FBI takeover of her office.

"I understand you're interested in the Stedman," Clark said.

Donovan said that he was.

"We traced it as far as Montana."

"Did you?"

"We learned that Deaver wanted to buy it and had an agent looking. And we heard that the weapon actually made it as far as Montana. But that's all we know."

"That's more than I have," Donovan said.

"Can we agree to share information?" Clark asked.

"You bet."

They shook on it.

"Who are at the top of your list?" Clark asked.

"The same guys you and I have just been talking about are right up there," Donovan replied.

"Any others?"

"One or two, but not developed to the point where I could talk about them."

"Can I give you a tip?" Clark asked.

"I'm always interested in what the FBI has to say."

"Take a closer look at George Halloran," Clark said, lowering his voice conspiratorially.

"Why him?"

"Just vague suspicions," Clark replied.

"He made my list, too."

"Good. I see we're *really* on the same wavelength."

"So what's your plan for today?" Donovan asked. "Tell me about the extortion note."

"It's a tape," Clark replied. "Made on her machine."

He nodded in the direction of Hummitz, who was watching the two men talk. She waved in a cursory sort of way at Donovan, adding a grim and fleeting smile. He returned a half-wave.

"It came in at seven-twenty this morning. Let's listen to it."

Clark snapped his fingers and one of his men—this one blond and especially young-looking—pressed a button on a hand-held tape player. An electronically altered voice said, "This is the Mountain Brigade. If you want the killings to stop so you can resume the course of your yearly plunder by rich corporations, leave ten million dollars in uncut diamonds beneath the elevated subway line at Thirty-seventh Avenue and Northern Boulevard at three o'clock this afternoon. You will notice that the plate covering the electrical circuits at the base of the northeast stanchion is held by only one screw. Remove that plate and put the diamonds inside. Replace the plate, leaving it as it was. We will retrieve the diamonds within twelve hours. Do not call the authorities. Any attempt to do so or to interfere with us as we pick up the diamonds will result in further bloodshed along your most gilded boulevard."

Clark said, "You can keep this copy of the tape." He took a cassette from his associate and handed it to the captain.

"Thanks."

"As I'm sure you know, that drop-off point is in a neighborhood with many Afghanistani residents."

"Asian, anyway," Donovan said.

"So we are, of course, most interested. And we will be making the drop. You don't want to do it, do you?"

Donovan shook his head. "My wife won't let me," he said. That remark earned him funny looks from the several FBI agents who were within earshot.

"Your wife must be a very strong woman," Clark said, a bit awkwardly.

"And a better shot than me, too."

"We'll be watching to see who picks up the jewels. We'll have extensive surveillance, of course. You're welcome to join us."

"Nah, you guys go it alone," Donovan said. "I'd only be in the way. I can tell you one thing, though. The Mountain Brigade guys—the Montana ones, that is—would stand out like moose in that neighborhood. Unless, of course, they have Asian allies."

"Not Deaver, never. He's too right-wing."

Donovan said, "Hitler had Asian allies, and it's tough to get farther to the right than him. Well anyway, have a ball. Are you about done here?"

"Jim?" Clark called to the fellow in shirtsleeves who was working behind the desk.

"The device is installed," the man replied, zipping up the cover on a small leather tool kit that he then slipped into his jacket pocket on the way out of the office.

Clark and Donovan exchanged business cards, with the

man from Washington saying, "I'll give you a shout later on today. Where will you be? At the hospital?"

"Oh, you know about that?"

"We *are* the Federal Bureau of Investigation."

Donovan thought, *Pilcrow told them.*

"I'm very aware of your reputation," Donovan said.

"This is your first child?" Clark asked.

"Barring someone unforeseen tumbling off the Greyhound from Tucson, our Christmas baby will be my first," Donovan said. "Our first."

"The baby is due on Christmas? That has to be good luck. Does that mean you will be at the hospital this afternoon?"

Donovan thought, *This man is more than casually interested in my schedule.* "Absolutely," he replied.

"Good. I'll call you there, then."

A few minutes later, the FBI had cleared out, leaving Donovan alone with Hummitz. He smiled at her and—his hands jammed deep into his jeans pockets as a way of showing the woman, who looked more than a little beaten up on, that he was being loose and casual—said, "So, how goes the revolution?"

Her eyes flashed up at his and they met in an exchange of . . . something . . . a kindred spirit, perhaps, a shared caustic outlook on life, before she looked back down at the table. She said, "So much upheaval."

Then she sighed and her day-to-day personality clicked on and she said, "Captain, I imagine you don't think that I should pay the money these extortionists and murderers are demanding."

"Not for a second," he replied. "Pay away. Pay *twice*. Indulge yourself in a little redistribution of wealth. Why should I care? The way I see it, your members can write off the loss and the money is going from folks on Fifth Avenue who don't need it to folks in Queens who do."

Hummitz looked slightly amazed, but before she could respond Donovan went to the table, plucked the Tuttle catalog from among those arrayed in front of her, and opened it to the page showing the $3,500 nightie that Paul Duke had borrowed for Marcy to wear for her TV interview.

"Tell me," he said. "Is this rag worth thirty-five hundred dollars?" He handed her the catalog.

She looked at the page, then replied, "*I* wouldn't pay it. But I'm old enough to know better." She sighed and said, "About lots of things. But if someone can, who cares?" She handed the catalog back to Donovan, who folded it inside a pocket.

"Where are the diamonds coming from?" he asked.

"I'm getting the note from the bank at nine," she said, glancing at her watch. "And one of our members is supplying the diamonds."

"Done as a tiara or as a brooch?" Donovan asked.

She smiled. "Loose stones in a small sack," she said.

Donovan noticed that Hummitz had softened in the weeks since he first saw her. Or maybe she had aged. She looked predatory no longer. And she had forsaken the scarf that previously hid the wrinkles around her neck. She looked her age.

She also opened her hand long enough to release another tissue ball. When she noticed him watching, she smiled sheepishly. "An old habit," she said.

"I noticed," Donovan replied.

"I do it when I'm nervous or hungry."

"I play with my car keys," Donovan said, sticking a hand in his pocket and illustrating. "Which are you now, nervous or hungry?"

"Both. I didn't get the chance to order breakfast before you-know-what hit the fan."

"Do you like Mexican?" Donovan asked.

"I *love* Mexican," she said, brightening.

"I know this place, but it's uptown."

"Which side?"

"East."

"I live uptown—Ninety-sixth and Second. The Beresford Towers."

"My wife and I looked at a two-bedroom there once, before deciding we could never be pried away from the West Side," Donovan said.

"I thought you looked like a West Sider," Hummitz replied.

"But while looking on East Ninety-sixth we found this good neighborhood Mexican restaurant."

"Not Paco's?" she asked, eyes agleam with the thought of tastes and sounds far removed from the sterile glitter of Fifth Avenue.

"That's the place. You know it?"

"I eat there all the time," she said.

"Marcy thinks that the chorizos are salty," Donovan said.

"Chorizos everywhere are salty," Hummitz replied. "That's part of the appeal. God, I could use a breakfast burrito right now. How could you do this to me, Captain?"

"I'm a beast," he said.

"I doubt that very much."

"As I was telling my wife just a little while ago, no one I've run into recently is exactly what they seem."

"You included?" she asked with a coy smile.

"Me especially," Donovan replied.

She looked at Donovan for a long moment, at the end of which he sensed there was something she wanted to say. But it passed. Hummitz stood, sighed, and said, "I guess I have my desk back. And there's lots to do."

She walked over and sat behind it.

"Seen Paul lately?" Donovan asked.

"Paul." She laughed bitterly. "Oh my, *Paul.* No, I haven't seen him. As far as I'm concerned, he disappeared."

"It's been all the rage lately."

"Has it? I doubt that Paul will ever change. I hope, for his sake . . . for a lot of people's sakes, that I'm wrong."

"Maybe he will," Donovan said. "Fear of being shot at is a powerful motivator."

"Actually being shot at is an even stronger one," Hummitz replied, opening her desk drawer and then slamming it shut with a resounding bang.

15. "THAT AND FIVE MILLION DOLLARS' WORTH OF ATTORNEYS WOULD HAVE GOTTEN YOU OFF," DONOVAN SAID

"You really aren't going out on the FBI surveillance this afternoon?" Marcy asked, finishing the bagel he had brought her after leaving Hummitz's office.

"I'm really not."

"I expected a fight from you."

"Let the Feds go and spend a pleasant afternoon and evening under the el in Queens," Donovan said. "They won't find anything."

"Why not?"

"Because nobody will come to pick up the diamonds. This is a fool's errand, I tell you. Not even *he's* interested in going."

Donovan had nodded in the direction of Moskowitz, who replied, "And a Merry Christmas to you, too, Boss." The sergeant sipped a cup of coffee brought up from the cafeteria.

"What are you going to be doing?" Marcy asked her husband's assistant.

"I got a lead on the gyro guy. I heard he's working in a pet shop in Queens, on Northern Boulevard."

"Where on Northern Boulevard?" Marcy asked.

"As if you would know anything about Queens," Mosko replied. "You never been outside Manhattan except maybe to visit your parents in . . . What's the name of that place? Crouton-on-Hudson?"

"Croton-on-Hudson," Marcy replied.

"Yeah, there. So what difference does it make where on Northern Boulevard the pet shop is?"

"OK," she said, a trace of exasperation in her voice. "*How far* is the pet shop from the drop site?"

"About fifteen blocks. A mile and a half."

"And you don't see a connection?"

Mosko did that thing that New Yorkers do by way of saying, "Maybe." He held his hand out flat, palm down, and waggled it from side to side.

"Where *do* the Afghans live in this town?" Marcy asked.

"All over," Donovan said. "But many live in Queens, along Northern Boulevard."

"So? There you have it. The Mountain Brigade *is* Afghan, they *are* behind the killings and the extortion attempt, and they *will* be there this afternoon, probably heavily armed, to pick up the diamonds. That's why my husband isn't going."

"Isn't it cute, the way she protects you?" Mosko said to Donovan. The sergeant leaned forward and, pretending to knock on her belly, said, "So what's going on in there? *Police!* Come out with your hands up!"

"Stop it," Marcy snapped, slapping his hand away.

"Daniel isn't moving much the past couple of days," Donovan said.

"It looks like it's getting cramped in there," Mosko replied.

Marcy said, "And *you* should stay away from the surveillance, too. What would your wife say?"

"My wife would say, 'Honey, what can I make you for dinner?' "

Marcy sighed and scrunched back into her pillows, nestling herself in and holding her belly proudly.

Donovan pulled an evidence bag off the end table where the phone was kept. The bag contained the Tuttle catalog he had got from Claudia Hummitz's office. Donovan gave it to Mosko, saying, "Send this downtown and have it checked for prints. Especially the page that shows the thirty-five-hundred-dollar nightie."

"You got that catalog this morning from Claudia Hummitz," Marcy said. "You're running prints on *her?*"

"You bet," he replied.

"Why? You *know* who she is."

"Oh, I know who she is. I just want proof."

"Who is she?" Mosko asked.

Donovan raised a finger admonishingly. "You keep running two paces behind me and you're never going to see that Christmas bonus. Aren't you two interested in why I'm so sure that nobody will pick up the diamonds this afternoon?"

" 'Cause this case isn't about money," Mosko said.

"I think it *is* about money," Marcy disagreed.

Donovan shook his head. "Sorry, honey, but you're wrong. The person who's behind these killings—"

"Note he said 'person,' not 'persons,'" Mosko said.

"—isn't in it for the loot. So the diamonds will just sit there, all ten million dollars of them, in the base of that stanchion under the el, until Clark and the rest of his FBI boys realize that their surveillance is colder than J. Edgar Hoover's pink taffeta party dress."

"Why the diamonds, then?" Marcy asked.

"To get the investigating team away from Fifth Avenue. To give us something to obsess on while he—the killer—does something. Probably kills Paul Duke."

Marcy's eyes widened. "What time is the drop?" she asked.

"Three or after," Mosko replied.

"Which means you'll be with Paul," Marcy said.

"No. But I left a message on his machine telling him to stay indoors and with people he trusts," Donovan replied. "I'll be talking to George Halloran at three. For one thing, I want to be with him at three o'clock. But first I have to go to Brighton Beach."

"Koslov?" Marcy asked. "The Russian mobster whose wife was seduced by Paul? You're going to talk to Koslov?"

Donovan shook his head. "Mdivani."

"Who?"

"Georgi Mdivani. You and I weren't talking at the time, so you never got to meet him. Too bad, 'cause you would have liked him."

"Which time that we weren't talking was it?" Marcy asked.

"The last. He's a former diplomat from a former Soviet Central Asian republic—"

"Anywhere near Afghanistan?" Mosko asked.

"Don't they teach geography in Brooklyn?" Donovan asked.

"You know what Brooklyn geography is?" Mosko replied.

"How to get to Kennedy Airport without going through East New York or Brownsville."

"Pamiristan is right near Afghanistan, now that you mention it," Donovan said. "Maybe I should rethink the Afghan connection. Anyway, Mdivani these days is a prominent bookie working in the Brighton Beach Russian émigré community. And I hear he bought into one of the nightclubs there."

"What's he going to do for you?" Marcy asked.

"Tell me about Koslov. At least he said he would."

"If you're going to be in that neighborhood, bring me something to eat."

"Not bagels from the place under the el. It went out of business and now is an Italian deli."

"Just what Brooklyn needs, another Italian deli. OK, how about a pint of decent borscht and a portion of chicken Kiev?"

"There's too much salt in chicken Kiev," Donovan said. "Almost as much as there is in chorizos. Think of your blood pressure."

"Isn't it cute how he's always protecting you?" Mosko asked her.

"Right," she said to her husband, making a sad face.

"I'll get you the borscht. What about a bottle or two of that Georgian mineral water? Didn't you say you liked that?"

"That stuff is vile, William," she replied. "What *were* you thinking about?"

"My case," he replied.

She shut her eyes and, clearly daydreaming, said, "I'm going to have a baby in four days."

"Merry Christmas, honey," Donovan said.

She made a growling sound. "I called the hospital's Jewish chaplain," she informed her husband. "The rabbi will stop by and talk to you before the baby is born."

"I'm not talking to any rabbi," Donovan said firmly. "I just blew off the cardinal, who also was trying to save me from the clear light of nonbelief. Why should I bother talking to a man—"

"Rabbi Weiss is a woman," Marcy said.

"God, a politically correct rabbi. It just gets better and better, doesn't it? From this point on, my mantra is 'Farther my God from thee.' "

Donovan got up, brushed some bran muffin crumbs from his lap and into a tissue, then balled up the tissue and left it on the end table, next to the telephone. He patted his laptop, which rested there quietly while the battery recharged.

"Wonderful invention," he said. "I'd be lost without it these days."

Donovan took his knish out into the bitter cold wind that was blowing sand across the boardwalk from the broad white strip that prevented the Atlantic Ocean from swallowing the garlicky take-out restaurants, gone-to-seed high-rises, and aging bungalows that lined Brighton Beach and neighboring Coney Island. He held the knish between cupped hands, nibbling on a corner while using the steaming pack of fried potatoes as if it were a hand warmer. The steam sifted between his fingers before whipping away in the morning wind that smelled of salt water and seaweed.

Donovan walked across the boardwalk to a bench that faced the sea. An ornate old cast-iron lamppost, painted black of course, rose from one side of it, the top of the stanchion curved around like a shepherd's crook, the bulb still burning despite the blinding December sun. There was a man on the bench, a barrel-chested man about a decade older than Donovan, huddled in a full-length suede-and-sheepskin coat worn beneath a black Russian hat the earflaps of which were turned down. He alternated furious puffs at a cigarette with sips at a cup of hot coffee that steamed like Donovan's knish, only hotter.

Donovan eased himself onto the wooden slats next to the man. "Hello, Georgi," he said, extending his hand.

"Good morning, Captain," the man replied, taking it. Georgi Mdivani's voice was thick and gravelly, the result of decades of bitter cold coffee-and-cigarette mornings spent toiling as a Communist Party apparatchik in Soviet Central Asia. Those days of the old Soviet Union also had given the beer-bellied former tractor-factory manager turned minor diplomat and, most recently, émigré entrepreneur operating on the fringes of the law in New York City, an attitude that was as callused as his hands.

A black tanker, its hold weighted down by a full load of number two home heating oil from Dhahran, chugged slowly and, as seen from a mile away in that morning of perfect visibility, silently toward the mouth of the Hudson.

"It is a bitter morning to be staring out to sea for a man of my age," Mdivani stated.

"I like Coney Island and Brighton Beach," Donovan said. "Where else can you see the sea, have a knish, talk to a Russian friend—"

"Georgian," Mdivani admonished.

"I know where you're from. I was teasing you, knowing your fondness for Russians."

Like many émigrés from the breakaway republics of the old Soviet Union, Mdivani claimed loudly and often to hate those members of the ethnic group that included many of his former masters. But his hatred didn't keep him from associating with many of them, particularly the criminal elements who were fast making Brighton Beach as famous in 1990s crime as Cicero, Illinois, had been in 1920s crime.

"As I was saying, where else can you have this scenery and talk to a *Georgian* friend?"

"The old country has its scenic points," Mdivani said expansively. "The Black Sea resorts are not so bad."

"If they were so good, you would still be there."

"There are too many Russians, even these days," Mdivani said, gesturing at the sky. "You know, when the ancien régime collapsed, we all thought, *That's it; the bastards will go home.* But, no, they stay on and on, like a bad toothache."

"They have no place to go in their own country," Donovan replied. "No job. No apartment. Nowhere to hide from the mafiosi who are shooting at each other across each street corner."

"Which brings us to the subject of your visit."

"Valery Koslov."

"Ah, yes, a Russian." Mdivani rolled his tongue around that *R,* his way of imparting extra meanness to the word. "What can I tell you about him? I know the man, of course. He comes into my club from time to time, insulting one and all with his arrogance and lack of manners. Me, since I left my country's service, I eke out a marginal living as a provider of gaming information to gentlemen."

"You're a bookie," Donovan said.

"I run a modest sports book."

"Now it's 'modest'? Three years ago you told me it was 'small.' "

Mdivani shrugged. "A man must seek to improve himself."

"And I hear that you bought the Gemini."

"My club? Sure. I got a deal on it. This is the land of opportunity, even today. Who do you think will be in the Super Bowl this year?"

"I couldn't care less," Donovan replied.

The Georgian seemed surprised. "Don't all Americans love the Super Bowl?" he asked.

"Should the opportunity present itself," Donovan said, sighing and settling into a parable, "a grown man will make love to the woman who rejected him when he was a boy. But the event is nearly always a disappointment. For both of them."

"Sad but true."

"To answer your question, in a month if there is nothing else to watch and nothing to read, I will watch the Super Bowl. An event notorious for failing to live up to expectations, formed when you were a kid and sports mattered to you. Now, about Valery Koslov—"

"I told him of your generous offer to preside over his surrender to the Manhattan district attorney. I told Valery Mikelovich that a man of your stature—who personally knows the mayor—would not let some staged catastrophe befall him on the way to the arraignment."

"Say what you will about America, it remains a nation of laws," Donovan said. "Thus O. J. Simpson is a free man."

Mdivani grunted and sipped his coffee. Then he pushed the cup in Donovan's direction, saying, "Take some. . . . It will warm your soul."

"What's in there?" the captain asked, taking the cardboard cup and sniffing suspiciously at the wedge-shaped opening in the white plastic cover.

Mdivani tossed his cigarette over the boardwalk railing and down to the frozen sand below. "Triple espresso. Four sugars. Two shots of vodka. Have a taste."

"You're a madman," Donovan said, handing the cup back.

Mdivani smiled. "We'll see who lives longer, the man who knows how to live life to the fullest or the man who gets shot at for a living."

"I want to talk about Valery Koslov," Donovan insisted.

"*He* is a madman. So why are we sitting here, freezing our asses, to save his? Because we are gentlemen, that's why."

Donovan said, "You're doing it because I cleared you of suspicion in the murder of Paolo Lucca. You owe me."

"I was innocent," Mdivani replied, jabbing the air with his hand.

"That and five million dollars' worth of attorneys would have gotten you off."

"God himself proclaimed my innocence," Mdivani insisted.

"Maybe. But it helped to have me rubber-stamp the document," Donovan replied.

Mdivani seemed to accept that notion. "I am grateful," he said, with a nod.

"I need to know where Koslov was the morning of November twenty-ninth and the evening of December sixth," Donovan said.

"In the first instance, he was at an associate's house in Coney Island all morning. I know because he placed bets with me several times. I was on and off the phone with him the whole time that German was killed at that store. And since *I* called Koslov several times, I know for sure he was there. You can check my phone records. On the second date, Koslov was slapping his wife around. Sent her to the emergency room at Coney Island Hospital, too, to have the bruises covered up. You can check that as well."

"Why'd he hit her?" Donovan asked.

"Why else? For sleeping with that TV pretty boy. You can ask her if you like. He left her. A man does these things when his wife is unfaithful. Slaps her around."

"Not when his wife has a black belt in kung fu," Donovan said. "Tell me, do you think Koslov would try to kill Paul Duke?"

Mdivani laughed heartily.

"I agree," Donovan said.

"The man faces a minor charge from the Manhattan DA. Nothing his lawyers can't handle. At the worst, they will delay and delay until he is safely back in Saint Petersburg. As you said, this is a nation of laws. And nobody knows how to get around laws better than Russians. I will give the bastards that much."

"So Koslov was accounted for at the times the killings occurred. He could just as well have ordered someone to do the dirty work for him."

"This is something Valery Mikelovich would not do," Mdivani said. "Were he to kill someone for revenge, he would want to do it himself. Besides, it is absolutely ridiculous to think that a professional man—even a professional thug, as some people might describe my friend—would destroy a rival by scaring him. Shooting tourists and businessmen to make him worry about his own health. Preposterous."

"It sounds nuts to me, too," Donovan agreed. "But I have heard stranger things."

"But not from a Russian. Think about why the Soviet Union collapsed. A Russian solves a problem by throwing numbers at it. The Soviet Union competed with America not by being clever but by throwing numbers at it—numbers of troops, tanks, ships, planes, and everything else—until at last they could not pay for the whole thing and the entire system fell apart. In the same way, a Russian thug will get rid of an enemy by gunning him down on the street corner or in his car in a hail of bullets. That is the Russian way. Not by trying to drive him mad first."

"Paul Duke is convinced that someone is trying to make him crazy before killing him," Donovan said.

Mdivani shook his head vigorously. "An Englishman would do that. Or a woman. But never a Russian."

Donovan thought for a moment, then said, "I'll need to have someone check what you told me about Koslov's whereabouts when those two men were killed."

"Of course you will. Have that man call me. What's his name? The weight lifter."

"Sergeant Moskowitz."

"Ah, yes, interesting man."

"My favorite kind," Donovan replied.

"Now, on to the other business. Koslov has agreed to surrender himself to you like we talked about, but he wants to do it on Christmas Day."

Donovan laughed. "What does he think he is, a gift from the Magi? Why can't I just walk him into Manhattan Criminal Court?"

"I am merely repeating what the man said," Mdivani replied. "Perhaps he believes that the importance generally attached to the day will protect him."

"Well then, he'll have to come to the hospital," Donovan said.

"You're not sick?" Mdivani seemed genuinely concerned.

Donovan said, "I'm becoming a father sometime in the next few weeks."

"Congratulations!" Mdivani replied, twisting his body toward Donovan and pumping the captain's hand. "A son, of course."

"Of course."

"Your first?"

Donovan tossed his hands up.

"I can remember my first, though it's been many years. And I can remember my seventh, my eighth—"

"You have been blessed."

"I have been blessed that I am still healthy—despite some of my habits," Mdivani said, finishing the last of the concoction in his paper cup and tossing the empty vessel over the rail and onto the sand below. "And that I can still work to pay for it all. Three of them are in college now."

Donovan groaned at the thought.

"So, it is done. Koslov will go to the hospital on Christmas Day. The district attorney will be there?"

Donovan said he would arrange it. "Tell Koslov not to show his face without something for the baby," Donovan added.

"I will make a special note of that. You will tell me what hospital and where and it shall be done. But tell me, how do you know that Christmas is the day the baby will come?"

"It *is* Marcy's due date," Donovan said.

"How did you arrange that?"

Donovan shrugged. "I needed something different to do on that day. The past several Christmases were washouts."

"You are a man of many talents," Mdivani replied. Then, glancing out to sea, he added, "Do you see that tanker over there?" He pointed at the black tanker that was moving slowly and silently up into the harbor, the smoke from its long stack whipping away, driven by a fierce and bitter wind.

"What of it?" Donovan asked.

"I will bet you anything, right now, that there are three illegal aliens aboard her."

"Only three?" Donovan said.

"Each one wants his crack at America. You know, streets paved with gold."

"Tin, a lot of the time."

"But, you see, tin is worth something to a starving man. Certainly it is worth more than the dirt and mud that paves the roads where they come from. Do you see what I'm saying?"

Donovan nodded. "You're trying to tell me that, in this

233

country, even Valery Mikelovich Koslov can thrive. Despite the district attorney and his petty concerns."

"Exactly," Mdivani said, slapping his knee with his right hand. This gesture caused his newly lit cigarette to go flying onto the boardwalk, where it quickly blew over the edge and fell to the sand to join the others. "Just what I am saying, that Koslov has no need to kill this pretty TV star. And he certainly has no need to shoot up store windows on Fifth Avenue. To the very best of my knowledge, he is not the man you're looking for. Now, I have told you everything I know about the man. There is no more."

"You are a good friend," Donovan replied, then finished his knish in silence. He balled up the bit of waxed paper it came in and tossed it up and down, trying to figure out whether to stick it in his pocket for eventual transfer to a trash can or to toss it over the railing, as Mdivani was doing with his garbage. A weather-beaten seagull stood nearby, hoping for a handout.

Suddenly Mdivani laughed. "I will tell you something funny," he said.

"I could use a good laugh," Donovan replied.

"You ask, does Valery Mikelovich plan to kill Paul Duke? I tell you, Valery Mikelovich is afraid of assassination himself."

"I know that. He's afraid of the cops summarily executing him on the way to the station house for arraignment. That's why I get to spend Christmas overseeing the process."

"That's not what I'm talking about. What I mean is that he is afraid that one of his rivals in the Russian mafia will shoot him through the window of his bulletproof limousine. And for that reason, Valery Mikelovich"—Mdivani laughed heartily, then slapped Donovan on the leg—"paid a lot of money to buy the only pistol capable of doing the job."

Donovan tossed the balled-up piece of litter over the railing and onto the pristine white December sand of Brighton Beach. The seagull took to the air and dived after it.

"Koslov bought a Kammacher Stedman?" he asked.

Mdivani bobbed his head up and down. "The only one on the market," he said, and laughed again.

"Where is Koslov now?" Donovan asked, standing.

"Don't you want to know what's funny?" Mdivani asked, standing also.

"Where's Koslov?" Donovan said again, more insistently the second time.

"At one of his apartments, I suppose. He has several. I can only point you at two of them. But I doubt he is there. Most certainly he is hiding out at a safe house that is nearby but well concealed. Why is this so important?"

"A Kammacher Stedman is the gun being used by the guy who's shooting up Fifth Avenue," Donovan replied.

"Oh. That's interesting, but I already pointed out how Koslov couldn't have committed those crimes. But what's funny," Mdivani said, "is that Koslov bought the gun so no one else could have it. Then, guess what?"

"What?"

"Someone stole it."

16. "MAYBE MRS. KOSLOV WANTED TO DRIVE HER HUSBAND CRAZY BEFORE KILLING HIM," MOSKO SAID

The second apartment that Mdivani took them to was like the first, a Russian mobster's version of American wealth, 1950s style. The colors were exaggerated, with reds and gold predominating, and nearly everything made of fabric seemed to have gold and silver fibers in it. The furniture was the best the chain furniture stores had to offer. A hot pink velvet sofa, with wood trimming that had been covered in gold leaf, sat below a mural oil painting of Gina Koslov. She was beautiful, all right. Blond, of course; whether born that way or created from a bottle, Brighton Beach wives were necessarily blond. In Gina Koslov's case, the hair was piled high in an elaborate series of symmetrical waves the likes of which had gone unseen in most of the rest of America for several decades. Around her neck was a glittering diamond necklace; below it, a push-up bra and a skintight gold lamé dress created a brand of sexiness that Ann-Margret might have been comfortable with on a Las Vegas evening in 1962.

"I wonder who gets the painting when this happy couple finally divorces," Donovan mused, scratching his chin.

"Maybe Paul Duke can pick it up cheap," Mosko replied, staring at his notebook computer, which he had set up atop the gold-flecked Formica bar.

"Where is she, still at Coney Island Hospital?" Donovan asked Mdivani, who had decided to plunk himself down on the couch and was puffing away at a Chesterfield.

"I hear that she's living with her mother," Mdivani said.

"Where's Mom?"

"Fair Lawn, New Jersey."

"Send somebody out to talk to her," Donovan said.

"You got it," Mosko replied.

Donovan picked up a chunk of polished glass, the size of a large eggplant, an anonymous artist had created to emulate an undulating patch of water. It was crystal clear save for a gold figure of a nude swimming woman that floated in the middle of the sculpture. Donovan put it back down where he had found it, atop a silver-and-glass coffee table also adorned with a fiber-optic flower burst. Its hundreds of illuminated strands waved gently with every blush of breeze stirred up by a passing detective, casting an electronic glow onto the deep-pile purple-and-gold carpet.

Donovan stared at the fiber-optic flower. "I'll bet if you play 'Raindrops Keep Falling on My Head' on the stereo this thing will move in synch," he said.

"Want to try it?" Mosko asked.

Donovan didn't. Instead, he looked back up at the oil painting. "I guess if you got rid of the hairdo and the Ann-Margret outfit that would be a beautiful woman," he said.

"She is," Mdivani replied. "She is."

"Are the rocks real?"

"Do you mean the diamonds? Of course they are. Valery Mikelovich buys only the best."

"So I see. Like the Kammacher Stedman."

"Like that. He is a man who likes to cover all bases, to use your American baseball metaphor. When that gun went on the market last year, he outbid all others. In secret, of course. He made a joke of the purchase, as if he wasn't really afraid that it otherwise might be used on him. But he was afraid, all right. I am sure of it."

"Where'd he keep it?" Mosko asked. "There's no gun cabinet in this apartment or in the other one you took us to."

"He kept the Stedman right here, in a walnut box on the cocktail table." Mdivani leaned forward and tapped a finger against the glass. "He used to call it his insurance policy."

"What happened to it?" Donovan asked.

"It was at last year's Brighton Beach Days festival. You know, where the chamber of commerce runs a big promotion to drum up business for local stores. Hires bands. Invites the press. The usual."

"Every ethnic neighborhood in New York has one of those street fairs," Donovan said.

"The press came. Somebody pulled a string—I think I know who—to get network television down here to do a story on the new rich of Brighton Beach."

"Who pulled a string?" Mosko asked.

"I'll bet that Gina Koslov pulled Paul Duke's string," Donovan said.

"Right you are, Captain," Mdivani confirmed.

"She wanted a videotape of this apartment and that painting on the TV news," Donovan said.

"The woman saw herself as the Marla Trump of Brighton Beach," Mdivani said.

"I hope she has a better prenuptial agreement. So down came Paul Duke with a TV crew to photograph this austere little love nest, among other things."

"On this point you are *almost* right," Mdivani said. "Paul Duke did not come here personally."

"That would have been too obvious, even for him," Mosko said.

"Who did he send?"

"The Irish weatherman. What's his name?"

"George Halloran," Donovan replied. "He specializes in trivial broadcasts from local celebrations. He also happens to be a gun nut."

"Now, what happened after then is a little uncertain," Mdivani went on. "Valery said the gun was stolen. But my suspicion is that Gina gave it to the weatherman to get it out of the house. Lest it be used on her."

"Or so that it could be used on her husband," Donovan mused. "Remember what you said before, Georgi? A Russian wouldn't try to drive a man crazy before killing him. But an Englishman would . . . or a woman."

"Maybe Mrs. Koslov wanted to drive her husband crazy before killing him," Mosko said. "After all, she knew he was afraid of that gun."

"Valery thought of all that, I assure you," Mdivani added. "And that is when the real trouble began between the two of them. Eventually he found out she was sleeping with Duke. But by then the marriage was over."

"All but the battering," Donovan commented.

Mosko broke away from the conversation to take reports from several detectives and make a call on his cell phone. When he came back to Donovan and Mdivani, he said, "There's nothing to help us here or in the first place we looked at, the apartment on Beach Fifth Street. There's no sign of Koslov. But George Halloran called you. Says he has some information."

"About time."

"Frankly, I don't think we're gonna have any more luck finding Koslov than the Brooklyn cops did."

"And you swear you don't know where he is," Donovan said to the Georgian.

"On my mother's grave."

"How do you contact him?"

"He calls me at my club. But always from a different pay phone, so tapping my line won't help you. I promise you, though, that he will show up to surrender on Christmas Day."

"Tell him not to bother with the bulletproof limo," Donovan replied.

Mosko looked up from his computer and said, "Here's how things look. Last year's Brighton Beach Days were June seventh through tenth. Halloran was here with a crew. The

Stedman disappeared. Last year's Moose Horn Billiards Tournament—"

"Moose Horn Billiards Tournament?" Mdivani questioned.

"Was June twenty-fourth through thirtieth. Halloran is reported to have been discussing the Kammacher Stedman with a bunch of Montana gun collectors."

"Yeah, one of whom Halloran described as being a rich Montana survivalist who is somewhere to the right of Hitler. Halloran was going to dig up his name and get back to me, but he never did. Maybe that's what he wants to talk about now."

"Why would this jolly pudgy weatherman take this famous gun from Gina Koslov—gift or no gift—and give it to the guy in Montana?" Mosko asked.

"If that's what happened," Donovan replied.

"And how did the gun get from Montana back to New York and in the hands of someone shooting Christmas shoppers?"

"It's a puzzlement."

"Could this mean that some right-wing survivalists from Montana are the ones claiming to be the Mountain Brigade?" Mosko asked.

Donovan shrugged. "Well, when the name 'Mountain Brigade' came up we all sort of assumed the mountains in question were in Afghanistan," he said. "Maybe we were getting ahead of ourselves."

"Maybe."

"They have mountains in Montana, don't they?" Donovan said.

"I think they're called 'the Rockies.' "

"I've got to talk to Halloran," Donovan replied.

Donovan didn't get into many bars in the years since he stopped drinking, but this one had the look and feel of an old friend. Hurley's was made of dark wood and leather and smelled of brandy and good cigars. It was an expensive smell, the scent of money. That was because Hurley's was the watering hole for the well-paid personnel of the NBC and Wolf networks.

George Halloran was hunkered down at the end of the bar, flicking cigar ashes into a brass tray conveniently placed adjacent to the rows of single-malt scotch. He wore clothes of the sort chosen by a man who can afford to go casual in style—a custom-made plaid shirt with equally expensive khakis fastened over his considerable girth by a Venetian leather belt. His hiking boots were brand-new and highly polished, as if the only trail they would ever see was the well-worn one to the automated teller machine. He was staring blankly at the brass ashtray when Donovan walked in the front door, but upon spotting the captain broke into a broad show-biz grin.

"Bill Donovan! Sit your weary bones down and have a drink."

"I'll sit," Donovan said, taking off his jacket and draping it over the back of the stool next to him before sitting.

"You're not a drinking man, my friend?"

"I'll have a Kaliber," Donovan said to the bartender, who sidled up wiping his hands on a towel.

"What is that, a brandy?" Halloran asked.

"Nonalcoholic beer."

"I like the sound of the name."

"It's made by Guinness," Donovan said.

"That, too."

Across the room, someone slipped a dollar bill into the jukebox and pressed some keys. Sinatra came on, singing "I've Got the World on a String." As Donovan's dark glass bottle was produced and poured, Halloran sipped a Johnnie Walker Black Label and asked, "Has this been as busy a week for you as it's been for me?"

"I've had worse. What have you been up to? How was the Utah Snow Festival?"

"Vertical and cold. Have you ever been on a ski slope?"

Donovan shook his head. "I'm a New Yorker. Going down a mountain at sixty miles an hour, standing on two planks, was never my idea of a fun time. How did your broadcast go? Did you do it from the lift?"

"Yeah, I went through with it. It was harder on my crew than me. I just sat there shivering and talked into a wireless mike. They had to pack into the chair after me and try to focus while swinging back and forth in a blizzard."

"I thought TV crews like challenges," Donovan said. "You know, offering to shinny up a flagpole to get a shot of a pigeon laying an egg."

Halloran nodded. "Yeah, but I think I wore my guys out last August shooting a remote from the Arkansas cow-chip-throwing championship. Do you have any idea what it's like in Arkansas in August with cow chips flying everywhere?"

"Sorry. My childhood playing in Riverside Park offers no parallels. So, my sergeant tells me you called. Do you have something?"

Halloran plucked a business card from his shirt pocket and handed it over. On the back, written in bold strokes that tilted precipitously to the right, was the name Harlan Deaver. Sinatra had begun singing "South of the Border."

"Ever hear the name Harlan Deaver?" Halloran asked.

"I read about him on the FBI's Web site," Donovan said. "He's the real-estate guy who became a multimillionaire by selling ranch land to rich Hollywood types of the Robert Redford and Jane Fonda ilk, then bought himself a thousand-acre parcel and set up a militia organization."

Halloran nodded. "Their main beef being that too much of Montana was being taken over by rich people from New York and California," he said.

"Does the word *chutzpah* come to mind?" Donovan asked.

"I was thinking of an earthier term. Anyway, the man has put out a lot of smoke about being dangerous, so the FBI says he is. His henchmen have roughed up a couple of marshals who came out to serve him with papers regarding nonpayment of taxes. Deaver has declared that his parcel of land is an independent nation no longer subject to the laws of the United States."

"And he's set up a kangaroo court and handed down death sentences upon a whole lot of people he doesn't like," Donovan said. "Of course, if they don't cross the border into his 'free and independent nation,' they're safe. The FBI has his parcel surrounded and is watching him, hoping to pick him up if he drives to the 7-Eleven for beer. But that's unlikely to happen, too. Deaver's militia—"

"He calls them 'the Mountain Brigade.' "

"—runs errands for him. George, I have to ask you a question."

"Shoot."

"Did you steal the Kammacher Stedman automatic from Valery Koslov's apartment and give it to Deaver? Or sell it to Deaver?"

Halloran looked surprised. Then he took a bolt of scotch and smiled. "No, no, and no," he said.

"You didn't steal it?"

"The dear woman gave it to me, and that's the God's honest truth."

"She gave it to you."

"Sure as the day is long. Gina was afraid that her husband would shoot her with it . . . would shoot her with *any* gun he might have in the house, so she got rid of the only one he had. It turns out that it was a famous one."

"Did you know she was having an affair with Paul Duke?" Donovan asked.

"*Everybody* at the network knew that. It was before management handed down its keep-it-in-your-pants ultimatum. Paul asked me to go to Brighton Beach to cover their little shindig because he was afraid that Koslov might have found out."

"He was afraid that Koslov would kill him."

"I suppose he was. Anyway, I do these kinds of festivals all the time. Sometimes five days a week I go to shoot my weather report at—"

"Little Suzie and Aunt May's Crawfish Festival and Cake Bake-off," Donovan said.

"Yeah, like that. This is how I got to be three hundred pounds. Anyway, I did it as a favor for Paul and because I can do it in my sleep. So Gina—she knew that I knew—asked me to ditch the gun for her."

"What do you think of the possibility that she gave you the gun hoping it would find its way into the hands of a rival who would use it on her husband?" Donovan asked.

"How might that happen? Through my exquisite set of contacts in the Russian mafia? Look at who you're talking to. A good-old-boy, ex-marine, all-American yahoo."

"Who's better acquainted with the Montana Mountain Brigade than the Afghanistan Mountain Brigade," Donovan said.

"Does Afghanistan have one, too?" Halloran asked.

"I feel pretty sure the two groups are unrelated. Why didn't you tell me all this the last time we spoke?"

Halloran sighed, then said, "We in network TV live a precarious existence that depends on public approval. We all have to be squeaky clean . . . or damned good liars. Paul isn't a very good liar. He likes women and makes no bones about it. It may get him fired yet. But me, it's easy for me to be squeaky clean, or at least pretend that I am. I drink. You see before you my one and only vice."

Halloran waggled the empty glass at the bartender, who came running with a bottle. "Something Wonderful Happens in the Summer" was on the jukebox.

"But if it got out that I knew something about—in fact, held in my hands—the gun that's doing all the killing on Fifth Avenue, management would fire me in an instant."

"And your golden parachute is no better than Paul's."

"Everyone's is better than his," Halloran said. "The man spends money like there was no tomorrow. Even now. But I still don't want to be fired. Nobody likes to be fired. It's no good for the reputation. You lose little perks, like lucrative endorsement deals."

"What did you do with the gun?" Donovan asked.

"Well, I heard that Deaver wanted to buy it but, as you can imagine, had even less of a likelihood of knowing someone in the Russian mob than I do. And, I think I told you, he wouldn't set foot in New York."

"In fact, can't run up to the 7-Eleven for beer."

"You got that right. So I made some calls and connected with the man. Sorry I lied to you about that. I arranged to bring him the Stedman when I was in Moose Horn covering the billiards tournament."

"How much was he going to pay you for it?" Donovan asked.

"Pay me? Nothing, of course."

Donovan's eyebrows arched toward the ceiling.

"The price I wanted for the gun was an exclusive interview with the man. You see, Captain, I'm as sick as you seem to be of this jazz with me always covering the catfish festival. To be absolutely, one hundred percent honest with you, if I have to do one more stand-up from a cake-baking contest I'm gonna toss my cookies."

Donovan smiled.

"I saw this as being my chance to be taken seriously as a reporter," Halloran said. "It's important to me."

"So you brought the gun to Montana."

"And therein hangs a tale. It disappeared from my hotel room."

"Wait a second," Donovan said. "The gun was stolen from *you?*"

"I assume one of his henchmen did it, so he wouldn't have to do the interview. That was the last I saw of the thing. I never even got to shoot it. Not that I would have at a hundred bucks a round for those fancy depleted-uranium bullets. Even I don't like spending money that fast."

Donovan had about finished his Kaliber and spent a moment peering into the near-empty glass. Then he asked, "Who was working with you in Montana? Besides Rose Waucqez."

"Just my crew. But one of them couldn't have done it. I've known these guys for years. Who else was there? The girl who books our flights. I can't even think of her name. And June dropped by for an afternoon on her way to San Francisco to interview the mayor. And Rose was there. But if you're think-ing of Rose, forget that, too. She's as honest as the day is long."

"And a good shot," Donovan added.

"I'm gonna tell you a secret, and I hope you take it alright. I *like* Rose."

"I'm not so sure it's reciprocated."

"Oh, you mean her dumping on me? That happens all the time. I know what it means."

"What's that?"

"It means she's sweet on me. Weren't you ever a kid?"

"Sure I was. In the sixties. Things worked differently then."

"Well, I'm older than you and remember a time when a girl kidded and teased you if she wanted you. I'm sure that Rose *really* likes me but can't bring herself to admit it because she thinks I'm a . . . What was that she called me?"

" 'An extra-chromosomal former marine,' " Donovan replied.

"So I want to do something to impress her."

"Like get an exclusive interview with the leader of the Mountain Brigade: Harlan Deaver."

"You got me cold. Well, as you can see, I blew my chance. Somebody stole the Kammacher Stedman from my hotel room."

"And after that happened, you never heard another word about the gun?" Donovan asked.

"Not until you brought up the subject," Halloran replied.

"Why didn't you tell me this before?" Donovan asked. "Why did I have to wait all this time to hear how the Sted-man got from Brighton Beach to Montana?"

Halloran looked embarrassed. He smiled and said, "Like I told you, guys in my line of work have to be squeaky clean.

You have two murders to solve. And here I am, the man who last saw the murder weapon. With the exception of the killer, of course."

"Who knows about Gina giving you the gun?" Donovan asked.

"Well, let's see. The guys in my crew. The boys in Montana—like Rosie says, 'the *rest* of the extra-chromosomal former marines'—I told them. But *after* the gun was stolen. Oh, and June."

"June Lake? You told her?"

"She's a good egg and a great listener. Been kicked around some in her life. Doesn't show it."

"You weren't worried about her telling on you to network brass?" Donovan asked.

"Nah. She's a true-blue friend. Everyone confides in her."

"Paul has."

"Yeah. I guess you know they had a thing for a while. Not that it means anything. Paul had a thing with everyone. Everyone except Rose, of course."

"Of course," Donovan responded.

"I have to ask one question," Halloran said.

Sinatra began singing "Here's That Rainy Day." Normally, that was one of Donovan's favorite songs. But the first verse wasn't out before Donovan's cell phone rang. He plucked the instrument from his pocket and said, "Either this is someone about to be born or someone who just died." And he brought the phone to his ear.

"Donovan," he said.

He listened in silence and, as he did, the lines in the corners of his eyes flattened and deepened. With his free hand he reached for his car keys—an old habit—and jingled them in his pocket. Then he said, "I'll be right over."

Halloran read him perfectly well. If the weatherman was

lacking in intelligence or sensitivity, it didn't show at that moment. He said, "That wasn't a birth."

Donovan laid a five-dollar bill on the bar and stood, slipping on his coat.

"I just got a report that Paul Duke was shot to death in the back of his limo."

"My God," Halloran said, making the sign of the cross over himself.

"When did this happen?"

"Ten minutes ago."

"Where?"

"On Fifth Avenue, half a block from the studio."

"I'm coming with you," Halloran said, abandoning his drink and, with a grunt, lifting himself off his bar stool.

It was midafternoon and once again a death had stopped traffic on Fifth Avenue. Blue police barricades and yellow crime-scene tape were just going up when Donovan finished hurrying, in a sort of half-jog, down the short block from the Avenue of the Americas. Halloran huffed and puffed along behind, great clouds of hot and weary breath coming from his lungs and crystallizing in the frosty air four days before Christmas.

Packed-in motorists honked their anger at the bumper-to-bumper traffic. Sirens converged on the scene, on the periphery of Rockefeller Center, from far and near. Already, a shoulder-to-shoulder crowd of tourists and shoppers surrounded Duke's white limousine, which was parked neatly against the curb between a posh boutique jewelry shop and the Brazilian Tourist Office.

With Halloran in tow, Donovan pushed his way through the crowd and squeezed between two blue sawhorses. Two uniformed cops approached, hands up, then recognized the two men and, blushing and smiling, backed away. The right rear door of the limo was open. The window was rolled up. A single neat hole had pierced it.

While holding Halloran back with one hand, Donovan stuck his head in the open door. What he saw was Duke's bodyguard and driver, lying on his left-hand side, a solitary hole piercing the side of his skull above and in front of his ear. The man wore the same blue uniform Donovan had seen on him a few weeks earlier. His white cap was in the front seat, though. At his feet were two paper bags, each holding a bottle of liquor. Johnnie Walker Black Label was in one, Jack Daniel's in the other. And there was a bag of supermarket ice propped up beneath the sliding Plexiglas door of the minibar.

Donovan pulled his head back into the afternoon air.

"Paul . . . ?" Halloran said.

Donovan shook his head. "Paul's driver," he replied.

"Thank God. I mean . . . Jesus, man, you know what I mean."

Donovan knew.

"Apparently he was sitting in the rear on the right-hand side restocking the minibar when he got hit," Donovan said. "The back door was closed. The killer must have mistaken the guy for Paul. Through that glass you can make out the outline of a head and maybe tell if it belongs to a man or a woman, but not who it is."

Donovan beckoned to the two cops who had come over a moment before. One of them, a sergeant, hurried up.

"Yeah, Captain?"

"Anybody see the perp?"

"Nobody we talked to," the man replied. "The closest we got to a witness is a couple from Pennsylvania who heard the shot and looked over."

"What did they see?" Donovan asked.

"They saw a whole lot of people running away. But ordinary people, mind you."

"No Santas or Santa's Angels."

"No, nothing like that. I specifically asked them that question."

Donovan thanked the man and told him he had done a good job, but nonetheless told him to introduce the couple to Moskowitz when he arrived. Maybe his aide, whose talent for friendly badgering had wrung additional memories out of many eyewitnesses, could do better.

Donovan's eyes were drawn to the storefronts where the driver had left the limo standing—in a NO STANDING zone, of course—while waiting for his boss and setting up the bar.

"Why did the guy pull up here?" Donovan asked.

"Why not?" Halloran replied.

"Why here, in front of the Brazilian Tourist Office, and not back there?" He pointed up Fifth Avenue to the spot, near the entrance to Channel Gardens, where he had seen the car waiting for Duke before.

"Because this is where Paul gets picked up every day," Halloran said, checking his watch. "Just about this time."

"Why not back there, where it's a quiet walk across the plaza?" Donovan looked around again, then spied the plain grey door with a buzzer and a peephole on it tucked away between the two stores. Were that a block zoned for apartments, the door would have led to several upstairs flats. "Is that a stage door?"

"You got it," Halloran replied. "That's our not-very-secret entrance."

"Who knows about it?"

"All the people at the network, although only the talent is supposed to use it."

"The talent?"

"The anchors and reporters and, of course, the weatherman. And the paparazzi know to wait out here if they want pictures of us. Not too many fans know about that door. They look in the studio window, as you know."

A clamor in the crowd heralded the arrival of several field detectives and Moskowitz. He spotted Donovan standing by the shot-up limousine and exclaimed, "Oh, no!"

"Not Duke," Donovan said. "His driver."

"And bodyguard, right? So much for half his talents."

"He's also parked in a NO STANDING zone," Donovan said dryly. "What happened at the pet shop?"

"You were complaining that I'm two steps behind you? Well, Mojadidi remains one step ahead of *us.* He did work at that pet shop but cleared out abruptly this morning."

"*This* morning? Interesting."

"Yeah, he got himself hired as Christmas-season help, then quit four days before Christmas. Coincidentally, on the same day the extortion attempt and the attempt on Paul Duke's life were going down. I don't know, Boss. I think Mojadidi is at the top of the list. Maybe he's the one who demanded a payoff as a way of getting the attention shifted to Queens long enough to take a close-range shot at Duke."

"You're suggesting that having cops on every corner dressed as Santa's Angels has helped," Donovan said.

"Well, it sure didn't help the bodyguard none," Mosko replied.

"I guess not."

"Say, what is it with hippies and pet shops? Every time I go into one there are these guys with long hair and rock-and-roll T-shirts gawking at the guppies."

"That's entertainment in their quadrant of the galaxy," Donovan replied.

"It's got to be," Mosko said, shaking his head.

Halloran appeared to be growing eager to get in on the conversation, so Donovan invited him over. "You didn't get to meet George Halloran, did you?" Donovan introduced them.

"Have you warmed up yet from that thing on the ski lift?" Moskowitz asked.

"Have you ever been skiing?" Halloran asked.

"They don't have it in Canarsie."

"Well, I'm still cold despite the liberal application of antifreeze."

Moskowitz peered in the back of the car and said, "One shot. Our boy's aim is improving. A good thing, too, 'cause he only has a handful of slugs left."

"Two, now," Donovan replied.

"So I guess this answers the question of whether Duke is the target or not."

"It would appear to."

"Damn, I hate when he does that," Mosko said.

"Does what?" Halloran asked.

"Says 'it would *appear* to.' "

"Oh, you mean that the captain is entertaining other theories."

"*Entertaining?* The captain has a whole senior prom's worth of suspects and theories going on in there." Mosko pointed at his boss's head, then asked him, "Has anybody seen the perp this time?"

"Not so's I can tell, but talk to the uniformed sergeant over there." Donovan pointed out the man, who stood by his pair of witnesses looking as eager to please as puppies. "He's got a couple of eyewitnesses who saw people running away. No Santa's Angels, though."

"Maybe I can get more out of them."

"I was hoping you could," Donovan replied.

Mosko went off to do it.

Another clamor—this one of sirens and blaring horns—announced the arrival of Bonaci's van. Soon the crime scene was filled with technicians and the uniformed cops were relegated to controlling the still-growing crowd.

"So Paul leaves every day at this time," Donovan said, returning his attention to the weatherman.

"He's late today," Halloran replied, again checking his watch. "Lately, he walks out this door and into the back of the limo."

"The driver holds the door open for him?"

"Yes. Paul hops right in."

"How do *you* get home?"

"By cab, most of the time."

"No limo?"

"I don't want to spend the money. Besides—"

"Half the time, Paul drops you off," Donovan said.

"How'd you know that? Did he tell you?"

"No. But he has a bottle of Black Label in there. That's pretty strong stuff."

"When you're a guy my size, nothing is too strong," Halloran said. "But you're right; Paul often drops me off at my place."

"Which is where?"

"East Sixty-fourth. Park and Lex."

"And Paul lives at . . ."

"Seventy-seventh and Madison."

"Nice neighborhoods. What's behind that door?"

"A corridor that the building maintenance people also use to put out the garbage in the middle of the night. It leads into an anteroom not far from Master Control."

"Is anything else along the route?"

"Storage rooms. One for props. Another for costumes."

"Costumes?" Donovan asked. "You mean like sequins and feather boas?"

"I mean like the blue blazers we wear on camera. And some other stuff. It's a cozy private room with a coffee machine and a small fridge. Sometimes we hang out in there."

"Of all the nice places to sit down in the studio, you hang out in a costume room?"

"That coffee machine is the best. You mean to tell me that you never went out of your way for good coffee?"

Donovan acknowledged the point.

"Want to see it?"

Donovan nodded and was about to start for the door when it flew open and Paul Duke and June Lake burst out, abruptly, into the crime scene, arm in arm and looking like the king and queen of the prom on their big night.

A flash of recognition and astonishment was followed by a scream. June Lake put her hand to her mouth and let out a high-pitched plaint while stamping her feet once and then freezing in place. The grey door that Paul had flung open swung back and smacked her on the shoulder, pushing her against Duke, who then held the door back and cradled her beneath his arm.

"Is that . . . Tony?" he asked Donovan, unable to pry his eyes away from the blood-spattered corpse in the back of his limo.

"It was supposed to have been you," Donovan said.

Lake's hands came away from her mouth and clutched at Duke's protecting arm. "My God, Paul, that man *is* trying to kill you!" she exclaimed.

"I knew it! I knew it! My God, poor Tony."

"He was sitting in back restocking the bar, when he got hit through the window," Donovan said.

Halloran came over then and the three TV people huddled together, exchanging tearful expressions of sympathy and support. Donovan thought they looked like a rugby scrum, bunched there on the sidewalk, arms around shoulders and waists, in front of the Brazilian Tourist Office. He gave them their moment, then broke up the meeting.

He said, "George, would you and June mind waiting over by the wall for a moment while I talk to Paul?"

"Sure thing, buddy," Halloran replied, before turning and steering Lake over by the big picture window—probably *not* bulletproof—that displayed huge color blowups of men in Carnival costumes in Rio and women in string bikinis on Ipanema Beach. She was dabbing at her eyes with a hankie.

Once alone with Duke, Donovan said, "We've got to stop meeting like this."

"What?" Duke asked, a bit dazed.

"At murder scenes."

"I can't believe Tony is dead."

"Where were you just now?" Donovan asked.

"Uh . . . why do you ask?"

"George said you normally leave about fifteen minutes ago."

"Sure," Duke said, checking his watch. "Every day at three."

"Why three?"

"I go to my health club and work out. With my personal trainer. He takes me at three-thirty." Duke patted himself on the tummy, which was remarkably flat for a man of his years, and said, "Got to stay in shape for the ladies."

Donovan scowled. "What does it take for you to learn your lesson—AIDS?"

"I'm not afraid of AIDS," Duke said. "I'm careful who I sleep with. I got chlamydia once, ten years ago, but I took some pills and it went away."

"What about a bullet?" Donovan asked. "Are you going to take pills that stop bullets? One way or another, my friend, your lifestyle is going to kill you."

He pointed at the limo, where a police photographer was taking snapshots of the corpse. That seemed to get through to Duke, the starkness of it, the made-for-TV reality of a man taking photographs of the body. Duke appeared to realize that he might actually be the target of the killer's rage. Duke gaped at the body of his bodyguard and the blood in the back of his white limo and the shot-up window. And it sank in that he, Paul Duke, could have been the one lying there with a bullet in his skull. He began to pale.

He said, mumbled rather, "I mean before all this stuff started happening I used to walk home. Not every day, but often. I walked right up Fifth Avenue. Then *People* called me 'the sexiest man alive' and, a while after, bodies started dropping."

After spotting the corpse and hearing June scream, Duke, Donovan figured, had been moved to play the tough guy. It seemed to come naturally to him, and that was how Duke had come to be famous, for shaking his fist at Russian helicopters. His stance was one actors take, a pose that was not backed up by any real backbone.

By the time he made his mumbling admission, however, Duke had got paler, a bit corpselike himself, same as he did a few weeks back when he was forced to face the prospect of a violent end. His knees seemed to weaken and his mouth fell open a crack and he breathed harder to get more air into his lungs.

"Brian!" Donovan shouted to his assistant while slipping an arm about Duke's waist to hold him up in case he keeled over.

Moskowitz came running and got a well-muscled arm around the anchorman just as his eyes rolled back into his skull and he fainted dead away.

June Lake screamed Duke's name. She, too, ran over, Halloran right behind, his grizzly-bear frame towering over her.

"What happened? Is Paul all right?"

"He fainted," Mosko told her.

"Stricken with grief at the death of his friend and body-guard," Donovan added, charitably and diplomatically, in case any reporters were within earshot.

"Let's get him to the hospital," Halloran said, trying, unnecessarily, to get a hand in to help the other guys in holding Duke up.

"I don't think he needs that, much as my wife would like to see him again," Donovan replied. "He just needs to lie down."

"We'll take him to my place," Lake said. "I'm close."

"How close?" Donovan asked.

"Central Park South."

"That will do."

"We need a car here!" Mosko bellowed, to no one in particular but in his best Brooklyn accent, the one sure to get results. Within a minute a squad car was through the crowd with its door flung open. Already Lake had her house keys out of her purse and jingling in her hand.

Efficient woman, Donovan thought, as he helped load Duke into the back of the car and got in along with him and his coanchor.

With Mosko's help and the connivance of the doorman, Donovan got Paul Duke's emotionally drained and temporarily inert body into the elevator and up to Lake's nineteenth-floor apartment overlooking Central Park. The apartment was shiny and modern, oddly sterile, all white Formica and stainless steel save for the occasional modern art flourishes that broke the monotony of eggshell-white walls. And since Lake appeared to admire the minimalists, those paintings tended to series of white-on-white or grey-on-grey or, in the case of an immense mural hung behind the white leather couch, a series of beige-on-beige triangles.

They laid him on the couch in Lake's office, a tufted-leather affair set across a smallish room otherwise furnished with a glass-and-stainless desk, several file cabinets, and a wall unit that held tapes, a TV, and a VCR. Once on the couch, Duke stirred and opened his eyes, a bit like a hatching chick peeking warily from the shell. They flashed around the room, seeking orientation.

"Where am I?" he asked.

"In June's study," Donovan replied.

"In her apartment?" he groaned, rubbing his eyes.

"I'm here for you, Paul," she said, sitting on the edge of the couch, her thigh touching his, her skirt riding up her legs with a swoosh of panty hose.

He lowered a hand from his eyes and left it where it was convenient for her to pick up and cradle in both of hers.

"My life is over," he said.

"Not when you compare it with Tony's," Donovan replied.

Duke shook his head and momentarily scrunched his eyes shut but otherwise ignored the remark. "I'll lose my job. They'll definitely fire me now. I have nowhere to go."

"I'll take care of you, honey," Lake replied, squeezing his hand for emphasis.

"I feel sick."

"Do you want a doctor?" she asked.

"God, no. Just time to rest and think. This is *awful*. Can I get a glass of water?"

"Sure."

"No, coffee."

"Anything."

"The way I like it," Duke added.

Lake stood, adjusted her skirt, and said, "You guys watch him while I go into the kitchen."

"Sure," Mosko replied, taking her place on the edge of the couch but farther down, by the stricken man's feet. She walked out of the room, leaving the three men.

"How *do* you take your coffee . . . honey?" Donovan asked, sticking his hands in his pockets and strolling over to her desk.

Duke groaned again, said, "Light, one sugar," and scrunched his eyes shut. When he opened them, he said, "The network will wait until after Tony is buried. They'll wait until after Christmas. Then they'll fire me. I'm ruined."

"It's beginning to look like you have an angel who will take you in," Donovan noted. "I hope you like the decor."

"This place is outstandingly warm," Mosko said, looking up at another painting, a beige circle inside a darker beige icosahedron. "It reminds me of this girl I dated before I met my wife. She was a weight lifter from Sheepshead Bay. Thirty-three and buns of steel. Lived in a one-bedroom apartment a block from the el. She had this bedroom set she bought from a place on Ralph Avenue. It was grey Formica."

"Sexy," Donovan said.

"Battleship grey. And on the matching vanity table she had this hockey puck she used to keep papers from blowing from the fan she had stuck in the window."

Donovan was fiddling with some papers on Lake's desk.

"I used to call this place 'the Winter Palace,'" Duke said, forcing a smile. "But listen; June is really a very warm and feeling woman. I've been horrible to her in the past."

"What did you do?" Donovan asked.

"She wanted a long-term relationship. I didn't."

"She wanted to marry you?"

"I've always had a problem with that word," Duke said.

"Me, too, until two years ago," Donovan replied. He had found a neatly stacked pile of financial records and was unable to resist prying.

"She also thought it would be good for our careers. You know—and this was her idea, not mine—June wanted the network to bill us as the married anchors, 'Duke and Lake.'"

"Sounds like the name of a prizefighter," Mosko said. "'Dukin' Lake.' Look, Cap; if you're done with me—"

"Take off," Donovan said.

"I'll get back to the stiff. So long, Mr. Duke."

"'Bye."

With a handshake and a shouted "Good-bye!" to the woman in the kitchen, Moskowitz disappeared through the living room and out the apartment door.

Duke said, "Maybe the way you did it is the right way. I'm over fifty, too. Maybe it *is* time to settle down with the right woman."

"June?" Donovan asked.

Duke sighed audibly enough to be heard across the room. He said, "I'd kind of like to have a kid. A little rug rat running around. A son to whom I can, someday, teach everything I know."

"I would pay to sit in on that lesson," Donovan said.

Duke frowned. "I want a son," he said nonetheless.

"But June is our age," Donovan replied. "The battery has run out on her biological clock."

"I'm a wretched man who deserves to be sent to the poorhouse alone and without a family," Duke said, perhaps realizing his misery, his voice rising into the plaintive range.

Donovan pulled a rectangular slip of paper from the pile he had been perusing and held it up. It was an old pay stub. "She makes thirty-eight thousand, four hundred sixty-one dollars, and fifty-four cents in take-home pay? How often do you guys get paid? Monthly?"

Duke shook his head, looking embarrassed, then proud. "Every two weeks," he replied. He held up two fingers in what looked like a *V*-for-victory sign.

"She makes more money in a month than I made in a year until recently," Donovan said. "What's *your* paycheck like? Are you in this league?"

"My friend, I *invented* this league," Duke answered proudly. "I make more than she does."

"How can you get a check like that every two weeks and still be broke? What do you spend it on? I don't recall seeing anything in the papers about mansions or yachts."

"I have houses in L.A. and East Hampton, an apartment here in town, and a pied-à-terre in London," Duke replied.

"Well, I guess that could eat up a buck or two."

"And I put money down on a little spread in Montana last year, but—"

"Where in Montana?" Donovan asked. "In Moose Horn?"

"Not far from there. But I changed my mind and got my money back."

"How come?"

"Call it bad vibes. I spent a few days out there last year, when George and some other people I know were singing the praises of Montana real estate, and came back to New York with the distinct feeling that the natives were unfriendly."

"Some of 'em are, I hear," Donovan said.

Duke looked pensive for a moment, then sighed and pulled himself into a sitting position, pausing to straighten his pants and tuck his shirt back in. "So that's where I've been spending my bread. Then there are the cars and . . ." He looked around to see if Lake had come back into the room. "And then there's the women. I guess I spend more than I should on them."

"How? Fur coats?"

"Sometimes."

"Jewels?"

"Definitely."

"Trips to Paris for lunch?"

"It's been known to happen," Duke replied.

"And what does June feel about all this?" Donovan asked.

Duke stretched and yawned. "She's a good friend these days. I'm sorry I didn't live up to her expectations for me. Now if I can just find some way to save my career."

"You're sure that Wolf will dump you?"

"As sure as the day is long. But maybe I can pick up something on cable. I'm not a bad-looking guy, even after all I've been through. Maybe I can sell stuff on the Home Shopping Channel."

"But kiss the big paydays good-bye, eh?" Donovan said, surreptitiously folding up Lake's old pay stub and slipping it into his pants pocket.

The rhythmic swooshing of panty hose announced the return of June Lake, bearing two mugs of coffee. If a tragedy had just befallen her TV family, such didn't show on her face or in her demeanor. The Barbie sheen was back and in full bloom.

Upon seeing Duke sitting up, she beamed and said, "You're up! How do you feel?"

"With my fingers," Duke replied, wiggling those on one hand.

"Your sense of humor is coming back. That's good. Here's your coffee."

She handed one mug to him, a plain white mug, and gave another to the captain. "You take milk and one sugar, don't you?" she said.

"That's fine. Thanks." Donovan had a sip and put the mug on the desk next to the stack of financial records.

Lake was back sitting on the couch next to Duke, one hand resting lightly on his leg. Her fingers were splayed out, delicately, like those of a harpist.

"What were you two doing in the costume room before?" Donovan asked.

"I don't know . . . talking," Duke said. "We were both running in and out,"

"Talking about what?"

"Is that important?" Lake asked—a bit defensively, Donovan thought.

Donovan said that it was.

"I don't know . . . stuff," Duke said.

"I was trying to pry him away from the city for the holidays," Lake added with a sigh.

"Christmas."

"The week between Christmas and New Year's. I was hoping to get him to come to the islands with me. I have to make reservations, so I wanted to pin him down today."

"Any island in particular?" Donovan asked.

"I have a villa on St. Bart's," she replied.

"God, you people sure know how to spend money. The last beach I spent any time at was Brighton Beach."

"I'm never going back to the Caribbean after last summer," Duke said.

Donovan smiled faintly, then commented, "When a volcano blew up and stranded you on Carricola for three weeks before the Coast Guard came and got you out."

"Oh, you know about that? Funny. I traveled incognito, with a beard, and it never made the papers. Except for a little mention when I was one of the Americans rescued."

"That little item remains on the AP Web site," Donovan said. "What did you do while you were down there?"

"God, what can you do *anywhere* for three weeks when you have only a few changes of clothes? I cooled my heels on the veranda with the other guests and ate too much. I put on five pounds." Duke patted his tummy. Then he added, "Dammit, I should have called my personal trainer and canceled."

"Did you hobnob with any royalty while you were in Carricola?" Donovan asked.

Duke hesitated for a second, and his eyes flashed to Donovan's, then away. "Oh, *heaps*," he replied, a bit too flippantly.

"You *did* have a horrible time last summer," Lake said then. "So, let's not go to St. Bart's. Let's go to Rio."

"Rio at Christmas?" Duke asked, interested.

"It will be totally different, and you need a change of pace to help settle your nerves."

"I'm not sure I can afford it, since I'm going to be losing my job."

"I have plenty enough money for both of us," she said.

Duke picked up her hand and squeezed it. Yet again she cupped his hand in both of hers.

"Remember when we talked—in the costume room,

come to think of it—after that German man was murdered. You told me about your 'desperation plan,' you called it."

"Desperation plan?" Donovan asked.

Duke's face took on a nearly childlike look that combined fear and helplessness. "I told June"—he held up her hands up so Donovan could see, out in the open now, the bond between them—"that if the network ever seemed on the verge of firing me, I mean actually doing it and not just leaking threats to *Variety,* I would bag it and quit."

"To do what? It seems to me we had a discussion along these lines and you didn't know how you would pay for everything," Donovan said.

"I'd dump everything," Duke replied. "Sell the houses and cars. Live a simple life."

"We'd get married," Lake said, tossing in the part of the plan Duke had neglected to mention.

Duke bobbed his head up and down, a bit like a two-year-old promising Mommy he would be good. "I'd write my memoirs. You know, *Tales of a TV Tough Guy.*" He laughed bitterly.

"Where would you live?" Donovan asked.

"Here, I guess," he said, looking around in a cursory manner.

"I have a country house, too," Lake added.

"I need to be straight on something," Donovan said. "You want this guy to be a househusband? To go from being TV's biggest hunk to being totally dependent on you?"

"I could keep an eye on him that way," she replied, her voice and expression tending to regard Duke as a scamp who was, nonetheless, adorable.

"I see," Donovan said. He walked away from them and to the window to look out at Central Park. The city's most famous patch of green was veiled behind fine snowflakes that had begun falling within the previous few minutes. They also floated down in front of Fifth Avenue Medical Center, off to the right across the corner of the park. For a moment Donovan tried to guess which of the dozens of windows was Marcy's.

Then Duke said, "That's it. That's what I'll do."

"I'm so proud of you," Lake responded.

"I'll call right now and quit—before they can fire me. Then I'll call my press agent and have her make the announcement. Then I'll call my lawyer and tell him to put everything I own on the block. I'll take a few days to arrange stuff. We'll have a quiet Christmas together and then get married in Rio."

The happy couple embraced, arms entwined, then kissed so passionately that Donovan wished he had a camera, knowing that such a snapshot was worth half a million dollars to the *Globe*. Duke and Lake: he dependent on her, helpless; she wearing the pants in the household. As fond as the captain was of strong women, having married one, the match he saw developing in front of him was too bizarre to be true. And not just because Duke had been ducking Lake only a few weeks earlier.

Donovan folded his arms and said, "I'm sorry, but you two aren't going anywhere."

"What?" they exclaimed, more or less in unison.

"You're not leaving town—certainly not leaving the country—till I find out who's killed three people, so far, on Fifth Avenue."

Lake bristled. No gloss covered her demeanor now. Instead, a hard edge, a frustrated and angry one, presented itself. "You can't stop us," she said.

"Watch me," Donovan replied.

"What's this about, Bill?" Duke asked. "Don't tell me I'm a *suspect.*"

"Everyone is a suspect at this point."

"But I was with June when Tony was killed."

"Did you hear the shot?"

"No."

"So you don't know when it happened. And June doesn't know where you were at the time your bodyguard was killed."

"You can't hear anything that goes on in the street when you're inside the studio," Duke said. "The walls are insulated to make sure you can't."

"So each of you doesn't know where the other one was when Tony was killed," Donovan stated.

Duke appeared to be astonished. "Well, now that you mention it—"

"Did anyone else see you guys in that room? Going to that room? Leaving it?"

Duke shook his head. "That corridor by the costume room is empty in the afternoon. You see, the whole studio is dedicated to *The Morning Show.* It shuts down a few hours after the show airs. Our typical day runs from five in the morning to noon. A few of us stay longer, mainly June and me. Sometimes George. And Rose, often."

"The redhead in Master Control. The one whose father taught her how to hunt with a pistol."

"Do you suspect her?" Duke asked.

Donovan shrugged.

Lake was still seething quietly, glaring at the captain while tightening her grip on her newly caught man.

Donovan said, "Let's talk about Carricola last summer."

Duke sighed, and then Lake and he exchanged glances. "He knows," Duke told her.

June softened then, the hard edge dissolving in favor of what seemed like a look of relieved honesty. Relieved at being able to tell the truth at last. Or was she acting? Donovan wondered.

She said, "I want you to know, Captain, that I know all about Paul's past. And I don't care. I truly don't."

"That's very modern of you," Donovan responded. "If it's true, then you won't mind listening while Paul and I talk about Princess Anna."

"I already know the story. Paul was trapped with this woman at the hotel in Carricola. They had an affair. Big deal."

Duke said, "Anna Hebbel seemed like a nice young woman. She was down in the islands having a final fling before getting engaged, getting married, and settling down. She chose me to have it with. She's European royalty. She could have had anyone. I was flattered. And, of course, in the hotel during the time we were trapped, there was nothing else to do. No TV. No radio."

"No morning-after pills," Donovan said.

Duke's eyes whitened and broadened. It was the deer-in-the-headlights look that Donovan knew so well. It was hard for the captain to avoid gloating.

"You don't know about the baby, do you?" he said.

"Baby?" Duke stammered.

"Your child. Daughter, to be accurate. Count back twenty weeks—well, twenty-three or so now—to Carricola, and you are the father-to-be. Congratulations, Dad."

Duke sort of laughed and shook his head. Then he caught a glimpse of Lake, who was not amused, and the glimmer of a smile vanished from his lips.

"Did she sleep with anyone else down there?" Donovan asked.

"No. Just me. I'm sure of it."

"She flew back to New York to be with Melmer, and very soon they announced their engagement. I suspect he knew about the baby but didn't care. Apparently, he was as 'modern' as you are." Donovan nodded in the direction of Lake.

"I had no idea about this baby, but it changes nothing," Lake said. "I still want to marry Paul. And Princess Anna didn't."

Duke added, "She's royalty. They cover up things like this."

"Wrong," Donovan said. "She's not royalty. Her real name is Anna Fritsch, and she's a penny-ante European scam artist who was born in prison, the daughter of a notorious sixties radical."

Duke had the deer look again. Donovan was less certain about the extent to which Lake was startled by the information.

And it was Lake who spoke. "What you're saying is, she'll be back," she said. "If she's a crook, no matter where she's gone, she will be in touch with Paul looking for money. In fact, I wouldn't be surprised if she slept with Paul deliberately to get pregnant."

Duke looked at Lake then, as if he was about to disagree. Donovan sensed a man about to stand up for the honor of the mother of his child. But the moment passed.

Donovan said, "If I'm not mistaken, Melmer had more money than Paul does, did, or ever will."

"He died before marrying her," Lake replied.

"This is true. Paul, she doesn't happen to be staying at one of your residences, does she?" Donovan asked.

"With me? No, of course not. I didn't even know she was missing."

"But you did show up at that second murder scene, not

out of general curiosity, but because you wanted to see if I would spill some information about her," Donovan said.

"I was concerned about Anna, that's true. Her fiancé had just been murdered. And like I told you, I was afraid that someone was gunning for me. Don't you see? I was right all along. It makes more sense now. Whoever is gunning for me must have thought that Melmer was me. I was supposed to be that first victim. God, I hope Anna is all right."

Lake looked sharply at him, and Duke said, "Just . . . you know . . . because she's been through so much."

"When you put the Lamborghini on the block, maybe you could give her a hubcap," Donovan remarked.

"I'm sure a payoff of some kind will be in the offing," Lake said. "Never mind. I can handle this . . . *princess*. Nothing will come between Paul and me now, certainly not some cheap hustler who got lucky and seduced my man when both were trapped in a hotel."

This time Duke said nothing but instead let his head roll to one side until it rested lightly atop hers. Then he began petting the back of her hand.

A short while and a few meaningless conversational exchanges later, Donovan excused himself and walked back to the crime scene. There he found that the body had been probed, prodded, and deemed fit for travel, then zipped into a body bag and driven the two dozen blocks south to the morgue. Traffic was moving again, though down to two lanes and creeping along. TV remote vans were everywhere, their telescoping antennae making the stretch of Fifth Avenue in front of the Brazilian Tourist Office resemble an asparagus patch.

Donovan found his aide sitting in the famous costume room, staring fixedly at a largish plastic evidence bag that he had placed next to the coffeemaker. Donovan couldn't see what was in it, there were so many labels printed or otherwise affixed to the parcel. But from Mosko's seriousness, Donovan felt he wasn't looking at lunch.

"I take it that's no prune Danish in there," he said.

"It's the Kammacher Stedman," Mosko responded, looking up in pride. "We found it under the car."

"Really? That's it, there? Amazing." Donovan was genuinely surprised, too. In his considerable experience, killers who went out of their way to acquire exotic weapons generally were separated from them only by deadly force. "You found it where?"

"Under the car, I told you."

"Where exactly?"

By way of reply, Moskowitz got to his feet, walked to the coffeemaker, formed his hands into a gun, went, "Pow," and pumped an imaginary bullet into the twelve-cup carafe. Then he flipped his right hand back and down around in a semicircle, as if to chuck a gun below the smallish table atop which sat the coffee machine.

"Right under the body?" Donovan asked.

"About where the head rested." Mosko sat back down.

"So the killer is right-handed."

"How do you figure that?"

Donovan said, "He shoots through the window. He yanks the door open. Sees the body. Chucks the gun. Left hand is on door. Splits. It's midafternoon on Fifth Avenue four days before Christmas and he needs to get away before the panic wears off and people start to remember things."

"I guess this means that Duke can stop being afraid of being shot through the window," Mosko said.

"His fears are over anyway," Donovan replied. "The man is quitting as of right now."

"What's he going to do? Open a gyro cart? The guy has some Greek blood. I'm sure of it."

Donovan shook his head, then filled in his assistant on the part of the conversation he had missed by leaving Lake's apartment.

When Donovan was done, Mosko said, "So Duke will have to sell the Lamborghini. Poor baby."

"I pretty much conveyed that sentiment to him."

"Did he listen?"

"Not that I noticed. You know, he said he's going to be flat broke and fully dependent on June Lake."

"Which is what she wants, you told me."

"She caught him. . . . She says she accepts him, warts and all . . . and she means to keep him."

"Seems to me I've heard of this happening before. A guy chases women and spends money until he wears himself out doing both. Then a good, simple woman comes along and takes him in, warts and all, like you say, and he's so grateful he stays forever."

Donovan nodded. "And it's not like Duke will be flat broke the way you and I might be flat broke."

"You've got plenty of money," Mosko said.

"I'm OK now. I wouldn't say I have plenty of money."

"Ever since you made captain and married Marcy—come on, admit it—her parents' money has been trickling down to you."

"My friend, captains make pretty good money these days, and my apartment is still on rent control," Donovan said. "So let's just say that, wherever it comes from, I can afford butter with my toast these days."

"You're saying that Duke will be able to afford butter *and* jam with his toast."

"At the very least, and good-quality jam, too. Even if he

declares bankruptcy, those laws let you keep a house and a car. Maybe you get to keep a Honda, not a Lamborghini."

"Poor baby. Duke has a Honda?"

"Beats me. And anyway, he's going to write his memoir, *Tales of a TV Tough Guy.*"

Mosko snickered. "He won't be doing it for free."

"No, he wouldn't. But if I read my June Lakes correctly, he sure won't be spending what money he may have on other women. Do you want to do something for me? Just for the hell of it? The Stedman fires depleted-uranium bullets. Is this depleted uranium radioactive?"

"You're asking me a science question? I got no idea, Cap."

"Me either," Donovan said.

"So what do you want me to do?"

"Get a guy with a Geiger counter and send him around this building. Send him around all the dressing rooms—Duke's, Lake's, and Halloran's—and around Master Control where Rose works. Send him to Tuttle's apartment in the East Village and to Koslov's apartments in Brighton Beach. Send him to that garage where the gyro guys park their carts and to Mojadidi's apartment in Long Island City. And let's not leave out the offices of the Midtown Merchants Association."

"What's he looking for?" Mosko asked.

"Radiation, of course. I doubt he'll find any, but that's really beside the point. Have the guy act like he's hot on the trail. Have him take lots of notes and look concerned but say nothing."

"Have him put on an act," Mosko said, getting it.

"And he needn't hide his activities from the press, either," Donovan added.

Rose Waucqez was in Master Control, editing a taped segment that had something to do with canoes and a swamp, when Donovan eased himself down into the chair beside her.

"Captain Donovan," she said pleasantly, without quite looking up.

"Ms. Waucqez, how are you today?"

"It's 'Rose,' and you know it's a sad day. That poor man. And poor Paul. I suppose he'll be leaving the network now."

She hadn't taken her eyes off the monitor except to acknowledge Donovan's arrival, so he said cheerily, "The Great American Canoe Festival, I guess?"

"Wrong. The Okefenokee Catfish Festival. It's going on all next week. This tape is from last year."

"Who's covering it?" Donovan asked.

"Who do you imagine?"

"George, but I don't think he'll be squeezing into a canoe without sinking it."

That got her to turn away from the monitor. "The man is a pig. And fat enough to sink the *Titanic,* if it hadn't already been sunk by that iceberg. Did you come here to ask me about George Halloran? Is he a suspect? If so, haul him off, lock him up, and throw away the key."

"He thinks you like him," Donovan said.

"The man is delusional. They let him stand in for the anchors a couple of times and he imagines he not only can fill Paul's shoes, he can wear his pants."

"George, stand in for the anchors?"

"Don't you watch the show?" she asked, looking Donovan up and down. "No, of course you don't. You have the look of a Public Television viewer."

"Thank you," he replied. "Why does the network let George stand in for the stars?"

"Because, in their reductionist vision, George is the wave of the future for them."

"Reductionist as in lowest common denominator?" Donovan asked.

"See; I was right about you. George has that slob-level appeal that the MBAs that run Wolf like. It's an open secret that we appeal to the Tonya Harding, professional wrestling, tractor-pull crowd to begin with. Adding a gigantic drunken ex-marine who waggles his eyebrows and leers at women is just their idea of the next network news superstar."

"I guess you don't like him much," Donovan said.

Waucqez reached over and shook Donovan's hand. "I guess I like you, Captain," she replied. "I'd go for you in a big way if you weren't already taken. The truth is I'm a committed feminist whose standards in men are so high I might as well move into a convent. Me go for George Halloran? I'd sooner go for George Wallace. And isn't he dead?"

"So much for Halloran's ability to guess what women are thinking," Donovan said.

"What did I tell you? He has the sensitivity of a kidney stone."

"Tell me this. Are you in any way suggesting that George might want to see Paul Duke lose his job?"

"Ha! *Might* want to! Would *love* to, that's more like it. But if you're thinking that George might kill to get the job, no, as much as I want to think ill of the man, I doubt it. He's a slob and an opportunist, but not a killer. Besides, how would you pack that fat body into a Santa's Angels costume?"

"You have a point," Donovan admitted.

She smiled and turned back to the screen. A few seconds later, the canoes, formerly seen sharply, were paddling off through the swamp, bathed in a misty glow that suggested early-morning fog. She said, "We're trying to tell a story about fog, and there wasn't any on this tape. So I just added it. The Wolf network. Integrity in journalism. George Halloran, future anchorperson."

"You're awfully hard on the network that pays your salary," Donovan said.

"And you never criticize the NYPD?"

"The other night, Marcy and I were watching *20/20* on ABC."

"Now, that is network news as it should be," Waucqez said.

"Is it? They ran a piece on a woman who gave up her wealthy lifestyle and her family to marry a convicted murderer currently residing on death row."

"I saw that; classic journalism."

Donovan shook his head. "In prime time and narrated by Barbara Walters, it looks classic. But run the same story at three in the afternoon on *Jenny Jones* and you have something like 'Men on Death Row and the Women Who Love Them.' "

"What are you trying to tell me? That Wolf Television isn't so bad? Or that all television is bad?"

"I'm telling you that there's a reason I read a lot," Donovan said. "I like information. Such as on dates and times. How are you on those?"

"You mean like when the murders took place?" she asked, turning back.

"Like then," he replied.

"Well, I keep track of all the comings and goings around

here, so yes, I can help you. You want to know where George was?"

"I want to know where all three of them were."

"The other two being Paul and June?" she asked, a little thrown by the possibilities.

"Yep."

She thought for a moment, then said, "Well, that *is* a shocker. The police want to know if Paul Duke and June Lake—"

"Dukin' Lake," Donovan said.

"—have alibis for the times of the murders. Let's see. As I recall, the first killing, where a man was shot through a store window, happened right after we went off the air, right?"

Donovan nodded. "Shortly after the stores opened. Nine-fifteen."

"And the date was?" She was calling up a screen on one of the half-dozen monitors in front of her.

"Friday, November twenty-ninth, is when Erik Melmer was killed," Donovan said. "Thursday, December fifth, is when Terry Seybold was murdered."

"That was the one at night."

"Right in the middle of the tree-lighting ceremony. At eight-seventeen. And the third murder, as you know, was about an hour ago. Around three."

"It's all right here," she said, smiling at the screen and her own record-keeping ability.

"Well?"

"Does the word *bupkes* resonate with you?" she said.

"If Marcy's mom is right, and I'm not going to be the one to argue with her, it means 'goat turd' in Yiddish."

"In other words, nothing. They have no alibis."

"You're sure of that?" Donovan asked.

"On November twenty-ninth we closed the show at nine A.M. Paul and June, as they always do, repaired to their dressing rooms. Which means that nobody saw them. Every day they do the same thing. They go to their rooms to unwind, lay down, kick the furniture, whatever they do in there. The point is, they are alone. Unless they happen to be with one another, and as you must have surmised, they don't get along that well. What happened before, by the way? I heard the rumor that she took him to her place?"

"She certainly did that. And I think she's keeping him, too."

"My, my. As Dorothy Parker said, 'Read a book, and sew a seam, and slumber if you can. All your life you wait around for some damn man.' Anyway, the corridor where the stars' dressing rooms reside is off-limits to all but the exalted themselves. So, in short, no one saw them on that day. And no one saw them at the time of the second killing, either."

"But that one was at night," Donovan said.

"Yes, but we were on the air that night, covering the tree-lighting ceremony. In fact, we preempted the *Marlboro Classic Monster Tractor Mash* to do so."

"What a shame."

"Yeah. You should have seen the letters. Paul and June introduced the personality who was covering the tree-lighting, then repaired to their dressing rooms per usual. So, once again, no alibi."

"Who covered the ceremony?" Donovan asked.

"George. So he's in the clear, at least for that murder. For the first one, he was in his dressing room. Which is on a different corridor but just as secluded. I heard that George was with you an hour ago when Paul's bodyguard was shot. So I suppose that the gigantic sot is off the hook for two-thirds of your murders. And as the poet said, 'two out of three ain't bad.' "

"Dorothy Parker again?" Donovan asked playfully.

"Meat Loaf," she replied.

They were interrupted by the ringing of Donovan's cell phone. He put the device to his ear and had a brief conversation, at the end of which he imagined that a smile must have crept across his lips. For Waucqez looked over at him and said, "You ought to bottle that look."

"Which look is that?" he asked, his mind swimming with entertaining possibilities.

"The cat-that-ate-the-canary look. I don't suppose you can tell me what fascinating tidbit you just learned."

Donovan shook his head. "I suppose you read *Moll Flanders*," he said.

"Many years ago."

"I love stories that take you from rags to riches but require thirty years to get there," Donovan said.

"Doesn't everyone?" she replied. "But what has that got to do with the murders?"

"Everything and nothing," he said, and headed for the door.

It was about seven in the evening when Donovan, having planted a suggestion at breakfast time, saw it come to life during the dinner hour. All he had to do, really, was be there to intercept the shipment. Consequently, it was Captain Bill Donovan of the NYPD, and not Jaime the delivery boy, who carried a sack of take-home food from Paco's Mexican Restaurant to a two-bedroom apartment in the Beresford Towers.

He rang the bell and, a moment later, heard Claudia Hummitz's voice, mellower than at any other time since he first heard it, say, "It's dinner, honey." And then footsteps approached the door.

She swung it open and, when her eyes met his, Donovan said, "Chorizos, anyone?" He held aloft the bag.

It was an awkward moment, at best, that could have led to tears or violence if the captain hadn't read the personalities correctly. But he had, and after a fleeting, surprised silence Hummitz laughed, shook her head, and laughed again.

"Damn, you're good," she said.

"Nah, just persistent. You aren't going to shoot me or anything, are you?"

"I haven't killed anyone in thirty years," Kirsten Fritsch replied. "What gave me away? I know; you got my fingerprints off that catalog."

"That and your habit of balling up tissues and leaving them all over the place, including your daughter's hospital room. Can I come in? I brought enough for three. How is your daughter? She *is* here, isn't she?"

"Of course she is. She came right to her mama after her fiancé, the only man who ever treated her with true love and absolute respect, was murdered. And she's been here ever since. Anna?"

The young woman was sitting on a floral print couch, her legs primly tucked under her, her pregnancy at last showing. She looked radiantly beautiful, but like an orchid does when it's slightly damaged. She had been through a lot, and looked up at Donovan with cat's eyes, full of fear. She said, tentatively, "I remember seeing you in the hospital. Your wife is multiracial, isn't she?"

"African-American and Jewish," Donovan replied.

"So you're not an ordinary policeman. Is my mom under arrest?"

"Not if she hasn't killed anyone in thirty years," Donovan said, helping himself to a seat on the couch next to the young woman. He put the bags on the coffee table, which was an old ship's hatch cover that a clever artisan had restored and converted. Claudia Hummitz—Kirsten Fritsch, that is—sat on his other side.

"Am *I* under arrest?" Anna asked.

"What for?" he replied.

"Running away?"

"It isn't illegal to run away from someone who's trying to kill you," Donovan said.

"Then it's true," Kirsten said. "What Anna and I have been assuming. That the madman who's killing people on Fifth Avenue wants her dead."

"I think she was one of the targets," Donovan replied.

"And the other target? Paul?"

"Definitely. That is Paul's baby, isn't it?" He waved a bag of food in the direction of Anna's tummy.

Anna nodded. "We had an affair in Carricola. Paul is very charming . . . and very attractive."

Kirsten looked away, but when her gaze turned back to Donovan it had an ironic smile.

Anna continued, "I didn't want to get pregnant, at least not by Paul. I slept with him, I don't know, out of boredom but also as the last gasp of my single days. I was going to get married, and here was my chance for a final fling, and with the man they're calling 'the sexiest man alive.' "

"And is he?"

"He'll do," Anna said, with a girlish giggle.

"What do *you* think?" Donovan asked her mother.

"Paul isn't bad for a man his age," she replied, shaking her head. "Do you know how *mad* I got at him when I learned?"

"I think I can imagine."

"There we were, in bed together, comparing notes about our love lives, when I found out he had slept with my daughter. Not only that, but he was the father of her unborn child.

And he didn't even know it. The man sleeps with so many women he isn't even aware of getting one of them pregnant."

"Did you tell him that Anna is your daughter?" Donovan asked.

"No. I was afraid he'd do something to fuck up her engagement. But I was still mad enough to throw him out of my apartment at four in the morning." She laughed and added, "I think that's the first time any woman threw him out."

"Well, he still doesn't know you two are mother and daughter. Only that he's going to have a child," Donovan said. "I told him."

"What did he say?" Anna asked.

"He seemed pretty amazed. My sense is he's giving that fact plenty of thought right about now."

"My God, a spark of decency," Kirsten said.

"Maybe more than a spark."

"I was mad enough to kill him, but like I said, I don't do that anymore. And I paid dearly for the one death I caused, over in Germany so many years ago."

"Just for the record, where were you on November twenty-ninth?" Donovan asked.

"When poor Erik was killed? I was in my office, with my secretary."

"On the evening of December fifth you were helping officiate over the tree-lighting ceremony. And this afternoon at three?"

"In my office, taking a call from that idiot FBI agent. God, can you believe it? The FBI trying to help *me?* What a fucking hoot. I only wish that J. Edgar Hoover had lived to discover that his minions were assisting Kirsten Fritsch, the notorious sixties radical and murderess."

"Where did you get that name?" Donovan asked.

"Claudia Hummitz was the name of my landlady when I

lived in Baden-Baden during the summer of 1967. When I got out of jail, I figured that if Jerry Rubin could transform himself into a Wall Street whatever-he-was and if Eldridge Cleaver can become a goddamn motivational speaker, then Kirsten Fritsch can transmogrify into the director of the Midtown Merchants Association. Where were *you* in 1967?"

"A man is entitled to a period of time that he doesn't have to account for," Donovan said.

"Ooh, a skeleton in the closet. And I'll bet I know what it is, too."

"No, you don't," Donovan said, opening the paper bags and distributing the Mexican food by way of changing the topic of conversation. A bit later, munching on a chorizo, he told Anna, "I'm sorry about Erik."

She looked down at her plate for a moment, then picked at her burrito. "Me too."

"You've been down one hell of a road," he said.

"A girl who's born in prison has to do whatever she can to survive," Anna said.

"So you became Princess Anna."

"Whatever works," she said. "The fake title got me into certain social circles, one result of which is that I met Erik." She hesitated for a second, then said, "I miss him."

"Did he know your real name?"

"I told him. It changed nothing. He fell in love with me, not my past."

"Erik must have been a remarkable man," Donovan said.

"I assume you know that he took care of me," Anna replied. "I'm actually a very wealthy woman right now."

"Your butler awaits your return."

"Bliley is a good man," Anna said.

"This time don't pretend to be royalty. I suspect he likes you better as you are."

"But I don't know if I could live in Trump Plaza."

"Oh, *I* could," Kirsten interjected. "I would savor the irony with every breath I took."

"Mom, let's go live there," Anna said, reaching across Donovan's lap long enough to touch her mother's hand. "We have nothing to hide from now."

"They'll fire me if they find out who I am," Kirsten said.

"Why should you care?" Donovan asked.

"True. . . . Why should I care?"

"Let's do it, then," Anna said.

Donovan held up his hand. "Wait a few days," he said.

"Why?"

"Let's not forget that someone still may be trying to kill you. We can protect you better here. I asked my associate, Brian Moskowitz, to join us tonight. Be absolutely honest with him. He'll put a twenty-four-hour guard on your door."

"It seems like a reasonable precaution," Kirsten said.

"And the four of us will sit down and come up with a plan to catch the man or woman who tried to kill you, Anna, and who is trying to kill Paul."

Nodding, Anna said, "Captain Donovan, I'd like to come see your wife in the hospital."

"She'd like that," Donovan replied.

"When is she due?"

"On Christmas Day. The doctor is going to deliver the baby then."

"You can count on us being there," Kirsten said. "But *who* are your suspects? Beyond the authors of the extortion demand."

"They're not even under consideration," Donovan replied. "Neither the Afghan bunch nor the Montana hoodlums. The FBI is chasing its own tail on this one."

"Pity," Kirsten said.

"As of an hour ago, no one had showed to pick up the diamonds. And there were more FBI agents waiting along Northern Boulevard than there were Afghan immigrants. By tomorrow morning I'm sure that even the FBI will realize it's been snookered and call home its dogs."

"In that case," Kirsten said, "who *is* trying to kill my daughter?"

"Paul can't be ruled out," Donovan replied.

Both women seemed shocked.

"But I consider him a long shot. As you said, the man has been showing a spark of humanity recently. Then there's June Lake. No alibi for any of the killings. A somewhat shaky motive."

"Which is?" Anna asked.

"To get Paul for herself. By scaring the daylights out of him and then giving him nowhere to turn but her."

"It seems somewhat extreme to imagine that a woman would kill three people to catch a man," Kirsten said. "Even that man."

"I agree," Anna added.

"Unless there's more to it, she's not the killer," Donovan said. "Next on the list is George Halloran."

"The weather buffoon," Kirsten said.

"He's ambitious and stands to gain a lot if Paul loses his job. However, he has an ironclad alibi for the most recent murder. He was having a drink with me."

"Who else?" Kirsten asked.

"Ever heard the name Valery Koslov?" Donovan asked.

Both women shook their heads.

"He's a Russian mobster and thug that the Manhattan DA is looking for."

"How did the Russian mafia get into this?" Anna asked.

"Koslov has a young and beautiful wife," Donovan explained.

"Oh," Kirsten replied, bobbing her head up and down.

"He also owned the murder weapon until quite recently," Donovan said. "However, he has alibis for two of the murders and I doubt he did the third. Now we come to Tom Tuttle."

"Who?" Anna asked.

"The son of the former owners of E & J Tuttle," Donovan said. "He's an army-trained sniper who was gassed during the Gulf War and subsequently snapped. Until recently he's been making a living by reciting poetry on the street while dressed as a Viking."

"Oh, Erik and I saw him," Anna said excitedly. "Erik gave him five dollars, for which he recited a poem. He seemed harmless."

"He's violent and has a huge grudge against the Japanese corporation that bought out his family store," Donovan informed them.

"I also heard about this man," Kirsten added. "I was told . . . This is sad, actually, or pathetic, depending on your point of view. Did you know that his family donated the Rockefeller Center Christmas tree?"

Donovan nodded.

"Did you know that Tuttle used to play in that tree during his childhood?"

Donovan hadn't known that.

"And that he actually had a tree house in it once? It's sad to think—"

"—that not only did he lose the family store, but he also lost the tree he used to play in as a child," Donovan said. "Which is now on display, dead as a doornail, around the corner from the store. No wonder the poor fool is howling mad."

Donovan made a note on a piece of brown paper bag and stuck it in his pocket. "Tuttle has gone up a notch on the suspect list," the captain explained. "I just wish we could find him."

"Is he your last suspect?" Kirsten asked.

"No. There's Yama Mojadidi."

"Who?" both women asked simultaneously.

"The Afghan enigma," Donovan said. "The only one on the list who's definitely going down for *something,* I assure you."

"Why?" Kirsten asked.

"He took a shot at me. Nothing gets my attention faster than being shot at. What did I tell you this morning? Especially since I'm about to become a father."

"Who is this man?" Anna asked.

"An Afghan immigrant who was running a gyro cart in front of F.A.O. Schwarz three weeks ago when Erik was killed. I was talking to the man when the shots were fired. He went for a gun; very jittery. By the time I got through at the crime scene he had disappeared. Curious, I went looking for him. And he shot at me."

"You said he was standing in front of Schwarz?" Kirsten asked. "Did you know that Paul used to walk to and from work passing by that spot?"

Donovan knew. "There's a good chance that Mojadidi was lying in wait for him, hoping to kill him. He was carrying a picture of a young woman, possibly a daughter."

"And Paul was in Afghanistan, covering the war there," Kirsten said. "Of course he seduced the daughter. Ergo the assassination attempt by the outraged father. They take family honor very seriously in Muslim countries."

"My God, you have five or six suspects on your list," Anna said.

"This *is* New York, after all," Donovan said. "And there used to be more names on the list."

"There were?"

"Your mom was on it," he replied.

Kirsten smiled sheepishly, putting down her fork. "Oh, the joys of being a retired murderess and murder suspect," she said. "You know, I think I *will* quit my job and go live in Trump Plaza. Fuck the Midtown Merchants Association and their money."

Donovan smiled and stood so mother and daughter could move together on the couch and hug. *Parenthood,* Donovan thought, *it looks good to me.*

After a minute, Kirsten looked up and asked, "What's next?"

"We wait for Moskowitz to get here from downtown," Donovan said. "Then I call Paul Duke and tell him that the mother of his unborn child wants to talk to him, on Christmas Day, at the Fifth Avenue Medical Center."

20. "YOU INVITED A SERIAL KILLER TO THE BIRTH OF OUR SON?"

Marcy's position was typically resolute, with only the slightest trace of hysteria. "I'm glad I'm going to be sedated most of the day," she said. "Because I've having trouble with the idea that you invited a serial killer to the birth of our son."

"I don't know if I'd put it that way," he said, keeping a wary eye on the door while browsing about in the medical records computer.

"What other way is there?" she asked. Marcy was sitting up in bed, brushing her hair, waiting for her doctor to come in and tell her that only an hour remained before she would be led off to be prepared for the delivery. It was ten on Christmas morning. A miniature version, maybe three feet tall, of the Barnes family Christmas tree stood on the end table. It was green plastic—no real evergreens allowed in the neonatal intensive care unit—and had an array of expensive miniature ornaments and was topped off by a crystal Star of David.

"For one thing, I could be wrong," he said.

"You, wrong?" He wasn't sure if her remark was a compliment or sarcasm. "What if Tuttle or Mojadidi did it? I couldn't even find them, let along invite them to drop by today."

"So the Viking who stands in the street and spouts poetry and the Afghan who took a shot at you—"

Donovan glanced at her, then back to the monitor as she gave him a dirty look.

"I heard about that. You didn't think I would hear about that?" Marcy said. "So these two men aren't going to make it to the birth of my son. I'm mortified."

"What does *chlamydia trachomatis* cause?" he asked, seeking to change the subject. "Is it pelvic inflammatory disease?"

"Don't try to ignore me," she said.

"I'm not ignoring you," he replied. "I'm trying to say that, maybe, someone else is the killer I'm looking for and not the people who are coming here today."

"Such as the Mountain Brigade? Whichever one."

"Such as them."

"The FBI folded its surveillance and went home two days ago," Marcy said. "The diamonds are back on Fifth Avenue, where they belong. Once again you were right."

"Let me explain how you came to have so many and colorful visitors," Donovan replied.

"I can hear my mother now."

"Koslov wanted to turn himself in, and it had to be today in Manhattan. So I said he would have to come here. Then, Anna and her mother asked if they could come to see you and the baby. Anna was a victim of this crime. Was I going to say no?"

"Not you," Marcy said.

"Duke and Lake have been here already, so they were naturals. Halloran more or less moves in Paul's shadow. All of a sudden, it turned into a crowd. Add family and guys from the office and it becomes a mob scene. Fortunately, the guys from the office all are cops, so I wouldn't worry too much about being shot or anything."

In fact, the policemen and policewomen—dozens of them, dressed as orderlies, nurses, or physicians—were everywhere, grateful to have shed the Santa's Angels getups, trying to remain unobtrusive but, in fact, giving the floor the look of a busy emergency room on New Year's Eve.

"Oh, that makes me feel reassured," she said. "These are the same guys who couldn't find Tuttle or Mojadidi? What makes you think they'll be able to stop someone from turning violent?"

"The violence, if any, will be directed at Paul Duke," Donovan told her. "And none of this will take place until visiting hours, which start at one this afternoon. Daniel will be several hours old by then, and I'll have plenty of time to pluck the killer from the crowd of also-rans and pack him or her off to the hoosegow."

"Would you stop playing with the computer and finish putting on your scrubs?" she asked.

Like many expectant dads who plan to be in the delivery room, Donovan told Dr. Campagna that he wanted to be a part of every aspect of the delivery. Then he donned yellow scrubs—paper ones that fitted over his regular clothes and rustled when he walked. But he had proven unable to get the paper booties over his sneakers. So he sat at the computer, working the mouse with one hand, holding the slip-on paper booties in the other.

"I'm almost done here," he said.

"Put on your booties."

"They don't fit over the sneakers."

"Then wear them over your socks," she replied.

He nodded in agreement, slipped off his sneakers, and pulled on the yellow paper shoes. "Now are you happy?" he asked.

"Rabbi Weiss came in this morning when you were in the shower," Marcy said.

"After this pregnancy, you know everything there is to know about reproduction," Donovan said. "Can chlamydia cause pelvic inflammatory disease?"

"Yes," she said sharply.

"And what can *that* do to you? Make you infertile? I mean—"

He was interrupted by the blaring of a warning signal. The alarm that was part of Marcy's fetal monitor went off; it was a sharp beeping sound that wasn't really all that loud but, given what it meant, seemed to dwarf the horn on a Mack truck.

"Oh my God!" she shouted, craning her neck to see the screen.

"What is it?" he asked, pressing the off switch on the computer and clambering to his feet, the paper coveralls rustling.

"The baby's heartbeat is dropping!" she said as nurses came running.

"What's that mean?"

"The fetus is under stress," said one nurse as the room filled up with medical people. Donovan went to his wife's side and held her hands as the sounds blared on and more people poured into the room from the hall. One of them was Dr. Campagna, for whom the crowd parted as did the Red Sea for Moses.

"Is he dying? Is he dying?" Marcy asked, frantic, squeezing her husband's hands so hard he could feel the bones crunching together.

The doctor peered at the monitor, looked at the strip of tape pouring out of the instrument, and felt Marcy's cervix. Then he said, "The heart rate is down. I don't know why. Sometimes it happens and you never know the reason. But I'm taking the baby now. Get Mrs. Donovan into the delivery room right away. She needs the epidural immediately."

Within half a minute, Marcy's bed was borne out of the room at the center of a moving cluster of doctors and nurses. As her hands pulled away from her husband's, she gasped, "William!"

"It will be all right," he said, his head spinning.

She was on her way down the hall then, but Campagna lingered momentarily in the doorway, looking at Donovan standing alone in the room. He said, "I'll need you in fifteen minutes. Be ready."

"Will everything be OK?" Donovan asked.

"I won't know until I get in there."

"What can I do?"

Campagna said, "If you want to go down to the chapel, it's on the first floor." He, too, then disappeared.

Donovan stood in the room alone for a minute, thinking of his wife and unborn child and the awful possibility that his son could draw so near to life only to die. Donovan looked around the empty room, which also was silent, the blaring monitor having disappeared along with his wife, and felt more alone than ever. He sat for a minute on the edge of the reclining chair that had been his bed in recent weeks. Then he got up and, feeling a bit ridiculous but unable to prevent himself, trudged down the hall in the direction of the elevator that led to the chapel.

The small, sedate, and wood-paneled room was scrupulously nondenominational. There was no cross, no Star of David, no Muslim crescent, but rather a backlit stained-glass panel that suggested tranquillity. In it were depicted leaves, flowers, soft and mosslike earth, and sky and clouds. Seven rows of leather-cushioned pews faced what passed for an altar—the stained-glass panel and a kneeling bench and rail that stood in front of it.

Half of the room was under renovation. A new floor was being put in. That area was separated from the rest by the same sort of red velvet rope that banks use to channel customers, and a smallish sign read: DANGER, CONSTRUCTION.

Donovan looked around to make sure no one was watching. Then he slipped into the chapel and let the door close behind him. He was alone again, or not alone, believers would say, but at least saw no other persons in the chapel. The scrubs rustling, he walked up the aisle, skirting the area under construction, and after a moment's hesitancy knelt on the bench.

He tried to think of a prayer. The Lord's Prayer should have come back to him from his childhood but didn't. He got as far as "Our Father, who . . ." and forgot the rest. Donovan had heard Marcy's mother say the Sh'ma, the Jewish prayer that affirmed one's belief in one God. Donovan always thought of the Sh'ma as being the perfect airplane crash prayer, for it could be said in five seconds—after the alarm sounded but before the 747 hit the mountain. But try as he might, Donovan couldn't remember the Jewish prayer, either.

At last he elevated his eyes to the ceiling and thought of what the cardinal had told him. That he would lose his atheism at the moment of his son's birth. *Well,* he thought, *this is the time.* Tears welling in his eyes, Donovan said, "I'm sorry if I did anything wrong. The best I can say for myself is that I tried hard and meant well always. Don't forgive me if you don't feel like it, but spare my wife and child."

Then he stood, the warmth of newfound belief filling his heart, and piously backed away from the altar. In so doing, Donovan backed through the red velvet ropes and into the construction area and stepped down firmly on a rusty nail.

"Shit!" he swore, hopping onto his other foot and off to one side and crashing down into a pew. He picked his foot up and looked at the bloodstain that grew quickly to the size of a quarter on the sole of his right foot.

He pressed two fingers against the wound in an attempt to stop the bleeding, but that didn't help much. So he gave up and, glancing at his watch, saw that his time was up. He got to his feet and limped out of the chapel and back to the elevator, leaving little spots of blood along the scrubbed floor.

"Captain Donovan! What happened?" asked a nurse as he hobbled up to the delivery room.

"God struck me down," Donovan muttered.

"You're bleeding. Let me see your foot."

"I stepped on a nail. The bleeding will stop on its own."

"You'll need a tetanus shot. Here, let me bandage it."

"How's my wife and child?"

"Your wife has had the epidural and is being prepped. The baby's heartbeat has stabilized, but Dr. Campagna still wants to deliver him right now. You have five minutes. Take off your sock."

Donovan did as he was told, standing on one foot and leaning against a supply cabinet as the nurse cleaned the wound and applied a patch of gauze. Then he pulled the sock back on and was given another slip-on bootie.

Marcy was lying on her back with all of her body below

her breasts hidden behind a blue curtain. The anesthesiologist stood by her head, alternating glances between his monitors, his patient, and what lay beyond the curtain. Donovan was waved into a folding chair by her head.

"Hi, honey, I'm having a baby," she said, a bit groggily.

"Can you feel anything?" he asked.

"Nothing."

"Daniel's heart rate stabilized. The nurse told me."

"I know. It's wonderful. I'm having a baby. After all those years, I'm having a baby. Hold my hand."

He did as he was told. He also petted her cheek with his other hand, and the two of them looked at one another and at the blue curtain while whatever the doctor was doing on the other side caused her body to lift up and down and rock from side to side, motions she swore later she was never aware of.

Fifteen minutes into the procedure Donovan heard the anesthesiologist say, "You have a baby boy," and break into a grin. Marcy began crying and Donovan asked, "Can I look?"

"No," said the anesthesiologist firmly.

"You're not a doctor yet," Campagna added.

Then came a baby's cry and assorted technical talk, all of it, Donovan noted with glee, spoken in matter-of-fact tones. Another couple of minutes and Campagna's head came around the curtain. He said, "There's a large fibroid—a benign tumor. That's why the baby didn't drop. I'm going to take it out."

"What difference does this tumor make?" Donovan asked.

"About nine thousand dollars to your insurance company."

"Take it out."

Another ten minutes later, Campagna's hand snaked around the curtain. It held a tangerine-size blob of red.

"Would you look at the size of that thing . . . Doctor," he said.

"Thank you for sharing," Donovan replied, a bit pale.

"Your wife and child are perfect. Here, let me show you." And with that a nurse brought the baby around, a perfect little blend of both Donovan and Marcy, with his chin and forehead but her amazing eyes and dark complexion, swaddled in white cloth.

" 'And unto this day a child is born,' " Donovan said. "To a wonderful mother and a not-so-bad father who just stepped on a nail."

Marcy didn't hear him. She was crying nonstop, holding her baby, laughing and crying, the tears soaking her face and neck and baby and the pillow below.

Later, as they were wheeling mother and child off to separate destinations—her to the recovery room, him to the nursery to be checked out more fully—Donovan took Campagna aside. "That fibroid, can it prevent her from having more babies?" he asked.

"No. Absolutely not. Only time can do that now, and more and more, we can negotiate with time."

"Fibroids aren't like pelvic inflammatory disease, are they?" Donovan asked. "*That* can make a woman infertile."

"It certainly can. Untreated PID is a major problem, especially considering the emotional issues attached to sudden infertility. Severe emotional stress is not uncommon. Why do you ask?"

"I have a friend. Well, you know Paul Duke. About ten years ago, he had chlamydia. He gave it to his girlfriend. But she wasn't properly treated and became infertile. She had a nervous breakdown as a result of it, too. Never quite got over the whole thing. I believe she was your patient."

Campagna was silent for a moment. Then he said, "I forgot you're Paul's friend. So they told you about it. Well, I guess that makes it OK for me to talk about it. June took that especially hard. In fact . . ." Here Campagna lowered his voice. "She had a complete mental collapse and was hospitalized for several months."

"The network portrayed it as being a leave of absence," Donovan remarked.

Campagna sighed. "She always wanted children. What a shame. But, as you can see, she rebounded. She became stronger than ever. Now she can have everything she wants."

Including revenge, Donovan thought. *"Whom the gods would destroy they would first make crazy."*

"Except children," he said.

"Except children," Campagna agreed.

21. "YOU DID RIGHT BY MY LITTLE GIRL"

Mother and child rested peacefully in the nursery, she on her gurney and he nestled under her arm. She slept lightly, and so did the baby, while nurses watched and total strangers admired the scene from behind plate-glass windows. Across the nursery from her, a woman of some importance from Kenya bottle-fed one of the quadruplets Campagna had delivered the day before. Her husband, a stout man with very expensive clothes and vaguely regal bearing, exchanged rapid-fire conversation, all totally unintelligible to Donovan, with several younger men, apparently aides.

Other visitors came and went, among them Kirsten Fritsch and Anna Hebel. They had dressed for the occasion, sort of, looking motherly and daughterly all in all, all other guises having been discarded. And following them around, carrying a basket of presents for the newborn, was George Bliley, his employment uninterrupted.

Donovan left the nursery and limped out into the hall, the door sliding shut behind him. A new bandage was on his wound and he had had a tetanus shot, but the foot had swollen enough so that the sneaker was a tight fit and limping remained a necessity.

Moskowitz joined him then, saying, "Mdivani and Koslov are still on the first floor with the lawyers, waiting in the chapel."

"Did you tell them to watch out for nails?"

"Yeah, and you should have heard the reaction I got from that mob of lawyers. Three of them gave me their business cards, and one told me, 'Fifth Avenue Medical Center has an endowment of one hundred million and that's exactly how much we should ask for.'"

"I'll take it under advisement," Donovan replied.

Mosko said, "The assistant DA is in the lobby, along with a handful of his investigators."

"Any assassins among them?" Donovan asked.

"Not one that I can see."

"So the deed is ready to be done. Do I have to be there?"

"It would be nice if you made the introductions," Mosko said.

"OK, here's the deal. You take Kirsten and Anna into that room I showed you, the residents' conference room. Let Bliley wait in Marcy's room with the goodies. When Duke and Lake appear, keep them here by the nursery until I return."

"How am I supposed to do that?" Mosko asked.

"I don't know. . . . Tell baby stories. Yes, tell lots of baby stories. How wonderful it is to be a parent. What a great mom Marcy will be."

"Rub it in good, huh?"

"You got it. Make her snap."

"She did that when she shot Erik Melmer," Moskowitz replied.

Donovan went downstairs, limping, with the assistance of a functional wooden cane that an orderly had brought up from the basement. He found Koslov and Mdivani sitting in a pew behind a phalanx of lawyers, all of whom were twisted around, the better to see their rich and dangerous client.

Upon seeing the captain enter, Koslov reached into a pocket and withdrew a small gift-wrapped box that he handed over. "This is for your son, with my best wishes for a long and prosperous life," Koslov said.

"Thank you."

"I understand that in a few minutes I will be in the custody of your criminal justice system. My lawyers assure me that it is a good system and that I have an excellent chance of . . . of beating the rap."

"I know your lawyers," Donovan said. "They don't lie." Then he thought for a moment, and added, "At least not about your chances of beating the rap. Well, good luck to you. I checked all the things you told me through my friend Georgi here"—Donovan patted Mdivani on the shoulder—"and it seems that you are entirely blameless in the murder investigation that is taking my time lately."

"It is foolish to kill a man over a woman," Koslov said. "There are so many other good reasons."

The chapel door opened and the representative of the DA's office walked in, followed by three of his detectives. Before too long, Koslov was on his way downtown to an arraignment at which it was fully expected he would make bail. Donovan thanked Mdivani and saw him to the door, then hobbled back into the medical staff elevator.

"Task two of the day accomplished," he said to Mosko when again they met.

"Task one being having a baby?"

"That's right," Donovan said, as the two men approached the anchorpersons, who waited by the nursery window. The onlookers formed a respectful halo around the stars, getting neither too close nor too far away. "Hello, Paul. Hello, June."

"That is one beautiful baby, Bill," Duke said. "Congratulations, Dad."

"Thank you," Donovan replied, shaking the man's hand.

"Your wife is more beautiful than before," Lake said, a bit formally, as if she were making a statement to the press.

"Daniel looks just like you," Duke added. "His eyes are your eyes."

"Including the bloodshot part, right?" Donovan replied. "No, he has Mom's eyes and complexion, my chin and forehead."

"And lips," Duke said. He seemed much more into the baby thing than his lady companion, who hadn't mentioned the child but was smiling more and more, the Barbie smile that had made her America's sweetheart. The smile, in fact, seemed painted on, a special effect or the product of really good makeup.

"We're delighted to see you and your lovely wife again," Lake began, "but we wonder about the reason for the invitation."

"I need to straighten some things out regarding the attempt on Paul's life," Donovan replied. "And you can help me."

"You can rely on us," she said crisply.

"To begin with, how did you get here today?" Donovan asked.

"Why, we walked . . . from my apartment on Central Park South," Lake said.

"Which way did you go?"

"Across Central Park South, past F.A.O. Schwarz, and here," she said.

"Weren't you afraid of being mobbed by fans?"

"You haven't been outdoors much lately, my friend," Duke said. "It's Christmas Day. All the shops are closed. There's no one on the streets."

"And no one followed you?"

"There was one man walking about a block behind us," Duke replied.

Lake gave him a look, and he quickly said, "I didn't want to worry you. Besides, the man looked familiar, so I assumed he was one of the captain's men."

"Did we have anyone tailing these two?" Donovan asked.

"Not on foot," Mosko replied.

"What did the guy look like?"

"Middle-aged, with a beard. But I couldn't really see him."

"When did you first notice him?"

Duke thought for a moment, then said, "After we passed Schwarz, I guess."

"Send somebody out on the street to look around," Donovan told Moskowitz. "You know who we're looking for."

"I do indeed," Mosko replied. He then gave an order to one of the field detectives.

"Paul has found it very liberating to be away from the pressure that this awful situation has put him under," Lake said, taking his arm.

"Have you?" Donovan asked.

Duke bobbed his head up and down. "When the news of my resignation hit the papers, we were mobbed with reporters. They were outside the studio and both our apartment buildings. But after two days they gave up and went home to spend Christmas with their families. It was fun to walk the street for a change. June has convinced me that whoever the madman was that wanted to kill me—probably one of the Mountain Brigade loonies—he has gone away and will never be back." Then Duke laughed, a bit nervously, perhaps, and added, "As long as I stay with her, that is. She says she's my guardian angel."

Donovan said, "Hmf," but doubted anyone heard. So he added, "Yes," and then asked, "Have you see George Halloran?"

"Is he coming here, too?" Duke asked.

"Yep. I'd like to talk to everybody, and the number of those unaccounted-for appears to be dwindling. Are we done here?"

"Done gawking at your beautiful family?" Duke said, looking again at Marcy and the baby. She opened her eyes a crack and, still groggy from the anesthetic, smiled a faint but loving smile at her husband. Then she went back to sleep.

" 'Cause if we are, there's someone I'd like you to meet, Paul."

"Who?" Lake asked.

"Two people, actually. Well, three. Walk this way."

With that he led them away from the nursery and around a corner and down the corridor to the residents' conference room. Three detectives stood guard outside the door. One of them, chosen because he looked especially technical and nerdy, held an official-looking black box that was covered with buttons, knobs, and displays.

"Open, please," Donovan said, and with Mosko's help ushered Duke and Lake into the same room with Kirsten Fritsch and Anna Hebbel. The other detectives followed, two of them keeping their hands on their weapons and not being very discreet about it.

The two women sat on the far side of a round conference table, sipping tea and nibbling at a plate of gingerbread cookies baked by the nurses' aides. They seemed in good moods, despite the bulletproof vests hidden beneath their jackets. They chorused, more or less in unison, "Hello, Paul."

Duke's eyes widened to saucerlike proportions. He said, "Anna! My God, it's you! You're all right. I'm . . . I'm so sorry what happened to your fiancé. Are you? I mean is that . . . ?"

"Our baby?" Anna replied, patting her tummy. "Yes, this is our baby girl."

Donovan watched closely as Duke and Lake changed. As he grew warmer, paternal, more open and misty-eyed, she hardened. The smile disappeared. Her normally full mouth became a thin slit drawn out across her face. And the skin at her temples tightened until Donovan could see the veins throbbing.

"Go to her," Donovan said, urging Duke to walk around the table. He did, and Anna rose, and the couple embraced, tears in their eyes, genuine tears, not Hollywood tears and not TV-studio tears.

At the same time, Lake's spine stiffened and she clutched at her purse with one hand and at the back of a chair with another. At last, she stared at Fritsch through the cold eyes of madness. "What is *she* doing here?" Lake asked.

Paul broke away from Anna then and looked down at Kirsten, who smiled the same ironic smile she had shown to Donovan and gave a half-wave.

"Claudia?" he asked. "Yes, what are you doing here?"

"She's another one who recently changed careers," Donovan said.

"My real name is Kirsten Fritsch," she said. "And I'm Anna's mother."

Paul looked at Anna, who smiled sheepishly and bobbed her head up and down, then over at Donovan, who shrugged. "I'm sure it happens more often than we think," he said.

Kirsten added, "Now you know why I threw you out that night."

Anna said, "I don't care, Paul, and neither does my mom. I just wanted to see you again, and to—"

It was at that point that Lake screamed, "No! Tell me you didn't sleep with *both of them!*"

Startled, Duke said, "It wasn't intentional."

"You bastard!" she shouted, backing away from the scene, against the wall next to the still-open door.

Then Donovan made a gesture, and the nerdy man with the fancy instrument poked a long and slender probe close to Lake's hand. The black box emitted a riot of peppery noises, causing her to look down at it and then jerk her hands away.

"What are you doing?" she shrieked.

"I'm getting a positive reading, Captain," the man said in a flat voice. "I'm reading depleted uranium here"—he poked the prod at her right hand, and again the noises filled the room—"and here. . . ." He did the same thing with her left, getting the same result.

Donovan commented, "The Kammacher Stedman that you used to kill Erik Melmer, Terry Seybold, and Tony DeStanzio fires depleted-uranium bullets that leave detectable traces wherever they touch. They last for weeks. We also found such traces in your dressing room."

"What?!"

"The television studio is a quick walk from all three murder sites. The hall past the dressing rooms is open only to the stars. The corridor that leads to the street is often deserted. You have no alibi for any of the murders. You have traces of radiation on your hands. And you have all the motive in the Western Hemisphere for wanting Paul Duke broke and ruined if not, in fact, dead."

"What's that?" asked an astonished Duke.

"Giving her the infection that made her infertile ten years ago, when what she wanted more than anything was to have a baby," Donovan said. "A baby like the one Anna is carrying for you."

"How'd you find out all that?" Duke asked.

"I got her Social Security number off that pay stub you and I talked about. After that, her medical records opened up like a ripe plum."

"That's . . . not . . . legal," Lake stammered, her face a mask of fury and her hand fumbling with the catch that opened her purse.

"Hire a lawyer and sue me," Donovan said. "There's a whole flock of 'em in the lobby."

With that Lake tore open her purse and pulled from it a small revolver. As Donovan and two other detectives went for their firearms, Lake fired two shots, missing Duke, who covered Anna with his body, protecting her. Furious and panicky, Lake fled into the hall.

It was still packed with people, most of them police. But she got a few paces down the hall, waving the gun around, her eyes ablaze with fury, Duke and Donovan chasing her, the captain limping with the help of the cane.

She fired two more shots that sent onlookers diving to the floor and behind the assortment of carts and gurneys left at various spots in the hall. Donovan pulled up ten feet from her; Duke was at his side but slightly behind.

"June, wait," Duke said, holding a hand up, as if the gesture would stop her.

"I went through hell for you," she replied, raising the gun and aiming it at him.

"Put that down," Donovan snapped. "I already have problems with my boss. Don't make me shoot America's sweetheart."

What escaped from Lake's mouth could only be described as a wail of anger and frustration, and she closed her eyes and was about to pull the trigger when she felt the cold steel of an automatic weapon at the back of her neck.

"Drop your gun," said a voice, a man's voice; to Donovan, an oddly familiar voice.

The wail turned to mere frustration; after a momentary hesitation, June Lake dropped her gun and immediately was swarmed over by police officers and dragged off. Duke came out from behind Donovan and stared across the circle at the man who had been following him on the way to the hospital that morning, Yama Mojadidi.

"Didi?" he asked, stepping forward, as did Donovan. "Didi, is that you?"

"You know this clown?" Donovan asked, without lowering his own weapon.

"Of course I do. He was my good friend when I was covering the war in Afghanistan. Didi was the leader of a mujahideen group that fought the Russians in the hills near the Great Buddhas of Bamiyan."

Mojadidi lowered his gun, the same automatic that Donovan had seen in his waistband outside F.A.O. Schwarz, and gave it to a detective. Then the Afghan went to Duke and the two friends embraced, crying and hugging. Donovan put away his Smith & Wesson and awaited the explanation.

"I'm sorry I shot at you, Captain," Mojadidi said at last.

"I was going to bring that up."

"But I thought you were an Immigration man who wanted to send me back to Afghanistan."

"That may happen anyway," Donovan replied. "I just became a father, and don't take my own mortality as lightly as I once did."

"Doesn't matter; I am going. I only came here to see Paul . . . and to thank him."

"For what?"

"My daughter, Melly. . . ."

Donovan rolled his eyes.

"No, it is not what you think," Mojadidi said quickly. "She was only seventeen when I brought Paul home to have dinner with my family. She was a bright girl, very bright, and wanted to go to university. But there was no chance of that, for I am a man of extremely modest means. Paul gave her the money for college . . . all four years . . . no strings attached. He is like that, you know, very selfless."

"I told you I spend lots of money on women, but I forgot that one detail," Duke added.

"And you didn't sleep with this one?" Donovan asked.

"On my honor," Duke said. And when that argument cut no ice with the captain, Duke added, "Not even I am crazy enough to sleep with the daughter of a mujahideen guerrilla leader. Didi, how is Melly?"

"Melly is dead," Mojadidi replied flatly.

Donovan said, "Your daughter is the girl in the photograph of the Great Buddhas."

"Yes. She was very beautiful, was she not?"

"Very beautiful," Donovan said.

"What happened?" Duke asked, grasping his friend's hands and holding them.

"She was killed by a stray rocket during a Taliban attack. It happened just last year, after she got her degree and came home. Before she died, she asked me to find you and give you this."

From his pocket he took a gold chain, from the end of which dangled a gold dog tag with Duke's name on it. He dropped the chain into Duke's palm.

Duke said, "The army gave me this after I raised my fist at that Russian chopper. I gave it to Melly as a memento."

The men embraced again.

"You helped her," Mojadidi said. "You did right by my little girl."

"Are you ready to do right by another little girl?" Donovan asked.

Duke nodded several times, tears running down his cheeks. And a while later Donovan reunited him with Anna and their unborn child.

Donovan held Daniel under his arm and played with his tiny hand, which fit neatly between the captain's thumb and forefinger. The infant made mewing sounds and looked up at his daddy, who wondered what he saw. Would this child, coming into the world in his papa's fifty-second year, mirror only the mature, thoughtful Donovan? Or would he carry some genetic resemblance to the old boozer and brawler who had wasted so many hours, months, and years hobnobbing with Broadway lowlifes? "I can't figure out if this kid will grow up to be a college professor or a punk rocker," Donovan said.

"Whatever he does, we'll always love him," Marcy replied, extending her hands to take the child.

Donovan handed her the baby, holding him as carefully as if he were a Ming vase, moving with the child and taking every precaution to avoid dropping the priceless little boy. She brought him to her breast and leaned back, letting out a satisfied sigh.

The family, hers, his, and theirs, had gone. Guys from the office and their wives had come and gone. George Kohler and the rest of the staff of Marcy's Home Cooking over on Broadway had come and gone. So, too, had several of the boys from Donovan's old life, scrubbed for the occasion and squeezed into clean clothes. Every one of the red-and-green Christmas cupcakes baked by Mosko's wife had been eaten, the paper cups littering the floor around a trash basket already stuffed with gift wrappings.

Donovan switched on the television. After surfing around the channels, he stumbled over the ten o'clock *Wolf News* and was startled, but not entirely displeased, to see George Halloran sitting in the anchor's chair. The lead item on the news that Christmas Day was, of course, the arrest of "America's sweetheart," June Lake, for the murder of three people on Fifth Avenue. But typically, Halloran had a personal touch. Tom Tuttle, bad-boy scion of the E & J Tuttle store chain, had been found, on Christmas Day, sitting beneath the tree in which he had played so happily as a child so very long ago. A Rockefeller Center guard found him, whimpering and reciting Keats's "On Melancholy." He was taken to Bellevue for psychiatric evaluation, after which his family was expected to take him in and nurse him back to health.

"Everyone is accounted for," Donovan said, switching to the Weather Channel.

"How is Paul?" Marcy asked. "*Where* is Paul?"

"OK at last, I think. And probably overnighting at Trump Plaza, busily tackling the first night of the rest of his life."

"How are the three of them going to work out the sleeping arrangements?" Marcy asked.

"Kirsten and him are sixties people. They'll think of something."

"So she's out of a job. He's out of a job. And all are filthy rich. There is a story here someplace."

"You bet, and that's the book that Paul intends to write instead of *Tales of a TV Tough Guy*," Donovan said. "The last I heard, he was asking around trying to find the name of Danielle Steel's agent."

"And the Afghan who shot at you? Mojadidi? What will happen to him? Are you going to charge him with attempted murder for shooting at you?"

"What for? The best I could do is get him deported, and he wants to go home anyway. The man has to fight the Taliban, after all. And I'll support anyone who fights religious fundamentalists."

To accent his point, he tapped his cane on his bandaged foot.

"I guess that's it for you and organized religion, isn't it?" Marcy said.

"Actually, you're wrong," he told a surprised wife. "I believe in Him now. That He *may be* out there someplace, in the clouds. What happened to me today was His warning. A shot across the bow."

The baby pulled his head off Marcy's nipple for a moment, long enough to make a mewing sort of sound, then resumed what he was doing.

"God knows that it's a safe bet that the Geiger counter stuff was all made up—"

"Entirely fictitious. But she bought it."

"And that you figured out how she disguised her voice and phoned in those extortion demands to throw you off."

"Any good computer can be equipped to alter voices," Donovan replied.

Marcy thought for a while, until the baby was finished eating and had fallen fast asleep. "I'm exhausted," she said. "I'm as tired as he is."

"You both have been through a lot."

"And your day was a cakewalk?"

"I do what I can," Donovan replied, a remark that was essentially meaningless but was the best platitude he could emit at that time of night.

"I don't want to let go of him, but you'd better take him back to the nursery," Marcy said.

She kissed the baby on both cheeks, both hands, and the top of his head, which was covered with a layer of fine dark brown hair, before handing him to her husband.

"Daniel Magid Donovan, whose name means 'storyteller,' let's go to bed," Donovan said, struggling to his feet while holding the baby safe in both arms.

"Good night, Daniel," Marcy said.

Unable to use the cane without trusting his son to the safety of just one arm, Donovan hobbled down the hall, wincing at every step, pausing halfway to the nursery to kiss the boy and whisper, "I love you," in his ear. And then he held his son to his heart and limped on.